Praise for the novels
of Elizabeth Bear

"A gritty and painstakingly well-informed peek inside a future world we'd all better hope we don't get, liberally seasoned with VR delights and enigmatically weird alien artifacts. . . . Elizabeth Bear builds her future nightmare tale with style and conviction and a constant return to the twists of the human heart."
— Richard Morgan, author of *Altered Carbon*

"Very exciting, very polished, very impressive."
— Mike Resnick, author of *Starship: Mutiny*

"Gritty, insightful, and daring."
— David Brin, author of the *Uplift* novels and *Kiln People*

"A glorious hybrid: hard science, dystopian geopolitics, and wide-eyed sense of wonder seamlessly blended into a single book."
— Peter Watts, author of *Starfish* and *Maelstrom*

"What Bear has done . . . is create a world that is all too plausible, one racked by environmental devastation and political chaos. . . . She conducts a tour of this society's darker corners, offering an unnerving peek into a future humankind would be wise to avoid."   — SciFi.com

"Elizabeth Bear has carved herself out a fantastic little world. . . . It's rare to find a book with so many characters you genuinely care about. It's a roller coaster of a good thriller, too."   — SF Crowsnest

"An enthralling roller-coaster ride through a dark and possible near future."   — *Starlog*

Blood and Iron

Elizabeth Bear

A ROC BOOK

ROC
Published by New American Library, a division of
Penguin Group (USA) Inc., 375 Hudson Street,
New York, New York 10014, USA
Penguin Group (Canada), 90 Eglinton Avenue East, Suite 700, Toronto,
Ontario M4P 2Y3, Canada (a division of Pearson Penguin Canada Inc.)
Penguin Books Ltd., 80 Strand, London WC2R 0RL, England
Penguin Ireland, 25 St. Stephen's Green, Dublin 2,
Ireland (a division of Penguin Books Ltd.)
Penguin Group (Australia), 250 Camberwell Road, Camberwell, Victoria 3124,
Australia (a division of Pearson Australia Group Pty. Ltd.)
Penguin Books India Pvt. Ltd., 11 Community Centre, Panchsheel Park,
New Delhi - 110 017, India
Penguin Group (NZ), cnr Airborne and Rosedale Roads, Albany,
Auckland 1310, New Zealand (a division of Pearson New Zealand Ltd.)
Penguin Books (South Africa) (Pty.) Ltd., 24 Sturdee Avenue,
Rosebank, Johannesburg 2196, South Africa

Penguin Books Ltd., Registered Offices:
80 Strand, London WC2R 0RL, England

First published by Roc, an imprint of New American Library,
a division of Penguin Group (USA) Inc.

First Printing, July 2006
10 9 8 7 6 5 4 3 2 1

RoC REGISTERED TRADEMARK — MARCA REGISTRADA

LIBRARY OF CONGRESS CATALOGING-IN-PUBLICATION DATA:

Bear, Elizabeth.
  Blood and iron / Elizabeth Bear.
    p. cm.
  ISBN 0-451-46092-8
  I. Title.
  PS3602.E2475B58 2005
  813'.6—dc22   2005033954

Printed in the United States of America

This book is for the Bad Poets
and for Jennifer Jackson,
who between them
made me keep writing it
until I got it right.

ACKNOWLEDGMENTS

The author wishes to thank a group of very patient, very dedicated, very painstaking friends, confidants, advisors, and musicians who shepherded this book and its writer through all its many incarnations. In no particular order: Chelsea Polk, Stella Evans, Kathryn Allen, Leah Bobet, Penelope Hardy, Jenni Smith-Gaynor, Dena Landon, Rhonda Garcia, Larry West, Jenny Tait, Jaime Voss, Kyri Freeman, Terri Trimble, Chris Coen, Jean Seok, David Williams, John Tremlett, Ruth Nestvold, Sarah Monette, Amanda Oestman, Nick Mamatas, Solomon Foster, Steve Wishnevsky, and others too numerous to name. Even more in-depth thanks are owed to Hannah Wolf Bowen, the Kelpie's wicked stepmother and resource for all things horsey, and Abigail Acland, the maintainer of www.tam-lin.org, one of the most outstanding examples of compulsive balladeering the Internet has ever known.

She would also like to thank her agent, Jennifer Jackson; her editor, Liz Scheier; her copy editor, Cherilyn Johnson; and her husband, Kit Kindred.

But first ye'll let the black gae by,
And then ye'll let the brown;
Then I'll ride on a milk-white steed,
You'll pull me to the ground.

—"Tam Lin," Child Ballad version #39C

Chapter One

Matthew the Magician leaned against a wrought iron lamp-post on Forty-second Street, idly picking at the edges of his ten iron rings and listening to his city breathe into the warm September night. That breath rippled up from underground, a hot draft exhaled in time with the harsh pulse of subway trains. A quiet night, as nights went in the belly of the beast . . .

. . . until his hands grew cold under the rings that focused his *otherwise* senses, and he raised his eyes to the night. *Trip trap, trip trap. Who's that tripping across my bridge, Brer Fox?*

Even before the vague sensation of cold resolved into something more defined, he had an idea who might have come to trouble him.

He tugged the placket of his camouflage coat together and stepped out of the shadows, into the dapples and patterns of light that were the substance of New York City at night. The coldness gave him direction; he followed it cautiously, although he could tell his targets were not nearby. And not together—which gave him pause. The stronger chill, the one that sank into the bones of his left hand, had the flavor of age and wildness about it. Ancient hunger, and the musk of a predator.

But the right-hand one was closer, and carried the blood-sharp sweetness he had expected. Besides, whatever was hunting the water-front was too old and too deep for one lone Mage to face. He dug his cell phone from his pocket as he moved, and called it in.

Then he picked up the trail of the Faerie huntress just off Broadway and followed her toward Times Square. She moved quickly, erratically, as obviously on a scent as Matthew himself—and, as obviously, she had not yet noticed *him*. He kept to the shadows, running when he had to, his hands balled into fists around the ice in his palms.

She flitted from shadow to shadow, but he finally caught sight of her silhouetted against the lights in the eye-shattering cacophony of Times Square. She was big-boned, too thin for her frame, in a green peacoat and blue jeans, her dark hair falling loose except for a few seemingly random braids swinging among the uncut tresses. Her nose was a stubborn, Grecian edifice, her chin notched as if by a thumb. She walked quickly, boots clicking, glancing up now and then at the buildings arrayed like broken teeth against the sky.

Only tourists look up in New York City, he thought, and noticed that she too drew her large long-fingered hands from the pockets of her peacoat to rub them as if they hurt. She wore no iron rings; the city itself pained her.

Slime splashed Matthew's boots as he followed. His quarry prowled past a pack of lean young men on a street corner, and one grabbed at her shoulder. She didn't turn, but Matthew—trotting to catch up—saw the shadows writhe around the man who reached, and saw him recoil, staring at his own hand.

Glamourie, Matthew diagnosed, before ice jabbed his palms, and he ran faster. *Don't touch that, boy. You don't know where it's been.*

That's the Seeker of the Daoine Sidhe. You're outclassed—

. . . and so am I.

A blur, another chill on the air, made Matthew turn. The cold of Faerie magic pierced the warmth of the night; the Seeker's will cast a shadow as she paused under a streetlight, again chafing her hands. He drew his own awareness tight as the coiled life inside an acorn, slowing to a trot as he sidestepped through crowds, hoping the magecraft in his rings would hide him from her *otherwise* senses—what the uninitiated might call *second sight*.

She raised her chin like a hound scenting the wind and turned on the ball of one booted foot. Matthew forced himself to keep walking, moving steadily, watching his quarry from the corner of his eye as she raised a hand and stepped from the light into a shadow—

—gone.

Dammit.

Her reappearance, three blocks distant, sent a twinge of cold through his bones. *Oh, no, you don't, my lady. Whatever you're after is* mine.

Matthew ran.

Seeker hated stepping out of the shadows almost as much as she hated the cold ache of the iron city in her bones. Shattered images taunted her: an inkblot silhouette settling on Liberty's torch; a gaunt and curious willow following a jogger through Central Park; demonlings leaping among the flashing LEDs of Times Square; a unicorn bowing its cold and final beauty to a savage, cage-eyed panther in the Central Park Zoo. *She* could not lay a hand on that cold silver neck without taking back a charred obscenity—could not have stroked that purity without leaving a smear of tarnish in her wake.

Seeker moved in a place of Names and glamours, of knotted hairs and deadly magics. Reaching into a silent blankness among the images that surrounded her, she found a Mage, dark-eyed and golden-haired and as human as she once was, wearing a jacket of army camouflage he'd no doubt chosen for symbolism over fashion, slipping along a filth-encrusted alleyway. He snarled into the shadows without stopping—*I see you too.* Sorceries hung around him on threads of cold iron and brass.

His glance was assured, mocking. The mortal Magi had a long and unpleasant rivalry with the Fair Folk. She riffled shadows faster: long ripples curled white foam and black against the wharves; that unicorn turned away, flickering silver through the night; the whole *otherwise* reality, magical and unseen by mortals, except a lucky—or unlucky—few. Seeker tossed her hair, braids moving among the strands. A man with a blade lashed out at a huddled girl. His image shuddered, a reflection split by a stone. His victim emerged brightly from the ripples.

Seeker stepped forward, shadow between shadow again and then out. She waited while the man noticed her and glanced from his prey. His gaze traveled up Seeker's boots and raked her face, tension becoming dismissal when he glimpsed dark, straight hair and her angular jaw. *Just a woman,* she read on his face.

"Leave her," Seeker said. "She's mine now."

He snarled, and lifted the knife.

"You are out of your depth. I warn you twice." She smiled at him, a very little smile that hurt the corners of her mouth.

He swiped. She stepped aside, her shadow lashing a tail on the concrete. As he overreached, her left hand stroked one of the braids binding thin sections of her hair.

She spoke a word.

A Name.

"Gharne!"

Casual with the blade as a butcher, the pimp slashed for Seeker's face—a feint at her vanity. She leaned away, fearless as the cat whose shadow she wore. Wingbeats sounded over her shoulder; her assailant's eyes widened. He threw up arms to protect his own pretty face.

In Faerie, you are granted three chances only. Never, never more. A winged black silhouette like an inkstain with teeth took him high on the chest. He sprawled across the girl still crying on the pavement. Seeker clawed after the shadow of that Mage, for safety's sake, and didn't find him.

Beak bloody, the inky thing gouged for the pimp's heart. The girl dragged herself away, his blood like a sash across her chest. Seeker's familiar demon hunkered over dying bubbles, hell-lit eyes focused on his mistress.

"Good hunting," he said.

She squatted and laid a gentling hand on his neck. "Enjoy your meal, Gharne. Thank you."

"Don't mention it." His beak dipped as she turned to collect the girl.

The girl, who had vanished into warrenlike alleys as if she had never been. Sure. *Now* she ran.

Seeker's footsteps followed comfortably; the scent of her quarry hung on the reeking air. The shadow that paced her was that of a running doe, four footsteps meeting Seeker's two.

"Seeker!" A voice like the crack of a whip. She stopped, made a midmotion spin on cat's-paws.

The human Mage grinned at her. "I know your Name," he said.

"Much good may it do you. It's claimed."

"Ah," he said. "What if it wasn't?" He stepped forward, extending his hand.

"Since when do Magi have any power over bindings?"

"We don't." His hair was a slick yellow ponytail revealing iron rings spiraling his ear. He wore round spectacles that hid his eyes in reflected twinkle.

"Then why ask? You exist to destroy Faerie, Magus, and I exist to defend it."

"That's *not* what we want."

"Don't lie to me, Magus," she snapped. "Trust me, I see no wrong in destroying Faerie. But you—*you* should know it's not safe to talk to fey things. This isn't a fucking fairy tale."

"Really?" That extended hand came down on her wrist. Something burned, searing her flesh. Cold iron rings on his fingers. "My name's Matthew. Szczegielniak. I'll give you that for free, not that it will help you; I'm a mortal man. And this looks like a fairy tale to me. What are you hunting tonight?"

She swore and jerked back. *"Seeker,"* she reminded him. "It takes more than blood and iron to wound me."

He shrugged. "It was worth a try. I have other allies." His hand slid under his jacket. *He has a knife,* she thought. *A gun.*

Before he could pull the weapon, Seeker crouched and leapt, over his head and away. "Look me up!" he yelled after her. "Szczegielniak! I'm in the book! We can help!"

Matthew watched her rise, his cell phone warm, winking in the palm of his hand. The number was on speed dial, even if he didn't have it memorized, and he was out of time—he could dial, or he could follow her up the fire escape and, as likely as not, he could lose her on the rooftops.

He pressed the button with his thumb. It rang one time.

"Matthew?"

"I lost her, Jane," he said, as the chill in his hands ebbed and eased. "I'm sorry."

"Her?"

"Yes. Elaine."

"Damn—" A pause, a whisper of breath he could picture, Jane's silver-black hair blown from her eyes. "That's the closest in some time. Did you speak to her, at least?"

"I gave her my name," Matthew said, unzipping his jacket one-handed as he walked out of the alley and toward the lights. "There's always the hope that she'll call."

"She can't," the transmitted voice of his archmage answered. "She would if she could. She's forbidden."

The shadow of an owl floated up the wall. Matthew was right. She should be put a stop to. Her footsteps fell light and level across the rooftop. She saw as the owl sees; she leapt the twenty feet from rooftop to rooftop as the doe leaps—until the cliff-edge of a warehouse brought her to a halt near the river.

Lifting her face, she sniffed the wind and sent her awareness *otherwise*, then leapt the roof-edge parapet into emptiness. The girl was below. Seeker smelled her. And another . . . *Damn that Mage for delaying me—*

—which was worth a wry grin. The Mage was less likely damned than she. She spread the owl's soft wings and floated down beside brick. She touched pavement. Predatory tunnel vision leached the edges of her awareness. She ran until the companion shadow of her doe deserted her, exhausted, and the shade of the cat ran beside her: hunter, leaper, stalker of prey.

Someone else stalked the same prey. The shadows showed her his footsteps: long black feet, pearly bare toenails, water dripping from his tattered cuff. A slow puddle spread where he passed, wet prints following him across the pavement.

Seeker pelted toward him, and he paced toward his prey.

The girl huddled in a doorway. Seeker glimpsed as much *otherwise*, and past her quarry saw the stalking enemy. Black of skin and long of face, clad in the rags of white pants and a shirt of archaic cut—and the very shadows seemed to recoil from his presence. He strode past the doorway and the girl.

Seeker turned the corner in time to see his sure steps hesitate. He paused, turned back. Delight or something passing for it creased his face as he smiled with square white teeth. "Are you hurt, child? Can I help you?"

She hesitated, but took his hand. As he helped her up, Seeker dug in and *ran*. The black cat still paced her; the tall man had not heard her footsteps. He turned the girl away, an arm around her shoulder, and she whispered something too soft to hear through the shadows.

When he replied, his voice was low but clear. "You're a pretty one to be out so late alone."

She glanced down and blushed: a child, vulnerable, whom the unicorn might once have adored. The dark man looked sideways at her, as if used to viewing life from only one eye at a time. White ringed his crystalline blue iris.

"Tell me, child," the thin man asked the girl, "have you ever ridden a horse?"

The exhausted cat-shadow vanished like a wind on water. Seeker's footsteps echoed, and she faltered to a stop. She had only the owl left, who couldn't help her now. And Gharne, but *this* would eat her familiar in half a bite, yawning.

But I know something he doesn't.

Shadows lay tangled on the ground behind man and girl, hers slight and mortal, his suddenly powerful, mane-tossing in fury.

"Kelpie!" Seeker shouted as he turned. A challenge, a demand. *Not his Name.* Kelpie came about to face her, his bare wet feet clattering on the stone.

He threw the girl down; she rolled and landed roughly, got her hands under her and started dragging herself away. Shadows twisted and writhed in Seeker's mind, slithering across her face. Kelpie relaxed, waiting.

"I charge you stay, child," Kelpie whispered. He stepped forward, his haunches and shoulders bulging.

Seeker shifted her weight, crouched, braced. *I'm dead. Even if I guess right, I'm not strong enough to bind that.*

They faced one another across ten cracked feet of asphalt. Seeker drew a brackish breath. "The child is claimed."

He snorted, vapor curling from nostrils grown broad and fierce. "Hardly by you, changeling. Or you should not leave your toys unattended, if she was."

Her hands shook. And he was deeper by far. He came on.

"The child is mine," Seeker repeated, "and the Mebd's."

"Contest me." Grotesquely swelling, and the girl's horror at last fixed on him. He towered. They stood in a shallow sea.

"By my hand and my heart," she replied. "By the name of your soul . . ." A gamble. A gamble, and maybe he would back down.

Hah.

You never knew.

The impact of Kelpie's hooves splattered Seeker's boots. His mane tossed froth-white. Pale hide shone under streetlights, wet and taut over muscle like bent and knotted ropes. He whinnied laughter, mane raining salt water, taste of the hurricane on his breath, as it was always meant to be.

He was glorious as he came to kill her, but Seeker remembered a teacher's voice in her ear. Calm. Maternal. *"Four things, if you forget all else, to be hoarded against need."*

He reared and Seeker cringed under his hooves, a lock of wet hair tangled between her fingers. Jewels of water shattered around her; behind Kelpie, the girl crouched in a puddle.

"To bind a thing, you must know its right Name," he said.

"By this lock of my hair, I know you to me. . . ." Her hands trembled. His weight bore her down—beyond control, beyond thought, beyond panic. *Four Names: Scian. Lile. Maat . . .*

The hooves came down.

There was no time to move and so she stood. Her will bent against his; strength crushed strength like blind, slick behemoths striving in the depths of the sea. Resilient, muscular, vast. *Please, please, please . . .*

". . . Uisgebaugh!"

Her fingers twisted the tangle into her hair as hooves shuddered above her. He all but *vibrated*—all power, all courage, and wilderness surged in his Caribbean eyes.

His shadow fell across her face. She reached out, gasping, and bent his power back like the fingers of a hand. Until he failed.

Squarely and sullen, his neck bent like a bow, he came to earth. Seeker wiped from her cheek, below the eye, some flecks of salt water that must have been thrown from his shaking mane.

"Mistress," he muttered.

She stepped away. "Fetch the girl."

The moon rose over the ocean, wearing a weary smile, her light reflected on billowing waves and Kelpie's sleek mane. His magic moved him quickly, for he was a part of this water and all water everywhere: all tides and currents, the great cycle that falls and flows and falls again into the vast blue cauldron of the ocean . . . and where there was water, there was also Kelpie.

And Seeker and the girl sat his back—Seeker shaking wet hair from her eyes, the girl growing stiffer in the cold.

Storm clouds massed on the horizon, black in the silver-lit sky. Distant lightning flashed, but Seeker didn't delight in its rumble. She saw the misery in her burden's face revealed in every flicker. The girl shivered and sobbed. She cried for water, and Kelpie gave her sweet water. She cried of the cold, and Seeker cloaked her. She cried for her pimp to come and save her, and Seeker bit her lip on a scathing *Gladly would I send you to join him.*

"Have courage, girl. There's worse to come."

They'd be rid of her soon. And then Kelpie and Seeker would continue their business. Though Seeker had bound him once, Kelpie might try two times more to kill her. If he failed thrice, he would belong to her—until she chose to unknot that lock of hair . . . or he died. Should she die first, his heart would stop with hers.

That was why Seeker was here, on his back, following his paths from the iron world to the moonlight one. If it had been merely her quarry and herself, she would have taken the thorn-tree road, her own path through the shadows not being made for sharing. But she judged it better to keep the Kelpie close and under her command, rather than trusting whatever devices he could get up to in her absence.

Waves pitched up and sideways, the sea hungry and unkempt. The ocean reached out contemptuously; the tips of the girl's fingers slid through Seeker's as a wave struck her from the Kelpie's back. She clawed upward, spluttering, shocked that the ocean should be so terrible.

Seeker leaned out, her fingers knotted perilously in Kelpie's pale mane, and clutched at the girl's grasping hand. She felt no fear, no rush of courage—only an overwhelming weariness that threatened to drown her as surely as the ocean would the girl. Seeker's fingers locked on her charge's wet wrist; she hauled the girl gasping and choking across Kelpie's withers. He tossed his head, eyes rolling, reflecting lightning as water sheeted down his face.

"Is this your storm?"

"Mistress, no." He might omit, but he could not fail to answer. And she had charged him to bring them safely to Annwn. "We are opposed."

"By whom?"

His shrug rolled his shoulders under her. "Magi? The Unseelie? I know not."

Seeker licked at the salt cracking her lips. "You need a name," she said.

"I have a Name."

"And shall I call you so before the court?"

He snorted and kept swimming, great muscles writhing under her thighs. She tightened her fingers in his mane.

Wet and wept out, the girl eventually curled into Seeker's arms. With her easy breathing, the storm subsided, and for a moment the Kelpie forgot himself enough to twist a look over his shoulder, one blue eye meeting Seeker's in surmise.

"Whiskey," he said. "Call me that."

The clouds shuddered to pieces before a setting moon and the easterly sky grayed. Seeker shook her charge awake. "Dawn and the clouds are breaking; you must see this."

The girl's eyes flickered open, the color of lichen: neither gray nor green nor hazel. Seeker had seen such eyes before, in the mirror and elsewhere. The girl seemed calmer now. Nothing was ever as bad in the morning as it had been in the night before. "Who . . . ?" and then her eyes registered Seeker and she sat up, squinting in mounting brightness.

"What do you see, girl?"

She grimaced.

"Water. Waves. The sky." She glanced over her shoulder, skin like honey once the makeup had washed away, her dark hair matted as stiff with salt as it had been with hair spray. "My name is Hope."

Seeker made an odd sound, a strangled laugh. "Certainly, it is." Then she leaned forward and kissed the girl's stone-colored eyes and her salt-wet mouth. The girl flinched, and when Seeker drew back, stared at her. Seeker pointed westward, where green hills welled up, visible to the *otherwise* eye. Taller swells on the ocean, hills like the call of the heart for home.

The sunlight touched those hills with gold.

Seeker's voice rose, off-key. " 'What are yonder high, high hills, the sun shines sweetly in? Those are the hills of Heaven, my love, where you will never win. . . .' "

Dawn in the Western Isles. How she'd grown to hate it.

Hope jerked against Seeker's grasp, her face lit in wonder as Seeker sighed once, quietly. They were lovely, high downs and the white faces of cliffs wrapped in rainbows struck from the golden mist. "The Westlands, Hope. Hy Bréàsil. Annwn. Tir Na Nog. Your home."

Whiskey snorted and surged forward—the end of his journey in sight. Seeker wondered if he truly swam so fast, or if his magic shortened the distance. Morgan would know. . . .

The Mebd's castle came into sight around a rocky curve of land, the reaching arm of stone protecting a half-moon of white sand at the base of a terraced, magical lawn. At the crest of the hill a beechwood harbored mist and chill morning. The line of trees vanished behind the palace, a fantasia of latticed golden stone translucent in the slanted light, green banners snapping in the stiff sea breeze.

A cluster of fair-haired fey ladies and Elf-knights waited along the beach. The impact of the Kelpie's hooves on the sand jarred his riders as he heaved himself from the ocean. Leaving the water was such an effort for his kind.

The courtiers of the Mebd came down to meet them, to receive Seeker's burden. Seeker handed the girl down willingly. And as she was off-balance, her steed melted beneath her with a breaking crash. Seeker rolled, scooping up a handful of sand. "An old trick, little treachery. And hardly your best . . ."

The wave struck before she saw it, knocking the precious bit of earth from her hand. It sucked her under, churning; she struggled for the surface, breathlessness an iron band across her chest, fingertips breaking into blessed air as she dragged herself upward. Sweet breath filled her lungs in the moment before he knocked her under. He was implacable as the bottomless lochs of Scotland, and he liked to play with his prey.

Violent currents twisted her. She struck for the bottom, hoping he would think her disoriented. One hand clawed through rocks, into sand. A sharp shell gashed her, blackness billowing. But she brought cupped hands to her mouth, blowing into them through the blood and watching the bubbles rise through water gone still and silent.

She drifted, knowing he could push her back if she struggled upward, wait for her to drown. Hoping that he needed a more *direct* vengeance—until a mammoth blow, a wall of water, slammed her chest, would have hammered the air from her lungs if she had any left, struck again. She spread her hands, the silvery net between them terribly frail.

She cast the net into the sea.

The ocean grew still, as if lost in memory. When she broke the surface, gasping and fuming, a cheer went up, and when the Kelpie arose behind her draped in her net as if in seaweed, a laugh. Seeker was not well loved. But nothing tamed is fond of that which still has freedom, and it amused the Mebd's courtiers to see one of the wild Fae bound.

Chapter Two

The Mebd awaited her, but Seeker did not hurry to dress. She stood before her mirror, feet bare on damp stone, a white linen shift brushing the tops of her knees. The tarnished silver backing of the looking glass mottled her reflection.

"Hurry," said Robin from the doorway. "Herself will not be pleased at the delay."

Seeker reflected an arch glance at the Puck. "The more you talk," she said, "the longer it takes." She turned back to the mirror and examined her face while Puck hopped on one foot, long ears twitching. She hid her smile, spread her arms, and spun thrice, hair flying about her.

Rippling folds of cloth of silver flared as she whirled, swaying heavily when she set her heel and stopped. Pewter-colored brocade skirts brushed the floor, the bodice pushing Seeker's bosom higher and cinching her waist.

She examined herself critically. Nothing but glamourie, and gone on the stroke of midnight. Fortunately, there were no clocks in Faerie. Seeker motioned as if tugging on gloves, and gloves appeared—darker gray than her gown, and of kid. Puck tapped his foot.

"Coming, Robin. Really, you'd think it was something important, and not the same audience every time."

He made no answer, and Seeker snorted in irritation. She too tapped her heel on the stones, but the third time she made the gesture she was greeted not by the *pat pat* of bare skin but by a musical jingle. She raised her skirts in one hand and thrust a foot out, inspecting a slipper of gray-and-white vair decked with tiny silver chimes.

" 'Rings on her fingers and bells on her toes—' " she commented, and Puck cut her off.

"And she'll be beheaded by morning if she delays longer."

"That doesn't rhyme, Robin."

"Or scan, either. It's *modern* poetry. Are you ready?"

"My hair's not done." Seeker angled her head and lifted her hands, running gloved fingers through glossy black strands. They fell into place, narrow braids twining accent to pearls and silver, the crude knot with which she had bound the Kelpie smoothing itself into a ladderlike four-strand braid bound with silver wire and a single pearl black and shining as a moonlit sea. Seeker touched her ears and throat to conjure quiet jewelry, and passed a hand across her face. "How do I look?"

"Well enough," Puck replied, tugging her toward the door. His legs were much shorter, but she had to step quickly to keep up. Her slippers jangled like sleigh bells; she took short breaths of air laden with the scents of wisteria and mist.

They hurried through vaulted corridors wrought of translucent golden stone, past the doorways of rooms that had stood empty for all the twenty-five years of Seeker's service, immaculately clean, waiting like grooms abandoned at the altar.

The Mebd's palace was bigger inside than out, and Seeker could not imagine it full. Its forlorn elegance spanned distances she associated with city neighborhoods and college campuses, and seemed designed for mourning. A certain misty forsakenness became it.

To think of these echoing passages teeming with Fae was daunting, both in the idea of that much alien extravagance, and the vivid realization of how much Faerie had lost.

The small ones had sickened first: the nature spirits, the little lives of brooks and trees. Some prospered, finding niches in wild places or under the aegis of sympathetic householders, but most limped, faltered, died. Imps and pixies, brownies and sprites, were not comfortable in kitchens full of stainless appliances and gardens sown with commercially propagated flowers. This was the true triumph of the

Prometheans: to turn even the red, red rose into a warding that kept the Fair Folk at bay. And if the roses lost their scent along the way, it was a small price for safety, for preeminence.

William Butler Yeats, who should have known, reported conflicting theories about the Fae. Some, he said, called them the last remnants of the Pagan gods, shrunk now and small, half-forgotten. Some said they were angels too bad to serve in Heaven, and too good to be damned to Hell. Other stories listed them with the Nephilim, among the children of angels who were tempted by the daughters of men, and so fell.

In any case, this much was true: they would not abide the name of the Divine; they preyed on the iron world to enslave knights, courtesans, paramours, poets, and lemans, and—as recorded in the ballad of Tam or Tom or Thomas Lin or Lynn or Lane or Line—at the end of every seven years, they paid a tithe to Hell. They brought home children of Fae descent as well, like young Hope, to replenish their fading line.

And they took mortals to pay that tribute.

Seeker's quarter-century in Faerie had taught her how worthwhile was the price—the scent of a rose, the life of a Fae—for human safety. Annwn's Queens were immoral as glaciers, righteous as stones. They locked their hearts in secret places, and they had learned to lock away the hearts of their lovers and playthings too.

Janet never would have won Tam Lin back from Queens so armed with bitter experience as the Mebd and the Cat Anna.

"Don't hum that," Robin said, and Seeker jerked guiltily.

"Hum what?"

He glanced over his shoulder, then whistled a few quick bars of music, his mulish ears wobbling flat.

> *If I had known, if I had known, Tam Lin*
> *I would have taken your heart*
> *And put in place of your heart, a stone—*

Seeker snorted. "Well, she knows better now, doesn't she?"

Robin Goodfellow answered her with a grimace, and picked up his pace. "She can see through the glamours, of course," he said, with a rude gesture to her dress.

"Of course," Seeker replied, "but she expects the courtesy." *And one day I would love to go before her in my robe and slippers. Especially when she insists on hauling me into court the instant I return, weary and salt-stained.*

"Aye," Puck answered, and fell silent until they stood before the dark Gothic doors leading to the throne room. An intricate relief worked into the panels cried out for hands to stroke its maidens and men at love and at war; hounds and horse in pursuit of wolves and stags; animal-headed spirals of three points, with the legs of hares or horses interwoven in the knotwork. On either side of the portal a grim guard stood, helm shuttered and a green-and-violet cloak slung around its shoulders, stiff as its own tasseled halberd. Seeker didn't know if they were men, Fae, or merely animate suits of armor. She'd never bothered to find out.

The Puck stepped away as she squared herself before the door, flicked illusory bell-skirts straight, and stiffened her spine. Mute on brazen hinges, the weighty doors swung open.

Her slippers chiming into the silence of a hundred broken conversations, Seeker entered the presence chamber of the Mebd of the Daoine Sidhe.

At first all Seeker saw was the jostle of silks and colors, the flutter of ribbons and cloaks adorning lords and ladies of the Fae—each taller and blonder than the next, and all taller and blonder than she. They had halted midstep in their dance, and as Seeker pressed forward into the vaulted hall the lines of the pavane parted before her. She stalked down their ranks, a solitary silver-clad figure amid a prismatic shimmer of green and gold and orange, of umber and periwinkle, ruby and cobalt. She heard the whispers as she passed, the rising murmur of voices over the rustle of stiff skirts and the jingle of her shoes. These were the high lords and ladies of the Fae, Elf-knights and green women—not the half-blood changelings that she was charged with returning to the nest, although even some of those rose among the ranks. Still, they drew back from her. *Word of the Kelpie has spread, I see.*

She tasted a bitter nugget of joy at seeing them afraid.

The last rows parted before her, revealing the Mebd, imperious on her gilded chair of estate, robed in a luxury of emerald and aubergine. A mantle of darkest forest-green silk swathed her, so brocaded with embroidery that the fabric was almost invisible. A wimple of finest white lawn hid her throat, and although the Mebd's hair was concealed by the veil of violet silk, Seeker knew it was golden as wheatstraw. *And knotted with more knots and braids and bindings than there are stars in the summer night.* Concealed behind velvet drapes and under a velvet pall, the shrouded figure of her throne hulked at the back of the dais—rarely used and never uncovered.

The Mebd's pet curled on a velvet cushion beside her chair of estate. A naked human boy who appeared perhaps six, green eyes bright beneath a fetching mop of ebony curls, he fiddled idly with his golden collar. Seeker's eyes avoided him, and she'd learned to hide the sting of tears in her eyes. It had been the same engaging lad curled there for a quarter of a mortal century—longer, in Faerie. The Mebd had ways of keeping things as they suited her.

Seeker came to the foot of the dais and dropped a curtsey that puddled her gown like spilled quicksilver on the azurite-and-malachite tiled floor. *Bound, like Whiskey. Poor little treachery.* Her throat burned with pity. Her eyes stayed lowered until the Mebd cleared her throat and said, softly, "Rise."

"Your Majesty." Seeker stood and looked into the eyes of her mistress. They shifted color when the Mebd smiled—perfect lips curving like a harvest moon—violet to jade and then violet again. Seeker was not invited to speak further.

The Mebd's voice was resonant as a dulcimer. "You've brought us charming gifts again, my Seeker, and we are well pleased with you. So well pleased that we have another task—one that, we think, will much challenge your skills."

Seeker concentrated on the formal rhythms of the Queen's speech. Where was the trap? "Your Majesty."

The Mebd inclined her magnificently encumbered head. "We have learned that a Merlin has come into his maturity."

She had thought herself ready for anything—any announcement, any task. Not so. Seeker's mouth fell open and she staggered back, tripping on the train of her gown. Silently, she cursed the bravado that had made her add chimes to her shoes; they jangled madly as a falcon's belled jesses.

The Mebd continued, imperturbable. "Your predecessors have had some success with previous Merlins, as you well know. Nimue, Viviane . . . their names are remembered. Merlins are rarer now than in days of old. One does not succeed the next so neatly. And *this* Merlin has not yet met his Dragon, has not yet grown into his power." The Mebd paused, waiting for Seeker, but all she could manage was a dry-mouthed nod.

Patient, the Mebd waited until Seeker found her voice. "You wish me to entrap him. Your Majesty."

The Mebd's smile warmed, reaching her eyes. "Bind the Merlin, Seeker, and we bind the Dragon. And *that* is a power that we have been too long without. You must hurry, of course. Doubtless our sister has taken an interest as well."

Seeker tried a breath, the next question seasick in the back of her mouth. "Majesty . . ."

The Mebd waited, eyebrow arched, while Seeker swallowed hard and tried again. "Majesty. Is there a . . . one of the other sort, as well?" Seeker waited for the slow oscillation of her liege's head, but denial did not come.

"Bind the Merlin," the Mebd said instead, leaning forward, "bind the Dragon. Bind the Dragon; bind the King."

Keith MacNeill waited in a place out of the moonlight, his nose stinging with the scent of roses, and watched as the woman he had loved seated herself on the carven bone bench beside a sleeping man's bier. He had been awaiting his moment. He had been watching her for hours.

The Seeker had exchanged her glamoured gown for slacks, boots and a tunic, her elaborate hairstyle for a single thick black braid with smaller braids wound through it. Emeralds glittered in her ears. They were real emeralds, set in white platinum, wrought by a mortal crafts-man. Keith remembered.

She bent over a book sewn into a doeskin binding, writing with a gold-pointed fountain pen. The little chapel was silent. Few came there anymore except attendants and caretakers.

Every so often, Seeker raised her head to glance at the bier, the moonlight falling through latticed walls across the sleeping man's face. Keith could see the sleeper clearly from his vantage place: a warrior in his middle years, perhaps, tall and broad of shoulder, no longer as narrow in the hip as a boy. His hair was reddish blond, graying beside closed eyes. Combed long and neat over his shoulders, it stirred in his breath where a lock lay across his face: his beard darker red and trimmed to follow the line of an arrogant jaw. Keith noticed the aquiline features and the fullness of his lips in repose, the way his big, scarred hands folded over the hilt of the bronze sword laid the length of his chest.

Bronze, and not the star-iron one he once had carried.

Seeker sucked the cap of her fountain pen and added a few more words. When she glanced up, her gaze fell on the sleeping man's face. She paused and marked her place in the book with the pen before standing. Moonlight caught on the twisted strands of her hair, casting her shadow like a stain on the alabaster floor as she came forward.

She laid her hands on the edge of the High King's bier and leaned forward, nostrils flaring. Keith's twitched in sympathy. A heavy funk of crushed roses surrounded the sleeper.

Tenderly, she brushed the disordered hair from his cheek. "Arthur, you son of a bitch."

Her voice came out low, snarled as neglected ribbons. "You could have been the best of all of them. I know the price. But did it have to be the babies?"

Of course he didn't answer. His eyelashes lay against his cheek without fluttering, undisturbed by her voice. She let her weight rest for a moment on her hands before turning aside, reaching for her notebook.

Soundless on cool tile, Keith stepped forward. "Elaine."

She stiffened, glancing back at the sleeping King. Keith bit down on a chuckle as Seeker raised her eyes to him.

He stood casually naked behind the bier and raised both hands to smooth back hair disarrayed by his previous run. Quarter-moon, and he could do as he pleased. Elaine would know that. He saw her glance at the sky. " 'The wind from one door closing opens another,' " she said, and the savagery in her voice as she quoted his own platitude pushed him a step back.

Keith drew a breath like boiling lead and looked down at Arthur. "He tried so hard, poor bastard. It's just not fair."

Seeker glared. He flinched; it had not always been so. "What are you doing here?"

His small, hopeful attempt at a smile slid from his lips. "I've a word for you, Seeker," he said, formally.

Her chin rose, her jaw etched in moonlight. "Your word?"

"A message."

"What's that?"

"Mist requests you attend her. Tonight."

"Mist . . . requests? How do *you* know what Mist requests?"

Keith began turning, his form blurring as he spoke. "It came to me in a dream." And nails clicked on pale marble as a powerful red-pelted wolf trotted back into the night.

Jane Andraste was already waiting when Matthew arrived. She held the door to her penthouse open, a rail-narrow woman with silver-streaked hair twisted precisely in a chignon to complement her pearls. Her suit fit as if tailored for her.

It probably had been. And only Jane would be so carefully dressed, even at home in the middle of the night.

Matthew glanced down at her shoes, fingering his rings. Jane caught him at it and winked . . . and then looked down at her own hand as she extended it to him. Her skin was soft with age, the bones and tendons visible.

"My apologies, Jane," he said, as she extricated her hand from his and turned to latch the door. "My failure—"

"Not a failure." She smiled. "Call it a qualified success."

Matthew wasn't quite so ready to forgive himself, but the tightness across his chest eased at her words.

"Are you hungry, Matthew?" Always gracious, even in declining to answer.

"I could eat," he admitted, as she led him over antique rugs toward the modern stainless steel and white-tile kitchen. "I laid hands on her, Jane."

The archmage shrugged, running water into the coffeepot. "Frustrating," she said, and then fell silent as she measured the coffee into the filter and turned the switch. She came back to the counter. "But anticipated. Trust an old wizard when she says you did well. Cream, no sugar, yes?"

"How do you manage to remember things like that?"

"Talent," she said, and tipped her head toward the breakfast table in the corner. "Sit, Matthew. If you hover, you're going to make me spill your coffee."

"I see." He pulled out a padded chair and sat, leaning against the back support gratefully. Despite the aroma of brewing coffee, his eyes kept trying to drift closed. "The Seeker—Elaine Andraste—"

"You'll have another chance at my daughter yet, I expect," Jane said. "We have rituals to set up, a spirit-trace on her and on the pointy-toothed Unseelie Seeker as well. Would you like the milk warmed in the microwave?"

"The hotter the better," Matthew answered, pressing fingertips to his throbbing temples. He loosened the elastic on his ponytail and finger-combed the chin-length locks that fell free, sighing in relief. A warrior or a wizard bound his hair and fastened his clothing and left no un-knotted strings about his person when he went into battle, but the ponytail always gave Matthew a headache. "Please don't play coy, archmage. I'm too tired for guessing games."

"Unfair of me," she conceded as the microwave beeped, and poured his coffee into the cup, atop the steaming milk.

"That's a speedy coffeemaker. Why the spirit-trace?"

"Isn't it great?" She slid the cup in front of him and started assembling her own. If she hadn't splashed the counter, he never would have known her hands were shaking. "The Unseelie Seeker has been in and out of North America on mysterious errands for the past two months. And now Elaine has joined her—"

"Elaine was strong enough to bind the Kelpie."

Jane cupped her coffee in both hands and blew across the steam so it curled from her lips like a musing dragon's breath. "Their competition can only help us," Jane said. "But whatever they're both seeking is something we must find first."

"Something? Or someone?"

"I suspect the latter," Jane Andraste said. Her cup clicked on the white-tile counter as she reached behind herself to set it down. "Soup or sandwich?"

"Soup and toast?" he said hopefully. She grinned.

"I envy a young man's appetite."

While she opened cans and clattered spoons, he waited for his coffee to cool enough to drink. "Someone," he reminded, when the aroma of chicken stock filled the kitchen.

She chuckled and turned back, raising her wooden spoon. "What could we do with a Merlin, Matthew?"

Matthew blinked. "What *couldn't* we do? But if you expect one, doesn't that mean a Dragon Prince won't be far behind?"

"Not necessarily," she answered, stirring the soup before it could scorch. "But it's time."

"That could be everything Prometheus needs—"

"Yes," she said, and reached for the ladle on the drainboard. "Everything we need to win this. Once, and finally."

The pain she hid so carefully spoke to a like pain in Matthew, and he leaned back, refusing to give in to it. *Everyone's lost someone,* he told himself firmly. *Your circumstances are not special.*

Seeker paused in the darkness at the base of the down, in a narrow valley overgrown with gorse and heather. The moon was slipping over the edge of the world and a cold fog coiled her ankles like an anxious cat; she closed her eyes and ducked her head. Three deep breaths brought little calm.

Seeker raised her face, looked around, and set off down the bank of a rocky stream that ran along the bottom of the vale. She saw in the dark with owl-eye facility, now that her shadow-bound familiars were rested. *If the sun would break through the mist once in a while. If it would thunder and rain. Why is it, I wonder, that we are permitted moonlight and not sunlight? What's so terrible about weather?* She laughed at the thought, her voice echoing strangely off the moss-and-ivy-hung rocks. The sound was eerie; it struck her to silence again.

Below a sheer escarpment, Seeker splashed through the brook, slick rocks turning under leather-soled boots. She could see the shadow of a greater darkness behind the thick tapestry of brier-rose and ivy. A frog jumped under her footstep; she recoiled, almost falling as she put her foot down hard. She windmilled her arms, regaining balance, and thought she heard the echo of a bubbling, neighing laugh.

She closed her lips on the first comment that came to mind, counting silently to five. "Behave yourself," she said softly, "unless you plan to challenge me again today, Uisgebaugh."

The narrow brook chortled over the rocks in answer. Seeker stepped onto the bank as the music of trickling water changed to the clatter of hooves. "I shall bide my time. I am patient."

"So the legends tell me." She glanced over her shoulder. Whiskey stood just as he must have risen, dripping, out of the chattering stream. He bowed his head to her with a little toss of his mane that made the gesture into mockery.

Then he snorted, a giant pale shape in the darkness, his black-splashed head raised, Roman nose in profile against the sky. "Walk into that cave, mistress, and you'll never walk out. There's something in there older, even, than I."

"Your concern flatters me."

"Hardly. Your death means my death, unless I kill you myself. I am knotted in your hair."

Seeker had heard the ritual words before. So close after the werewolf's visit, they all but burned her. "I am sorry." She turned back to the green-shrouded entrance of the cave. She reached out and took a handful of hanging vines, careful to grab the canes of brier-rose between the thorns.

It was in bloom, out of season or not. The roses never faded in the Blessed Isles. Seeker was tempted to strip the five-petaled blossoms from it with her bare hands for spite.

"Permit me to protect you."

"If you want to protect me," Seeker answered, lifting greenery aside, "don't tell the Mebd." She pushed into the cave.

When the curtain of vines fell behind her, shutting the Kelpie and the starlight away, the darkness was absolute. Even her cat's vision could not penetrate it. Seeker felt the dry stone of the cave under her boots and raised her right hand, calling foxlight around her fingers. It cast a flickering St. Elmo's fire throughout the arched stone tunnel, revealing the marks of chisels and hammers and the gold-flecked veins of quartz for which the dwarves had delved. Vapor coiled her limbs.

Cool air redolent of moldering leaves and old charred wood filling her lungs, Seeker started down the tunnel. It descended to a shallow, spiraling slope broad enough for two lanes of traffic. The floor was almost polished, chiseled with patterns of ivy and roses to echo those that hung by the entryway. In the souls of the craftsmen who carved this mine, utility was no excuse for a thing to be anything but beautiful.

The odors of rot and burning grew stronger as she crept under the earth. She let the foxlight die off her fingers when a dull crimson glow began to cast relief shadows along the carvings. When the threads of mist lit orange-red, she almost hesitated. But if she stopped, she wouldn't start again.

Seeker took a final step around the corner into a painful light. The tunnel opened halfway up the wall of a cavern as vast and changeable as a view of the sea. Mist coiled within it like twisted pennants, drifting in banners and streams on cool currents of air. And within the mist . . . lay *Mist*.

Fog-white tendrils scrolled about her face, a face that transformed from moment to moment while the Dragon lifted her massive head. Eyes gleaming in streaked planes of hot light, translucent as fire opals, considered Seeker. When the Dragon bent her neck to shift a wing long as a battlefield, an ashen sheen rippled over char-dark scales. The hide between glared golden, scarlet, lava cracking as it flowed.

Stirring the sea of gold and jewels on which she nested with one lazy five-taloned hand, the Dragon blinked. She shifted again—scales now more black, like sharp-chipped obsidian; now red as magma; now a dark hot gold like molten steel. The wings first spread wide and then the body coiled sinuous and narrow—the head horned and then maned and then antlered a moment later.

The eyes remained unchanged.

The Dragon's voice rang like forged iron. "Elaine Elizabeth Andraste, Seeker of the Changed. Enter freely into my domain, secure in love and trust."

"Dana," Seeker tried to say, or one of the Dragon's other Names. "Mist." Her knees went to water. She fell under the density of the Dragon's presence, ducking her face toward bedrock. Carven stone scored her palms; the heat of blood smeared the petals on the bas-relief briers. She managed one breath, and then another, and then her voice. "Grandmother Dragon. I am not Elaine Andraste. I have no Name."

Hot breath surrounded her, fragrant of summer. The voice was tolerant and amused, maternal in its enormity. "Of course you have a name, child. Your mother gave it you, did she not?"

"I am the Seeker of the Changed. The Queen of the Daoine Sidhe has me tangled in her hair." Something stiffened her spine as she said the words, however, and Seeker raised her eyes to meet Mist's. "She's stripped me of such insignificant things."

The Dragon chuckled, rattling small stones loose from the tunnel roof. Seeker felt the vibration between her teeth. "Foolish child. Has no one ever explained the rules to you?"

"Yes." *It's no worse than being condescended to by the Mebd, and you bow your head to her.* But another rogue voice whispered, *But here you have a choice,* and Seeker pressed her slashed hand against the stone and, wincing with pain, pushed herself to her feet. "I know the rules. I've spent my three chances, Grandmother Dragon."

"Chances are nothing. These are the older rules, and even the Mebd must abide them—that in life one may be bound or bought, but in the end you go to judgment naked, clad only in what you were born with and what you have earned, lessened only by what you have sold or given away. That which is taken by force, for good or for ill, goes unconsidered. Understand?"

It is perilous to admit weakness. It is even more perilous to lie to dragons. "Mist, I do not."

"No matter. You will. For mortal men, immortality is of the soul—but for Faerie immortality is of the body only, as they have no souls. And you were born mortal, Elaine Andraste." The ever-changing head rocked from side to side.

"I was born a changeling. I am of Faerie now."

Mist seemed to ignore the statement. Pricked ears swiveled forward at the top of the mountainous head—then they smoothed into scales and antlers emerged in their place. *The Dragon that is all dragons.* Seeker thought the Dragon smiled.

"Perhaps that is as it is." Wryness colored the voice, and a forked tongue thick as a hawser darted forward to taste Seeker's sweat. And then a lightning shift, quick as the flicker of that tongue. "Your task is to bind me."

Seeker blinked at the suddenness of it. "Yes." A sour taste filled her mouth, her heart hammering in her chest. *If she slays me, I don't have to worry about the Mebd—or my crimes in her service—anymore.* Another realization, a heartbeat later, like a ragged follower to the first—*But I don't want to die.*

And if I die, Gharne and Uisgebaugh die with me.

"Here, in this place, you stand in the heart of my power. Even your Queen cannot protect you."

"Yes." A cold fear, like a dagger pressed up through the diaphragm and under Seeker's breastbone.

"And despite this, you came before me."

Seeker swallowed. *Dangerous to lie to dragons.* Gold coins rattled like beach pebbles beneath the Dragon's feet. Seeker thought of the sound of a shaken length of chain. She understood that she was being tested, but she did not know the nature of the test. "Yes."

"Why?"

What is the right answer? Quickly, without thinking, Seeker closed her eyes and blurted, "Because you asked nicely."

Silence—a great and echoing silence—followed by laughter that knocked Seeker from her feet again and rolled her aside, literal gales of laughter. Seeker curled into a ball, huddled on the knotty carven granite, arms drawn up to protect her face. It went on for a long time, smelling of roses and the end of winter, and at last trailed off with a satisfied sigh.

Seeker risked uncoiling enough to open her eyes and look out. The Dragon's enormous red-shattered eye hung over her, blinking lazily. "You'll do," the Dragon said. "When the time comes, remember this conversation. What I have told you will prove useful. And take some pains to conceal it from your mistress—she would be angry."

Chapter Three

Grass stems bent cool under the pads of Keith's feet as he paused on a hillside in Scotland, a northern outpost of the iron world. He crouched behind a shaggy line of meadow plants, his elbows barely brushing the earth as he tasted the wind and observed the long, exposed slope he must descend. Wolves don't live long, who walk heedlessly into a moonlit field. Even one that amounts to their own backyard.

A house—a romantic old heap, more properly—dominated the valley below, straddling the narrow zone of safety between the hillside and where the marshy burn might flood when it rose. Neither precisely a manor house nor a castle, its outline described an irregular rectangle of mortared stone with chimneys and additions and gables protruding at odd angles like the spines of a hedgehog. It was the same color in moonlight or sunlight or overcast: dappled silver and charcoal, a few of the boulders nearest the foundation glinting with mica when the light slanted against them.

The sea tossed against a rocky beach; the village was a little way off. The house had the look of a gentleman farmer's abode, and the lawns were indeed cropped close by sheep and shaggy Highland cattle—*coos*, in Eoghan MacNeill's parlance—but there were those who knew the deeper truth: that there were no more wolves in Scotland, except the wolves who dwelled here.

Keith let his tail rise cockily, picture of a returning Prince, and trotted down the slope through cold reflected moonlight to his father's door.

He passed through late summer herbs—the mint gone to flower, the dill setting seed—and scratched and whined at the kitchen door rather than the big main entrance that faced the road and the sea. Stout gray-haired Morag was there to let him in, the dressing gown in her hands draped over his shoulders deftly even as he began to change. His paws became hands as he fumbled with the belt; Morag stepped back to stir the soup pot on the stove.

"Welcome home, young master," she said. "You were missed a bit. The bread's in the oven. Your father is in his study, and I imagine he'd be glad of ye."

"I'd have thought he wouldna be at home," Keith answered, bending down to kiss her on the part of her hair. "Isn't it his Glasgow week?"

She hesitated, the thick stock curling around her wooden spoon. "Och. He's not well, Keith my love . . ."

"Ah." Keith stepped back, thrusting his fists into the pockets of the dressing gown.

Morag dropped her spoon on the ceramic spoonrest—shaped like a chicken—and turned to face Keith. She craned her neck back, hands on her hips, her frown twisting the tip of her nose to one side. "You sound like a damned American, laddie."

" 'Tis a thicket of deception," he answered, grinning. "*Some* of us have to leave Scotland once in a while, Morag. Or there'd be not a soul left in the country but wolves and their brides."

"And would that be such a bad thing?" She *tch'd*, cocking her head to one side like a bird, eyes glittering bright enough to make him laugh. "Go, see your father, young master. It would be a kindness of you."

"He's that poorly?"

"Aye."

"I've nowhere else I need to be," he answered. "Of course I'll stay. And I'll go up and see him as soon as I get some clothes on. Will that suit?"

"It will," she said, and stood on tiptoe to kiss the air beside his cheek.

Keith joined his father fifteen minutes later, having taken the time to clean the mud from under his nails and change his dressing gown for blue jeans and a cable-knit sweater. The study was only loosely so

termed; Eoghan MacNeill had lavished more attention on this room
than any other in his slow restoration of the old manor house, and its
rugged tapestry-hung walls framed a view of the moonlit ocean through
broad modern windows. The massive table that served as Eoghan's desk
was butted up against the outside wall. As Keith entered the room, he
saw his father's head framed by the window, silver hairs picked out by
the green-blue glow of twinned monitors and the remaining ginger
strands sidelit by the amber warmth of the fireplace.

And when did he get so much gray in his hair? "Your Highness," Keith said,
and paused just within the door, sorting the aromas of the room through
his inadequate human nose. Smoke and whiskey, mothballs and his father's human sweat . . .

. . . and in that sweat, a sourness Keith recognized all too well.
Eoghan turned in his swivel chair and smiled like a wolf, lips closed
over his teeth, but did not rise. He looked drastically thinner than when
Keith had seen him last, his cheekbones standing high under papery
skin, and his eyes had sunken over them and were smeared with darkness like kohl. Keith came across the carpet, sandalwood and camphor
rising from the wool compressed under his loafers, and crouched to take
his father's hand. The old wolf's nails were yellowed and sharply
hooked; Keith saw the marks of the file along their edges, and the
cramped-looking bulges of Eoghan's knuckles as he tightened his
grip—a grip still strong enough to make Keith set his jaw to endure it.
Not quite ready for his deathbed yet, Keith thought, and squeezed right back.

"Stand up, stand up. Get a chair. We don't see you enough at home
anymore, my boy." Eoghan released his grip and turned back to his
computer long enough to save his document. "Pour me a wee dram
while you're up, there's a good lad."

Keith did as he was bid, smiling into his beard, and tried not to notice how his father braced both hands on the edge of his desk in order
to gain his feet. Eoghan met him by the fire, gesturing him into one of
the twin wing chairs set before it, and shrugged Keith's hand off when
Keith would have helped him to sit. "I smell that wench of yours on ye,"
he said, after Keith pushed the tumbler of whiskey into his hand. "I
don't suppose that means there's word of your son?"

Keith shook his head. "Things are . . ." His voice trailed off, and the old wolf snorted and leaned forward, hands dangling between his knees and the glass pressed between his palms, staring into the fire. Keith pressed into the overstuffed chair, as if in contravention of his father's posture. ". . . no better."

"You'll need that lad when I'm gone," Eoghan said. Keith shot him a startled look, and saw his father complacently sipping whiskey, eyes twinkling like peridots in the firelight.

"Gone?"

"Aye, or did you mean to let the princedom of the pack desert our lineage? Tell me you'll fight in my memory, lad."

The fire was warm on the soles of Keith's feet, even through the leather of his shoes. "I haven't thought of it," he said, pretending the nauseating twist of panic was someone else's emotion. "I hadn't thought of it at all."

"Think on it now," Eoghan said. He leaned back with a sigh, and rested his glass on his leg. "It won't be long—"

"You're strong yet." Said as a dismissal, and Keith could not stop the oblique twist of his right hand that brushed the issue aside, and away.

"Deny it if you like," Eoghan answered. "I'll be dead before the New Year; I can feel the weariness in my bones when the moon changes. And I'd like to meet my grandson before I go."

"It won't be easy," Keith said.

The old wolf shrugged. "What in life is? A wolf who won't claim his own offspring won't be seen as fit to lead the pack."

"Who said I wanted to lead the pack, father?"

Eoghan tilted his head to one side and smiled, and this time he showed Keith the edge of his teeth. Just enough to make an impression, and no more. "Did ye think you had a choice?"

Whiskey awaited Seeker in the predawn light, head bowed, nosing listlessly among the waterweeds. He lifted black-socked feet aimlessly from the stream and set them down. *Waiting to be struck dead.* Seeker felt pity like an edge of glass parting her skin, until she recalled his many murders.

"Uisgebaugh," she said from the mouth of the cavern.

His head came up. He snorted and thrust himself up the bank, water puddling from his lower legs and feet. It dripped from his mane as well, spotting the shoulder of her tunic as he lowered his head to look her in the eye. "You are well."

"More or less. Bend a knee for me, water-horse." She reached up and grasped his mane, sliding belly first over his broad back before slinging her right leg across his rump. Water streaked her front and soaked her thighs, running in streams over her fingers where she clutched the mane. "I don't suppose you can shut that off, can you?"

From the shadows that lay all around them, she saw *otherwise* as his head went down; she was ready. Big hooves left the ground; he rocked forward, sunfishing halfheartedly. She held on, feeling water stream between her legs and his hide, smacking him once on the neck with her open hand. "Enough."

He pawed the earth, but his hide was abruptly dry.

She tugged his mane so he sat back obediently on his haunches and spun like a cattle pony, hooves carving gullies in the streambank. He leapt the water, snorting, and set off at a trot that was harder than it had to be, grinding her groin against his backbone and rattling her teeth. She kicked him in the ribs, twice, and he settled into a canter gentle as a rocking horse. "You ride well," he said grudgingly.

"I'm from Wyoming." As if that explained everything.

"Where are we going, mistress?"

"You heard of the task the Mebd set for me?"

He shook his mane, ears flickering. Bladderwort squelched between her fingers, tangling his mane. "Everyone has."

"We're looking for a mortal man to seduce and betray. Your specialty." His hoofbeats echoed from the face of the down. She turned him with the pressure of her knees and started up the flank of the big hill at an angle, toward a copse of trees that crested it. East, the sky shone pink and silver, ephemeral.

She leaned into the beat as he picked up speed, powerful hindquarters propelling them. Big as he was, he moved like a quarter horse, bunching and extending, covering the ground in fast, jerky strides. His feathers, the dark long hair on his fetlocks, flared and floated.

"This is the way to the Weyland Smithy."

"It is," she answered. "We're seeing about shoes."

He stopped short, head-tossing. She squeezed with her legs and he danced backward.

"You will go on," she said. "Our hunt will lead us into the iron realm. They lay iron under the roadways."

He shivered beneath her, ears laid flat. "I went into the mortals' city barefooted. You saw."

"Indeed. Barely ten feet from the water, dripping oceans with every step, and weak enough that something like me could bind you. You will have shoes."

He pawed another gully, water flooding from his hoofprint. His head dipped and Seeker held tight to the mane, expecting him to kick out again or to rear. The final contest.

Instead, a great breath heaved from his barrel. "As you wish." Docile, he turned toward the copse.

Rowan, hazel, ash and willow: she knew their flowering branches. As Whiskey bore her to the edge of the glade, a heavy hammer thundered, faster than any smith should have swung it. She slid down, sighing as her feet touched the greensward. The scent of burning coke and scorched metal reminded her of Mist.

One hand on Whiskey's neck, she led him forward.

Trees completely enclosed the rough clearing. Beside a rock-rimmed well a bandy-legged little man bent over his forge, naked except for a leather apron. Terrible scars marked the back of his leg where a jealous god had lamed him. He wore his long matted beard parted and braided, the ends knotted behind his back; the hammer he swung with such ease bore a head as big as a breadloaf. Other tools hung like offerings from the branches of the trees.

Weyland Smith turned at the sound of Whiskey's hooves and set his tongs and hammer aside. He cocked his head, bald at the center as if tonsured, and sucked his cheeks in as he looked from Seeker to

Whiskey and back again. "Well," he said, and turned his head to spit into the grass, "what have we here?"

"A horse for the shoeing, mastersmith." Seeker walked forward, holding out a hand with two silver coins glittering in the palm. Weyland Smith's geas—the rule that bound him—was simple: he could refuse no commission, no matter how daunting. His little eyes glittered like stars as he reached a gnarled hand for the money.

He bit down on the silver and then dropped one coin each in the two pockets of his apron. "I've not shod a horse like that one before. It'll be silver, shall it? Silver for the moon-horse, silver for the horse of the water."

"Silver will do nicely." Seeker turned and beckoned Whiskey. He came stamping, pied tail swishing, his nostrils flaring wet red in his face—a piebald who was almost a horse white as milk, black-legged and splashed with black on face and breast, with black strands lacing the pale mane and tail.

The little smith ignored him and bent to his bellows, nattering away as if Seeker had not spoken. "So it will be! Silver as the wheels of Arianrhod's chariot. Gold for collars and bindings. Silver for protection. Werewolves and wampyrs and such. And protection from iron, of course."

Gold is for collars. Oh, indeed. Seeker swallowed, and did not think of werewolves.

Weyland Smith lifted his hammer and his tongs, singing as he pounded out the heated metal. *"Tam Lin."* And the Mebd would be as terrible in her displeasure at him as she would have been at Seeker. But the rules were different for the ones that were gods. What could the Mebd do to the Weyland Smith? They were both descended of Dana.

Seeker walked to the well and peered over the smooth white stones that marked the edge in the grass. Water rippled and reflected as more hammer blows and the scent of scorching hoof revealed that Weyland had fitted the first silver crescent to Whiskey's foot. Whiskey snorted in protest; Seeker looked over her shoulder to check. But he stood patiently as Weyland drove the nails through the hoof wall and clipped them short.

"That'll be a fine silver ring in your man form," Weyland said. "Next foot."

Seeker blinked to clear her vision and gazed back into the water. The rippled surface now shivered with the pale circle of her own face, distorted by dim light and water. She bent closer, fascinated by the twisted image—and jerked back when a gout of icy water struck her face. Blinking, about to curse Whiskey, she glimpsed the spined back of a rose-and-green fish as it slid into the depths.

The water on her lips tasted cool and sweet, and she had just dipped up a handful when the hammering stopped. "Finished, m'lady," the smith pronounced. "Best be on your way."

"Already?"

He smiled and nodded, cheeks like ripe crab apples under waggling eyebrows. He set his hammer aside and made her a stirrup. Whiskey stood foursquare, testing the unfamiliar weight. The clipped ends of silver nails shone against hooves gleaming black as if shoe-polished. Weyland all but threw Seeker onto Whiskey's back.

Before she was fairly settled, Whiskey broke into a flying trot, footfalls light and his knees rising as if racking in the show ring. He threw his head up. Seeker, clutching his mane, turned to call back thanks to the smith—but the forge under the hazel tree was gone, and she couldn't see the outline of the well in the grass.

Whiskey floated on his new-shod hooves. He was behaving himself, so she leaned low over his neck and let him stretch into the gallop.

There wasn't anyplace for them to run to, Seeker and steed; the Blessed Lands were vast but quickly spanned if one knew the proper routes, and the paths to return to the mortal world lay nowhere and everywhere. But there was running for its own sake, and there was a task before her and a rival Queen's Seeker to address. So she knotted her hands in Whiskey's weed-matted mane and threw her weight as high on his withers as she could without a saddle, and they raced through mist and over downs and dales. He snorted once, a sound like a hiss, as she kneed him into a river that ran red and warm between the banks—*"for all the blood that's spilled on earth runs through the springs of that countrie"*—but he did not fight her.

Blood-heat swirled around her thighs, staining her leggings and Whiskey's white hide. *I could release him.* She tasted the idea for a moment. *I could. And then, on the very slim chance that he didn't kill me for having had the temerity to bind him in the first place, I wouldn't have him to use on the Merlin.*

Whiskey swam strongly, although the river of blood was no more his element than hers, and brought them safe to the other bank. He clambered up, spattering red across the crisped, sere earth. Seeker did not complain, this time, when a freshet welled from his hide and washed the sticky droplets from them both.

Whiskey snorted and stamped, resting at the top of the bank, and Seeker almost relaxed into the companionable silence of horse and rider—until Whiskey turned his head and fixed her with a cold, sidelong stare. Water welled up like tears in his china-blue eye, tracking the sculptured veins and bones of his muzzle. A chill closed her throat. *I am looking my death in the eye.*

They stood poised a moment longer, until she brought him around with a hand on his neck and a word in his ear. "Stand steady," she commanded, throwing a leg across his haunches to slide down. He stamped before she was well clear, but the dinner-plate hoof did not brush her. She patted Whiskey on the shoulder as she might any horse.

"Shall I wait here, mistress?"

"I'll make my own way home." A risk to let him go. More of a risk to let him overhear. She waited until the clop of his hoofbeats died away, and started walking. The moors beyond the river of blood lay silent and smiling in the dim afternoon. Seeker called out, "Seeker of the Unseelie Fae! It is I, the Seeker of the Daoine Sidhe."

Two Queens ruled Faerie, a kingdom divided between them. One Queen for the dark things, and one for the bright. The elder was the Mebd, the Summer Queen. The younger was the Cat Anna, the Queen of Winter, the White Witch. There had been others, Queens and Kings of air and darkness, ghosts and shadows: Oonagh, Titania, Oberon, Niamh, Finnvarra.

All were gone.

A cold wind sighed across the moor, flicking the ends of Seeker's hair like snakes' tongues. In this land, the Cat Anna's land, the shadows showed her nothing. Something small, clad in a pointed cap and a layer of filth, scurried into winter-bleak brush. Seeker flexed her fingers, shadows of a cat's claws dancing at the tips. With an effort, she straightened her hands; the talons fled.

"Bold, sister." Someone unraveled from the shadows under a gorse shrub, uncoiling taller than anything had a right to from such a small hiding place. The woman swayed like a cobra, standing clad only in a deluge of golden bracelets and necklaces and a bright patterned sarong that stood out like blood on black marble against her skin. Rubies glittered in her ears, her nose, her navel. Rows of tiny beadlike scars shiny as drops of sweat covered her breasts, her arms, her forehead.

Seeker thought if she laid a hand on the other's cheek, she could cut her palm on the bone. "Kadiska," she said, bowing.

The Seeker of the Unseelie came forward. "We are watched," she whispered, bending in a matching bow. Her shadow flared a hood, balanced long and supple, stretching its length into the grass, and then broadened, widened, flaring ears and massive shoulders. "Your skin is cold. I see your fear." Her tongue tasted the air, and she smiled from bottomless eyes.

"It's good to see you."

"And you as well." The other's formal tones fell away. "I heard you bound the Kelpie."

"I did." Seeker came forward and laid her hand on Kadiska's arm. "And your own hunting has been rich?"

Kadiska's legends were not Elaine's, and neither of theirs were the legends of Britain. But stories twine like the web of a spider, taken deep enough. And the Fae had spread their blood wide. The two Seekers might be cousins. Changelings, once taken, were rarely told who their Faerie ancestors might be, no matter how far removed.

Their Queens were sisters. And enemies born.

"Let us walk," Kadiska said. Her shadow tail-lashed, flattening ears more tufted and longer than those of Seeker's cat-shadow. "Someplace with fewer ears."

She spoke in the language of cats, which is not really speaking, and then she led Seeker along the riverbank until they came to a copse of rowan and thorn. "Here."

A bench perched there, above the river, as if someone might want to take in the vista. Kadiska seated herself and gestured that Seeker do the same. For a long moment, they sat companionably thigh-to-thigh and made sure nothing fey was close enough to overhear. Then Kadiska turned with a rustle of gold chains and tilted her head. "Word of your mission travels fast, sister. I will compete with you."

"I had assumed you would. It's too good to pass up."

"Aye." Kadiska rolled her shoulders. "Of course, our Queens know we will conspire against them. And each other." A musical laugh revealed teeth filed sharp as a snake's.

Seeker laughed too. "It's the nature of bondage. Do you have a starting place?"

Kadiska bent and scooped up a stone, then tossed it into the crimson river. "America," she said. "The previous Princes—there has been a general, if erratic, progress westerly."

"There has?"

She showed Seeker her teeth. "I know of one or two perhaps you don't. You Americans think you invented civilization."

"We invented the Big Mac. That has to be worth something."

"Hegemony isn't civilization." But Kadiska still smiled as she turned away.

Not the next day, nor the day after that, Matthew was forced to admit that the spirit-trace had failed—had not revealed the movements either of the Seeker of the Daoine Sidhe, or of the Seeker of the Unseelie Fae. As if their souls were given into soul-jars. As if they left no trace at all. *Hell of a way to find a Merlin, this.*

And if I were a modern Merlin, Matthew thought, rising to lock the door of his office after the last of the students left, *and I were not already a Promethean Mage, who and where would I be? And what would I be doing with my life?*

How is a Merlin different than a Mage, in any case? He paused with his hand on the latch, and shook his head. "Start from a point, Matthew," he said under his breath, and reached up to grab his jacket from the peg upon the wall. "How do we find new Magi? How did Jane find *me*?"

His office hours weren't technically over for another fifteen minutes, but he didn't glance at the clock as he tugged the door shut behind himself and started down the tiled corridor with his hands stuffed into his pockets. And stopped, suddenly enough that an undergrad stepped on the backs of his shoes. "Dr. S, I'm sorry—"

"If you want to know something, and you don't know where to look it up, who do you ask?" Matthew turned around, looking down at the freckled redheaded girl who had almost run him over. He recognized her from his Critical Theory section, and smiled. "Hypothetically speaking."

She blinked and stepped back, tilting her chin up to meet his eyes. Melissa. Her name was Melissa. "An expert?" she hazarded, uncertainly.

"Say you don't know any experts. Say it's an obscure fact."

"Reference librarian," she said. "Go to the library."

Matthew grinned, and pushed both of his hands through his unbound hair. Echoing his gesture, she tugged on one of the braided pigtails that did nothing to make her seem like a little girl, and lifted an eyebrow hopefully, and something deep in his heart that he'd thought healed—or at least scarred over—broke into fresh blood. "Excellent, Miss Martinchek," he said, and nodded. And turned away quickly, before his queasiness could show in his face. "I'll see you in class, won't I?"

A reference librarian. Smart girl.

He glanced back over his shoulder to see her standing, frown line between her eyebrows as she watched him walk away, one thumb hooked under the padded strap of her knapsack. Something in her gray-blue eyes snagged his attention and drew it back. *That's who we do it for. Smart girls like her.*

How do you find a Mage, Matthew? That's how. You look a little more carefully, is all. Whistling now, and telling himself the sound filled the emptiness under his breastbone and made his footsteps light, Matthew let those footsteps lead him to Patience, and to Fortitude.

The streets bustled on a sunny September afternoon as Matthew left

Hunter College. He played a game as he walked, reading unreliable futures in the flight of pigeons and the scud of clouds. Anything to distract his mind from worrying over old disappointments. Such a denatured term, *disappointments*. But Matthew was a Mage, who knew the value of the true meaning of a word. *Disappointed in love, disappointed in career, disappointed in one's suit upon a lady—the Victorians had it right.*

The Victorians also had brain fever, fates worse than death, and women who were no better than they should be, honesty constrained him to recall. And they did not have Patience and Fortitude. Matthew's footsteps halted at the base of the wide white steps leading up to the main entrance of the New York City Public Library building, where he pushed his spectacles up his nose and nodded left and right—once at each of the lions crouching in guard by the portals of knowledge.

Patience and Fortitude dated from 1911: no earlier. They had not gained their modern names until the Great Depression. Their true names were no deep secret, though, and Matthew knew a great number of Names.

Matthew dug in his breast pocket for the silver flask he carried and climbed the steps until he stood on the south end, dwarfed beside Patience's enormous paw. *Ask a librarian. Of course.* He spilled a little brandy on his fingers, and dabbed it on the lion's nose, then stretched to touch anointing fingers to its eyes, its breast, its massive gentle paws, and slipped the flask back inside his camouflage jacket, which he zipped to the neck before he bound his hair. "Leo Lenox," he said, and—having glanced over his shoulder to see if he was observed—he leaned forward and blew into Patience's alcohol-scented marble mouth. "In my Name, in the Name of Matthew Patrick Szczegielniak Magus and all the angels of God, I command thee: *Awake.*"

Almost nothing: a trickle of his own slight strength, no more, and the lion's cold marble eye blinked once. And then once again. Patience— Leo Lenox—was so steeped in love and tradition and the heartbeat of the living city that he was very, very nearly awake already. Very nearly a Genius. All Matthew had done was reach out just a little, and shake his shoulder. *:Matthew Patrick Szczegielniak Magus:* Patience said, his soft eye tracking Matthew's movements. *:You have a question for Me?:*

"Leo Lenox, I have," Matthew said, and felt as if the stone under his fingers took on some of the character of coarse black mane. "Warden of knowledge, I come to ask of you a question."

:Will you dare my riddle?:

"What is the price if I fail?" He kept his voice low, though the lion's voice boomed in his chest like a drum.

:Only that your question goes unanswered:

"Will it be answered if I choose not to play at riddles, Leo Lenox?"

:No:

"Then ask." Matthew drew a breath, listening closely.

:Where do you go to sell your soul, mortal man?:

"To the crossroads," Matthew said automatically. And blinked. "Times Square."

:The crossroads of the world: the lion said. *:The answer to the question you have not asked is, you must follow the magic and the music to their source, and face what you have lost therein:* And once again, the beast was stone.

Chapter Four

Promontory Summit, Utah: not Cheyenne, but the West nonetheless, and Seeker felt less weary for it. She stepped from a red rock's shadow under a sky pale as the Kelpie's eye and stretched, raising her face to the sun. Old pain lay like dust across the desert. This was the place where the New World had been struck in chains, old magics manacled by new subtleties; the reek of that binding still rose from the dun-colored land.

The grade of the old railway, torn up for scrap steel during the Second World War, hosted a party of hikers eastbound in the light of an October noon. The day held cool and bright. Seeker turned the flannel collar of her shirt up and smiled. If there was anywhere in the Americas she would find traces of a Merlin not yet come to his power, it was here. Here where the spell still lived—although roadways and highways laid the bindings now, a more intricate set of chains.

Seeker crouched, boots creaking, and laid her hand flat on the dust between her feet. *"Your predecessors have had some success with this,"* the Mebd had said. Nimue convinced Merlin Ambrosius to take her as a student; she seduced and entrapped him. The wisdom was taught from priest to priestess and back to priest, in the old days. But that trick wouldn't work this time, if this Merlin was in fact untaught, untried.

I'll have to be the teacher. Her fingers spiderwebbed trails across dry earth. *The seducer.* Air redolent of sage and creosote turned bitter in her lungs. *As Keith was to me.*

She frowned, and sketched another word in the dust. Ogham, the writing an uneven ladder above and below the centerline. But there was only blankness. It might have been Kadiska, here before her, but it didn't feel like the other Seeker's touch—the power wasn't used or drained. Just—gone. Walled away.

And who has such strength? Seeker didn't like the answers. She scraped fingers through her writing, obliterating the form of the ancient letters, and raised her eyes to the glaring sun. *Otherwise* glimpses of the hikers caught her attention, seen from the depths of shadows salted here and there on the barren plain: images of a jackrabbit, a roadrunner, a floating dragonfly windblown from some oasis.

Seeker moved westward along the old line of the track. A coyote ghost winked from beneath a rock and she offered it a sideways smile. Out of touch with the land that remained, but the old spirits still stalked here as elsewhere. And the rules were different, for the ones who had been gods. She kicked a pebble. There might be other places she could look, places where the power of men crossed the power of the Fae as that of the Merlin was made to do.

America. A big place. Full of ancient, chained magic and stains of spilt blood. No worse than the Old World, certainly. But no better. *How am I supposed to find one man in all of this?*

Blocked. Which meant someone had blocked it.

"Why can't she ever just *ask?*" Seeker said to the wind, and went unanswered. "I wanted to talk to her about the Kelpie anyway."

She stepped back into shadows and sought the third Queen in Faerie: the one who ruled no kingdom, and wore no crown.

On Seeker's first visit, she had expected some gaunt wildwood-wrapped tower or a castle on a cliff overlooking a tempestuous sea. But Morgan le Fey lived in a cottage tidy with thatch in a wildflower meadow. Although the skies of Faerie were gray overhead, Morgan's doorpath bloomed with jonquils and mayflower, drifts of bluets and forget-me-not. And those eternal roses, tumbling over the cottage in a damasked waterfall.

Dragon colors, Seeker thought. *King's colors too.*

A raven with a crooked wing perched on an eave, smiling as well as could be expected. "I've come," Seeker said to him.

"I knew you would," someone else replied. Seeker turned to regard the witch framed inside the red-and-gold-painted door.

Morgan was fair as her sleeping half brother, as her legended son and her sister's four were remembered to be fair, even fifteen centuries later. She came to Faerie alongside her brother's body, one of three Queens, old debts forgiven. And the blood of an Elf-knight ran in Morgan's veins as well as the blood of a mortal Queen: twice cuckold, Ygraine's husband. *Ygraine, whose name I bear. Another spiral, like the spirals carven on the doors of the Mebd's great hall.*

 The sorceress pushed a graying red-blond lock behind her ear and stepped from the shadow of the doorway. "Seeker," she said. "Have a cup of tisane."

Morgan wore a cable-knit heathered sweater and canvas trousers dirty at the knees with gardening. She held the vermilion door open, stepping aside so Seeker could precede her.

The doorframe was polished bone-white trunks, waxed shining and lashed together at the crosspiece. The door opened inward and Seeker entered the little house under a tapestry hooked to one side. "It keeps out the draft," Morgan said, closing the door. Daylight shone through the cracks.

Inside, the cottage was one clean, spacious room. Slates in a dozen colors tiled a rammed-earth floor, half-hidden under woven rush mats, and the unlofted half of the rafters hung thick with ropes of garlic and onions and hanks of herbs. Two wolfhounds cuddled in elegant twin sine curves by the fire, the dog red and the bitch silver. They did not lift their narrow heads when Seeker entered, but lashes long as a girl's flickered over amber eyes. A cauldron of iron hulked lightlessly in the hearth corner, chilling Seeker's bones.

The fieldstone walls were also thick with tapestries: one in particular caught Seeker's eye, showing a white hart and a black in lathered, eye-rolling detail, pursued by hounds and men on horseback. "This is new, isn't it?"

"It is." The sorceress gestured to the frame that stood in the corner farthest from the hearth, spanning floor to rafters on the unlofted side. "Few see them. The Fae won't venture here, where there's iron. But I need the cauldron for my work." She strode to the hearth and took two wooden mugs from a peg. While Morgan measured herbs and ladled steaming water from a silver kettle with a dipper made of horn, Seeker walked along the wall, touching the tapestries and examining the other odd objects hooked in among them: a crimson-glazed Japanese tile emblazoned in black with the character for *love;* an iron horseshoe hung to mimic a crescent moon; a sword in an embroidered tapestry sheath, the style of the embroidery matching that of the surrounding tapestries so it almost vanished against the wall. There were bundles of rosemary and strings of glass witch-globes—blue and red and violet, catching the glimmer of light from the hearth and the overcast glow from the un-shuttered windows—and a dusty cloak in black-and-gold brocade that Seeker knew better than to take down and try on.

Morgan came up beside her and slid the mug of tisane into her hand. "You admire the sword?"

"It's very old, isn't it?" Seeker reached out with her free hand to touch the leather-wrapped bronze hilt. Serpents chased each other around the abbreviated crosspiece.

"It's a spatha," Morgan said. "A Roman-style blade. There is a leaf-blade here"—she crossed the floor, rush mats rustling under her foot-steps; the fire popped on the hearth—"and here, this one is older. My favorite of the three, a furrowed Celtic blade with the man-hilts. See his head and arms?" She took the sword down from the wall and ex-tended it.

This one was sheathed in plain leather. Seeker took it by the dark wood hilt and slid it from the scabbard. The polished bronze blade gleamed richly in the faltering light. "Interesting symbolism," she said, and sipped her herbal tea. It tasted of moss, the steam coiling up redo-lent of leaf mold and memories. The sword's blade protruded from be-tween the legs of the figure that made up the sword's pommel, hilt, and crosspiece.

"Men," Morgan answered. "You'd think they invented sex. Or vio-lence, for that matter."

Seeker reversed the blade one-handed and gave it back to the witch, who sheathed it and returned it to the wall. "I thought the Fair Folk invented those things."

Morgan's hair tumbled in a rippling tawny-red curtain over her shoulders when she laughed, the liquid in her mug splashing her hand. "Perhaps they did," she gasped. Her eyes met Seeker's, and Seeker looked down from that piercing light.

"Which brings me to my question—"

"How did I know where you were going? I didn't," Morgan answered. "You realize your mistress has set you up as a stalking-horse, I hope?"

"What mean you?" Seeker paused with her mug at her lips.

"Her public announcement of your task and quest. Foolish, unless she wanted all of Faerie to know. Thus, she must. And she must hope the knowledge will provoke someone to action."

"And of course, Morgan, you have a theory."

"I have enough theories to build a bigger house than this from. They avail me not. But your Queen's magic will not reach here and so here we may speak freely." Morgan pulled a stool away from the narrow table and gestured Seeker to it before seating herself opposite.

"I don't understand your motives." Seeker hooked her bootheels on the bottom rung of the stool.

The statement drew another of Morgan's rich, enigmatic laughs. The sorceress rolled it on her tongue as if savoring the flavor. "No one has *ever* understood my motives, Seeker. I see no reason why I should become uncomplicated with age."

I wonder what it is that pleases her so greatly. Not that she'd ever tell me. "I wondered about the Kelpie's magic."

"Ah, and the Kelpie may be half the reason the Queen sent you now. Binding him, even though he was weakened and out of place, shows your maturing power."

"It was you taught me his Name, Morgan. How did you know I would have need of it?"

"It's not the only Name I've taught you. And you'll have need of more." Morgan rose, taking the two empty mugs with her as she went to freshen the fire. Baskets of wool huddled beside the hearth, a heathered gray and ivory that matched the sweater Morgan wore. The knitting needles protruded from the basket. Morgan tucked them to the side with sinewy hands, stepped over the enormous dogs, and squatted before the fire.

"You've seen these things?"

"Many things," Morgan answered. The scent of brewing herbs filled the cottage; she pushed her hair behind her ear. "You're thinking," she said through the smile marking her narrow face, "that the Morgan of the stories surely could not have been me, homely and house-proud, knitting sweaters by the fire."

Seeker nodded, turning on her stool to face the fire and the woman beside it. "But then, I know the divide between my own office and who I wish I were."

"Ah. There is that. But I am a woman and not an office." She stood, vapor coiling like dragon's breath from a mug in either hand. "Have you asked yourself how I came by those swords?"

"I imagine," Seeker answered, "that I know those stories as well. Which one was Lancelot's?"

It was a risk, of course. But the witch was in a mood for laughing, and she continued as she had begun. "None of them," she answered around a chuckle. "His I gave back when I was done with it." Morgan grinned wider, amused by her own pun. "Few now remember that twist of the tale."

"I've had time for some reading." Seeker pushed her own dark hair back, mirroring Morgan's gesture without thought.

"I imagine you have."

I see why men wanted her, Seeker thought. *You want to make her laugh and look at you. She was famed for her conquests, was she not? Morgan the Enchantress. I'll wager she needed no magic to bring men to her bed.* "I thought he was a later invention."

"Oh, he was and he wasn't. Bard's tales shape history as much as history shapes the tales. Especially here, where will is the shape of the world. No, you have the lay aright. He came to me in grief, that I would keep him from Gwenhwyfar." She slid a mug onto the table by Seeker's hand and sipped her own.

"And?"

"And I did. For a time." She rolled her shoulders back. "As Calypso kept Odysseus. For a time. Neither Lance nor Arthur had much to recommend them as lovers, though. Gwenhwyfar could have chosen better. But for all her beauty, she was not clever." And Seeker thought she heard in Morgan's voice a trace of the old disdain of the brilliant — and lonely — woman for the one who is simple, and sought. "No matter. I wanted to warn you of the hands raised against you. And offer assistance."

"In trade for what?" The tea was hot and soothing; Seeker cradled the mug close in her hands.

"Whatever may come. Alliances are not based solely on an even trade of resources, you realize. Besides, I'd like to meet this Merlin of yours once you catch him."

"You seem to have no doubts that I'll bend him to my will."

"Ha." The witch leaned her shoulder against the tapestried wall. "You will do. Or the Cat Anna will. You know he cannot be bound — not like the fey folk. Not bound with a Name."

"I know."

"You'll have to make him *want* to serve you."

"I know."

"As Nimue did before you. There are ways and there are ways, Seeker of the Daoine Sidhe."

"Just tell me where to find him," Seeker said, pushing her mug aside. "I'll worry at the rest when the time comes."

Seeker returned to the iron world on a busy, winding, mostly residential street in Connecticut. A cold wind sailed maple leaves in tawny, cinnabar, and crimson through the outside lights of a housefront bar. The same night breeze ruffled Seeker's dark hair and set the green, orange, and gold sign above the door swinging. *"A place called the Hungry Tiger,"* Morgan had said, pale lips curving beneath her aristocratic nose.

Seeker climbed three narrow steps to the jade-colored door, paid the bouncer eight paper dollars that would crumble into dead leaves in the morning, and stepped through the entryway and inside.

She paused as she entered, extending her awareness *otherwise,* wondering if she would feel *this* quarry. The bar was dark and smoky, paneled in raw oak and divided lengthwise by an awkward half-wall. Morgan's cottage was bigger inside than the main part of the bar, although there was an extension out back—a greenhouse of sorts, cantilevered off the hill, arranged as a dining room. Seeker knew the layout from the shadows: the kitchen, the narrow basement, the rooms upstairs; the couple kissing in the corner near the stage and the flannel-shirted steamfitter who shot her an admiring glance as he lit a cigarette beside the bar.

Ripples. Ripples and shadows, shattered visions not-quite-resolving into the crystalline clarity, the reality of prey. Seeker blinked, shook her head, and stepped toward the bar, her blue jeans and boots blending with the crowd. The bar was busy for a Thursday night; the sharp vinegar tang of buffalo wings reached her through the reek of smoke. The girl behind the bar wore black jeans and a knotted shirt. Seeker leaned over the scarred wood surface and ordered a Ballantine's.

The camouflage of the beer in her hand, she straightened and scanned the room, her eye skipping over men and women in blue jeans, boots, and leather or denim jackets. Beyond the half-height partition a five-member band was setting up on a stage roughly the size of a lap desk. Quarters were so tight the keyboardist was crammed half behind the drummer in the corner; two guitarists and a bass player paced the dime-sized space between their amps, taping and tie-wrapping cords.

Seeker stepped forward, leaning over the partition between support pillars and pretending to watch the musicians. The bassist caught her eye: a rugged-looking blond, neat beard redder, with broad shoulders and nimble hands. *It could be one of the musicians.* The lead guitarist was too old, she guessed—a stocky round-cheeked black man in his fifties—and so was the rhythm guitar. The keyboardist had an islander look and might have been thirty, thirty-three, but she was a woman, balancing a snifter of brandy in one hand while she crawled under patch cords. The drummer was another possibility, burly and swarthy, black curls poking through the open collar of his shirt.

The shadows showed her nothing. She pushed off the wall and passed through the bar into the fern-hung greenhouse. Something little moved in the shadows, scampered away under a bench, but Seeker shrugged. Brownies or bogeys: she didn't care tonight that they'd found a corner to persist in. She sauntered to the back wall and stared over the moonlit parking lot and the darkness of a municipal park beyond. The night lay motionless and cold beyond the glass, and Seeker cast her awareness out into the shadows beyond it.

In the front room of the bar, the music began. And Seeker, picking the unmistakable strain of magic out of the hard-driving melody of an old blues standard, turned lightly on her toes and walked back into the bar as if drawn on a thread, leaving her beer forgotten on the window ledge.

Seeker stood between greenhouse and tavern, motionless as if the music were a pin thrust through her heart. Men and women jostled her, turning sideways to slip past, headed for the bathrooms or the bar. She did not move. She did not blink. She barely breathed.

Eyes unfocused, she hung in the sound of the music, caressed by the melody, the rhythm of the drums deep as the rhythm of her heart. The lead guitarist's fingers danced, clutched, fought the neck of his guitar—he tangoed with the blue-swirled axe and made it cry. The bass line and the rhythm buoyed her up and swept her along, until Seeker felt like she was bodysurfing the music. It reminded her of Whiskey, and the thought seared like a match struck down her breastbone.

Pity. What right have you to pity him?

And then the keyboardist leaned forward and growled into the microphone bent like a black swan's neck toward her lips, and the world lit red behind Seeker's eyes.

Her.

No.

Her.

The Merlin is a woman.

Seeker rocked on her feet and fell hard against the wall. She craned her head to steal another glance at the keyboardist. The woman pulled her hands off the keys, sharing a smile with the drummer as she bent for her water—

—and her gaze brushed Seeker's, and she stopped. Drew a breath. Picked up the glass in her right hand and settled back in her chair, never looking down. Seeker was trapped, unable to break a regard that pulled like wire drawn through a die. The musician's face seared itself in Seeker's vision: a mask impassive as an Egyptian empress', lips blooming fat and sensual as orchids beneath the flat, aristocratic nose; skin red-black as the famous bust of Queen Tiy; hair braided in a thousand beaded Medusa serpents. *I wonder if a Pegasus would spring from her blood if I spilled it.*

Those eyes were opaque opals set in creamy, ancient ivory. Bottomless and appraising, and she seemed to sort through Seeker's soul like riffling a deck of cards—and then she broke the contact, nodded once, and looked down at her hands as if gathering her thoughts. She half stood, drained off her glass, and leaned forward over the keyboards to talk to the bassist, who nodded and whispered in the guitarists' ears. The three men shared a glance, and the lead guitarist pivoted and gave the keyboardist a careful look until both of them nodded. And the guitarist very carefully, very quietly, began to play.

Seeker pressed her open hand to her own throat, fingers curved as if easing a chain.

The keyboardist's voice was soprano, silken and ice, rivers of gold and green, fish flashing in the sunlit depths and subtlety and the taste of hazelnuts and . . . Seeker licked her lips, savoring coolness and wet, the leaf-mold flavor of splashed water on her mouth. She leaned forward over the partition and let go, at last, tasting salt.

Chains of gold. Chains of silver. Chains of iron. *Chains, bending you back in a circle. A spiral walked around the stake. No freedom. No answers.*

Just wearing a circle at the end of a chain.

"Ian," Seeker said. She bit her tongue. She had to push through the crowd to get a clear view of the band, but the keyboardist didn't glance her way again, even as she sang the final verse and brought the song down to a shivering finale.

When it ended, the silence hung on the air for seconds; Seeker was not the first to applaud. She raised her hands, half-dizzy, feeling like a collar had been ripped from *her* neck. Lighter, stranger, as if she could step out of the spiral and drop the chain on the bare earth where the grass had been worn away. *Pacing, pacing.*

The Merlin looked up, twisted her open magic closed, smiled into Seeker's eyes one last time . . . then winked and looked away.

The set lasted forty-five minutes. Seven songs. Every one of them, Seeker thought, was sung *for* someone, and she could usually tell who. The edges of the sung spell that had held Seeker lifted, curling like paper steamed from a wall—as if the veil over some ancient grief had cracked and begun to flake. *Picking scabs,* she thought, almost reaching after the muffling darkness that had covered the raw new pain to pull it back around her shoulders like a comforting cloak.

Almost. She rubbed her hands across her face and recollected herself. *Pain is pain. It can be endured.*

And what cannot be mended must be borne.

So much power in her. A bard, like Ambrosius. Like Cairbre, like Taliesin. Thomas the Rhymer, Orfeo. A true singer, who could raise emotion, stir the hearts of men to fear or love or courage. Seeker shook her head, the braids in her hair snaking across her neck heavy as a chain. What a power. What a gift.

And she was here to break it to the will of her Queen.

Seven songs, and at the end of them Seeker gathered herself and pulled her hands off the partition. Her fingers snagged in a braid as she ran them through her hair. She tucked it behind her left ear. *First learn. Then act. No hurry—no hurry at all.*

Seeker blinked and frowned, watching the keyboardist laughing, leaning on the arm of the tall bass player, cupping her brandy snifter in her free hand. She moved with a willowy grace—*ballet,* Seeker thought—but her gaze was endlessly mobile, always touching the faces in the crowd. Aware.

And not the innocent I thought she'd be. The innocent I was. Once upon a time. Seeker felt the compulsion of the Mebd's will upon her, a pressure that could bend her until she broke, make a puppet of her body if she opposed it fiercely enough. At first, she had.

At first. For a little. Seeker turned away from the laughing Merlin and moved down the bar, into the shadows, where there was darkness at least, if still no peace.

Seeker blinked, frowning against the images the music piled into her mind. The night crested over midnight and crashed down the leeward side, and the band swung into their last set. The music had an edge to it, now: a tang of sorrow sweet and pure and focusing in its agony.

She stood when the last song came to an end. Her eyes stung. A weary moment hung on silence before conversation resumed, and Seeker garbed herself in shadows before she started forward. For safety, or just for something to hide behind.

The keyboardist walked toward the restrooms, and Seeker appeared at her elbow. Braids swung and beads clicked as she turned to Seeker, smelling of patchouli and clove cigarettes. Her eyes were even more bottomless, up close. "Excuse me," Seeker said.

"Yes?" Her accent wasn't island at all. Pure mainland, and educated. Local.

Seeker focused on the smaller woman's eyes and put all her sincerity and power into her words. "I'm the Seeker of the Daoine Sidhe. I'm here to teach you how to use your magic."

The woman blinked. Her mouth fell open, and if she shaped words, no sound came out. *Lost her. Too much, too fast.* It had been a gamble, and an easier path than stalking her like a fish to be tickled from the stream. Seeker swallowed on a dry mouth. "You do know you have magic, don't you?"

The room seemed suddenly distant as the two women stared into one another's eyes. "Yes," the Merlin said finally, and took an unwilling step toward Seeker. "I know."

" 'Face what you have lost,' " Matthew murmured, although he was alone in his automobile on a dark highway in Connecticut. "I'm not sure I like the sound of that."

He shrugged off the chill between his shoulders and pushed random buttons on his radio until he found a Providence classic rock station halfway through an old Doors standard. *Providence?*

An aptly named city. Magi learned to pay attention to minor details such as names and synchronicities; portents were where you found them. In the interstices where reality and story touched, a man—a Mage—could find clues to which shaped which, and follow them to surprising destinations.

Stories had a way of telling themselves.

Matthew took the 384 exit eastbound, toward Providence via the University of Connecticut, but he never made it that far. The road was quiet and dark except for the intermittent flicker of headlights in the oncoming lane across the barrier. Most of the highway was shielded from habitations by a curving tunnel of maples and oaks; near one of the Manchester exits, a glimpse of a main street and a row of houses beyond a park off to the left caught his attention due to their brilliance in the darkness, but one structure among them in particular was unique. The first story of a two-story house, with a walkout basement built into the side of a hill, had been extended into a greenhouse on stilts, the whole structure glowing with a white, peaceful light.

The Jethro Tull song on his car radio cut out the instant his eyes settled on the greenhouse.

"Well," Matthew said into the darkness, as he put his blinker on, "that wasn't very subtle at all." He allowed a bit of a grin; he was past the exit and had to proceed up the highway and loop back. Just to convince him the forces of the universe were serious, his radio died again in the same place.

I hope you're out there listening somewhere, Kelly. The thought tightened his smile. He swallowed it, and downshifted to fourth as he hit the exit ramp, before rolling down the window to let the night air in. The end of summer was coming; a sharpness under the warmth carried the musky snake-smell of leaves.

The house was actually a bar. He turned down the steep narrow driveway and parked in the lot behind it, settling his camouflage jacket over his shoulders before he closed and locked the Volkswagen. He scraped his hair back into the ponytail as he climbed the hill beside the drive, made sure his jacket was zipped, and brushed the back of his hand across his clean-shaven jaw. It would do.

It was almost last call, and the bouncer let him into the narrow entryway without collecting the cover charge. There were pegs along the wall and the heat in the cramped bar was stifling, but a tingle across Matthew's nape and the backs of his forearms stilled him when he would have unzipped the jacket.

He stepped to one side so he wouldn't be framed in the doorway and leaned against the wall. Too late, the rings on his fingers chilled enough to sting, reacting to the fey presence. Across the crowded room, he saw the Seeker's dark head come up—and knew by the way the cold burned in the iron piercing his ear when she found him through the shadows, although she never turned. The profile of the woman on the Seeker's right hit him like a jolt of cold water on an empty stomach, and it wasn't just the beauty of her face; she burned against the darkness of the room as if someone had sketched over her outline with a silver-gilt pen. She lifted a cased keyboard in her right hand, a folding chair and the stand slung over the crook of her left arm. The power in her made his fingers curl.

The Merlin's a girl. Who would have guessed it?

Matthew saw the grasp of her hand on the Seeker's sleeve, the way she looked sidelong at the Seeker's profile, and swore.

Yes, the Fae are lovely, aren't they, Matty? Kelly's dry, dark voice in his ear, and Matthew shook his head at the memory of his brother's cropped blond hair and the razor-edge blackness of the ink patterning the back of his neck, his shoulders.

Leave me alone, Kell.

I can't do that until you let me go . . .

The chill up his spine had nothing to do with the Seeker's slow turn, the tilt of her head as her gaze fell on him, her long neck gleaming dull gold where the lights over the bar touched it, or the breadth of her shoulders under her black turtleneck. When she smiled, lines sprang into relief from the corners of her mouth to her aquiline nose, and the unlikely angles of her face rearranged themselves into vibrancy.

She's Fae. Half-Fae. It only follows that she's lovely.

And then, unbidden: *She looks like her mother, doesn't she?*

The woman beside the Seeker shifted a quarter step closer, hugging her various burdens to her side, when Seeker glanced away from Matthew and turned a dazzling smile on her. Cursing himself for an idiot, Matthew stepped in front of the door as the Seeker and the Merlin strolled toward him, checked quickly to be sure his shoelaces were tied and his hair still bound, and pushed his spectacles up his nose with a fingertip.

"Matthew. Szczegielniak," the Seeker said, pronouncing his name better than he did himself.

"Elaine Elizabeth Andraste," he replied, smiling with a confidence he didn't feel. Her footsteps hesitated, though, and he stepped within the doorway's frame. There was strength in the places between places, just as there was strength in the forged iron on his hands and the fastenings of his clothes.

I should have turned my jacket inside out, he thought, and looked past the Seeker to her prey. "Greetings, wizard," he said to the Merlin, watching her eyes widen. He glanced down to flick an imaginary bit of lint from his sleeve. "Before you go with this one, my lady, would you like to hear competing offers?"

"Matthew," the Seeker said, more kindly than he would have expected, "did you follow me here?"

"You are untraceable, of course," he said, returning the gentle tone. "Synchronicity. Or Prometheus' guidance, perhaps . . ."

"Oh, *that* explains it." She shook her head, one hand on the Merlin's shoulder. The Merlin shot her a glance, but did not move away. "You Magi lost your Prometheus four hundred years ago, Matthew Magus. After such a messy divorce, most brides would give back the name."

She was Fae, and not to be trusted. And he could tell by the twist of her lips that she wanted him to ask —*lost Prometheus?*— or at least hesitate. It was a diversion. And he didn't believe she knew anything worth telling. Prometheus was a symbol, a legend. Not a person.

"We Magi have done nothing but defend our species from yours," he answered, tilting his head so that the flash of light off his spectacles would hide his eyes.

"And I have done nothing but recoup in some small way the losses you mortals have inflicted upon Faerie," the Seeker answered, with a sidelong glance at the Merlin that told Matthew she knew it wasn't as simple as that, no matter what she said. That maybe she didn't believe it herself. "One might argue that it's the Prometheus Club's *fault*. When Faerie was stronger, the Seekers were farther between."

"When Faerie was stronger," Matthew countered, "there wasn't a cradle without iron and thorn hung over it that did not go unplundered, and Elf-knights and Elf-queens stole men and women off horseback and out of their beds."

The Seeker shrugged. "Is your argument that there is wrong on both sides of the war? I've heard that before—"

"War?" The Merlin's first word into the conversation that she'd watched with the bright intentness of a bird. Her voice was rich and soft and deep, lovelier than her face or the velvet of her skin, and he shivered and took an involuntary step forward until the Seeker blocked him with an upraised hand.

Spooky.

Matthew shook his head to clear it, iron clinking in his ear. "My argument is that the greater wrong is yours, and that the lady should know the facts before she chooses."

The lady in question glanced from his eyes to the Seeker's and back again.

"It's hers to decide," Seeker said. Her sidestep reinserted her between Merlin and Mage, irony sly on her expression when the Merlin couldn't see it. *Of course the wrong is Faerie's*, the expression said. *Of course I know it.*

What she could *say* was another story. And Matthew didn't miss the curve of the Merlin's lips as she considered Seeker's gesture. *Half-besotted already.* But of course that was a Seeker's gift—and curse, as much as the cool eyes he could feel regarding him from the shadows, and the deadly insubstantial claws that curved at her fingertips.

"I'm Matthew—"

"—Szczegielniak," the Merlin finished, and Matthew blinked. For proof of magic afoot in the world, meeting two people in the space of a few days who didn't screw up his name was a start. "Yes, I heard. And I'm Carel, and I'm afraid you have both mistaken me for someone else."

"No mistake," Matthew said, his sentence interrupted as someone behind him cleared his throat—the bouncer—and Matthew was all too aware what he looked like: a tattooed, ponytailed, pierced bit of rough trade blocking two women on their way out the door. Even if one of those women was Matthew's size, and carried herself like a black belt. "But if you feel a bit like a spider with everyone pulling on a different leg—"

"More like the best-dowered girl at the debutantes' ball," the Merlin answered. Utterly fearless, and her eyes looked through him as if she saw his scars and strengths and they were both the same to her. "I might find this a little spooky." Her darkly opalescent eyes flickered up, over Matthew's shoulder.

"Is there a problem here?"

Such an original line. Matthew opened his mouth, turned his head to explain. The bouncer wasn't looking at him, though, but rather at the two women. *Dangerous if I had plans to put a knife in his ribs.*

"Just a conversation," Seeker answered, her gaze still meeting Matthew's through the flimsy barrier of his spectacles, and he felt that rush of charm and compulsion again. *And you not even Fae,* he thought, and wondered if this was what it had been like for Kelly—this intoxication and sudden undertow like swift water. Magic was the only thing Matthew knew to compare. "I'm sure we'll see you somewhere later, Matthew."

"Yes," he said, stepping aside—and incidentally sidling out from under the bouncer's grasp. "I'm sure." And slipped his business card into the Merlin's pocket as she and the Seeker walked past him and the bouncer, out the open door and into the streetlit darkness beyond.

Seeker swirled weak coffee in a too-small mug, leaning over the Formica tabletop in a narrow booth. Across from her, the Merlin—

Carel Bierce—pushed biscuits and gravy around with her fork, frowning. She'd twisted her beaded braids back in a purple velveteen scrunchie, and she too was drinking the offensive Denny's coffee because it was there, and hot.

They were alone except for the staff. At least the waitress had left the carafe.

"This is disgusting," the Merlin said, pushing her plate away. "I should have had the pie."

"It's Denny's." Seeker hadn't ordered. She waved the waitress, who looked as if she wished she were chewing gum, closer. "My friend would like some pie."

"What kind?"

"Peanut butter," the Merlin said. She lifted the carafe and refilled her mug, her other hand encircling its narrow waist. "I'm done with the sausage gravy, thanks."

The waitress picked it up and shot a glance at Seeker. "Apple, please," Seeker said. "With ice cream."

"It'll be terrible." The Merlin peeled open a packet of creamer and dripped it into her coffee, pearl after pearl. She shot a glance at the waitress as if worried of giving offense.

"It always was," Seeker answered.

"Do you pay with fairy money?" She swirled the coffee, watching the ribbons of creamer make spirals in her mug.

"Of course." Seeker pulled the carafe over, but it rattled empty. She opened the lid and set it on the edge of the table. The last swallow in her mug was cold. The Merlin stared at her.

"Who was that man in the Tiger?" But her eyes held another name— *Elaine Elizabeth Andraste*—and Seeker could have cursed Matthew for sharing that name with this . . . this dream made real, this elegant, vibrating creature across the scarred beige table.

Seeker pushed herself back against the red plastic padding of the booth and shrugged. "A Mage," she answered. "A member of a thing called the Prometheus Club, which has been at war with Faerie for hundreds of years."

"He doesn't look that old." Dry and sharp.

Seeker laughed, and spindled a paper napkin between her hands. "It's a stupid war—"

"Are there any wars that aren't?"

"Some." Seeker shook her head. "When you're fighting to protect yourself."

"And yet you had a civil conversation with him."

"It's not that kind of a fight. More a . . . cold war. Move and countermove, politics and sorcery."

"The Iron Curtain," Carel said, brief flash of white teeth behind the burgundy of her lips.

Seeker nodded slowly.

"Why should I trust you over him? Matthew, I mean?"

"You shouldn't trust either of us." Seeker pushed at her geasa, wondering how much truth she could get away with. She nibbled her thumbnail, feeling no pressure back. *Control the Merlin—well, if truth will let me do it . . .* "Tell me what you know about magic, Carel."

"I just . . ." Her eyes changed, away from the music—dark as moss-covered stones, now, and as prosaic. "Sometimes I look at somebody, and I know what they need to hear. Sometimes I find a song, and it seems to mean something, and I sing it. And things happen. People react. But I don't know where it comes from."

"I felt you reading me tonight," Seeker said after a pause.

She nodded. "Sometimes I just know," she said. Seeker's eye was drawn to the sway of a knotty lump of blue-and-gold glass that finished one escaped braid. It clicked on the edge of the Formica tabletop, and the Merlin tossed it absently behind her shoulder. "I've—this is going to sound crazy."

"Nothing sounds crazy to me anymore." The pie came, along with more coffee, and Seeker picked up her stainless steel fork. Her fingertips tingled. She set it down again.

"I see things." The Merlin began peeling the cookie-crumb crust away from the filling of her pie. "Like now." Her gaze on Seeker's hands was intent. "You—when you picked up that fork, the light around your fingertips went bruised. I could see that it hurt you. At the bar—I looked at you and I saw . . . chains." Her voice trailed off. "And ghosts," she added after a silence.

"Yes," Seeker answered when she had finished her coffee. She felt a press of *need*—the Mebd's will. But the Merlin had to choose her side. She was mortal, and couldn't be bound . . . which led Seeker briefly into musing: if Morgan's father was truly an Elf-knight, how was it that she had escaped binding, all those long centuries? And how could she bear the touch of iron? *Magic. And Morgan. They're practically synonyms, after all.* "Do you ever see things that don't exist?"

"Like what?" The Merlin's hand trembled, and she spun the fork nimbly. Her nails were filed short, French manicured.

"You said ghosts. Mythical beasts? Griffins, chimerae . . ."

"I saw a unicorn once. When I was in high school." The Merlin let her shoulders rise and fall in a fluid, expressive shrug. Her neck twisted to the side, waterbird-graceful. "Why am I telling you this?"

Seeker turned her hands over, showing the palms. Movement in the shadows distracted her; she narrowed her awareness with an effort. "Because I'll believe you. And because you've been lonely for a long time, and the neo-Pagans and the witches can't offer the thing that you need. Because your magic is not their magic. And you know I have something to offer."

"Ah, what's in it for you? I sing enough ballads to know the Elf-knight and the demon lover always make a girl pay."

Seeker hadn't an answer, so she forced herself to pick up her fork and take a bite of metal-poisoned pie. It wouldn't hurt her badly . . . which was why she was Seeker, and other Fae were not. *Otherwise* sight showed her footsteps beyond the door, and Seeker frowned and swallowed. She'd known she wouldn't have long. Still. *Already.* She didn't stand, but she turned to face Kadiska as the other Seeker padded up to the booth. The Merlin's eyes grew wide as she looked up at the new arrival.

Kadiska wore red velvet pantaloons slung low across her belly, showing her navel and the beaded lines of scars. Gold cloth wound her breasts, golden sandals wound her ankles, and a shawl of cloudlike wool wrapped her shoulders and muffled her arms. Except when she reached out, as she did now, and ran her fingers through Seeker's hair, tucking the dark strands behind an ear in which an emerald still glittered.

The waitress was staring.

"I hope you haven't entrusted this one with too many secrets," Kadiska said to the Merlin. "What the Faeries touch cannot be trusted, and they tell naught but lies wrapped in the skin of truth. Wolves in wool coats." Her filed teeth flashed as she smiled and drew her arm back inside her pashmina.

"And who might you be?" The Merlin poured herself more coffee. "Someone else come to explain magic to me?"

"I represent a competing offer," Kadiska said.

Seeker blinked: Matthew's words, almost exactly. *How long* has *she been following us?*

Kadiska settled herself back on her heels and crossed her arms. "You have power, lady, and that power is of interest to my Queen. As it is to the one who holds my esteemed counterpart's leash." Kadiska grinned wolfishly at Seeker, who sighed and drank more coffee.

The Merlin's silence shattered into a laugh. "I begin to see. So I do have something you want."

"It's always about bargains," Seeker said. "Your power makes you a target."

The Merlin lifted her chin, cord-fine braids whispering across her shirt. "I'm expected to choose a side?"

"The sides are going to force you to choose. Now that we know you exist." Seeker raised her gaze to Kadiska, daring the Unseelie Seeker to say something.

Kadiska tilted her head slightly and shrugged acquiescence.

"Well." The Merlin sidled out of the booth and stood. Kadiska stepped aside to give her room, and she dug in her wallet for money, tossing it on the table next to the picked-over pie. Seeker blinked at the warm aroma of sandalwood and myrrh that rose from the gesture. "I'm not looking for a job. I like the ones I have, and I'm not interested in being bargained for. Or with. So if you ladies will excuse me . . ."

"Bargained for?" Seeker scrambled to her feet. "*Taught* is still the offer on the table."

The Merlin, walking away, did not answer.

"Thanks," Seeker said, when the glass door shut behind their quarry.

Kadiska dropped a warm arm around Seeker's shoulders. "Where would the fun be if the chase were easy? Besides, I think she likes you."

"Oh, wonderful. Maybe she'd like you too, if you got those teeth capped. Want my pie?"

Kadiska's necklaces rasped on one another as she stepped away. "No, thank you," she said. "But I'll bet you an amber ring you'll have her in bed before I will."

Chapter Five

The lake drained into a stream which tumbled over a cement dam and through a culvert under the road. Below the culvert was a secret place, a miniature valley full of wildflowers and overhung by willows. Someone—some student from a nearby dormitory, no doubt—had knotted a single-board rope swing to a high branch of one of the willows, so it swayed over the brook.

It was midafternoon of the next day and a few miles northeast. Seeker straddled the rope, her feet dragging on the bank of the stream, her head leaned against her forearms. She swallowed what would have been the next in a series of sighs.

Despite the deliberate footsteps on the bank, Seeker did not turn her head. The aroma of salt sea air would have given her the newcomer's identity a moment before his hand fell on her neck, even if she hadn't seen him coming from the shadows.

Her hair was twisted up with a plastic clip, but a few strands escaped. Whiskey twined them around his fingers. She lifted her head to regard him, clad in his ragged white.

"Seduction now, little treachery?"

He smiled, showing even white teeth. "There is an art to it, mistress. An art I can teach you. Besides, I'd hate to lose my touch. Someday you'll be gone, and I mean to be in at the kill." He didn't move his hand, and she didn't quite pull away. "In the meantime, let me tend your aches. The stronger you are, the less likely you are to die at anyone's hand but mine."

"A nice justification. Why would I let you put your hands around my throat?"

"Because I'll offer you my oath that you will come to no harm this hour if it be in my power to prevent it."

Seeker chewed her lip a moment before she bowed her head. Whiskey slid both thumbs the length of her neck. "Does it hurt?"

"Yes. Keep going."

He was strong, thumbnails thick as scallop shells and the dark pads of his fingers soft as crushed velvet. A thick silver band encircled each of his thumbs: horseshoes, transformed by the Weyland Smith's magic and his own.

The network of old pain beneath her skin loosened ever so slowly as his hands slid under the collar of her knotted blouse. He unclipped her hair and combed his fingers through it, pressing her temples. His fingers snarled on a braid, and he disentangled them carefully. "Unbind me, Seeker. Better to have me gone than always at your back waiting for the weakness."

She sighed against the rope. "And I could trust you then?"

He chuckled, a sound like a nicker. She felt his breath on her hair, scented of seaweed and new-mown grass. "Mistress, I would go into the ocean and never trouble you again. I would promise to do your bidding three times without fail, in exchange for my freedom. I'd help you with this task you're given."

She hung silent, swaying.

"Why came you to this place, mistress?"

"I went to school here. It looked different then."

"You could show me the college. I think you loved it here."

Keith, she thought. "I do not trust you, little treachery."

"I could make it worth your while in so many ways." His hands were gentle, his voice very close to her ear. "Surely, you don't think I borrowed all those lovely young girls only to *drown* them. Horses are . . . very symbolic, and I know many tricks."

"I'm sure you know tricks I've never even heard of. You're all about trickery, aren't you?" She laughed bitterly. His hands slid along her arms.

"Yes. And I've heard you're fond of shapeshifters too."

She yanked free, spinning to place the heavy rope between them. "Whiskey."

"Aye, mistress?"

"You're not to mention that individual in my presence again. Are we understood?"

His eyes darkened, a storm-shadowed ocean. "Aye, mistress."

"Go, then. Find Kadiska, and play your little tricks on her. Keep her away from the Merlin for seven days. I'm sure you have the *tricks* to do it."

"Aye. Mistress."

She waved him away, and he went.

Once Whiskey departed, the smaller spirits of dale and streambed peered tentatively out of ferns and willow roots. They scampered free of their hiding places, some of them limping, some raw-skinned and welted. Seeker kicked off the raised, bare-scuffed bank and let her feet swing over chortling water, closing her eyes again to submerge herself in shadows.

It seemed strange to her, strange as if fated, that the course of time and this hunt had brought her back to the very doorstep where she'd met Keith: a venerable state university, modern brick and steel buildings interspersed with gray granite and hewn red stone, to a campus dotted with trees as old as the young American nation. There were new buildings since the seventies, but the soul of the place remained. The shadows teemed with haunts.

She had Carel's scent now, so it was the work of moments to find the Merlin's shadow among many. She picked up a trace of Kadiska, also watching, and pressed a smile against the roughspun manila rope. Old magics and petty spectres saturated the campus and its environs. Eerie things moved through Connecticut hills flame-and-ash-kissed with autumn, but Seeker knew them for what they were, touched them and let them pass. Something antique and dark—a cracked, leonine form— inhabited the woods east of the campus' hilltop graveyard. Seeker felt as well the ghosts of colicked horses haunting the stables a half-mile farther north, beyond the curve of a great, smooth-scraped teardrop of a hill, legacy of a long-forgotten glacier. Sprites and boggans explored the steam tunnels under the School of Engineering and the ether-scented hallways of the old chemistry building with its precipitous lecture halls. Spirits of chalk and dust, spirits of the greenhouses scented of loam and chlorophyll. And through it, a silver wire twisted through a tapestry woven in russet and bronze, the presence of the Merlin.

Seeker drew her shadows around her and, half a mile distant, watched Dr. Carel Bierce, Merlin, Dragonborn, stand before her dusty green chalkboard and teach a freshman lecture on geology, pointing out the classroom window to the curved silhouette of that hill. Seeker slid *otherwise* carefully, afraid the Merlin or Kadiska would sense her presence. But the elder Seeker showed no concern, watching boldly, though Seeker saw the Merlin's attention drift more than once to the shadows.

Seeker sighed and settled herself to relearn the wonders of pyroxene and potassium feldspar. *Dammit, Mist. Why couldn't you just tell me what you wanted me to do? Riddles within riddles, and oh.* And then her eyes opened wide and she tilted her head back, looking at a sky of thin-sliced sapphire set in the beaten gold and copper of the leaves. *And since when is the werewolf running errands for the Mother of Dragons? I should have thought of that right away.*

There's a clue there, and I missed it.

Seeker squinted into the brightness of the sky, most of her awareness stretched out *otherwise*. The Merlin wore a crimson silk blouse with a black velvet vest picked out in bugle beads, and Seeker watched her through the dance of shadows as she raised her left arm and marked a big, arcing curve on the chalkboard. The wooden frame rattled as she got her chalk-stained fingers under it and heaved upward, revealing a clean board behind. *Scientist, musician, dancer, wizard.*

Seeker's shadow swayed on the surface of the stream over which she swung, a suggestion of soft-feathered wings melting into a lashing tail and then just the rippled shape of a woman. *Why is Keith running errands for dragons?*

The waves wet Keith's paws as he trotted along their ragged margin, and swept his footprints into the sea. He could not have outrun the dreams and the dragons that pursued him, and he frankly didn't try; he just paced beside the cold, cold sea and felt its spray soak his coat and hiss between the stones.

Something pale, elevated on a wet stone, caught his eye; Keith slowed to an amble. He knew the silhouette and the scent, even over the salt-rich, half-rotten scent of the sea. He stood upright, wolf melding into man, stones that were nothing to callused pads sharp on bare feet.

The woman in the white gown watched him amusedly, seeming impervious to the wind that pinned the cloth against her wiry body and raised her coarse gray hair like a ragged banner. He wasn't surprised. He didn't feel the cold, either. "Fionnghuala."

"Keith," she said, and slithered off her rocky perch with a smile and an outstretched hand, unfazed by his nakedness. He caught her hand, a steadying grasp she did not need, and squeezed her long fingers lightly. Her skin was translucent as silk in the moonlight, and the bones underneath delicate as reed flutes. She winced when her bare feet touched the stones. "Welcome home. Where have you been?"

"Did you walk all this way in bare feet, Nuala?" An odd fey-seeming woman: a mortal who clambered about like a child, who bled red when she scraped her shins or elbows on the stones. The name was Irish — and ancient — and the accent was American, and she lived in a little cottage up the clifftop and was rarely at home.

"You walked farther on your bare feet, wolfling," she answered, leaning on his arm.

"My feet are suited to it." He winced as he stubbed his toe on a stone. "When I'm a wolf, in any case. How is it that you never feel the cold, Nuala?"

"My heart froze long ago," she answered, giving him a smile that said it was a lie. Her voice was a little too casual when she leaned close and continued, "When my husband died. Have you spoken with your father yet?"

"Yes," Keith said, a hand on the old woman's waist to lift her over a ridge of jagged stones. "He says he's dying."

"He's right. Does this mean you'll be putting some thought into marrying?"

"Nuala!" He glanced down quickly, caught the twinkle in her eye as she regained her feet. "Not you too."

"I merely meant that I have a granddaughter or three." That roguish grin, and so roguishly delivered. "And some likely nieces, come to think of it."

"How do you come to know so much about the pack?"

"Who do I have to have tea with but Morag, and your father when he's at home? It's a lonely coast, Keith." She gestured across the ocean, a dark ring glinting on her slender finger. They came to the foot of the stairs hewn in the cliff face, and Keith fell in behind her as she began to climb. "What are you going to do, young master? About your father dying?"

"Not so young anymore," he answered. "I've never been much of a Prince."

"Neither was Hal." She didn't turn back to see his expression, but climbed, holding her hair out of her eyes with her hand. "I understand that turned out all right. In the end."

Keith shrugged, letting his hand trail along the stones they climbed beside. "My sympathy was always with Falstaff."

"He did sort of get the thin end of the stick, didn't he?"

"My father thinks there's something I can do to reconcile with the mother of my son."

The old woman stepped aside at the top, and then paused, her hands on her hips as she drew a deep breath. "Then you'd have the issue of the heir sorted out, at least—"

"It's not quite so simple as that, Nuala."

She chuckled, low and rich. "No. It never is, is it? You *do* know Fyodor means to challenge you."

"I did not know until recently that there was anything to challenge for," Keith replied, taking her arm again. She patted his hand with paper-soft fingers. "Fyodor Stephanovich Danilov. A Russian wolf, here?"

"Is that any stranger than an American woman?" She held the door to her cottage open for him.

Keith shook his head and stepped back. "No," he said. "I don't suppose it is. Are you really an American?"

"I became one. You should meet him," Fionnghuala said, through the crack in the closing door. "Fyodor, I mean. While Eoghan is still alive. Because you're going to have to kill him when Eoghan dies."

"Nuala—" Keith said, but the door was already shut, and with a finality that precluded knocking. He shivered and collapsed into the warm familiarity of his wolf form.

He had forgotten to ask her about his dreams.

Three days later, Seeker contacted the Merlin again. A park bench rested under a big magnolia tree by the rear door of the geology building, and Seeker spread her lunch out there and waited, entertaining herself with comics in the student paper. They were not significantly more puerile than the ones she'd read as an undergraduate, thirty years before. There hadn't been a truck serving gyros on campus then, however, or anyplace to get cold vinegary dolmas.

The Merlin almost danced past her, cobalt and ruby-glass beads clattering with every balanced stride, but Seeker looked up and caught the other woman's eye. "I'm not going to believe this is an accident," the Merlin said, but she stopped on the walk and turned back around, half-unwilling. A canvas bag drooped heavily from her hand; she was obviously thinking of swinging it at Seeker's head.

"No," Seeker said. "I'm stalking you. You could come and eat with me. I have too much food. And I'll try to explain."

"I know better than to eat fairy food."

"It's from the roach coach," Seeker replied. She held a scrap of paper out in grease-stained fingers, sucking yogurt and cucumber off her other thumb. "There's the receipt."

The Merlin glanced at it, chuckled, and sat—stiffly—on the corner of the bench. "I shouldn't be talking to you."

Seeker nodded. "But the curiosity is driving you crazy, isn't it? That's part of what makes you what you are. Driven to learn things. Master them. Are you a risk taker, Carel?"

"Most geologists like adventure. We spend a good deal of time peering into volcanoes and spelunking in dark caverns." The Merlin smiled, cautious. "How did you find me? Web search?"

"Magic," Seeker answered. "Do you want proof?"

The Merlin, whose ripe-berry mouth was half-open to demand just that, simply nodded. "My second sight—if that's what it is. It would be so easy to explain it away. Borderline schizophrenia. Hallucinations. Synesthesia."

"And you have."

"All part of justifying my existence."

Which made Seeker laugh out loud. Their eyes met; warmth spread through the Seeker's chest. She missed *friends*; she'd been Seeker as long as she'd been mortal, now.

A rattle on the roof slates of the hulking neo-Gothic geology building drew Seeker's attention. She glanced up to see Gharne curled against a chimney like a shadow cast by the afternoon sunlight. The Merlin followed Seeker's gaze and blinked. "What is that?"

"A servant," Seeker said. "Most can't see him. He's sideways in the world."

"Seeing auras is trendy."

"True enough. I could show you some things, but you might want privacy for it."

"If you think I'm going anyplace alone with you, you're crazy." The Merlin leaned forward and examined the dolmas, but did not touch them. "Who was that woman with you the other night, by the way?"

"Another Seeker. The Seeker of the Unseelie court."

"The bad fairies."

"All the Fae are . . . inhuman in their morality. I'm sure you know the ballads about that as well. I represent the Queen of the Daoine Sidhe. She is very powerful, and very bright. Kadiska's mistress is a Queen called the Cat Anna—"

"Isn't that a Celtic goddess of some sort?"

"Her name has been used so, yes." Seeker bit into a stuffed grape leaf, savoring tomatoes, rice, the tang of dressing.

"Please continue." The Merlin's tone was rich with mockery, but it lay uncertain over a brittleness like sugared glass.

She's been lonely too, Seeker realized. *Accomplished in so many ways. And who can she tell what she sees in the dark of the moon?* "—a much darker figure," Seeker finished, as if she had not been interrupted.

"Tell me more about the Mage. Dr. Szczegielniak."

It crossed Seeker's mind to wonder how the Merlin knew that Matthew held a doctorate. *Prescience or research, what does it matter?* "What more is there to say?"

"What does he want with me?"

"The same thing I do," Seeker answered, picking at the edge of the bench with a thumbnail. "Your wisdom. Your power."

"Girl—" Carel stopped herself midspeech, drew a deep breath, and planted her free hand on her hip. "My wisdom isn't anything to speak of. Maybe a bit more levelheaded than most—"

"Is *that* all."

Carel laughed, a rich dark sound that crested up into her singing range. "You expected some panic-stricken Hollywood reaction? I get weirder things than you in my cereal box."

Seeker swallowed the last bite of the dolmas. "Really?"

Carel cocked her head left and right, a falcon considering whether to peck. "Not so much weirder," she allowed. "I could freak out theatrically if it would make you feel better."

" 'Come with me if you want to live,' " Seeker quoted, drawing another laugh.

"You get many recent releases in Faerie?"

"We learn all the stories, sooner or later. Especially once they start growing into myths. Here's another one: Haven't you ever wanted to see elves, Carel Bierce?"

The Merlin threw back her head and laughed that much harder, allowing herself to be disarmed. "Who hasn't?" she answered after her laughter trailed off, bubbling like that little stream. "I see elves all the time. Every day. There's one picking around in the flower bed up there." Carel pointed, and sure enough, there was. A gnome, anyway, but it didn't seem the time to correct her.

"Come with me," Seeker said, letting her power and a little of her position vibrate in her voice, "and I will show you things more terrible than you imagine. Darkness and the Dragon at the bottom of the world: the magic that makes all things whole and then rends them again, bit from bit." *Keith. Damn you, what are you doing with the Dragon?* "I will show you terrifying truths."

"And what will your colleague show me should I go to her?"

"Lovely things, no doubt," Seeker said softly. "The lie is always prettier."

The Merlin pursed her lips, her eyes like black jade. "What is this thing you feel I might want privacy for?"

"I'll have to kiss you." *Which is half a lie, and half a truth that isn't really.*

"And you're scared if you kiss a woman in public, you'll be tarred as a lesbian forever." The Merlin's laugh frothed up again, a wave effervescing over the breakwater.

"You're the one with a reputation to worry about," Seeker said mildly, provoking more laughter.

"Honey," the Merlin answered, "the whole campus already knows which way I swing. So if you think you've got something that's worth taking risks for, show it to me. Then maybe we can deal." She stood. "Or leave me the hell alone. I've got a full plate already. So convince me. And then you can explain to me what you get out of it. I still don't believe in free lunches."

"No," Seeker answered. "What's in it for me?" She stood as well, wadding the remains of her lunch in paper and pitching them underhanded into the trash. "Better to ask what's in it for my Queen. The prestige of having a human wizard of such power and promise attached to her court. Your strength and wisdom to counsel her, when you grow into it. Alliance. What does the university offer you?"

"Tenure, eventually. I see your point. They protect me, provide for me, and have a claim on my research and my teaching time. Patronage. So what does it get me, and what does it cost?"

Seeker gestured toward Gharne's languid form. He blinked sleepily, eyes like hurricane lamps with the candles flickering inside, and spread inkblot wings across the red-and-gray slates, soaking in the heat of the sun. A mockingbird improvised arpeggios in the branches of the magnolia. Whatever Seeker had been about to say died on her lips.

"What?"

"Nothing," Seeker said. But she had heard the birdsong, and heard in it meaning plain as words. *Fine fellow, fine fellow—see me; I'm a good provider, strong and smart and fat.*

The leaf-mold taste of springwater filled her mouth. She swallowed it and forced a smile. "Hold still. Close your eyes." She kissed the Merlin on both eyes and then her mouth, awkwardly letting the kiss linger a moment before she backed away.

"Okay," Seeker said, and Carel opened her eyes and looked around.

"What should I be seeing?" she said, and startled at the sound of her own voice. "What's that?!"

The second sentence came out in English, but the first had been in the fey tongue. "A small magic," Seeker answered, lapsing into the same formal language. "The gift of tongues. And the Sight, which you had in small measure already." She pointed across the gardens and the walkways and the lawns.

"I'd think you slipped me a hallucinogen," Carel said after a long time. "Everything looks so . . . real."

"It does, doesn't it? Come with me."

"Where are we going?"

"To talk to a tree," Seeker said, and, taking the Merlin's hand in her own, led her along an asphalt path and by the water.

Seeker brought the Merlin around the edge of the little lake at the bottom of a bowl-shaped lawn, holding the smaller woman's hand. A family of three stood beside a white metal sign announcing a forty-five-dollar fine for feeding the waterfowl. The little girl shook bread crumbs to the Canada geese, laughing at the big birds' squabbles. She was blond and fair-skinned, perhaps ten years old. Seeker glanced quickly away anyway, longing twisting inside her. "Tell me what you see," she said to the Merlin.

Carel struggled for focus. "Everything." She spread her hands helplessly. "Only brighter."

Seeker nodded, encouraging.

The Merlin's hands tumbled one over the other like courting butterflies. "It's like . . . late afternoon. When the light is at a slant and the shadows make everything look very *real*."

"Good," Seeker said. "That's how it should look."

Carel stood in silence for a moment, turning her head as if surveying the winter's first snowfall. "Well." She dusted her hands on her trousers. "Where's this magic tree?"

"Not magic." Seeker extended a finger up the slope of the lawn. "Just friendly."

The weeping willow stood at the top of a sweep of moss-green grass, across the street from the English and social sciences buildings. It wasn't one tree, precisely, but rather five trunks grown together in the communal fashion of willows, the cup where they forked making a bower large enough to cradle several people in the palm of its enormous hand.

"When I was here, we called him Old Man Willow." Seeker walked under cascading, autumn-bright leaves. The willow's massive boughs lofted skyward, ribboning back toward earth in plumes echoed by the fountain. "He likes company."

"When you were here . . . ?" Carel began, but her voice trailed off into softness. "Oh. My."

Because the wizened old giant looked up, saw the women coming toward him, and smiled. Or perhaps more accurately, gave the appearance of smiling, because the physical tree did not move or change. Nevertheless, Seeker saw it gaze a welcome as if over the edge of a newspaper. Carel froze, and then took a single hesitant step.

The weeping branches stirred in a wind Seeker did not feel, brushing her hair and then the Merlin's, leaves cool against her cheek. "Welcome, ladies," the willow whispered, a sound like the rasp of moist earth along the belly of a worm.

Seeker held her tongue and waited.

Carel's eyebrows went up. *You're testing me.*

Seeker smiled. *You're right.*

The Merlin squared her shoulders. "Good afternoon."

The big tree chuckled and seemed to settle himself, an old man leaning against the back of a bench. "It is indeed," he answered. "I've seen you before, but you never stopped to chat. Climb up into my branches. I'm told it's comfortable."

Seeker moved forward, taking the Merlin by the elbow. "It's polite," she said. The crotch of the tree was three feet up; Seeker set one boot on a conveniently gnarled root so polished with footsteps that it resembled a waxed door lintel. Grasping rough bark with both hands, she jumped lightly into the tree.

"I'm tripping," Carel said.

Seeker offered the Merlin a hand. *"Allez-oop."*

A moment later, and the two women were ensconced among sheltering trunks. "Like a bee in a flower," Carel said, wonderingly. She laid a hand on the rough, sun-warmed bark. "Are all willow trees so friendly?"

"Most of us," he answered. "Haven't you ever noticed how many birds and insects make us home?" The branches wavered, and Seeker was struck by how much it resembled the sway of the Merlin's braids. "You'll be able to talk to birds too, soon."

"Can you do that?" Carel leaned toward Seeker.

"No," Seeker said, but she remembered the mockingbird and wondered. "But I am Fae, and you're a wizard. I don't know the rules for wizards."

"She's more than a wizard, little one," the willow said. "And you! I remember you. Twenty, thirty summers ago. You sat in my branches with a red-haired man. You weren't Fae then."

"Part Fae," Seeker answered, more curtly than she intended. "They found me the summer I graduated and brought me home."

The willow seemed unruffled by her tone. "Welcome back," he said, and she had an impression that the branches offered her a brief and warm embrace. "Too few of my old friends come back to visit. But there are always new ones."

"I never knew," Carel began, and cleared her throat, "that trees were so . . . talkative."

The willow chuckled gently. "I'm special." He eased himself on his roots like a storyteller warming to a tale. "Willows have always been more restless than other trees. In the old days, the willow-folk were known for walking at night, even following unwary travelers on the road." He sighed. "Things are different now. But people do come and talk to me."

"I'm sorry I never did before." The Merlin seemed at a loss for words. "What sort of things do you like to talk about?"

"Oh, all sorts of things. There was a girl who used to come and read me Brer Rabbit and poetry. There was a dark-haired boy who liked to sit in my branches and write, and a blond boy with a bicycle who brought his friends here. None of them could hear me. But they weren't what you are, after all."

"What I am? A . . . wizard?" She still tripped over the word.

Seeker started to interrupt, but she wasn't fast enough.

"A Merlin," the tree said.

"A . . . like Merlin the Magician. Like that?"

"Like that," Seeker said. She hadn't been back to talk to the tree since she *changed*. Most willow trees weren't so well educated. *Most willow trees aren't the focal point of a university campus.*

"I haven't noticed myself living backwards," Carel said tartly, studying her fingernails.

Seeker laughed. "I suspect that was a convenient fiction Ambrosius put about to explain his propensity for telling the future and knowing creepy things about people. Most Merlins are prophets of one sort or another."

"So how is being a Merlin different from being a wizard?"

The tree seemed to cock his head, thinking. "Wizards, Magi . . . they *learn* magic. Wizards *generate* magic," he said. "Magi *use* magic. Merlins . . . they *are* magic."

"Like you two are magic."

"No," Seeker answered. *In for a penny,* she thought. "We contain magic, Old Man Willow and I. You—" She paused. Carel watched her, dark eyes glistening intent as a bird's, motionless as a heron stalking a fish. "—are the personification of magic. One to a generation. And not every generation gets one."

"Ah." The Merlin seemed to be chewing that thought over. She frowned and sighed, twisting her boot against the bark. The tree wriggled without moving, delighted as a tickled puppy. "What am I supposed to do with this . . . power?"

She didn't try to deny it, Seeker noticed, as if something in her bones told her the truth of every word. *Good. That makes it easier. Maybe the tree wasn't such a bad idea after all.* "Oh, the usual," she answered dryly. "Ordain Kings. Foresee the future. If you're lucky, save the world."

"And if I'm not lucky?"

Seeker coughed into her hand. "Remember the Dark Ages?"

"That's"—Carel stopped and let herself slide down the concave limb of the willow until she crouched in the cradle of its trunk—"a lot of responsibility. Why me?"

Seeker shrugged, and leaned back against another branch of the trunk, bracing her legs against an opposite branch. What sunlight filtered between the tree's golden leaves dappled the backs of her hands as she examined her fingernails. " 'Why me?' " she mocked. "I don't know, Carel. I don't know why me, either. Except that we're born to it, and the world is a stranger, wilder place than I ever imagined, when I thought I was mortal."

"Are you telling me I'm . . . immortal?"

Seeker wasn't sure what emotion the other woman's tone betrayed. She shook her head judiciously. "No. You're spared that. Although wizards generally live a long time."

"Oh." Considering silence and the tree speechless too, humming of warm days and wet autumn breezes. "You're unhappy."

"Observant." Seeker straightened and tucked a braid behind her ear, swallowing defiance. "Will you come to Faerie with me?"

"Can I leave again?"

She's sharp.

"Anytime you want to." Seeker's mind went to Mist, though, and the shattered eye of the Mother of Dragons. *The Mebd does not know all the rules. I wonder what she meant.*

You can't be seriously considering going against her.

But she was. Except her very blood and bones would prevent her. And if that wasn't enough . . .

Ian.

"Hah," said the willow abruptly, as if his musing had led him to a better answer. "Also, Magi . . . well, some of their practices are bitter."

"Bitter?" Seeker leaned forward.

"Like metal in the earth, like soured stinking water. They prickle. Not all of them, but some." The branches gestured like a graceful hand. "Some of them do not love the old things."

"I know," Seeker said. She patted the tree's bark, thinking of the Promethean Mage with his ten iron rings. "Some of them work for the freedom of man, as they call it. What they *mean* is the *elevation* of man. Power as a zero-sum game."

"Dr. Szczegielniak. He seemed very earnest."

"Earnest. Yes, you could call it that."

The Merlin drew breath in some sudden understanding. Seeker saw her advantage and looked at Carel with beseeching eyes. *Everyone likes to feel special.* "We need the help," she said plainly. "Come with me today, and we will visit Faerie, only. I vow."

And Carel laid a warm, strong hand on Seeker's shoulder, fingers just brushing the skin of her neck, and smiled. "This, I gotta see. But I'm not eating any pomegranates. Where do we go?"

Seeker raised a hand and pointed northeast, toward the arcing shape of the massive drumlin concealed by buildings and the tree line. Thorn-break grew on it, between the cattle fields and alfalfa: native rose and blackberry brambles. "To the land under the hills," she said, "and over the westering sea."

Carel grinned, shaking out her braids. " 'What is yonder mountain high,' " she sang, " 'where cold winds crack and blow?' "

" 'Yonder's the mountain of Hell,' " Seeker answered, without taking her eyes from the thorn-topped hill. " 'Where you and I must go.' "

"You've been following her," Jane said, crossing her legs in tailored, pin-striped pants. She fussed idly with the toast Matthew had made for her, picking crumbs from the edge with a fingernail, but didn't taste anything. Sunlight fell through the window of his tidy kitchenette, highlighting avocado and harvest-gold decor that hadn't changed in two and a half decades.

"Better," Matthew said. "I found out who the Merlin is. I met her, briefly. I gave her a business card."

The archmage's eyes sparkled over the rim of her teacup. "*She.* Interesting. Has *she* called?"

"She may not have found it yet," Matthew answered with a shrug. "Elaine was standing next to me when I slipped it into her pocket. But I was able to use it as an anchor to follow her, and I know where she lives and works now. She's a college professor. And as soon as I can figure out how to meet her without presenting the appearance of a creepy stalker type—"

"Excellent," Jane said. She set her cup aside and rose. She washed the grease from her fingertips at the kitchen sink, then crossed her arms on the countertop and leaned toward the window.

As if she can't look me in the eye. Matthew set his mug down too, and pushed his chair back, the feet on the metal legs skipping slightly as they snagged on textured tile. "Out with it, fearless leader," he said, crossing the kitchen to stand shoulder to shoulder beside her.

"You haven't asked to see Kelly recently," she said.

He didn't glance at her, but let their sleeves brush. "You're my mother now?"

Her sly smile in response shocked him. "I'm everybody's mother," she answered. "This thing. This Merlin, and the five-hundred-year mark— if there's going to be a Dragon Prince, Matthew, things are going to change. The last upheaval brought our chapter into existence, and five hundred years of work have given us a great deal of strength and control. We're safer from wild magic than ever before in the history of the human race."

"We?"

"Men, most mortal," she said. "The old strange powers do not rule us anymore. We've bound the dragons to our chariot."

"Poetic," he answered, and sidestepped closer, taking comfort in her warmth.

She sighed and pressed her ear against his shoulder, leaning into his rough, spontaneous hug. She might be more than twice his age, but she wasn't fragile in the least. He knew she felt strongly—about Elaine, for him. She never let it rule her. "Yes. The Dragon Prince could change all that."

"He could. And even if he doesn't, how can we call it a victory when disasters like Kelly still happen?"

"Like Kelly. Like Elaine." She rose on her tiptoes to plant a motherly kiss on his cheek, and brushed her hands over the tattooed patterns that peeked over his collar. "I'm glad you agreed to this. You'll need all the protection you can get."

"It helped Kelly so much." He stepped back, head shaking.

"He lived," she said. She held Matthew's gaze on her own, unrelenting. "It's a hell of a business. And there are going to have to be sacrifices made."

"I know." He did know, that was the worst of it. And knew in his bones why it was so.

Jane twisted her fingers together. "Make sure you spend some time with Kelly soon, all right? And see what you can do about the Merlin while you're about it. Maybe there's some way to combine the two—"

"All right," he answered, as she smiled and stepped away.

Chapter Six

Keith waited for Eoghan at the bottom of the stairs. Dinner in the MacNeill house was served late and formally, with the ceremony of a bygone age, and guests were welcomed and usually present. And Keith had no intention of confronting the wolves in the parlor until he could walk in at his father's right hand as befitted a dutiful son.

He pretended he didn't see his father clinging to the banister. *Coward,* he accused himself.

Keith frowned ruefully and ascended the stair, offering Eoghan his arm. They came down together, the old wolf in his kilt and dinner jacket leaning on the young one in his cedar-smelling tuxedo. "Have you thought about what we spoke of?"

Keith chuckled. "If Fyodor Stephanovich wants the princedom of the pack so badly, father—"

"You've spoken with Nuala."

"How did you know?"

"It was her, or Morag. You'd hand the proud traditions of the pack to that tea-swilling *oborotni?* That Cossack? *Keith.*" Eoghan's disappointment almost dripped from his voice. "Besides, he's too young."

Not that much younger than I am.

Nay, another voice seemed to answer. *Only a few decades, and what's that to a wolf?* It was the same voice that had called him coward earlier, and touched him in the dreams that sent him to summon Elaine into the presence of the Dragon. Keith shivered when he realized it. *Mist?*

Fyodor Stephanovich. Were he my Prince, would you still follow him, Keith MacNeill? Even knowing the price he would pay?

Would I follow your Prince, Mother of Dragons? What sane man would, had he something to lose?

Ah, she answered. *Something to lose. Something to win. And thus we speak of Princes, and thereby hangs the tale.* A dark chuckle and the sensation of shifting earth, of a crimson eye splintering darkness, and the presence was gone as suddenly as it had come. Keith bit the inside of his cheek and struggled to keep his face bland as he steadied his father to the landing. His scent peaked, though, and he knew from Eoghan's sidelong glance that his father smelled it as well. Eoghan sighed. "Lord a'mercy, Keith. Where's your ambition, son?"

Keith smiled as they paced across the flagstoned hall, toward the parlor. Already he smelled woodsmoke and whiskey and the scents of three or four wolves. "You should have had another son, father. One to follow in your footsteps."

"I've one," Eoghan said calmly. "And a fine sense of duty he has, even if he's lacking in ambition. He'll serve."

And if Fyodor's a Dragon Prince, what then? Keith wasn't fool enough to think he could stand against *that.* But then, it was unlikely in the extreme that anyone would believe that Dragons spoke to Keith Mac-Neill, werewolf and expatriate. He released his father's arm as they came up on the door of the parlor, leaving Eoghan his pride. Keith tugged the door open, the brazen handle cool and finger-polished. There was a shallow dip in the flagstones in the center of the corridor, a passage worn by hundreds of feet and hundreds of years.

Side by side, Keith and his father entered the parlor.

Fyodor Stephanovich dominated the room with the careless ease that one would expect of a Prince among wolves. He leaned casually beside the mantel of his Prince's fireplace, surrounded by a court of two. There was a snifter of brandy cupped in one daddy-longlegs hand, an inch of bare wrist and knobby bone showing beyond his shirtsleeve. His wild dark hair, though glazed into ringlets, had defeated whatever product he'd worked through it, and the curls tumbled over his forehead to brush his brows. Deep-set eyes glittered like mica chips on either side of a scar-bridged gypsy nose, and he straightened and smiled as Keith and Eoghan entered.

"Sire," Fyodor said. The Russian wolf lowered his glass with his hand, the other hanging flat by his hip, and drew himself to a stately height, turning his head to show his long, ridged throat to Eoghan. "Elder Brother." This to Keith, with a respectful nod, but he did not turn his head. Instead he came across the floor, switching his glass to his left hand and extending the right.

Keith took it.

Keith topped six feet, broad chest and thick limbs showing the heritage of the same Norse raiders who had left Scotland his burnished red hair and the feral gleam in his eyes. Those eyes were level with Fyodor's chin, when Fyodor straightened to his full height. The black Russian wolf—the *oborotni*—seemed wired together out of broomsticks, but the grip that matched Keith's was as unyielding as the ambition in his eyes.

"Younger Brother," Keith answered, and didn't let the growl constricting his throat color his voice. His father's presence at his shoulder was all that kept him from stepping back. "I don't believe I know all your friends."

There were two other wolves, both wearing the same wary, powerful look as Fyodor. The black wolf angled his head at a stocky man with ash-colored hair and a trimmed beard. "Sire, Elder Brother. May I present Younger Brother Ivan Ilyich."

"Please, call me Vanya, Elder Brother," Ivan Ilyich said, a perfectly unaccented voice and a close-mouthed smile belying his modulated handshake and his unwolflike refusal to stand on formality. His eyes were a blue pale as a sled dog's, a cold dawning color like a shadow on snow.

Unwolflike. Un-Russian, for that matter.

Surnames were a recent enough thing in their country that the Russian wolves rarely bothered with them except when dealing with false papers and mortal society, and Keith didn't ask for one. Particularly once Ivan Ilyich *did* show Keith his throat—just an angling of his jaw, but enough. He stepped back at the same moment Keith did, not quite giving ground. "Welcome to Scotland . . . Vanya. I am Keith MacNeill." He hesitated. "Keith."

And the younger packmate squeezed his eyes half shut and smiled through the lashes.

Keith ignored the stiff prickle of Eoghan's disapproval. *If he wants me to be a Prince, I'm not sure I can prevent it. But I'll be my own sort of Prince. I will.*

Perfect politeness, perfect dignity. And the tension in the room was enough to raise Keith's hackles and make his eyeteeth itch. He turned his gaze on the youngest wolf—Fyodor followed propriety even in the order of the introductions—and blinked. The boy could have been the black wolf's younger, more beautiful twin. Keith caught Eoghan's subtle nod out of the corner of his eye, and showed teeth. "Eremei Fyodorovich," Fyodor said, and Keith smiled more at the tentative way the cub took his hand.

"Your son." As blatant a declaration of intent as a wolf could make, without a challenge snarled.

"My own," Fyodor agreed, with a quirk of smile that transformed his lined face into radiant beauty.

"Elder Brother," Eremei Fyodorovich said, stepping back and folding one arm across his belly for a bow that would have done a Tsar's son proud. His tight-curled hair shone dark against the nape of his neck; Keith hurt to look at him.

"Younger Brother," Keith answered, and bit back his smile, and returned the bow, Eoghan's shoulder brushing his sleeve. The old wolf stood very close, and Keith breathed silent encouragement on his father's scent. *Coward,* he thought again, meeting Eremei Fyodorovich's laughter-sweet eyes. He wondered briefly if Ian's would be as changeable as Elaine's, or if they were green, like his own. And then, *Oh, pity. The Dragon Prince has a son.*

That will cost him, before this is over.

"Come along," Eoghan said, with a gesture that included Keith and the Russian wolves. "Dinner should be ready."

Keith tasted nothing. *Elaine. Ian. I am going to have to talk to Elaine.*

❀   ❀   ❀

Morgan served the Merlin and the Seeker green tea in cylindrical mugs without handles. Seeker traced the green-on-beige outline of the Japanese symbols that ran in tidy rows from rim to base. The Merlin, she noticed, turned her mug with her fingertips but did not raise it to her mouth. *If only she weren't so wary.*

If she weren't so wary, she wouldn't be much of a Merlin. Seeker, on the other hand, drank her jasmine-scented tea and smiled. The Merlin had taken the trip into Faerie as much in her stride as she seemed to take everything: imperturbable, or simply in shock. *"For forty days and forty nights / they rode through bluid red to the knee."* Seeker caught herself humming when the Merlin turned and lifted an eyebrow. Seeker could only presume she knew the tune.

"You're Morgan le Fey," the Merlin said when Morgan finished fussing with her kettle, settling across the trestle.

The witch pushed a trencher of bread, cheese, and sliced apples across the table. "I am. Am I not what you expected?"

"Not exactly."

"May you never cease to be surprised," Morgan said. It sounded like a benediction.

The silver wolfhound came up beside the table and slipped a black nose into Morgan's palm. Morgan tousled the dog's ears. It raised its head and rested a wise gaze on Seeker, eyes on a level with her own. Morgan noticed the regard and smiled, matching it with one of her own. "Her kind are the reason there are no wolves left in Ireland."

Seeker looked down and took a slice of cheese, but did not taste it. "What is her name?" the Merlin asked.

"Ah. This is Evèr. Her son is called Connla."

"Interesting choices," Seeker said. Carel looked puzzled.

"Terrible jokes, you mean." Morgan flashed a white-toothed smile. "Cuchulainn's wife and son," she explained to Carel. "He was called the Hound of Ulster."

"Oh." The Merlin pushed her mug away. "I have the feeling," she said when the other two turned, "that this is supposed to be a historic meeting. Fraught with significance. The sort of thing bards might sing of, if there were bards anymore."

"And it feels a little anticlimactic?"

"Yes."

Morgan pushed her chair back from the table and steepled her fingers. "Seeker, would you leave the Merlin and me alone for a moment or three, please? I believe I need to explain some things to her."

"She's already forewarned against me," Seeker said, but stood. She and Morgan shared a glance until Evèr came and leaned against Seeker's thighs. "But tell her what you will. She knows my task already." *The half of it. But Morgan will know that. I cannot afford to win. And I will not be allowed to fail.*

I wonder if the Kelpie is still keeping Kadiska busy.

Seeker turned slowly and walked under the high-draped tapestry and outside. She stopped by the rosebushes, taking in well-tended gardens and a mist-silver sky. The shadows were dim in the even lighting. Seeker could have peered inside Morgan's cottage, but some perversity moved her to play fair.

I could trust Morgan to figure something out. She snorted laughter. *That's always worked out so well in the past.*

Evèr followed her outside. "Don't worry," the great silver hound said, looking up at her face.

Seeker jumped. "You speak?"

"You're only just now hearing me," the dog answered. "I wonder what's changed." She scanned the tree line, head up and tulip ears attentive. Wolfhounds were sight hounds, bred to follow their prey not by scent but by vision, bred to outspeed and outmuscle any wolf in the world.

"I don't know," Seeker admitted. "Nothing that I can think of, except binding a Kelpie."

"No, that wouldn't do it." She lowered a dartlike head, narrow-muzzled and broad across the cranium, and nosed the tail-lashing shadow that followed Seeker down the garden path. A low whine rose in her throat. "Where are they, Seeker?"

"Where are who, Evèr?" She'd done stranger things than talk to hounds, and the dog had an alert, interested, caring tone.

"The shadows. The beasts bound to you—doe, cat, owl. You've stolen their strengths. Where are their bodies?"

"Dead," Seeker answered, and turned aside. "I killed them." A thrush sang. *My tree! My mate! My chicks!*

"It is your special gift," Evèr replied. "What you are. Is it worse than running down a hare to taste its blood?"

"Yes," Seeker answered, following the contorted canes of the rose-bush around to the place where it rooted beside the chimney. The stones were warm with the fire within, and Seeker leaned against them. "How would you feel if I took your shadow?"

"I wouldn't like it any better than you would if I tore out your throat," the dog said, her tongue lolling over capable teeth. "Or any worse, I warrant." Laughter floated through the thick wall of Morgan's cottage, muffled but still audible. "The wolves weren't much fond of my kind either. We are what we are."

"Easy enough for you to say."

"True." Evèr's plumed tail wagged twice. Seeker laid a hand on her neck. The wolfhound's coat felt like wire mixed with wool, at once coarse and butter-soft, and slightly greasy. The big dog sighed and leaned against the Seeker's hip.

Evèr looked back up at Seeker, eyes kind under Leo G. Carroll brows, and widened her doggy smile. "Speaking of wolves," she said, "I should be off. You seem to have a visitor." She pointed with her nose, after the fashion of sight hounds. Seeker followed around the corner of the cottage.

The other wolfhound, the red one, paced down the trail alongside a wolf of even ruddier coat. A wolf that stopped in his tracks as Seeker came into view, and then sat down on his haunches and curled his tail neatly over his toes. "Set up," Seeker muttered. She turned to frown at Evèr, but the wolfhound had vanished, and by the time she turned back, Connla was moving away as well, pretending nonchalance. "All right then."

Squaring her shoulders, she advanced on the wolf.

"Keith MacNeill." His ears were forward. He waited. Something prickled in her chest; she told herself it was irritation. *What is he doing, running errands for Mist? There's something afoot here bigger than the rivalry between the Mebd and the Cat Anna*, she thought. *Morgan set this meeting up.*

"Well," she said. "If you've aught to say to me, get up on your two feet and say it." She crossed her arms and scowled.

And he did. The red wolf blurred and stretched, a smooth reshaping of form that left him standing, nude, facing her. Seeker bit her lip and kept her gaze on his eyes, telling herself the breathless pain she felt was nothing but nervousness.

"What do you want, Keith?"

"Peace," he said bluntly. "I want an alliance." But his eyes slid off hers, and she turned away, raising one hand to touch the thorn-prickled cane of the climbing rose.

That isn't all. "What else?"

"I want you to talk to the Mebd."

"You want to see Ian."

"Of course I do." He came up alongside her, close enough that she could feel the heat of his body against her arm, even through the denim jacket that she wore over her shirt.

"You know what the Mebd has done to him, I presume."

"I've heard." His breath stirred her hair. "Let me treat with her, E— Seeker. I understand better than you do how to use your power."

"I haven't any." She spat vile-tasting words on the ground.

"You have power you can't imagine," he replied. "If you would only choose to wield it—" He stopped short, sharp accusation in his voice. "No. I'm sorry."

She held her breath.

"I failed you, Elaine."

"You screwed me over, you mean."

He sighed. "I hurt you out of weakness. I . . . betrayed you."

"Damn straight." She pressed venom into her voice, wishing she had Kadiska's cobra-shadow, to turn that venom into a bite. She could have pushed him, reminded him who had given the Mebd her Name. But it was history they both knew, and whatever his reasons, the deed was done.

But he bulled on. "What the man would do out of fear, the wolf should refuse to do, out of loyalty."

"Are you saying that you were afraid of the Mebd? You owed her no service, no more than any of the wild Fae do." *Like the Kelpie.* "Except you're not Fae, and she couldn't even have bound you! You owed her nothing."

"No," he said, and heard the frown in his voice. She turned back and lifted her eyes to meet his, wolf-green, with the lines of old sorrows at their corners. "I'm saying that I couldn't bear to see you get old."

If there were a sun in the sky, it might have moved the width of a finger before Seeker found her voice, standing there in front of Keith, looking up into his unblinking eyes. A werewolf might live two hundred years or more. A human woman, half that.

The Seeker of the Daoine Sidhe need never die.

"I'll ask her to lift the prohibition," Elaine said.

He inclined his head and placed a hand on her shoulder. She struck it aside, her lip curling. "Find a way," she said. "Get me my son back. Get him free of her. Do that thing, Keith MacNeill, and we'll talk again."

"Done," he said, and slowly backed away.

The grass beside the stone wall at the edge of Morgan's garden was wet with mist. Seeker sat on it anyway and pressed her face against her knees. She reached into the shadows, groping toward Morgan's cottage, and felt as if her fingers brushed slick, opaque ice. *You will not pass.*

She sighed, resting her chin against the back of her hand. *Some of us are not going to survive this.* Keith's quiet confidence that he could, in fact, *do* something only made her more certain of that. She dug at the ground absently, fingers burrowing like worms in the cool earth, stopping when brittle grass broke between them. She picked her head up and looked, frowning. Burned-gold stalks powdered and crumbled, friable as moldy hay when she rubbed them.

"That's not right," she said. The grass smelled like high summer and high prairie drought when she raised it to her nostrils, but—yes—the ground was wet. And the grass was green and soft, on the surface at least; but when Seeker parted the stems and peered between them, she could see it was dying at the root. She thrust a finger down into the soil, feeling grains under her nail, and rubbed some between thumb and forefinger.

A susurrus as of small voices caught her attention, and she was about to bend her head to listen closer when the crunch of feet on a leaf-littered path turned her head. Morgan crouched beside her and extended a hand. "You could have sat on the wall," the sorceress said.

Seeker reached out muddy fingers and let Morgan pull her to her feet. Carel stood under the crimson and bone-white shower of the rambling roses, breathing deeply. She turned to face them as Seeker and Morgan walked back. "I think of roses as a summer flower." Carel fingered the petals of one half-open bloom.

"They are," Morgan said. "Summer and again in the fall."

"What were you two discussing?" Seeker wondered if they would lie. *Don't trust me,* she thought, meeting Carel's eyes.

"Wizards." Morgan's face gave away nothing, smooth as a mirror. "Their instruction and training. Meanwhile, I think your guest would like to go home."

"Carel?"

"Yes," the Merlin confirmed. "Take me home."

"I had thought to bring you to meet my Queen."

"Perhaps later." Confidence surrounded her. "I should talk to the other side as well. If"—the Merlin hesitated—"I am, as you assure me, free to make my own decision." She shook a clatter of braids over her shoulder, the sweep of her hand encompassing the dale and the line of the forest beyond, before she tucked it into her pocket.

Seeker drew herself up short. "You always have been." *Is this Morgan's game, or the Merlin's test? Oh, I am not meant to swim in waters this deep* . . . which made her think of the Kelpie, which made her think of Mist, which made her think of Keith.

Am I really what they seem to think I am?

"Then you'll take me home."

"I'll take you home. Let me set my familiar to watch over you, at least?"

"The inkstain thing?" The Merlin pursed her lips, seeming to consider. Seeker heard Morgan breathing, but the sorceress did not speak. "No," she said, and forestalled Seeker's protest with an upraised hand. "I believe I'm what you say I am . . . which means I have to learn to take care of myself, doesn't it? And as Morgan has kindly offered to tutor me, I think I should hear what both sides have to offer."

Seeker sighed.

It was going to be a long autumn.

A day or two later—time was not always predictable, in Faerie—Seeker called Whiskey to her, away from Kadiska, and set Gharne to watch the other Seeker. From a safe distance, she warned him. "And don't let the Merlin see you." They spoke on the lawn of the palace; Whiskey cropped the greensward a few yards away, blunt white teeth tearing the grass with a sound of ripped paper. Slow rivulets of water dripped down his flanks like beads of sweat, plastered his mane to the high white arch of his neck, slicked dark feathers against his fetlocks as if he waded through dewy meadows.

Seeker strolled across the grass and crouched before him. An ebony swath dripped down his face from ears to muzzle as if smeared on with a paint roller, surrounding his eyes and his nostrils in black, spatters of shining darkness marking his cheeks. Black strands mingled the white at the top of his mane. "You had no problems?" She picked a teasel out of his forelock.

" 'She turned about her milk-white steed, and pulled True Thomas up behind,' " he quoted through a mouthful of grass. "She was amenable."

"Amenable? I thought I told you to keep her busy."

"I did," he snorted. "Pleasant company. Sharp teeth." A big hoof landed next to Seeker's knee.

"Don't step on me." She saw something under the fall of his mane and stood, lifting the wet coarse-matted hairs. He shuddered irritably, twitching her away as he might a fly. "I owe you a currying. Be still." A red perforated wound adorned the crest of his neck. "Sharp teeth indeed."

"It's less satisfying when you cannot eat them, after."

"Poor horsey." She withdrew, rubbing her hand on her jeans.

"Why are they always milk-white steeds?" He raised his shining wet head, Roman-nosed and noble, to look her in the eye. " 'First came by the black steed / then came by the brown.' "

" 'Then Tam Lin on a milk-white steed, with a gold crown on his brow.' " Seeker smiled, pretending her unease forgotten. "White horses are a symbol of death, as well you know. And is half your fault, I suspect."

"Rhiannon," he said.

"The White Mare. Second wife of Manannan mac Llyr, who is said by some to have been the father or the grandfather of the Queens of Faerie. Rhiannon, the unjustly accused."

"She is remembered." He stamped and sidled away, lowering his head as if distracted by the grass, but Seeker did not see him chewing. "Have you another task for me then, my mistress?"

She reached up and tucked her braids behind her ear. Her fingers lingered for a moment; she jerked them away once she noticed. "You'll accompany me to court," she said. "I need someone to watch my back."

The clipped ends of silver nails winked in his hooves as he straightened and turned toward her, shifting restively, his neck a fine long arch into the draft-horse power of his chest. "How deep is the danger?"

"I don't know."

Whiskey's tail smacked flies. He crouched back, light on the forehand, ready to rear, ready to whirl. "I like that answer less than I might."

"It would be easier if you'd just get the third challenge out of the way, so we could be sure what lies between us."

Droplets of water flew as he shook his head. "I'll get around to it eventually. Get up if you're going to ride."

Matthew unhooked his toes from the foot bar of the incline board as his phone began to ring. He slid a twenty-pound weight off his chest and laid it on the mat, digging in the pocket of his shorts for his rings with one hand while he unhooked the cell from his waistband with the other. "Szczegielniak."

A soft, listening silence on the other end of the line. Something made him hesitate before he pressed the disconnect button: a feeling, a tingle in his fingertips. "Matthew Szczegielniak," he tried again. "Is this a wrong number?"

"Dr. Szczegielniak." A low woman's voice, musical enough to send a thrill up his spine.

He knew who was on the other end of that line. "Dr. Bierce. Call me Matthew. I'm very pleased you called." The mat dented under his soft-soled gym shoes as he stood. He cradled the phone between hunched shoulder and ear while pushing his rings onto each finger. *And he shall have music wherever he goes.*

"This may amaze you, but you're not the first white boy to slip me his number in a bar."

Startled, reaching for his towel, Matthew laughed. His glasses were in their case in the mesh pocket of his gym bag, and once his hands were dry he fished them out and slid them up his nose. "No," he answered. "I imagine I'm not. I imagine also that you're not calling me because you have a taste for blonds."

"You don't think so?"

Not by the hair on my chinny-chin-chin, he thought. Which was a pity, he decided. Because given half a chance, he could develop a taste for her laugh. He spoke before she could quite stop laughing and sink him with a comeback. And he was certain, even on brief acquaintance, that she could indeed sink him with a comeback. "Can I help you, Dr. Bierce?"

"I want to hear the other side of the story." Calmly, with a lilting inflection. "Are you busy for dinner tonight? I can come down to the city . . ."

Matthew hesitated and checked his watch as he stretched the metal band over his wrist. A big man nearby dropped free weights with a clatter; Matthew turned away, blocking the noise with his body. "I have Circle tonight," he said. "And plans to visit my brother beforehand. How about a somewhat early dinner? Or . . ."

"Or?" Still musical, but a rising inflection now that betrayed her curiosity.

"Or you could come with me," Matthew said, proud of how smoothly his voice came out, without defensiveness or tension. "And I can show you what I'm fighting against."

Chapter Seven

Whiskey's hooves rang satisfactorily on the flagstones of the palace as Seeker brought her weight back and eased him to a halt. Unbridled, unsaddled, he tossed his sharp-etched head and peered imperiously through a waterfall of forelock that Seeker had brushed until it shone like wet silk. Greater and lesser Faeries withdrew from the courtyard, stealing glances at the giant pale stallion from the white edges of their eyes.

"They fear you," he said under his breath as Seeker threw her leg over his haunches and slid down his side.

"They fear you more. Come and see the Queen."

He chuckled bitterly. "I'd rather not be displayed before *that* one as a trophy, if it's all the same to you."

"Come, little treachery," Seeker said. "Think of yourself as my loyal retainer. Shift, if you please. Dress nicely." *And why is it that Whiskey's clothes come and go with him when he changes, when Keith's do not?*

He shook himself once, and reared up on his hind legs. A murmur ran through the observers as he collapsed into himself and stood before her, a handsome, narrow man nattily dressed in a raw-silk suit. He swept a mocking barefoot bow. "Loyal retainer," he said, and, stepping closer, "How is it that you came to know my Name?"

"Morgan taught me," she replied in an undertone. The doormen stepped aside, bowing as they opened the great double portal. The gilded wood was only a little brighter than the translucent golden stone of the palace's high, graceful walls. Seeker hung glamouries on herself as she walked, making herself presentable for her Queen. "I don't know how she learned it."

"From my father, no doubt." He fell into step beside her, a frown in his voice. The rings on his toes clattered on the cobbles like tiny horseshoes. "She has her ways of getting men to tell her things."

"Women too," Seeker admitted as they climbed the steps and entered the door.

"Has she taught you any other Names?"

"Three or four others. Never told me whose they were, however."

He seemed as if he would add something, but two figures hurried across the checkered stone floor of the entryway toward them, seeming slight in the scope of the lofty, pillared space. One *was* small, froglike in silhouette except the hair-tufted head with its ridiculous ears. The other, Seeker took a moment to recognize: a slender young High Faerie with hair like moonlit water and flawless golden skin. "Hope," she said, gaping.

Hope dropped a competent curtsey. "It's been too long."

Seeker rolled her shoulders, trying to ease the tightness between them. "The Queen's speeded time while I was away," she said. "How long has it been, Hope?" Whiskey weighed at her shoulder, a swordlike burden, both comforting and uneasy.

"Some few years," Puck said, coming up. "Your young acquaintance shows quite the talent for music and glamourie."

"Really?" Seeker frowned at her own surprise. "Tell me more. I am going to importune Her Majesty now, if she's available."

Hope let one shoulder lift and fall beneath gold-and-brown brocade. "The Mebd had me apprenticed to Cairbre. I'm to be ready to become her *rigbardðan,* she says, eventually."

"It will take you a few hundred years to learn every poem the royal poet knows." *And a few hundred more before she's bored with the position.* But Hope had to know that by now. In the few days Seeker had been away, Hope had grown from abused girl to aristocratic young woman. It was in every line as she tilted her head to the side, listening to laughter floating down the sweeping stairwell—in the calluses on her fingertips and the smile at the edge of her eyes. *And Cairbre's more to her than teacher, or I miss my guess.*

Seeker sighed. She looked up and sideways at Whiskey. The wound on his neck was still visible, a serrated circle that could never be mistaken for anything but the imprint of pointed teeth. *You've a Merlin to seduce and betray,* she reminded herself. *That should keep you busy for a while.*

"Seeker," Hope said.

"Yes?"

"Thank you." She stopped Seeker's disclaimer with an upraised palm. "Just thank you. That's all."

The Puck cleared his throat. "Politics," he said.

Seeker nodded. "Can we speak after I meet with the Queen?" And then she realized what had been troubling her about his manner. "You're quiet, Robin. And very stern, for a jester."

He touched the back of her hand with knobby, black-nailed fingers. "There are emissaries at court."

Seeker shut her teeth on her initial reply and lowered her voice. "Emissaries."

"From Àine. And I am barred from the councils, Seeker. And there are rumors afoot that the Mebd plans to name an heir." The Puck turned aside and summoned a page, sending the child ahead.

"Ah." She'd never heard of such a thing. She could tell from the way Whiskey shifted from foot to foot that it troubled him too. "She's got no children."

"Nary one living. But she has a sister."

"Barren too," Hope reminded them. Puck shot her a smile, and Seeker could see he had been testing her.

"Like Gwenhwyfar." It just came out, and Seeker regretted the words at once. She concentrated on the sound of her bootheels falling on the stone. The other three kept pace with her, even little Puck hobbling on his twisted limbs.

"Do you know the story of Gwenhwyfach?"

"Gwenhwyfar's wicked sister, according to some." Seeker paused in the hallway, not far from the Queen's study. Between guardposts, incidentally. "According to others, a cousin. Why?"

"The Mebd had a daughter," Hope said, her voice dropping to tones that would not carry, but would not attract the attention a whisper might. "One. Although the lays that speak of it are not sung here, Cairbre tells me they are heard in the Cat Anna's hall. She married a mortal King. Her name was Findabair."

Seeker's jaw dropped. "Gwenhwyfar."

The silence that followed was broken by Whiskey's laughter, a mocking nicker. "You mean you didn't *know* that? Oh, human memory is shorter than I thought."

Hope and Robin left Seeker at the Mebd's waiting room, but Whiskey accompanied her inside. Seeker paced restlessly across intricate mosaic tile and piled carpets, wearing a path from the outer door to the inner one; the water-horse stood beside the first of those portals unmoving, his eyes locked on the gold-framed oil painting hanging on the wall. She imagined she could see his tail flicking invisible midges, tension in the line of his neck and the square of his shoulders. In his other shape, his ears would be laid back hard against his skull.

It's not the threat to me, she realized. *It's something about the Mebd.*

Seeker composed herself when the latch lifted. The door opened into the waiting room, and behind its ivory-inlaid frame the Mebd stood with her white hands folded before the jeweled embroidery of her kirtle. A human-looking Fae who seemed perhaps seventeen came into the room before her to hold the door. He was black of hair and pale of skin, slender as a rapier in ebony velvet picked out with silver. Sour old Peaseblossom, the Mebd's councilor, stood at her left hand, his twiggy face drawn down in a frown and his antlers draped with jeweled velvet cords.

She dropped a low curtsey, illusory skirts pooling on the tile around her boots. "Your Majesty."

The Mebd slipped into the room. "Seeker," she said, as the lad beside her took her arm.

Seeker kept her eyes downcast. "I bring you news that might best be discussed in private, Majesty."

Peaseblossom rustled into the room, the dags on his houppelande fluttering red and black as he closed the inlaid door. "A little courtesy to the Queen, Each-Uisge." *Water-horse.* An eyebrow tendriled like a creeper rose, and he stared over Seeker's bowed shoulder at the Kelpie.

The Mebd sighed. "See to it," she said wearily.

Seeker felt it for a command and lanced a sharp look at Whiskey. He glowered beside the door. "Whiskey," Seeker hissed.

He opened his mouth to speak, and she half turned to confront him, raising her right hand warningly. "Whiskey."

A muscle along the side of his long horsey jaw knotted, and she clearly heard teeth like chipped quartz slide one over another. Shoulders square, with infinite dignity, he bowed from the waist and stayed there, his eyes fixed on the toes of Seeker's boots—or perhaps the hem of her glamoured dress.

"You may rise," the Queen said negligently. "Anything that must be said may be said in front of Peaseblossom."

Seeker straightened, waiting as the black-haired lad guided the Mebd to a chair by the window. Peaseblossom remained by one door, Whiskey before the other. Seeker heard the clatter of silver on tiles as he shifted from foot to foot, barely restraining himself from pawing the patterned floor. She stole a glance at him. Nostrils flared. His irises were rimmed with white. *Peaseblossom, sure. And the lad?* But she knew better than to ask. The Mebd was playing a game. If she was breathing, she was playing games.

The dim light from the diamond windows sparkled on the Mebd's crown: on amethyst and tanzanite shaped into the clustered blossoms of wisteria, on rubies and red garnet and the oil-green sheen of peridot like the newest leaves of spring.

"Your Majesty," Seeker said, "I have contacted the Merlin and befriended her. She came as far into the Westlands as Morgan's cottage, but turned back. I mean to see her again."

"She? Interesting." The Mebd inclined her head. "I'll wish you to remain by my side for a little while. I have arranged for your convenience, and the Merlin's, that time will flow more quickly here. She"—and the Mebd tasted the word again, and smiled—"will be able to complete her training while maintaining her duties in the mortal realm."

"Kadiska has located her as well, Your Majesty," Seeker said. "But I spoke with her first, and believe her inclination is to trust me, though she is wary."

"Excellent on both counts. I will deal with Àine. As you claimed the mortal first, she will withdraw her Seeker. Of course, there will be subtler ploys to win her away from us."

"Yes, Your Majesty." Tension quivered from Whiskey, silken and heavy as the air before a thunderstorm. "May I inquire as to the nature of the delegation from Queen Àine?"

"They are present to witness an announcement," the Mebd replied. She stood, as if her chair had grown tiresome, and turned to the windows and the rolling mist beyond. The fog coiled like a dancer's veils through yellow trees in an autumn wood, and a slow pensive rain that was barely a rain fell. The leaves swayed and brushed one another in an unfelt breeze, gold coins on a gypsy's dress. "Time grows short, and there is that afoot in the world of men which may trouble us even here."

"Yes, mistress." Seeker swallowed bitterness and took a half step toward the Mebd. "Your Majesty, I ask a boon."

The Mebd did not turn, but she nodded. Seeker saw something sorrowful in the line of the Queen's neck and shoulders, but she poked her old rotten hatred up hot and burned whatever scrap of pity might have followed the thought.

"Keith MacNeill. I wish him permitted at court."

Behind the Mebd, the black-haired youth glanced up, startled. Peaseblossom leaned over and whispered in the lad's ear, and his eyes grew wider. Seeker caught the amber-green glitter of his gaze—and the matching glitter of the long, smooth collar of golden mesh that lay behind the open neckline of his shirt, low upon his breastbone.

"Mother?" Ian said, his voice so different from a child's that she never would have known it.

It might have been blood roaring in Seeker's ears. She wasn't certain. But she nodded nonetheless.

"Ah, yes," the Mebd said. "You two have not seen each other in some time. My apologies. I'm sure you'll have time to reacquaint yourselves." She laid a lily-white hand on steamed glass. "The boon is granted. You will attend court tonight."

Seeker nodded, as she was constrained to, and stole another glance at Ian. Peaseblossom restrained him, a hand like a naked tree limb on the boy's shoulder, but Ian vibrated with potential action. "Of course."

"I shall see you then. Rested. There will be a ball."

It was a dismissal. Seeker nodded once, murmured a "Your Majesty," and fled, Whiskey sulking behind her.

Seeker paced over the flagstones, her back stiffly upright, acutely aware of Whiskey following. *Show no weakness,* she thought, and almost summoned Gharne. Not that Gharne would have been able to so much as slow the water-horse down if he'd decided to challenge her then. She didn't understand why he didn't. Didn't understand why he caught her by the arm when she tripped and would have gone to her knees, would have buried her face in her fists and wailed like a bean sidhe.

"No weakness," he snarled like the voice of her own conscience, and tugged her up. The ridge of his ring, the edge of his nail bruised her as he lifted her to her feet. "Never show weakness, mistress. Stand up. Walk. Where are your rooms?"

She pointed, and he led her, making it look like a solemn escort. She unlocked the door and brought him in. The chamber was cold, the fire unkindled, and as Whiskey dragged a chair before the door Seeker steadied herself against the mantel. She wobbled like a newborn colt but managed to turn and face him. "Challenge me not today," she commanded, leveling her voice.

"I'd rather not see you dead." The water-horse circled her to kneel before the grate. He laid kindling and larger wood together before taking up a lucifer match and setting fire against it. It bloomed, and he backed away without haste.

"You can't tell me you're professing affection," she said. He supported her to another chair, and sat her down within its green-embroidered wings.

"Affection?" He nickered, and his voice took on the rhythm of poetry. "I've no soul to love with, mistress, nor kindness to give. I am of the Fae so old we blur into things that are ancienter still, and I will tell you true that there is nothing in me that cares for you." Strong fingers combed her hair, avoided the braids.

"Then what?"

"Self-interest. You're powerful. And I want my freedom given, and you as an ally. My offer stands. I'll swear on my father Manannan's domain, which is also my own, and on the justice so long denied my mother. I'll swear. By the white shoulders of my father's sister, Fionnghuala the Swan Maid—"

"No." Seeker leaned forward. She would have pulled away, had Whiskey's hand not cupped her chin and stroked her throat. "Release me."

He did, and she stood. "Challenge me," she said. "Get it over with."

He came a step closer. "That is the one command I cannot be made to obey."

"And if I bid you importune me no more, little treachery?"

"I should obey, of course." His voice was level and cool but she sensed something dark moving under it, a shadow in the depths. "But you know what I am, mistress. What I am for. I am but a petty godling, it's true, but I am the god of the dark depths of passion, the sea that drowns and gives back life. Tell me you don't crave the attention. How long have you been alone?"

"I . . ."

"Lie to me," he encouraged. "Put yourself that little bit in my power. Tell me nothing in you chafes at the cool certainty of Faerie. That there is no human soul in you, craving touch, craving passion and emotion."

Seeker's hands clenched into fists. She didn't move, still swaying on her feet. He closed the distance between them, lifted her hair, let it fall between his fingers. "Lie to me," he said.

"Fuck you."

His nostrils flared, as if he scented prey. "It hurts, doesn't it?"

She thought of court, a few scant hours away, and feared it. It would be good to rest. Not to worry about Keith, about Mist, about the Merlin. About the Cat Anna's machinations and Ian's safety. If she did have a soul left, as Mist and Uisgebaugh insisted, she was certainly going to Hell.

The rules were different for the ones who were gods. Not for the ones born after the Christian days.

And thank you for that, Arthur, too.

Just tell him begone, she thought. *Third time tempted.* But the command died on her tongue. "Why don't you just try to snap my neck? Get it over with. Today, you could win. I'd probably *let* you win," she snarled.

"I like to play with my food, mistress mine. They're no fun that don't fight."

She raised a hand against the smooth-rough ivory silk of his suit when he came up to her. His breath tickled her ear; she felt the heart beating in his chest with a slow, calm rhythm that she wanted to lean into and weep. Shivers trembled across her neck when he brushed her earlobe with his lips. A salt-grass aroma surrounded her, touched with the copper scent of blood from the scabbed-over wound on his neck. "Not so cold and fey after all," he whispered.

Seeker sighed once, softly, and closed her eyes. "No, Uisgebaugh." She pressed her face against his breast and let him hold her for a long and silent moment. He kissed her ear, the downy place under the fall of her hair. His hands slid up her body from her waist.

Then she leaned her head back and looked up at him, his strange pale eyes and his smiling mouth. "No, Uisgebaugh," she said once more, and drove her elbow up under his ribs. "Act like a studhorse, and I'll treat you like one, dammit."

"Understood," he said, eyeing her with wary respect. "You were vulnerable."

"Like a shark scenting blood," she answered, and sighed. "Whiskey. After the Merlin. After that. We'll talk again, about arrangements. But you know, even if I set you free . . . now that the Mebd knows I know your Name, she can force me to tell her."

"Then I shall have to kill her, shan't I?" He smiled and swept another bow, turned away and went to sit by the fire.

"Kill her, kill me," Seeker answered. "And half of Faerie. Unless you were bound to her instead of to me, of course."

"But I'm not that, am I?"

"No." She sighed. "Not that at all."

Carel Bierce took the train into the city from Hartford, and Matthew met her at Penn Station. The train was five minutes late. He stood on the greasy granite-paved platform in a cavern that pounded like the hollow, chambered heart of the city with train wheels, and tugged his tweed jacket irritably over a steel-banded watch the third time he caught himself checking it. *She'll come if she comes.*

He half hoped she wouldn't. But she was the third one down precarious steel steps, a swirl of heavy cinnamon velvet skirts brushing the calves of her boots like a beautiful woman's hair falling across her neck, and Matthew walked forward to meet her. He extended a hand as she turned, smiling as she folded it in her own. "Welcome to New York." His words had the ring of formality, and he knew she understood them for what they were. The sideways twitch of her head told him as much, and the slight smile that touched the corners of her eyes but didn't curve her lips.

"I am pleased to be your guest." She had a suede knapsack slung over one shoulder. Swags of love beads strung across its surface rustled as she dropped it from her shoulder to the crook of her elbow and dug inside, frowning until she came up with a sunglasses case. She slipped the glasses up her nose, and Matthew smiled in recognition of the gesture.

"You wear contacts."

"How can you tell?"

"Because you handle your glasses like somebody who wore them constantly for years," he answered, suddenly self-conscious about adjusting his own. He hadn't ponytailed his hair, and the ends brushed the underside of his jaw when he turned to lead her between yellow-painted metal beams. "Hungry, Dr. Bierce?"

"Carel." A small lowering of the walls. The curious tilt of her head remained. "I could eat. Where are you taking me?"

"To dinner," he answered, leading her toward the escalators that would raise them out of the hollow darkness and into the bustle of the station proper. "And then to meet my brother."

She ate the way Matthew imagined a raptor would eat: delicately, ravenously, with sharp and total concentration. She used the fork in the European manner and chewed each bite precisely. Matthew found himself watching her hands, the way the tendons moved across their backs, and he fussed at his own chicken Caesar salad while she worked methodically through hers.

"And who might your brother be?" She hummed lightly under her breath when she looked at him, seemed to catch herself, and ended the music with a sip of beer.

"A man who was kissed by Faeries," he said. She arched an eyebrow at him. He shrugged. "You'll see."

Five hundred years of conspiracy had left the Prometheus Club unworried about funding. Kelly's care was not *quite* the best that New York City's medical establishment could offer, but it was certainly more than Matthew or his parents could have managed on their own.

It was just as well that Matthew had the help.

Kelly needed it.

Carel must have picked up on Matthew's mood; her politely aimless conversation—about movies, music, politics, anything but magic and the truth—halted as they passed through the scrolling doors of the elevator. She cast a sidelong glance at him and frowned, but bit her tongue; Matthew had the strangest feeling that she was looking *past* him as much as *at* him, and only with effort forced himself not to turn to check the angle of her gaze. She stood beside him, her shoulders rising and falling with her breath, and said nothing at all until the half-second before the doors slid open. "What's his name?"

"Kelly." Matthew put his hand through the electric eye to hold the door, gesturing her past. "His name is Kelly."

Matthew had been in enough hospitals to know that it's untrue that they all smell the same. The ventilation differs, the smell of the cleansers, the top note of the air freshener sharp over the bottom note of human musk and adhesive and gauze. Some hospitals smell of desperation and rot and unchanged sheets. Some smell of hope.

To Matthew, this one smelled of guilty consciences and delayed vengeance, and by the way Carel stiffened as they stepped into the tiled corridor, she caught the aroma too. She paced by his side, skirt rippling with her strides, her chin held high, her knapsack slung casually over one shoulder. If he hadn't noticed the way her free hand tugged the hem of her embroidered tunic down, he never would have recognized her fear for what it was. He would have seen only the arrogance.

She carries herself like a Mage already. He paused, his hand on the door to Kelly's room, and turned to her. The darkness of her irises flickered with splintered color for a moment as she met his gaze, and she smiled. "You're so very, very angry at them."

He jerked away, burned. His hand dropped back to his side. *Not a Mage,* he corrected himself. *The Merlin. And don't you ever dare let yourself forget it.*

"Yes," he said, stepping back to give her precedence. He gestured her hand to the doorknob. "In a moment, you'll see."

Her eyes dropped, her beads clinking as she tilted her head. "As you wish."

"Go in."

Carel pushed open the door. "Private room," she whispered. "Professordom pay better in New York than out in the boondocks?"

"Not significantly."

"*You* must introduce *me.*" Said firmly, and she stood against the door panel to permit him to enter first.

Straightening his shoulders in a parody of pride, he walked past the Merlin and into his brother's sickroom. "Kelly?"

I wonder how he'll be today. There was a narrow corridor between the door and the room itself, like the entryway to a hotel room. A mirrored door concealed the bathroom on his left. On his right was the louvered slide of a closet, tidily shut. "Kell, it's Matthew."

Faintly, Matthew heard his brother singing. He jammed his hands into his pockets, walking forward as if it didn't hurt. Surprised to find Carel's hand resting on the crook of his arm, steadying him while making it seem he was leading her. She peered around his shoulder. "He's singing?"

"He sings a lot," Matthew answered, and moved away from her hand. Kelly sat in his wheelchair, facing the window, the light of a sunset flushing the sky. "Kell?"

" 'Light down, light down, true Thomas.' " Kelly's voice rose off-key, on a strange high warble. " 'And lean your head upon my knee / Abide and rest a little space / And I will show you ferlies three. . . .' "

Carel slid her hand free and swayed forward, in time to the limping rhythm of the ballad. Matthew kicked the door shut and followed, waiting to see if Kelly would turn his head. Carel's intake of breath was sharp as she finally got a good look.

"He can't be your brother." She cast a glance sideways to confirm it. Matthew caught himself leaning forward so his hair would cover his face. "Unless you're older than you look."

"No," Matthew answered. "But he's much younger than he looks, Lady Merlin." He crouched beside Kelly's chair, and took his brother's papery claw in his fingers. Kelly's head wobbled on an old man's plucked-chicken neck; his rheumy eyes were cloudy between the red edges of his eyelids. Softly, Matthew stroked a thumb across the bumpy back of his brother's hand, and reached up to brush greasy yellowed wisps away from Kelly's forehead. "Kelly's two years older than I am."

Kelly's voice was a buzzing mumble. " 'Oh, see you not yon narrow road / So thick beset with thorn and briers / That is the path of righteousness / Though after it but few enquire. . . .' "

The Merlin blinked. She set her back against the narrow strip of eggshell sheetrock between the window and the side wall and folded her arms across her chest. "Strange days," she muttered, fingering a black opal ring. "What happened to him?"

"Stolen away by Faeries. Kelly, can you hear me?"

" 'And see you not that broad, broad road . . .' "

"And the Faeries brought him back?"

" 'That lies across that lily leven?' "

"When he couldn't dance anymore," Matthew answered, and gently tugged at the blankets wrapping his brother's knees. Carel stepped forward; Kelly's head lolled.

"Have you sung to him?"

"When he sings so well to himself?" Sharper than Matthew had intended, but he felt skin below the blankets now, and it was hard enough to talk at all.

The Merlin laid a callused hand on Matthew's shoulder and drew a breath, and came in on the second word of Kelly's next warbling line.

" 'That is the path of wickedness / Though some call it the road to Heaven. / And see you not that bonnie road / That winds about the fernie brae / That is the road to fair Elfland / Where thou and I this night maun gae. . . .' "

Kelly's voice faltered. Lashes flickered across his glazed, empty eyes, and he turned toward the sound as Carel kept singing, her voice hitching softly as if she bore some secret pain.

" 'But Thomas, you must hold your tongue / Whatever you may hear or see / For if you speak word in Elfin land / You'll ne'er get back to your ain country.' "

Carel glanced down and the song died. "Oh, dear lord."

Withered claws protruded from the cuffs of Kelly's pajamas, leathery hooks resting uselessly against the stirrups of the wheelchair. The only thing Matthew had ever seen to compare with it were photos of Chinese foot-binding, the deformed and folded extremities of women intentionally crippled for life. "They took him for a night. One night, and all his life — Kelly! No!"

His brother hadn't looked down from Carel's face, and now, instantly, he moved. His twisted right hand lashed out and caught the sleeve of Carel's tunic before she could step back, and he used that grip to haul himself to his ruined feet. His face showed no pain — only transcendence, as Matthew grasped his waist, trying to take his weight. The wheelchair glided backward; Matthew's grip was all that kept Kelly from crashing to his knees, his hand straining the fabric.

"Lady," Kelly whimpered. "Lady, I see you."

Carel got her free hand up, an arm under Kelly's arm, her hand splayed across his back as Matthew held his feet away from the floor. She bent her knees and lifted, taking Kelly's weight. Her knapsack struck Matthew alongside his head. Something hard inside it — a ceramic mug? — clinked against his skull; he saw stars, heaved, got his brother deposited on the bed and almost fell backward himself. "Lady!" Kelly wailed.

Carel's grip on Matthew's shoulder saved him, something shattering with a crunching sound as she dropped her knapsack on the tiles. He reached out blindly with some idea of clasping her hand in thanks, but she wasn't looking at him. She seemed, in fact, to have forgotten his presence as she moved forward, crouching beside Kelly on the white chenille hospital bedspread and wrapping his hand in both of her own. "What do you see?" she asked, as Matthew came up beside her, close enough to feel the warmth of her body through her velvet tunic.

"Lady, I see *you*," Kelly answered, in a clear, crisp voice that brought blood to Matthew's mouth. "I see the light all around you. The shattered light. And I hear the song."

"The song?" Matthew laid his hands over Carel's. She let him, without looking up.

Kelly didn't answer, but Carel hummed a bar of "Thomas the Rhymer," and he nodded. "Yes." He blinked and lifted his head from the pillow. Bruises were already darkening beneath Kelly's fragile skin. He smelled sweet and stale, the mustiness of age clinging to his skin.

"Kelly," Matthew said, hopelessly.

"Matt?"

His name. Which Kelly hadn't said in a decade and a half, now. The blood in Matthew's mouth was sweet as his brother's eyes flickered, cleared, focused on his own. "Kell—"

"Has she come to take me back?"

"Kelly?"

Kelly shook his head, turned back to Carel. "Lady," he said. "Have you come to take me home?" He didn't seem to notice as Matthew squeezed his hand once, chest burning, and then had to—*had to*—step away, unable to breathe, his fingers prickling numb as he scrubbed his hands against his trousers and Kelly whispered to the Merlin, "Please. Please, my lady. I can still hear the music. Please won't you take me back home?"

Chapter Eight

Keith dreamed of dragons again, and awoke cold in his bed, curled into a ball that would have had his tail tucked tight across his nose and eyes if he had been in wolf's shape. It was still dark, the night air cold through the open window and scented heavily with the sea. Keith tautened, head up, weak human ears straining as if he could still hear the scrape of scales on stone, the rustle of leathery wings unfolded and resettled. The hiss of the waves and the susurrus of wind across the window sash could have been a giant, rhythmic breathing. His breath steamed into the air as he lifted his head; in the moonlight, the shadows moved as if they had weight.

"Mist?"

Nothing. Silence, and the ocean moving below, the chuckle of the waves against the stone. The clouds blew across the moon like a great eye closing, and Keith rolled out of bed and padded to the clothes chest in the testicle-shrinking cold. He pulled out wool socks and thick trousers, a rag wool sweater that he dragged on over a thick cotton turtleneck. The trousers needed braces; he edged the sweater up around his shoulders to get them on and then tugged it down again.

It would have been easier to shift into a wolf, of course—but hardly conducive to a lengthy visit if he arrived naked and chilled to the bone. Keith stomped his heavy boots on and tugged open the door, mindful of creaking hinges in the night. The stairs, at least, were stone, and the house slept on.

He let himself out the kitchen door, glancing up once at the windows on the east side of the house. The several rooms shared by the Russian wolves were silent and dark. Keith turned away and set out down the beach, not just wandering tonight. He didn't expect to find peace, precisely. But perhaps a cup of tea and a warm fireside, away from the pack and its demands.

He never doubted that Fionnghuala would be awake and awaiting him. And lights gleamed in her windows as he approached. He could see her moving about the table in the kitchen, the steam rising from the spout of her cosied teapot as she lifted and poured. The wind brought him the scent of orange pekoe and woodsmoke, and Fionnghuala's perfume—

And the scent of a man. A wolf.

Ivan Ilyich. Keith smoothed his lips over bared teeth, raised his fist to the door, and knocked. It opened smoothly, on silent hinges; the werewolf tilted his head and smiled. He could see Vanya behind Fionnghuala, leaning forward over the wax-finished table, his elbows on either side of a mug of tea. "You have company, Nuala. I'm sorry—"

"I have room for one more," she said, and shuffled aside to let him enter through the close-cracked door. She shut it crisply, trapping the warm air inside, and rolled her shoulders back. "Keith, you couldn't sleep?"

Keith shook his head slightly, wry agreement, and moved forward until he was standing across the table from the Russian wolf. Ivan Ilyich tipped his head back, showing his throat as if unconsciously, and didn't stand. "I did not know you were a friend of Nuala's," he said. "Good morning, Elder Brother."

"Good morning, Vanya," Keith answered, and pulled out the bench opposite to sit, with a glance at Fionnghuala for permission. He repeated her question to the younger wolf. "Couldn't sleep?"

"I don't sleep much," Vanya answered, with a self-deprecating shrug. "And my Elder Brother's nightmares would keep any wolf awake."

Nightmares. Fyodor. Interesting. "So you come to sit with our American witch." Keith grinned at Fionnghuala, a doggy showing of teeth, and looked down when she grinned back.

"Best conversation on *this* seaside," Vanya answered, with an arch look.

Oh, the wolf has a sense of whimsy, does he? Keith accepted the pottery mug their hostess slipped in front of him and shrugged. "I tend to find it so. And your eyes are full of questions, wolf."

"Are they?" Vanya leaned back in his chair, tension cabling across his face even as Fionnghuala kicked the far bench out from under the table and arranged her gray-brown skirt over it, settling herself. She wore an apron as white as a patch of snow on lichen-covered rock; Keith resisted the urge to reach out and stroke his fingers across it to see if it was cold.

She laced her fingers around her own mug and smiled without teeth. "I'll not have you fencing at my table, with words or with blades," she said. "This is not the pack's ground."

"No." Keith blew across his tea to cool it. "It isn't, is it? All right, then, Vanya. What's your first question for a Scottish wolf?"

"Why do you want to be Sire?"

"I don't," Keith answered calmly. *There is the matter of the Faerie Queen.* But that was not the sort of thing that one could say. "But my father expects it."

"Your father will be dead before the issue comes to a . . . *discussion*." A delicately chosen word, and Vanya made sure that Keith appreciated the delicacy with which he had chosen it. Yes, a discussion that would end with one wolf dead upon the earth.

"I'm aware of that," Keith answered. "You've heard the expression that no man should be King who wishes it?"

Vanya smiled. "I would follow Fyodor Stephanovich whether he were my cousin or not, Elder Brother."

"And what of the Scottish wolves? And our French and American brethren? The Russian wolves have not been known for their attention to politics—"

"No, nor our interest in the outside world," Vanya answered. "That has always been a very Slavic failing. But Fyodor is—"

"A leader?" Keith could see that for himself; the black wolf had charisma.

"A visionary," Vanya answered. "And I could wish you would not call us Russian. We're not, all, any more than you are Irish."

Keith sipped his tea. It smelled of smoke and summer. He rolled it over his tongue while he thought. "Is there anything more frightening? Than a visionary, I mean."

Fionnghuala cleared her throat, sliding one hand forward across the dark, waxed tabletop. "Keith," she said. "If you do not wish to be King for any reason but your father's legacy . . ."

Keith smiled, the question hanging on the air between them. "There is another reason," he said.

"And that is?" Vanya, leaning forward now, an interested negotiator. No lead wolf, Ivan Ilyich, but perhaps that made him the better at compromise.

"I have promised the Mebd that I would bring about an alliance between her folk and the pack."

"You'd draw us into an outside war?"

"It's too early to be certain there will be war, Vanya."

Fionnghuala leaned back on her bench, stretching her legs. Her expression showed incomprehension, but Keith suspected she understood more than she revealed. "War, Keith?"

"There is a human faction that is not fond of the Fae Folk, Nuala. And never has been: they are largely responsible for the reduced circumstances in which the Faerie court finds itself. I spoke with the Mebd, and her word is that the Prometheus Club, as they call themselves—"

"An odd name."

"They date from an era where such names were de rigueur, for occult societies." Keith's lips twitched.

"Like the Hellfire Club?" she asked. "The Order of the Golden Dawn? That sort of thing?"

"Older. Think the School of Night," Keith answered, the chuckle finally escaping. "They are Elizabethan, at the least. And rumor has it there once was a Prometheus, or an individual bearing that name, but the Mebd defeated him or won him away sometime in James the Sixth's reign."

"And they exist to protect the mortal realm from Faerie?"

"They existed, then, to exalt God," Vanya interjected, leaning forward. "And through the exaltation of God, to attract power to themselves: to claim Him. In recent years, they have become interested in the magical power of the material world—iron and steel. Computers and aeroplanes. They are no friends to Faerie. But. They have presented no threat to wolves."

"Because the wolves present no threat to anyone," Keith answered. "We live quietly and apart, and have for centuries."

"And you would bring us into this fight between the Fae, who do not love us, and the mortal men, who love us less?"

No. "Yes."

"Why?"

"For the sake of my son," Keith said, fiddling his mug with his fingertips. "Surely a wolf can understand so much?"

Silence, until Vanya pushed Keith's tea back three careful inches. "I will speak to Fyodor Stephanovich," he said, his hair falling across his forehead as he tilted his head. "It is possible indeed that a wolf can understand that much."

Whiskey still seemed well pleased with himself when a knock sounded against the door. Seeker crossed the carpet-scattered flagstones and dragged the wedged chair aside. She opened the portal and peered through it.

Hope stood beyond, dressed in trews and a white muslin shirt. A patchwork vest, gaudy in brown and orange, hung over her shoulders. "I brought wine," she said, holding up two bottles and a pair of goblets.

Seeker stood back and let her come into the room. "We'll need another glass," she said, and Hope noticed Whiskey sitting by the fire and blushed.

"Sorry."

"Not at all." He stood gallantly and offered her the chair.

Seeker found another goblet on the clothespress, although the crystal pattern didn't match, and brought it over while Whiskey retrieved the second chair. Hope caught Seeker's eye as she arranged bottles and glasses on the little table before the fire. *Is it safe to talk in front of him?* she mouthed.

"My life is his life," Seeker answered.

Hope considered while Seeker fetched the stool from her vanity, claiming it for herself even when Whiskey tried to gesture her into the more comfortable chair. When the three of them were situated, Hope made a little ceremony out of pouring wine and handing it around.

Whiskey tasted his suspiciously. "Surprisingly nice."

"I've learned a few things," Hope said. "Like what you would have done with me if I had gone with you, that night."

Whiskey inclined his head. "I make no apologies for what I am," he said. "The sea does not change its coat because the world changes around it."

"No," Hope answered. "The sea never changes. And yet, it never stops changing. Shall I sing you the song?"

"No," Whiskey said. But he seemed unaccountably unsettled.

"As well."

Seeker marveled at the girl's self-possession. *It has been years,* she reminded herself. *A few days, and half a lifetime.*

Hope sipped her wine and flicked the edge of the glass to make the crystal sing. "Seeker, the rumor you've missed while you were away is that the Mebd will name an heir."

Seeker sat up straighter. She'd taken the odd glass, with its pattern of forget-me-nots. She ran a thumb over engraved petals. "I heard. She fears for her life? Or plans to abdicate?"

"I only know rumors."

"What sparked them?"

Hope shrugged. "Cairbre. She asked my master to find all the links and branches of her family. To run down the descendants of Manannan mac Llyr, through all his children."

Whiskey shifted forward. "What did he discover?"

"I was not made privy. But the lineage as I know it—there are no others of her father's blood remaining, they say, except Morgan and the sister Queens. Findabair was barren. Mordred left no get. And she'll not name Morgan to the throne."

"Indeed. It would have to be someone the Mebd had a hold over. Even if she has—I am sure she has—reasons and subtleties of her own. She'll want to own whoever she names. But unless Cairbre found a lost blood relative . . ." Seeker let her right hand fall open, sifting ashes to the wind.

"It must be a blood relative?"

"Aye."

Whiskey cleared his throat and finished his wine. "Your knowledge is incomplete."

Seeker spun her glass between her fingers. "What?"

He smiled mysteriously and reached for the bottle, refilling his glass.

"Tell me," she said, levelly.

He sighed and sipped his wine. "There's no playing mystery with you. I too am the son of Manannan mac Llyr, and born in wedlock, although he denied it and punished my mother Rhiannon for an adultery she never committed. Perhaps the Mebd intends to name me to her throne."

"Perhaps," Seeker said, and did not dispute when Hope raised the bottle and refilled glasses. "Are there no others?"

"My father had a sister." The Kelpie shrugged. "And Morgan had a younger son, named Murchaud. But they both went to the teind."

Carel watched him with the wariness you'd give someone you expected to crumble into hysteria. Disconcerting, especially as she matched his stride easily, all the while wide-eyed and watchful as a cat. Matthew wondered if he looked as fragile as her regard made him feel.

"Where are we going?" she asked.

"Where else?" Matthew answered. "I did say I had Circle tonight."

"You hold Circle in the city?" The Merlin pursed her lips, intrigued. Glass beads clattered as she slid a hand under her braids and lifted them away from her neck and over her shoulder. "Most witches I know try to get as far out in the country—"

"Ah," Matthew said, pausing in an ebb of foot traffic, "we are not witches." He gestured Carel into the lee of a mailbox and raised his hands slowly, fingers open, palms flat, as if offering a sniff to a potentially unfriendly dog. Her hand snapped shut, and she stripped his shirt-sleeve back to show the stark patterns that ran down to the bones of his wrist.

"Nice ink."

"Thanks." Kelly had them too, but Kelly's were faded now.

"Have you got those all over?" A quirk of a smile. From another woman, the comment might have been flirtatious. From Carel, it came with level appraisal and a touch of a frown.

"More or less."

"That must have hurt." She touched his ten iron rings with a curious fingertip, brushed his hair aside and tilted his cheek to examine the ones in his ear. "To keep the Faeries at bay."

This time he smiled, to soften the conversation if she wouldn't. "More or less." *They might even have helped Kelly, if he hadn't been so eager to hand away consent.*

"So afraid of the wilderness, Matthew?"

If it's anything like what's in your eyes, my lady Merlin — "Is that what I'm scared of?"

"It's what mortal men have always been scared of," she answered. "It's what drove the very first one to pick up a smoldering stick from a lightning scar and learn to cultivate fire. Fear of the wolves in the dark." She smiled, and released his wrist. "Do you wear your underwear inside out?"

"Is it any of your business if I do?"

" 'More or less,' " she mocked, and Matthew felt for a moment as if the shadow of something larger fell across his face. He glanced up; there was nothing there.

"You've seen the price," he answered, with a shrug. "What's Fae is not safe for mortal men."

"Ah." She leaned back, ample hip against the letter box, and swung her braids. "Do you think if you gave Dylan Thomas a plain choice of his poetry or his life, he would have chosen differently than he did?"

It wasn't a new question for Matthew; rather, it was the sort of thing that students and Magi stayed up late to argue over. "You're asking me who I am to decide."

"We are all the ones who decide. But there will be always those who choose forest and forge over hearth and home, Matthew. Try not to look too surprised when the time comes."

Simple words. Things he knew, and they shouldn't have troubled him. "Come on," he said, and dug in his pocket for a green velour scrunchie, which he handed over.

She took it dubiously and sniffed the cloth.

"Put it on."

"Because?"

He was pulling his own hair back into a ponytail, twisting a yellow-wrapped steel-bound elastic around it. "Because it's the only way past the bindings, and your braids won't be enough."

She obeyed him, elbows akimbo as she yanked her braids through the elastic, her head ducking and then rising again on a long, powerful neck. "We're going in?"

"We are."

"Nice address."

"Nothing but the best."

The doorman recognized him, nodding slightly as they passed. Matthew kept a hand lightly on Carel's sleeve as they stepped into the private penthouse elevator, wondering if she too felt the tingle of the wards against her skin. From the way she glanced over her shoulder and frowned, she did. "Down the rabbit hole again."

"You're taking it well."

She chuckled, rich crumbling chocolate, and rocked forward on the balls of her feet to watch as he touched the heat-sensitive elevator button. It lit up dark gold around the black-and-silver numeral. "Taking things well is a trademark, apparently; I'm not what any of you expected."

"Any of us?" He turned his back to the walnut paneling and folded his arms. The iron rings pinched his fingers when he tucked them into the creases of his elbows.

"You, the Fae. All you people who want something from me." She swallowed, just as Matthew's own ears popped. "You expected someone . . . naive. More easily impressed. Less worldly."

His lips twitched. "Almost everyone is less worldly than you, I imagine. And no, you're not what I expected."

"What did you expect?"

He shrugged as the elevator slowed. "Not you. I'm not sure if I expected a wise old master calling me *grasshopper,* or a guileless innocent, but—"

"You didn't expect someone powerful." She nodded. "I've picked up on that. Everyone I've spoken to since the Seeker found me has an agenda, and seems to think I can be bent to fit that agenda."

"You're a prize," Matthew said as the doors scrolled open.

Carel shot him a look as she fell into step. "Oh, Matthew," she said, a wry twist to her tone. "That ain't what it's about at all, my friend."

They emerged from the elevator into the foyer of the Prometheus Club's penthouse suite. Jane stood from a plush chair beside tall arched windows and smoothed her skirt over her thighs, her tailored navy suit contrasting with Carel's flowing velvet as if it had been chosen to do so. Carel strode toward her, soft brown boots scuffing on the marble floor, and settled on her heels a measured four feet away.

Jane drew herself up, chin high and shoulders back, and extended her hand. It was half the gesture of a Queen to a Queen, and half an offering to a wild animal, and Matthew bit his lip on a smile when he noticed. Carel eyed the hand as though she were in point of fact some wild, too-cautious thing, then glided a step closer and extended her own. "Carel Bierce."

"Jane Andraste," Jane answered, giving Carel a quick, delicate squeeze before withdrawing her hand, the considering gesture of a cat that has tapped something of interest and is waiting to see if it will jump, and in which direction.

Carel smiled and let her hand hang in the air for a moment longer, making it plain that Jane had broken the contact first. "I understand I'm here to observe a ritual."

"If you like," Jane said. She glanced at Matthew. "We're raising power for another Circle."

Jane pivoted in her designer shoes and pressed one side of the double doors open with her fingertips; solid oak swung away from her touch, hung so perfectly it moved like rice paper. "One that won't happen for some time. You'll find this interesting."

Carel's wariness was a dance, a bride's hesitation-march or the scoop and sway of a pavane. As they walked from the foyer into the lounge, she inspected the marble-tiled floors and the pale furniture distributed in cozy conversation groups, around which clustered a dozen or so Promethean Magi dressed as executives, schoolteachers, artists, Bohemians. Neither Carel nor Jane looked out of place among them; one would be hard pressed to find a broader spectrum of intriguing-looking people.

Carel ignored the Magi, most of whom glanced up only briefly when she entered. She paused out of the sunlight, in front of an abstract canvas, angling her head to follow the textured splashes of gray and silver and pewter and platinum gracing its cream-pale surface.

"Beautiful."

Jane smiled. "Isn't it? One of our members in Paris."

Carel smiled. "And what's your talent, Matthew?"

"Alas . . ." He shrugged. "I am peculiarly suited to the appreciation of art, having none of my own."

Jane snorted, her cool facade cracking into charm. Carel glanced at her, surprised. "Oh, don't think we're all seriousness and stealth, Merlin. Can I fetch you coffee?"

"I notice," Carel said, turning her back on the painting, "that you are rather unforthcoming about the actual purposes of your ritual. The one you're raising power for, I should say, and not this evening's event."

"Oh," Jane said. "We mean to go into Faerie and take back all the children they've stolen."

Fyodor was not drinking vodka. Almost, Keith thought, as if that might be too much the stereotype. Instead, the black wolf leaned back in his chair, spidery hands cupped around the bell of a brandy glass full of slivovitz, and chewed his lower lip with crooked ivory teeth. "There aren't many of us left, Elder Brother," he said, his thumb leaving a faint oily smudge as it stroked the curve of his glass. "And you'd risk the pack for one cub. A cub not even blooded in the pack, at that."

"What the man fails out of fear," Keith answered, his own glass—

ginger beer, and he wasn't ashamed to admit it—sweating on the sandstone coaster before him, "the wolf must persevere, out of loyalty." Giving the proverb its proper form this time, and not the revised version he had offered Elaine. "Vanya thought you might have sympathy."

They were alone in the second-floor study, an odd-shaped little space that had been a retiring-room at some point in the house's long and checkered career, and Keith had his boots up on the table. Fyodor, a study in angles and elbows, leaned forward with his wrists on his knees and his drink dangling between them, caressed and examined, but untasted. "I have a great deal of sympathy," he replied. "For loss, most of all." His shrug rearranged bony shoulders like a ridgeline shifting; the light of the lamp glinted amber in the depths of his eyes.

"Vanya wants to see us allies," Keith said.

Fyodor nodded. "*I* want to see us allies, Elder Brother. We each have things to offer, yes?"

"Yes," Keith said, watching a droplet roll down the side of his glass. When he glanced up, Fyodor's eyes were still expectant as a hound's. "I am not a warrior."

"All men are warriors when pressed to it. Or else they are victims. And I do not think you are a victim, Keith MacNeill."

"Of my own stupidity, perhaps." Keith shrugged to soften the words, his posture as relaxed as possible without submission. "Convince me."

"Of what shall I convince you, my friend?"

"Convince me of why you are a man who should be King."

Fyodor chuckled, a low rattle in his throat. "Sire."

"As it were." Keith dismissed the title with a wave. "Why?"

"Because," Fyodor said, and sipped the plum brandy in his glass before he set it on the coffee table. He stood, his long hands sliding into his pockets, and took the two cramped strides that the room permitted. "I have lost a family, yes? A human family, and an *oborotni* family. And I will not lose the pack."

"Vanya said you were cousins." Keith debated standing, and decided it would weaken his authority to show too much concern.

"We are," Fyodor answered. The fabric of his trousers stretched across his knuckles as his hands twisted into fists. "He is all I have left of Kiev—"

"Kiev." Keith shook his head. "Have you been to America?"

"No."

"You should go. It gives one revolutionary ideas." He grinned up at Fyodor, half human reassurance and half baring of teeth.

Fyodor twisted over his shoulder to stare at Keith, one curl falling across his forehead. "I have had enough of revolution, I think."

"And enough of war?"

"Oh," Fyodor said, "I can still fight." The dark gold eyes went slitted with the black wolf's smile.

"*Can* and *will* are different words—"

"How ironic that the competition should come down to the claims of two wolves who are not keen on a fight, yes?"

"Ah." Keith pulled his feet down, finally, and leaned forward to claim his glass. "Yes. What if I offer that the appearance of strength is often enough to dissuade the enemy?"

Fyodor pulled his hands from his pockets. He slouched against the wall and folded his arms, left over right, and his smile melted into a frown. "It is your son."

"It is."

"He's of the pack."

"He is."

"And I do not wish to fight you, Keith MacNeill."

Keith finished his soft drink and left the glass behind when he stood. "Fyodor Stephanovich, the feeling is mutual. For one thing, it would only weaken the pack to lose you."

"Lose me?"

"Are you confident, Younger Brother?"

"*Da.*"

Keith smiled, close-lipped, and turned it into a shrug. "Good enough. So am I."

There were dark lines of blood on the Merlin's wrist, where Kelly's fingernails had broken her skin. She rubbed them absently as she watched Jane walk away. "That's the lieutenant governor of New York, isn't it?"

"It's a day job. To us she's the archmage."

"How does she manage to keep a secret life like this out of the media?" Carel's gesture took in the workroom, as the Prometheans dismissively called it: the former ballroom to which the gallery served as antechamber and reception room.

"Have you ever heard of a politician who *didn't* belong to some sort of private club?"

"Not one quite like this." Her hands swept wider, indicating the tall windows lining three walls. The workroom encompassed the width of the building and most of the length, a city block of satiny hardwood floor with an inlaid border and a scattered design of oriental dragons worked in cherry, purpleheart, and woods Matthew didn't even know the names of. There was no furniture, and the focal point was an iron spiral stair at the far end, wide enough for three to climb abreast.

"This is something," the Merlin said, and crouched down beside one of the inlaid dragons, tracing the detail work with her fingertips. "His eyes are steel."

"The better to see you with, my dear," Matthew answered, offering her a hand up again. She barely leaned on it as she rose, all calculated power. "They're all different, you know."

"The dragons?"

"Everything, really. Would you like to sit with me?"

She turned in place, watching the rest of the Magi begin to trickle into the workroom. "Are you going to make me dress up in a black robe and chant?"

"Not at all. But you will have to button your collar."

She tilted her chin, lips paling where they pressed together, but she allowed him to fasten the top button on her tunic. "All part of your ritual, I take it?"

"Everything is ritual if you look at it right," he answered, rubbing his hands together as cold started to creep through his rings. "The comings and goings of the trains, the patterns of traffic, the routines of life. Even the way the city breathes at night means something. Our magic is the opportunistic sort. We use what we find . . ."

Carel nodded. "Someone told me once that Magi used magic rather than making it. And you also put your members in positions of power and influence?"

"What secret society doesn't?"

"Indeed." She smoothed a braid behind her ear; it had wriggled loose of the scrunchie. "Do you read conflicting portents in entrails and in the flights of birds?"

"When they conflict." Matthew shrugged, uncomfortable under the intentness of her gaze. *Does she ever flinch?* He knew the answer; her tempered ruthlessness was not all that different from Jane's. He led Carel to a place by the wall and settled down against it. "The floor's clean. Pull some up."

She folded her legs and plunked down beside him, velvet skirts spreading over the inlaid wood. "Tell me about your tattoos," she said, reaching out to run a thumb across the back of his wrist, her fingers folding around the heel of his hand to steady her touch. Despite himself, he turned and raised his eyes to the light falling past the curtains, through the windows. "Are they part of your magic, Matthew Magus?"

"Something like that," he said, shifting uncomfortably. She had the eyes of a predator. *What did you expect?*

"Kelly has them too."

"Kelly was a wizard before me. He taught me." *At first. Until he ran out of things to teach.* Unwilling to explain, and she knew it and pressed him anyway, knowing he would be equally unwilling to risk offending her. He couldn't look away from the splintering light in her eyes, although the chill from his hands contracted his shoulders as if a shadow fell across him.

"The tattoos aren't Promethean—"

"They are, though," Matthew said. "They were supposed to link us together. Make our power one. And protect us."

"But you're not twins."

"Symbolically speaking, we were, after we got the artwork done," he said, and leaned his back against the wall, lacing his fingers together. The cold in his hands was nothing, was expected . . . wasn't the sort of Fae thing he would have to jump up and oppose. And if it needed opposing, there were those here far more equipped to do so than he. He smoothed his hair with both hands, making sure it remained tucked into its tight ponytail. It had stayed put, for once. He folded his arms, knowing exactly how defensive he must seem.

Carel sighed and sat back against the wall beside him, tucking her skirts around her legs and drawing up her knees. "I suppose I should make sure you don't mean me to be a sacrifice."

"Perish the thought." Jane stood over them, a tall familiar man beside her. "I'm afraid that honor is long claimed," she continued. "And today is about taking rather than giving. Merlin, if you don't mind . . ."

Matthew was rising to his feet, and Carel had already proved how adept she was at reading a situation. She stood beside him, extending her hand. Matthew kept his balled up and shoved them into his pockets. A scent hung on the Merlin's hair, green and rich, elusive. Ylang-ylang and jasmine, perhaps. Or lavender and marjoram.

"Charmed," Carel said, looking directly into the tall man's eyes. Even Matthew, whose taste did not run that way at all, could see that he was beautiful, his black hair slicked back, his suit impeccably tailored and his claret tie fastened with a silver stickpin, a fleur-de-lis that matched the discreet medallions on his cordovan loafers. "And you might be . . . ?"

"You may call me Murchaud," he said.

She examined him from shoes to chin, and deliberately raised her gaze to his eyes. Jane cleared her throat. "Did you enjoy your visit with Matthew's brother?"

Carel turned her head and looked at Jane—as much as looked *through* Jane—and slowly rolled her shoulders. "And what have you lost to the Faeries, Jane Andraste, to pull you into this war? You're very far and a very long time from where you grew up, or my talent placing accents deserts me. . . ."

Jane actually blanched, and for one awed moment Matthew thought she might even step back, but she held her ground and met the Merlin's challenge smiling. He could imagine how it must sting. "A child," she said. "Like any mother, I'll do what's needful to get her back."

"You are a driven woman."

"I've had a very long time to work at it," Jane answered, smoothing the pockets of her suitcoat absently. "And where are you from, then?"

"All over," Carel said. "New York and Texas, mostly. I was an army brat. And touché, as they say. And you, Murchaud? A Fae lord in New York City, at the side of the Promethean archmage?"

"Not Fae," he answered, bending over her hand. "No longer. If you called me a Duke of Hell, my lady, t'would not be far off. Fortunate we are to have so lovely a Merlin to treat with."

"A Duke of . . . Hell."

"It's not quite what the stories would paint it," he answered, after his lips had brushed her skin and their eyes met over twin calm smiles. "They say Hell is the absence of God. And the presence of the Morningstar."

"You have known other Merlins, Murchaud?" Slowly but definitely, Carel withdrew her hand.

"Ah," he said. "Two or three. Never one so determined not to be wooed, I warrant." But he smiled when he said it, and turned his attention to Matthew. And was wise enough not to extend his hand. "Dr. Szczegielniak. Are you well?"

"Very well, Your Grace," Matthew answered, with the odd formality that always came over him when he was confronted face-to-face with their strangest ally. "And yourself?"

"Well enough, for one in Hell," he answered, the way he always did. He bowed to Carel again, and nodded to Matthew, and took Jane's arm in a courtly hand and squired her away.

"Well." Carel watched them go. "That was a surprising thing to find here. Where does he enter into the equation?"

"An equation is balanced," Matthew said. "We're at a disadvantage, and always have been. But as I understand it, Murchaud's master also has an interest in seeing the power of Faerie contained. Strange bedfellows, and all of us have made sacrifices. In addition to what we've lost less willingly."

Carel's eyes were unwinking as a snake's when she turned them on him. She touched his hand again, and again he felt it up the inside of his arm, in the hollow of his throat. "And what have you sacrificed, Matthew Magus? Children? A home, a wife?"

"More or less." He stuffed his fists into his pockets. "We should make ourselves comfortable. It might be a little while."

The Circle was an anticlimax, as it always was; Promethean rituals were usually efficient, rarely dramatic, and mostly without pomp. Matthew sat and chatted with Carel, introduced her to a few more friends and acquaintances among the New York and Connecticut Magi, and when it was his turn he walked up to the front of the workroom, laid his hand on the iron helix that curled from floor to ceiling, and murmured the words of consent. The rush of strength out of his body left him light-headed and weak as if with hunger; he staggered back to Carel, who was standing, framed by a window in the failing light.

"See?" he said, rubbing his aching hands together. "Nothing to it. Shall I walk you back to your train?"

"I think the Fae are not the only seducers about," she said, and offered him her arm to lean on.

He accepted shamelessly. "How fortunate I'm immune."

Chapter Nine

At dinnertime, Seeker sat on the Puck's left, toying with her jewelry, deflecting his forays into curiosity, and watching courtiers ply their trade while she waited for the Mebd to arrive and begin their meal. The hall was long and tiled like a checkerboard, heavy tables ranged on either side of an open dance floor strewn with flowers. Cairbre and Hope played softly upon a small stage by the wall. Outside, black night pressed against the soaring windows, hanging over the roof that arched overhead like a clerestory made of glass and the branches of golden trees.

Both Seeker and Puck started up when the doors swung open, but it was not the Queen. Rather the Mebd's herald entered, flanked by dignitaries. On his left slunk a Leannan Sidhe, jet hair wound around her proud head like a braided crown, her long neck white as alabaster. Whiskey turned to watch her walk: like quicksilver puddling and flowing. The water-horse's head came up high and proud, nostrils flaring red.

Seeker didn't need a little bird to warn her of trouble. Not when the Unseelie emissary arched an eyebrow black as squid ink and narrow as night, watching Whiskey watching her, and acknowledged him with a wink. Leannan Sidhe were not, generally speaking, known for their good intentions.

But then, neither was Whiskey.

The Mebd's herald drew a breath and announced the Leannan Sidhe by name as Cliodhna. Cairbre, his waved dark hair and beard neatly trimmed, his shoulders wrapped in a bard's patchwork, left the stage in Hope's care and came to the Leannan Sidhe; she allowed him to hand her down the broad stairs, her robes dripping from her body in diaphanous folds. Puck watched.

"She'd eat you alive."

"What a way to go," he said with a grin that split his face from ear to ear. "And what bragging rights, if she didn't. Tell me you haven't been tempted to sample . . ." He jerked his head at the Whiskey, his long ears waggling lasciviously. "Even a little."

"Even a little," she said, and changed the subject. "The Mebd can't be far behind."

"Indeed." He helped her to her feet. "We should find a good spot as soon as possible. Oh, and what's that?"

Seeker turned at the clatter of Whiskey's horseshoe rings on the floor. The great doors at the far end of the hall swung open silently, framing a figure clad in red velvet and silk who gazed about with obvious wonder. "Hell," Seeker said, because it seemed like the only thing she could say, and began walking across the wide-open space in the middle of the floor to intercept the Merlin, leaving Robin behind.

Whiskey got to Carel first, claiming her arm as if it were the most natural thing in the world. They made a handsome if mismatched couple, the ivory of his garments dramatic against the crimson of her swirling skirt and tunic, his skin only a shade or two darker than hers. She didn't tug against his grip, nor did she move closer, while her eyes scanned the crowd.

Looking for me, Seeker thought, and it was confirmed when Carel's eyes met hers and the other woman smiled.

Heads turned to track Seeker's arrow-straight path across the floor. The last voice Seeker heard was that of Cairbre the bard, cut off mid-sentence, offering his temporary companion a glass of wine. Then he too fell silent.

A curt gesture brought the herald across the floor at a near run. She heard the patter of the herald's hooves and the jingle of Cairbre's bells. The walk the length of the hall was interminable, even as Whiskey guided the Merlin toward her—or, more precisely, was swept along in her wake.

"Carel," Seeker said. "How did you get here?"

The Merlin giggled like a satisfied schoolgirl, trying to gawk unobviously. "I watched you do it, and the other Seeker—Kadiska. Simple once you know the trick. And Morgan told me—among other things—how to find the palace when I went to visit her. But I seem to have crashed a party."

"A big party, yes. Thank you, Whiskey."

"A pleasure as always to serve, mistress." Irony soaked his tone, but she couldn't be bothered to glare.

Seeker took Carel's arm, but made no protest as Whiskey fell into step behind them. "It's dangerous."

"So I've heard." Carel ducked her head and nodded to a tall gray-limbed being who stepped aside to let them pass. She put up a reasonable front, but Seeker saw dilated pupils and felt the Merlin's pulse shuddering against her skin. "This is all real." Around them, the rustle of conversation resumed.

She just parted the veils and walked here. Into Annwn, as if walking to the corner store. "Since you're here," Seeker said, "you'll be expected to meet the Queen. Later. She's making an announcement tonight. In the meantime, have some wine."

Cairbre caught up with them, the Mebd's herald dogging his heels. Seeker, turning to face them, saw Cliodhna standing nearby but separate, watching in silence. "Herald," Seeker said over the chatter. "Master bard. This lady is Dr. Carel Bierce, the Merlin. Announce her, if you will?"

The herald took a step back, his green-and-violet livery catching the torchlight just so. He pawed the floor and shot a look at the dais. But the bard Cairbre merely nodded, his resonant baritone taking on a flirtatious tone that Seeker knew was entirely affected. "As the lady commands." The bard's hair fell over his shoulders as he turned to face the room. "Oyez! Oyez!" he cried, casting the hand unencumbered by a wineglass out wide. "My lords and ladies, sprites and Faeries, elves and spriggans. Sidhe, Annwn, and noble Fae! Attend, pray, attend!"

Conversation halted. The rafters groaned, dust sifting down from the vault, and Carel started. "What?"

"Spriggan," Seeker muttered. "Don't worry."

"It is my pleasure and my honor to introduce one who has traveled far and hard on a weary road to reach our shores. Lords and ladies of the Daoine Sidhe, honored guests"—he nodded to Cliodhna and, surprising Seeker, to Whiskey—"may I present Merlin the Magician." His voice rose at the end and he bowed with a flourish, spilling not a drop.

Silence hung thickly. Seeker held her breath, feeling every eye upon her. No, brushing past her, pinning the woman whose arm she held. As if they could peel the Merlin open, uncover her secrets, learn her Name.

Collectedly, Carel freed herself from Seeker's grip and bowed from the waist. "A great pleasure indeed," she said, and turned to Seeker as if their talk had not been interrupted.

Seeker saw the Unseelie coming, limiting her strides to a casual stroll, and caught the barbs of tension flowing from her. The wall of silence cracked and voices rose in a tumult cut by crystalline tones. "And very welcome you are, my dear Merlin."

What else could possibly go wrong? Seeker lifted her head to regard the Mebd, who had slipped through the crowd and stood just behind Whiskey, crowned in radiance. Whiskey snorted and shied, banging the herald. Seeker glanced around for Ian, and did not see him.

The Mebd chuckled softly. "Merlin," she said, extending her milk-white hand. "How good of you to come. May you always be welcome in my court, and come and go as you please." Her hair was uncovered, and it fell around her shoulders in silken plaits thin as ribbons. Seeker looked from the Queen to the Merlin, watching their braids swing as they spoke.

Carel took the Mebd's hand cautiously and bent over it. "Your Highness, thank you."

Seeker caught Cairbre's eye, and he nodded. Carel would need to be taught court titles on top of everything else.

"Not at all, magician. But I see your colleague approaches, so I will leave you to her tender mercies. Master bard, I will need your services, and those of your apprentice as well." She released Carel's hand

and let her golden eyelashes dust her cheek, looked back up coyly and smiled. And then she turned imperially and moved toward the dais, trailing Cairbre and the herald, stopping to speak to Cliodhna along the way.

Carel watched her go, and slowly shook her head. "So that's the Queen of Faerie."

"One of them." Whiskey answered.

The Merlin breathed in Seeker's ear. "Colleague?"

Seeker pointed with her chin. "Cliodhna, I presume. She's beholden to the Cat Anna, Kadiska's Queen."

"A usurper?"

"Nay. Another kingdom within the Kingdom of the West. Be careful. She's a Leannan Sidhe."

"Leannan Sidhe?"

"A Faerie muse," Whiskey answered, licking his lips. "The sort that burns mortals up in the fires of creation."

Seeker took Carel's arm and led her toward the tapestry-hung wall, each breath an effort. The stones were cold and hard under her slippers, people slipping out of focus as if she were already drunk, the confusion of voices and presences making her eyes in the shadows more distraction than use.

Whiskey leaned against the wall, watching a footman serve the women. "Is it safe to drink this?" Carel asked.

"The Mebd has promised you may come and go as you please," Seeker answered. "Her word is binding."

"Ah." Carel raised the wine to her lips, breathing the aroma from a mouth-blown spindle of red glass wound with golden filigree, delicate as a soap bubble. "It's lovely."

Seeker wasn't sure if she meant the wine or the glass. But she nodded anyway, and turned to greet Cliodhna.

"The Merlin," Cliodhna said, a smile narrowing dark eyes. Her voice was furred like catkins and chimed like silver. "I had not thought, forgive me, that you would be a lady."

"Have there been no others?" Carel sipped her wine, and did not extend her hand for the Leannan Sidhe to touch.

"No," she said. "And I have known some few Merlins. Do they still teach magecraft in the mortal lands? Are you a musician?"

"I am a musician," she answered. "Would you like me to sing something for you?" Her eyes sparkled, and she was looking at Seeker, not at Cliodhna.

"Yes," the Sidhe said, and licked her lips.

She's charmed by Carel, Seeker thought. *We all are.* "Not 'Tam Lin,' " Seeker whispered aside to the Merlin.

Carel winked. "Of course not," she answered low, and sipped her wine. And then she tilted back her head, half closed her eyes, and let her sweet high singing voice, such a contrast to her spoken tones, roll from an open throat.

And the vast reaches of the ballroom fell silent again.

> *"Alas, my love, you do me wrong*
> *To cast me off discourteously*
> *When I have loved you for so long*
> *Delighting in your company."*

Cliodhna turned slowly on her heel and raised her black-maned head like a startled swan. Whiskey leaned forward, his big human hands twined together, his blue eyes glistening. Seeker felt the ache in her chest grow to something she thought would consume her, and bit back the tears.

And then another voice rose up, plain and unornamented, from before the dais. A baritone, resonant as a cello, strong and controlled. Cairbre, wearing the strangest expression as he took the following chorus.

The Mebd stood, now, her green gown draped upon her still as if on a statue, her face frozen in a mask like pain or like peace too terrible to be spoken of. Carel picked up the second verse as Cairbre's chorus was dying away, and she leaned into the song as if it were a strong wind over the bow of a ship.

Seeker, watching the Mebd, saw something she had never thought to see. A single tear glistened in the corner of the Faerie Queen's eye and laid a gleaming track down her porcelain cheek. Eight verses and eight choruses, and bard and Merlin sang them all, while the guests stood frozen and the Queen of the Summerlands wept before her chair. Until the end.

The bitter end.

There was something more than magic in the Merlin's voice, for each time in the lyrics that the name of the Divine was repeated, Seeker flinched, expecting pain. But the pain never came, and she saw wonder on Cairbre's face as well.

The bard finished the final chorus and leaned back against a spiraling pillar at the foot of the broad, sweeping steps, closing his eyes in exhaustion. The magic—the *sorcery*—in that song hung over the ballroom, and not so much as a breath stirred it until the Mebd closed her eyes and sat back on her chair. When she opened them again she blinked, oblivious to the tears still marking her face and spotting her gown, and raised her right hand. "For that, Lady Merlin," she said in light sweet tones, "for that gift, I grant you one boon, any boon within my power to grant, with the stipulation that it harm not my kingdom nor any subject to me. And you, Cairbre, as well."

"Thank you, Your Highness."

"Whiskey," Seeker said, leaning close to his ear. "There's some significance to that song that I don't understand."

"Aye," he said. "There is."

She lifted her chin and glared, keeping her voice to a murmur. "Little treachery—"

"Alas, that you must ruin my entertainment." He sulked elaborately, so she almost forgot herself and laughed. "The last time that song was sung here, the singer's next trick was to steal the Mebd's husband away."

"Murchaud. For the tithe?"

"Before that. But yes, Murchaud."

The Mebd smiled. "And as we have silence, and everyone's attention . . . Ian, you will attend me, please?"

The hush came over the room anew, and Seeker's heart squeezed. *Ian. No. Is she going to place a binding on him too? Or send him for the teind?*

Seeker's son came forward from the tapestried shadows behind the chair and took his place beside it. He wore black, velvet and linen, his doublet girdled by a heavy golden belt set with emeralds and amethysts half as big as Seeker's palm. There was a blade at his belt and a thick-linked chain around his neck. *She's knighted him. And he goes armed in her presence.*

She tasted bittersweet. *Has she taken him as a lover, then?*

The Mebd glanced up at the slender boy fondly. "I have a royal pro-nouncement to all gathered here," she said, and her clear voice carried like bells. *She can't mean to marry him. . . .*

She can mean anything she wishes, Seeker reminded herself. Whiskey's hand rested on her shoulder, but the numbness surging through her all but made her forget. Carel shifted restlessly.

The Mebd waited for the silence to become profound. "This lad is Ian MacNeill. I tell you he is blood of my blood, child of my father's line through my half sister Morgan le Fey."

Seeker blinked and touched her ear with cold fingertips, but the words did not change. Carel stroked her arm in concern.

Seeker shook the gentle hand off, and Whiskey's when he would have steadied her, and stumbled forward. "Your Majesty," she said, when she stood before the chair, "I don't see how that can be true."

"But it is, good Seeker. Your true father—not your mother's hus-band, but your sire—was my husband Murchaud, who was the son of Morgan of Cornwall and the half-Fae knight Lancelot du Lac."

"The Queen just named your son her heir, and acknowledged you her grandniece," Whiskey said an hour later, buttering bread with a knife wrought of heavy silver. "I don't understand what you're upset about." He'd devoured everything set before him—fowl and fish, roast and veg-etables—and was eyeing Seeker's untouched plate.

Carel sat beside them at the banquet table, toying with her wine. She'd played with her food as well, making Seeker go over—and over—the significance of the Mebd's pronouncement. "But if she's been a few thousand years without one, why does she suddenly need an heir now?"

Seeker had no appetite. She pushed her dinner toward Whiskey, while continuing to watch from the shadows clustering the room. "That's part of what worries me, Merlin." She glanced down the length of the table. Ian sat on the Queen's right hand. He caught her looking and offered her a smile. She looked away.

"It's power," Whiskey said. "You'll be dealing now from a position of strength. And she's granted his father right of return. Who knows what could happen?"

Seeker formed some rebuttal in her mind, but before it reached her lips, the Merlin's eyes came up. Her head followed, and she stood, darkened for a moment as if a shadow fell across her, surrounded by the scent of roses, trailing dappled velvet. "Who . . ." she said, not looking at Seeker.

Seeker's eyes followed the Merlin's. Her goblet shattered on the stones before she knew it had slipped between her fingers.

"No," Seeker whispered. *Ah. No.* But it was too late, and the Merlin was already walking, moving like a marionette, her skirt fluttering behind her. Her long fingers reached out, casually disarming an Elf-knight who happened to be between her and the door, slipping his scabbarded sword from his belt.

She flowed forward to where Keith MacNeill stood, framed in the great carven doors, blinking in the light of ten thousand candles. In one fluid motion, the Merlin skinned the blade clear of its sheath and dropped the scabbard on the marble to echo like a slap in the silence. Another step bore her up to the tall, red-haired werewolf; she uncoiled like a cobra. The silver blade whistled toward his neck.

Seeker lunged to her feet, shouting—*"No!"*—but the Merlin was already in motion.

Keith never flinched. Even when the edge of the silver blade parted the white skin of his throat, and red blood stained the blade, he stood unmoving. Impassive, as the Merlin stopped her swing with the strength and control of the dancer she was. She stood facing the werewolf, unblinking, the edge of her blade resting on his neck, a crimson blot spreading over his shoulder.

"You'll do," the Merlin said, and went to her knees before falling hard, senseless, on the stones.

Seeker stood frozen, watching blood thread the white cloth of Keith's shirt. No one moved, no one spoke, no one's heart so much as hazarded a beat. And then Seeker unfurled *otherwise* wings and leapt, passing over the table, an owl in flight the length of the hall and then stooping like a falcon to earth before him. She crouched and placed her hand on the Merlin's throat, fingers seeking the flutter of her pulse. Then she stood. Keith stared, wordless, blood trickling over his fingers.

A clatter on the marble alerted her that Whiskey had followed; she issued her commands quietly, without turning.

"Get Ian. And the Queen. Keith . . ." Her voice trailed off as she met his eyes. "How long have you known?"

"Known what? Who is this?"

"Never mind. Help me carry her." The rest of the Fae were closing in around them, Cairbre nearest, dark eyes worried. Seeker saw the Mebd above the crowd, standing on her dais, her hands clenched skeletal and white on her gilded chair.

Keith stooped and lifted Carel in bloodstained hands. "Silver. It won't heal quickly."

"It's not bad," Seeker said, leaning to check as she spoke. "More bloody than dangerous. Do you feel dizzy?"

"No."

"Then follow me." She saw Whiskey speaking in the herald's ear, saw him turn and lead the way to the Mebd. And then her attention was taken up by the way the ring of Fae drew back against the walls as she led Keith forward, crimson droplets spattering the sage-and-rose tiles. Only Cairbre and Cliodhna did not withdraw; the bard came up along-side the taller werewolf, and the Leannan Sidhe stood where they would pass close before her, and waited.

"I'll summon a physician," Cairbre said. "Is she . . . ?"

"Fainted," Seeker answered.

"It would be a pity if—" Cairbre stopped himself. "—anything happened to that voice," he finished, walking away.

"What was that about?" Keith looked around at the crowd as a low mutter swept the room, rising over still forms clad in persimmon and periwinkle and a thousand other colors.

"Damned if I know."

Cliodhna reached out as they passed and caught Keith's sleeve. "Wolf-prince."

"What?" He kept moving, forcing her to trot to keep her grip. Seeker swallowed a grin before she remembered her worry, implications making her temples throb.

"Protection," the Leannan Sidhe hissed. "Sanctuary if you need it. Think of us when the time comes."

"Perhaps." Keith pulled free of her. "Shark tank," he said in Seeker's ear.

"You got me into it." And was then sorry she had said it. They were almost to the door, and music rose—the notes of a harpsichord—and the Merlin stirred in Keith's arms and moaned. Seeker risked a glance at the room. Hope was stretched over the keyboards, and Robin led a bog Faerie with hair like marsh weed out on the dance floor. Seeker couldn't see the Mebd anymore, or Ian. "Why the hell did you come here tonight?"

"I heard it would be permitted," Keith answered. Seeker pushed past the doorman, shoving the double-hung portal back on silent hinges.

"Of course." She started laughing as the door closed behind them. "And you were late. It's too perfect."

She wanted to sag against the wall and slide down it, laughing, holding her head in her hands. Keith kept striding unerringly toward her chambers, and she had to keep up. "Keith, she made Ian her heir."

"Who did?"

"The Mebd."

He didn't stop, but he closed his eyes briefly and then looked down at her, the movement causing a thin line of scarlet to crack the fragile scab. "But he's not her child."

Seeker opened the door to her rooms. "No. But I'm her grandniece. Bring Carel in here and I'll tell you about it."

Keith had barely laid Carel down on the coverlet when a light tap rattled the door. "Come in," Seeker called, expecting Whiskey or a servant— not expecting a slender boy with black curls and green eyes to slip into the room on quick, silent strides, turn, and shoot the bolt behind. He put his back to the door and paused inside, hands curling and uncurling at his sides.

And despite everything, Seeker froze for a moment, staring, while Keith waited in uncomprehending silence at her back. She'd avoided looking, avoided seeing Ian, for years. And now she couldn't look away, couldn't move, and neither could he. Both stood transfixed, gaping at each other.

Until he breathed, and the light shifted on the golden collar under the open neck of his shirt. As if some sorcery had freed her from stupefaction, she stepped forward, grasped Ian's shoulders, and pulled him into her arms.

He was cold, stiff as if with stress or exposure, but she warmed him as best she could. He stood unmoving until she touched his hair, and then his breath came out on a long, shuddering sob, and he clung to her, one arm around her waist and the other crossing her shoulders.

And then he stepped back, his features compressing, then smoothing, as he mastered his expression. "I got away as soon as I could," he said. "Mother, the Mebd says she must entertain Cliodhna, and begs your indulgence and your care of the Merlin."

"Where's Whiskey?" Seeker began, before Keith cut her off.

"Merlin?" he demanded, and then, *"Mother?"*

Seeker covered her eyes with her hand and steadied herself against the carven bedpost. The Merlin's chest rose and fell slowly, seeming the only motion in a quiet room. "Keith MacNeill, meet your firstborn son, Ian, heir to the throne of the Daoine Sidhe. Ian, this is your father. He's a werewolf, and given tonight's display"—Seeker gestured vaguely at Carel—"the living incarnation of the Dragon Prince. So I don't know about you, but I am going to have a glass of wine." *Or a bottle.*

Ian, Keith, and Seeker stood, each waiting for the next to speak. Ian toyed with the chain at his neck, looking from his mother's face to his father's. Keith leaned on the bedpost, pressing at the sword cut. "That might scar," Seeker said.

"I expect it will," he answered, and in a carefully casual tone, added, "Dragon Prince?"

"It's time—" she began, but another tap on the door interrupted her. "We'll talk when the procession ends," she said, rolling her eyes.

The physician entered, garbed in healer's red. He cleaned and bandaged Keith's wound and nodded over the Merlin. A page arrived with wine before the chirurgeon finished; Seeker sent him back after hot water and a clean shirt for Keith. Ian poked up the banked embers and laid birch logs white as wedding dresses on the fire.

Hot water came, and Keith stripped with his usual disregard for propriety and washed the blood from his chest and hands, leaving the water in the ceramic basin roped with pink. He reclothed himself while page and physician withdrew, and took the wine that Seeker poured and Ian brought to him. "Now," he said. "Dragon Prince?"

"That's the Merlin passed out in my bed," Seeker answered. She brought her glass with her, and led Keith to the chairs by the fire. Her stool was still there, but she settled into the green wing chair and leaned forward, an elbow on her knee, watching the flames because she couldn't bear to look at the man, or the boy either. "She marked you, Keith. And it's time."

"For an heir to Arthur. And you think I'm it?" He did not sit. His eyes stayed fixed on Ian, who had returned to crouch before the fire. The birch logs burned incandescent, crackling bark flaring brighter and hotter than strips of paper.

"Not an heir to Arthur. A . . ." She shrugged hopelessly. "The prince is always a *drighten,* a warlord. He comes in a time of turmoil, and changes everything. Unites the beleaguered against their foes, pays some terrible price through his own greed or shortsightedness or cruelty. Is betrayed by someone who should love him, and dies bloodily."

"I know all that," Keith said. He closed his eyes. "It cannot be. I have it from Mist that the Dragon Prince is another—"

"—and you have it from the Merlin, with Mist's shadow on her hair, that it is you. They used to say Merlins lived backward, you know, because they knew so many things they shouldn't have had ways to know."

"I know." He hesitated, rubbed both palms across his face before he opened his eyes again, stretching and smoothing freckled skin. "Dammit. No, the Dragon said *if,* not *is.* 'If he is a Dragon Prince.' I just assumed."

A cold tingle in Seeker's fingertips, and she turned away so she would not have to see Keith's eyes. "How did you come to talk to dragons, Keith?"

"I—" He stopped and lifted his wineglass again. "Dreams, first. And then she spoke to me. I thought—"

"Conquered any kingdoms lately?"

"My father's ill," he answered, and took that chair after all. "He stands at the head of the pack. But I haven't any brothers and I won't do what Arthur did. Or what Vlad did, either. From what the Dragon said to me, I thought I knew who the Prince was to be, and he's . . . fit to lead. I've all but promised not to stand in his way."

Ian stood and turned to them, his green eyes wide and the pupils dark. "Father." As if the word felt strange on his tongue. As if he had not been listening to the conversation at all. "I don't even know you," he said. "I want to know you. I won't do it, whatever it is that I'm supposed to do to betray you. We're here, all in the same room, finally. We're talking. And we know things that Vlad and Arthur did not know. Who cares about a stupid prophecy?"

"It's not a prophecy," Seeker said. "It's a pattern. A story. Keith, have you other children?" She held her breath over the answer.

And he shook his head, picking at his trousers.

How did I come to be living in a Faerie tale? "It's a pattern repeated with variations. And it means that—if the pattern holds, and it always has— either Ian or I, or both of us, is going to betray you."

"Not before I kill a lot of other people," he answered, and scrubbed his free hand across his face, wincing as the motion tugged his stiffening injury. "Is there anything we can do about this right now?"

"Worry ourselves sick," Seeker answered.

"Yes." He set the glass aside and looked over at her. "I gathered." He sighed and stood back up. "Ian."

The boy's face was curiously still, unfrightened. "Yes?"

"I haven't been here. It hasn't been my choice. But it was my fault." He stopped. In the silence that followed, Seeker looked into the still-rising flames. "I'd like to be friends."

"I don't need a friend." Ian fingered the bulky golden belt, adjusting the hang of his sword. "I'm going to wind up on a throne of my own eventually, unless my life gets any more like a ballad. Ballads"—he shook his head—"rarely end well."

"I'm sorry, then."

Seeker heard the pain in Keith's voice; it twined around the guilt in her heart, enough to strangle her. "It's my fault, really," she said, but Ian stopped her with a gesture.

"I need a family. Not friends. I'll have all the friends I need, every one of them waiting to be thrown some tidbit. From pet to Prince in half an hour." Cool resignation. "I'll manage. But I want to know you both."

"Yes," Keith said.

Seeker couldn't find the words to go with what was rising inside her, so she nodded and kept nodding, her head jerking up and down erratically until it filled her and ran over into hiccuping sobs. She didn't push Keith away when he came and pulled her into his embrace, warm and smelling of soap and blood, and a few moments later Ian came and wrapped cool arms around her as well.

Keith's clean shirt wasn't clean anymore by the time her sobs faltered. She looked up as a page rapped on the door and summoned Ian away to attend the Mebd. The boy glanced back over his shoulder guiltily, and Seeker looked up long enough to see Keith give Ian a worried smile over her tangled hair. *Go.* She wiped salt from her face.

He went, and Keith pulled her back into his arms. "I'm sorry," she said, her voice still taut and strange. She leaned against his shoulder, an old command to silence stilling her tongue when she would have explained more, about the Merlin and the Dragon and a thousand other things.

"I'm sorry too." He leaned against the wing chair; after a moment she sighed and rolled her head back, cracking her neck.

She turned and sat beside him, letting him drape his arm over her shoulders. *I should get up. I shouldn't let this happen. Cold and stern, and show no weakness. No emotion, no fear and especially no love.* She leaned back into the embrace.

"You were so . . . *fey*," he said, his voice wondering. "More fey than the full-Fae themselves."

"They can smell pain," she said.

"So can I." He smoothed her hair back from her face. "We still work well together in a crisis."

"We do." She sat beside him, watching the Merlin sprawled across her bed. Carel muttered and turned on her side, her eyelashes fluttering. "That looks like natural sleep."

"It does. Should we wake her?"

"No." Her hair tangled against his sleeve as she shook her head. "I haven't the energy to explain to her what happened. Her power of prophecy is manifesting. Before long she'll be speaking for the Dragon." *And then I'll have failed in my task, unless I can find a way to control a Merlin at the height of her power.*

She shivered. "What's wrong?" Keith asked.

"The Mebd is scared," Seeker said. "And I don't know why, but I think she's trying to consolidate power, and she's trying to get her sisters to commit to the same plan. Which means something's going on. Something above and beyond their game."

"Ah," he said, as if he thought of something, and was silent while the quick-burning birch logs flickered down. "You know," he said, "Ian looks like you."

"He has your eyes," she answered.

Time passed, and before too long the sun rose behind the clouds and morning came.

The Mebd summoned Seeker at the breakfast hour, when servants came to bring Carel to her new chambers. The werewolf laid a hand on Seeker's arm after she dressed herself—too tired to attempt a glamourie—and headed for the door. She turned to look into eyes yellow-green as peridot.

"Elaine."

"Don't." She didn't shake his arm off, though—instead pinned him with a look as wide and dark as the sea. "Keith, what can you possibly want from me?"

"I . . ." His voice fell apart. "We loved each other."

She snorted laughter, and then she did pull away. "You're going to die, Keith. And I'm probably going to be the one to betray you to that death. Doesn't that mean anything to you?"

"No," he said, but he didn't reach out to her again. "No. Because the pack is loyal to the pack, and families are loyal to each other."

"I'm not a werewolf."

"Of course not."

"And you're the fucking Dragon Prince."

"I know that too."

"So what the hell do you want from me?" Her voice was dead and calm.

The silence hung between them like the pall on Arthur's bier, like the tapestries on Morgan's walls. She stopped, turned, looked up into his eyes. "I want you to love me the way you used to," he said.

"I do," she answered, and slammed the door in his face.

Chapter Ten

It wasn't the first time Keith had stood, his fists clenched at his sides, and watched a door close between them. He suspected that it wouldn't be the last.

"So." A throaty drawl from the window: a cold draft as the diamond-paned casement swung open. "*You're* the competition."

Keith turned. Rain-kissed breeze brought with it three yellowed leaves and the rich sharp scent of the sea. Black-skinned fingers gripped the window ledge, silver rings glinting on the thick-nailed thumbs, and a tall lean man in a ragged white shirt climbed over the sill to stand, dripping rain, at the edge of the rug.

"Competition?" Keith wrinkled his nose. Even in man form, the Fae smelled of wilderness, of seashore and stallion and hay bales curing in the autumn sun. "You're the Kelpie."

"Call me Whiskey," the Kelpie answered. "And I will call you my Prince, my Prince —"

"I am no one's Prince." Keith's gut clenched as he said it, knowing it for a lie. He flexed his hands, sidestepping slightly as the Kelpie moved into the room. *Will it come to a fight?*

"Oh," Whiskey answered, tossing his head so that jeweled droplets spattered, "but you are. The whole hall knows it. My Prince, and our Prince, and my mistress's true love . . ."

"You're here to warn me off, I take it?" Keith smiled, a curl of his lip and a showing of teeth. He stepped sideways again, circling, getting his back to Elaine's enormous bedstead. The Kelpie turned to keep them face-to-face. "I am not Fae, Whiskey. But I am no mere mortal to be threatened and bullied."

The Kelpie crossed his arms and leaned back on his heels, seeming at ease, his back to the wall now, the window on his right. His eyes glittered gray-blue in the watery light. " *'Tell her to find me an acre of land / between the shore and the salt sea strand.'* Really, my Prince. I am but a bondservant, and have nothing with which to threaten *you*. No, I merely came to introduce myself, and meet the man who will lead us."

"My leadership is not a settled thing," Keith said. He eyed the Kelpie a moment longer, his hackles bristling, and suddenly came to a decision—not to trust, exactly, but to risk—and turned his back on the stallion and strode back to the fireside. He crouched, warming his palms by the embers. "And I am a wolf, not a man. Do you want a drink, Whiskey?"

"Whiskey," Whiskey answered, coming to join him. Keith shuffled sideways. They squatted knee to knee, Whiskey's damp sleeve steaming slightly, until Keith stood again and moved to the cabinet to find Elaine's glasses and liquor.

He spoke over his shoulder as he poured. "I know it's Fae to speak around an issue in epic spirals, Whiskey, but do you think you could take pity on an old wolf and say what it is you came to say, if you're not here to kill me?" He turned as Whiskey came up, and pressed a glass into the stallion's hand.

Whiskey lowered his head over the rim, nostrils flaring as he sniffed. "We wish her to live."

"Elaine?"

"Yes."

"But you will kill her if you can," Keith answered, cupping his own glass between his hands instead of tasting its contents.

"I am divided." A shrug. "I will kill for my freedom. But I would rather have it given than take it, Dragon Prince. Surely, you have some influence on the lady—"

"Whiskey," Keith said, "how much strength—how much power in magic—does it take to bind something like you? You are not a little wild thing, a sprite of the rocks or moors, to be bound by what knows your Name. Are you?"

". . . No."

"It would take a great deal of strength, wouldn't it? Not merely skill. Or luck. Raw power."

"Yes," Whiskey answered, and swirled liquor in his glass. "I'll kill her if need be."

"You wouldn't be much of a Faerie if you didn't," Keith answered. "You're not actually offering me fealty in exchange for your freedom."

The water-horse looked up at him and smiled, and tapped one silver-ringed toe on the floor. "If you were in my shoes, wouldn't you?"

"What is she?"

"Her father's daughter," Whiskey said, with a shrug. "And her father is his mother's son."

Matthew's headphones were camouflage. His own internal monologue provided the beat his footsteps syncopated. He ran to get away from magic, not to find portents and hints in the way his Walkman chose to pick up one local station and let another dissolve into static on any given day. If Jane wouldn't have had his hide for it, he would have left his cell phone home as well; instead, he turned the ringer off and made sure the carry case was zipped tight.

His feet sparkled in white, white sneakers, his legs content to be doing what legs were meant to do, over a rolling path with the strength of a body in motion, under yellowing edges of the overreaching leaves. A blur, and he kept just enough awareness to scan through the dusk — not true dark yet — for obstacles and potential enemies. Too cold already for the shorts he was wearing, and too warm yet for sweatpants. Cold wind prickled on sweat, his hair working loose of his ponytail and sticking to his face. His water bottle was halfway empty and he wasn't thinking of Merlin the Magician and her blatant and totally insincere seduction attempt.

He still had three miles to run.

Matthew tripped on the rubber sole of his own running shoe when he saw the unicorn. He recovered, drew up limping, favoring his stubbed toe, and regarded the mythical beast. It stood in the center of the jogging path, tail lashing like an irritated cat's and head raised to stare. No point in being coy with himself about it: there it was, horn like a twisted sword blade glittering steel-blue in the gloom, eyes flatly metallic as the darkening city sky.

The unicorn swung around, lining its body behind that deadly horn. Matthew felt it like a pressure on his skin, how easily the fine-honed point could pierce cloth and flesh and slide past bone. He wondered if he would feel anything at all.

The unicorn pawed the path, hoof glancing off concrete. Matthew raised his hands reflexively, aware of the futility. *Don't flinch. Don't show fear.* Ridiculous to treat a unicorn like a wild animal, of course, but how else? Even if it was no bigger than a whitetail doe. Which wasn't big for a horselike creature, but more than big enough for something with a horn leveled at one's breast.

It snorted, slow coils of steam in the fragile crispness of autumn, and lowered its head. A mane tangled with crumbling willow leaves fell across its eyes; it was white enough to silhouette against the concrete, white enough that even in dusk it was hard to see except in outline.

"The Fae are sending assassins now?" Another jogger swept past him with a curious look and ran right through the body of the unicorn. The unicorn ignored him, rolling both steely eyes at Matthew. "A logical development." *Pity I won't get a chance to warn Jane about it. Of course, my body might be enough to do the trick.* He backed away slowly, one hand outstretched, the other feeling for his phone. At least Jane was on speed dial . . .

The unicorn tossed its mane again, lifted its horn in a gesture like a cat sheathing its claws, ears forward, hooves clattering on the walk. He held his breath and fumbled the zipper on his phone case, failed to get it unfastened before the animal was close enough to touch. The narrow neck came up; he saw the line of its throttle clearly delineated under softly whorled white hair. Its breath smelled of apples and bruised roses, a sharper scent over the goatiness of its skin. The horn *was* steel, not just the color of steel, down to the fine dark tracery of rust like dried blood inside the curve of its spiral. Matthew dropped his hands and clenched his fingers against his rings.

It paused eye to eye with him, only the length of its muzzle away. Its nose was silver, freckled in pink, its ears more deer than horse, and in addition to the snarled beard it had quivering whiskers like a mare's. Matthew held himself still as it brushed them across his face, inquisitive. *It's not a Fae thing, with a horn like that.* A horn that didn't even touch his skin as the unicorn nudged him, gently first and then harder, its nose soft but the shove as hard as if he were straight-armed by a man twice his size. A demand as unsubtle as a dog pushing its nose under its master's hand.

Matthew let his breath trickle between his teeth, realizing only then by the ache that he had been holding it in. "I suppose you would know, at that," he said quietly, and reached up to scratch behind its ear.

It didn't move away.

The flesh was warm and yielded softly over bone. The hair felt coarse and soft and a bit gritty, as if there were sand caught in it. Warm, yes. Solid, and startlingly real where he had expected stuffed-animal softness, or perhaps for his hand to pass through it as had the other jogger. Instead, the unicorn whuffed like a horse, moaned a little, and leaned into his touch, white lashes closing over flat blue eyes.

Matthew swallowed in disbelief, remembering what Carel had asked him about sacrifices. Thinking perhaps a moment like this made everything worthwhile. He stroked its neck with his other hand, leaning closer to breathe the thick animal smell.

A siren cut the moment, and the unicorn startled and shuddered, jumped back, eyes wide now and black in the failing light. It stared at Matthew, snorted, shifting its weight as if it meant to whirl and kick, or lunge forward as it had failed to do before. Footsteps behind him; another runner, he assumed, but didn't turn to check. "Don't go—"

As if his voice were the last straw, it broke, bolted off the path, and was gone. Matthew stood, blinking, the smell of the unicorn on his gritty fingertips. He could have searched for it, stepped off the path and followed.

He finished his run and went home.

The Mebd wore white, a diaphanous gown shot through with strands of silver. She met with Seeker alone in the Queen's offices—and Seeker, laced into court dress, felt bulky and awkward in comparison. She curt-seyed, but the Queen gestured her upright in irritation.

"We are pleased with your progress." She paused, and studied Seeker's face. "Is not your son handsome and well made?"

Seeker could not raise her eyes. "Yes, Your Majesty."

"Stop." The Mebd held up her bone-china hand, palm flat. "If you're to be a member of our family, you will comport yourself as one."

The threads of the binding spun spider-tight around the Seeker, drawing her upright, lifting her chin. She glared at the Mebd, and the Mebd laughed.

"Excellent." The Queen lowered her arm, and the translucent samite drifted across her wrist. "We mean what we say. In addition to all the others you've returned to our court, you've brought us the Merlin and identified the Dragon Prince. And gifted us as well with a claim on him by blood. Even your grandmother could have done no better."

Seeker took a breath, the question burning in her. As much as she hated to ask the Mebd for anything . . . "How are you certain she is my grandmother? My mother—"

The Mebd tossed back the golden ropes of her hair. "Many an other-wise virtuous woman is seduced by an Elf-knight, and your father did not hide his conquests from me. And my husband was a knight among knights. He is much missed; the Devil has cost us dear these many years."

Some more than others, Seeker almost said, but gave it no voice. *And the tithe comes due again.* "Morgan knew all along."

"Why do you think she agreed to teach you?"

"And said nothing."

"She too was a Queen, was Morgan of Cornwall. She understands these things, and knew you came to us unwilling. Knew also the neces-sity of raising you to strength. To which the Daoine Sidhe have in no small measure contributed. What you are, we made you."

"Then you must need me." The words left Seeker wondering at her own arrogance. Was this what the Mebd had commanded her to, in cor-recting her deportment?

The Mebd offered an angled smile, proffered like a chocolate. "Faerie is dying."

"I know."

"Faster than you imagine. Faerie is being killed. The Prometheus Club wishes more than to contain us. They wish to eradicate us."

"I . . . Matthew," Seeker said.

"The apostle?"

"The Mage," Seeker answered, "who tried to stop me from taking Hope. And who has been pursuing our Merlin."

The Mebd inclined a graceful head. "The tithe does not protect us as it once did," she said. "Even Hell is beset. Men do not believe in the Devil anymore. The Dragon Prince . . . Seeker, I believe the Dragon Prince is here for us. For Faerie. And you must bring him to heel, or our kingdom is foredoomed."

"Your Majesty. Would you return to the days when humans lived in fear of us, and marked their houses with salt and iron to keep us at bay?"

"It would be nice, wouldn't it? To come and go as we pleased, to take what we wished when we wished it?" The Mebd's eyes twinkled. She turned away in dismissal. "Sadly, that's unlikely. Go. You know your task. You know the stakes. Go to it, and do not forget you are the grand-daughter of a Queen who made men do her bidding whether they willed it or no."

When Seeker returned to her chambers Keith had gone, and she was torn between anger and gratitude to be able to strip off her gown in peace and anticipate the waiting tub. She didn't know who had drawn it, or scented it with rose petals and peppermint, and she didn't care. The lavishly embroidered gown lay slick on the flagstones; Seeker threw her shift and shoes on top before sliding into the steaming water, her neck relaxing against the scrolled headpiece.

Exhaustion buoyed her like the water, numbing her arms. Her flesh felt wooden. The water was dizzyingly hot, speeding her heartbeat until blood rang in her ears. She slipped lower. Something danced in the shadows, some *otherwise* trace of unease and warning. She reached after it, but it slipped beyond her fingertips, something she could brush but not grasp, slippery as a wet marble — and heat lulled her, pulling the tension from her shoulders. The water on her lips tasted of bath salts and roses. Her head drifted to the side. She sighed; it trailed into a whisper. Almost, Seeker slipped into sleep.

She blinked against exhaustion and gripped the sides of the tub, pulling herself forward on the second try. There was Carel to attend to. She reached blindly for the soap and the rag.

She yelped in shock when a hand brushed hers, dropping the verbena-scented soap into her palm. Her head jerked up and she met Whiskey's crystalline eyes.

"I almost had you that time."

She threw the soap in his face, sinking lower in the water. He caught it before it touched him, and laughed. "It was a good trap, you have to admit. People drown in bathtubs every day."

"Where have you been?"

"Wandering the halls." He set the scented bar on the rack again and began unbuttoning his collar. "You didn't summon me, so after I carried out your instructions I entertained myself. I did see Ian hurrying to the Mebd's quarters halfway through the night, amid mysterious comings and goings. But of course, you were watching *otherwise* and you know that."

She hadn't been. Had been too caught up in Keith and Ian to extend her power. *Careless.* "You're not getting in this tub," she said. He dropped his shirt atop the tangle of her clothing.

"I already am." He splashed the water with his fingertips, a boiled-looking rose petal clinging to his skin. "I thought I'd wash your back, if you permit. Since we're already so intimate."

Hot water swirled between her thighs, over her belly like a hand. She gasped and struck out at him. "Stop that!"

"As you wish. Mistress." Whiskey tossed his head in horsey laughter and picked up the soap. "Lean forward, please."

"I want an oath," she said.

"If you'd waited until my hands were on your throat, you could have claimed it my third attempt."

"If I'd waited, I'd be dead."

A great snort of warm air blew his nostrils wide. He dipped his hands into the bathwater, which shone like black pearls on his skin. "No harm will come to you by my hand today, mistress."

It might have been the leaden weariness deadening her limbs or the released grief deadening her soul, but Seeker nodded and leaned forward, wrapping her arms around her drawn-up knees and laying down her face. His hands were big and warm, but they seemed cool after the water and they were slick with lather as they worked the length of her back. Some of the pain fled before his touch, and more of it vanished when he ran his thumbs along the length of her spine. She let him wash her back and then her hair, clean hot water flowing from his hands to rinse the soapy strands and rewarm what filled the tub. He passed her the soap and she washed her arms while he rinsed the lather from her shoulders. It seemed natural that his hands would slip below the water, brush her waist and encircle her torso. "Whiskey."

"What harm is in it?" he whispered against the wet skin of her neck as he palmed her floating breasts. "Women have come back to me, you know. Ones I let escape. I could show you."

"Why would you let one escape?" she muttered, but her face fell forward as he stroked her with soft palms, rough fingers.

"For the joy in a brave girl." He nuzzled her hair aside and lipped the nape of her neck, pressing against the unyielding wood of the tub. "How long *has* it been, mistress? Just think: I offer what another cannot. I am what I am, and no apologies. I will not lie to you, promise to protect you, take my use of you and leave. I cannot, and you will always have control of me."

The softness of his voice hypnotized. The water caressed her with myriad immaterial fingers, tingling on her skin. She stifled a whimper. *I could make him stop with half a word.* "Until you kill me."

"Doesn't that make it better?" He drew her back against the tub, his hands still gentle on her breasts. She started to pull away, but she didn't command him to stop, and her breath came faster when he resisted her movement, his touches coaxing and soft. "If I'm to serve you," he said, "let me serve you."

What does it harm? she wondered. She leaned back against the unyielding curve of the wood separating his chest from her shoulders. He took up the soap again and lathered her hair a second time, massaging her scalp and letting his fingers trace the outline of her ears. *I'll never have Keith back. Never find a lover I could care about. Not in Annwn. They cannot care for me, none of them, and the one I want I cannot have.*

Whiskey sang in her ear, his voice whiskery and thoughtful, that dangerous tune, "Tam Lin." Seeker basked in his laughter as he sang it, and when he came to the verse about the roses of Carterhaugh, he scooped the limp petals from the tub and stroked them by handfuls along the skin of her neck.

> *"She had not pulled a rose, a rose*
> *A rose, but barely one*
> *When up gat brisk young Tam Lin*
> *Said, 'Lady, let alone.*
> *How dare you pluck a rose, Madame?*
> *How dare you break a wand . . . ?' "*

The Mebd has no soul; she cannot love. Does she go untouched?
She does not.

Despite the heat of the water and the caress of Whiskey's hands, Seeker followed the thread of the song. The water-horse's voice was a baritone, breathy and soft, and did not hold a note well, but Seeker relaxed into his touch as he told her of Tam Lin's seduction of young Janet. And his plea that she save him from his service to the Queen of Faeries, and his inevitable fate as a part of the seven-year's tithe to Hell.

And how Janet went into the cold night and broke in on the Queen's progress, and pulled Tam Lin down from the shoulders of his milk-white steed—Seeker and Whiskey both chuckled, remembering their earlier conversation—and held him through transformations into a mad hound, a viper, a bar of red-hot iron, until the Faerie Queen's magic was exhausted and Tam Lin stood before her wrapped in Janet's own green mantle. And so Janet defeated the Faerie Queen, and was cursed by her, and won Tam Lin away.

> *"Out then spak the Queen of Faeries,*
> *an angry Queen was she,*
> *'Shame betide her ill-far'd face,*
> *and an ill death may she die,*
> *For she's ta'en the bonniest knight*
> *in all my companie.' "*

So the story ended. How the tithe was met that year was not recorded, but it must have *been* met. And the Mebd had learned a thing or two about holding on to men's bodies and souls since.

But even the Queen of Faerie couldn't shake the echoes, the tug of Tam Lin's thread on the pattern of the whole damned tapestry. One never can, when one is made of stories. And as long as Tam Lin was sung, reimagined, or remembered, the Mebd's failures would also be.

The ballads were a true history of Faerie, and a false one. They were true because all stories are true, and false because stories have echoes and interplay and Faerie is the result of the tension between those. The pattern of a tapestry was not the substance of the strands.

But pattern could be manipulated by how the strands were woven — which pulled taut, which brought to the surface, which drawn beneath. And more than one version of a story could be true at once. And moreover, the stories of the past affect the future, and echo and repeat and replay themselves over and over again, in infinite variation, through courage and determination.

It's been so long, Seeker thought. "Only this," she said, "and nothing more."

Whiskey whickered against her neck. Water sloshed in the tub, splattering the flagstones, and her body curved like a bow under its touch, and the touch of its master.

> *"If I had known, if I had known, Tam Lin,*
> *That for a lady you would leave*
> *I would have taken your heart*
> *And put in a heart of stone.*
> *I would have plucked your two gray e'en*
> *And put two wrought from a tree."*

"Shall we sing another?" he asked, long moments later. "She doesn't hate 'Thomas the Rhymer' quite so much. Perhaps 'Scarborough Faire'?"

Seeker sat upright in the sudsy water, wetting the floor further. "Janet was Fae."

"Yes. She always wears green."

"And claims the roses he guards for her own. Wait. It's a true story, Whiskey? That's why the Queen won't hear it."

"The Queen hates losing. And all stories are true."

"But Tam Lin was bound to her."

"He was." He spoke against her neck, letting her feel the pinch of his even white teeth. She floated, still lulled despite wild ideas tickling the back of her mind. Fatigue held her like gray cotton wool, and the water was warm as blood.

"Was he human?"

"As human as you are. Which is to say, human in some part."

"His eyes were gray. He was one of us, you mean. A changeling, this man Thomas. A knight and a bard."

"So it is recorded." She felt him smile against her neck.

"And yet Janet won him free." Seeker knew she was restating the obvious. She was on the verge of something, and didn't know what. Didn't know how to get there from where she was, or from what angle to examine what Whiskey had handed her. She thought about raising her hand, and it barely stirred in the water.

"She will not hear it sung," Whiskey reminded her.

"How did she do it? Janet, I mean."

" 'I fear you go with child. . . .' " he sang softly. "It wouldn't be in the song if it wasn't important. 'She held him fast and feared him not, the father of her child.' And there it is again. She had a greater claim than the Mebd."

Seeker pulled away and stood, water sheeting down her body. She wobbled and caught the edge of the tub. "Help me dress."

He kissed her neck and brought a towel. "You must sleep."

"I must *be* somewhere. I can't leave Carel alone without at least checking on her."

"Mistress. As you wish it."

She stepped out of the water and accepted the clothes he pulled from her wardrobe. He had to steady her so she could drag the trousers on, but she wouldn't meet his gaze. "Be good while I'm gone," she said, and padded away, barefoot, her wet hair darkening the shoulders of her blouse.

She pretended not to hear him humming the chorus to "Scarborough Faire" as the door closed between them.

Chapter Eleven

Matthew paused, key in the lock, as the warmth in his hands gave way to aching cold. His sweat had chilled on his skin, but the stable sweetness of apples and animal lingered like a woman's perfume. He cursed, pulling out his cell phone, kicking the door shut, and hooking his sweat-soaked shorts down with his thumb before toeing off his running shoes. "Jane," he said, when she answered on the first ring. "The wards. I'm rolling."

"On the island?"

"Close," he said. "Just got in from a run; I'm half-naked. Let me drag some pants on and I'm all over it. Can I come by after? I have something I need to tell you." He pinned the phone between his jaw and his shoulder, wrinkling his nose at the reek of his own cold sweat as he yanked jeans on.

"I'm in Albany," she said, muffled against his ear. "I'll meet you, unless you want to come to the penthouse."

His boots were on their sides under the bed. He crouched on the edge and started stuffing his feet inside. "Here is good. If you wanted to pick up takeout—ow!" His hands twinged, hard. "Jane, I have to go. It's a Seeker."

"Go," she said, and he flipped the phone closed and grabbed a sweater off a chairback on his way out the door.

He felt her moving, tasted her sweetness like venomed blood. Traffic was at its worst and he would have to run it, but she was close. So very close.

The coldness was pain like arthritis by the time he shortened his stride in a floodlit alley and checked his hair with both hands, smoothing stray strands and tightening the elastic. Not Elaine, which meant he wouldn't have to explain to Jane how Elaine had slipped through his fingers again.

He curled those fingers tight, tilting his head back, already knowing what he would see. A fire escape, yes, and an open window at the top of it, pale curtains printed with bright cartoon dinosaurs blowing out into the cold, cold night . . . *and pray God we are not too late*, Matthew thought, and crouched, and leapt, the iron of the fire escape gritting under his palms, rasping on his rings. They cut his hands as he chinned himself, rust shaking across his face. Enough iron to keep any Fae at a distance. *Any Fae but a Seeker, that is.*

Matthew got his feet up onto the escape and stood. He couldn't manage the Seekers' trick of moving in profound silence, or Elaine's ability to spread shadowy wings and glide, but he thought he managed the rickety contraption with admirable silence, wishing all the while that he had his camouflage jacket to hang a pass-unseen upon.

Blistered paint slid as he laid a hand on either side of the open window frame and swung his legs up over the sill, not pausing to check the layout of the room. The good news was, Kadiska couldn't step through shadows with the human prey; she had to hunt in the mortal world, and she had to return to Faerie the hard way, through the path under the thorns.

Small mercies, Matthew thought, as his boots scuffed carpet and he came down in a crouch, one hand spidered for balance. *Christ. That's a cradle.*

"Who's been sleeping in my bed?" he asked, rising, his right hand spread to grab. The Seeker was waiting for him in the narrow room, back to the corner between the crib and a single bed with two huddled dark heads. *Shit.*

The Seeker rolled her shoulders, lifting her head on a strong neck. Light trickled through the window along with the cold night air, casting a shadow on the wall behind her. It rose and flared, cobra hood, the sigil on its neck visible as an interference pattern, a curve of lesser darkness. The Seeker hissed, and her shadow hissed with her.

Matthew had attention only for the bundle clutched to her breast. "You'll not pass me. Not with that child, you won't—"

"Matthew Magus. How will you stop me, mortal man?"

He clawed both hands and spread them wide, a wrestler moving for a grip. "Come find out. Here, kitty, kitty—"

The teeth she showed when she laughed were filed to points. "Such a pretty lad," she said. "I remember your brother very well. Good sport in that one."

He stepped back, hesitated, bootheel snagged on the rucked, water-damaged carpet. "Don't talk about him," Matthew said. "You don't deserve to talk about him."

"Good sport indeed," she continued, moving toward him.

The baby in her arms was silent: ensorceled, and there would be a simulacrum left in the crib, a changeling. A fey mockery to die by sunrise, and leave the grieving family to wonder. Crib death. Elf-stroke. *How little we remember.*

"Kelly, wasn't it?" Her shadow towered, from the snake to a shape with tufted ears laid flat, a lynx. Her bare footsteps could not have been more silent. She lowered her arms, showing him the dark beaded skin of her breasts, holding the child to one side. "I remember him."

"You're lying." Matthew moved to block the window. "You will not pass me, Seeker. Not while you hold that mortal child."

"Not mortal," the Seeker answered. A crimson scarf bound her hair back from her face. Tiny mirrors sewn to it flashed when she angled her head. "Not mortal. Mine." She smiled, showing flesh-tearing teeth, and undressed him quite meticulously with her eyes. "Your brother had lovely patterns from his shoulders to his thighs. Very black, on so much white, white skin. Do you have marks like that?"

"I wouldn't show you if I did," Matthew said softly, through the rage that wanted to take the bit and run. "Give me back that child."

"You're all red," she said, a half step closer. He leaned closer, for all he willed himself not to, feeling her power, the serpent's hypnotic romance. Her perfume should have dizzied him, but suddenly all he could smell was the clean animal heat of the unicorn. "Let me lick the rust from your skin, Matthew Magus."

"Birds should know about snakes," he said.

The Seeker smiled. The baby in her arms might have been a corpse, but Matthew heard it breathing: a thin, slow sound like the rattle of a poltergeist's chains. "Snakes know all about birds." She leaned close as if to press her lips to his.

He grabbed her by the chin, one-handed, snatched at cloth with the other and brought a steel-toed boot down hard on her bare, horny foot. She jerked away; he felt the savagery of ice in his fingers, across his palm where the rust pressed between his flesh and hers. Felt the blankets in his left hand slipping and released the Seeker, abandoned the knee-crushing side-kick that would have been his next move. Slipping—

Falling.

In pain and shock, the Seeker hurled the baby at him, and Matthew didn't have a grip on it. Just a brushing contact, fuzzy cloth against his fingertips, and he turned the momentum that would have been a kick into a pratfall, went down hard, striking on the arch of his back. Agony kicked his breath away, a rattle rather than a shout. It didn't matter, because the thing that struck his chest on the way down was the blanket-swaddled infant, and he landed on the bottom, and when he did the child began to scream.

And scream, and scream, and scream.

From the corner of his black-edged vision, he saw the shadows flicker as the Seeker made her exit. Pushed himself painfully over onto both knees and a hand, the motion making him gag as if he'd been kicked in the kidney.

Which I more or less was. Except with a floor. Way to take a fall, Matthew.

Knees, check. Hand down, and sound of a door opening elsewhere. Two bodies in the twin bed awake now and one of them screaming, each of them clinging to the other. Knees, feet, move. He set the baby in the cradle, rust-stain handprints all over the white of the blanket reminding him to chant a quick mantra and blur his fingerprints, his DNA. The infant's scrunched and screaming face was engraved into his memory as —.

gagging on his own pain—he tore apart the changeling construct with iron-ringed hands. *Fire escape. Fire escape. Go, go, go—*

The bedroom door rattled. Matthew dove for the window at a hobble more than a run, leaving the screaming children behind.

By the time Seeker tracked down a page who could show her to Carel's room, the door was standing open, the Merlin reading at a rolltop desk. She looked up when Seeker tapped on the doorframe and nodded her in. The Mebd—or her castellan—had provided a fine, airy room for the Merlin's use. Gray-and-green patterned silk curtains coiled in a light breeze from the open windows; the air was damp with rising mist. The walls were carven to resemble the slender trunks of trees, blending into the arches overhead like the vaults of branches in an open wood.

The Merlin pushed her crackling book aside and stood. "It's been an interesting morning. You look . . ."

"Terrible?"

Concern folded lines between Carel's brows. She caught Seeker by the elbow. "Sit. What happened?"

"No sleep," Seeker answered.

She let Carel guide her to a chair, the warm smell of vanilla following the swing of Carel's braids. After the vanilla came the scent of roses: pouchong tea. Carel wiped out the gray stoneware mug sitting on her desktop and poured from a tea cozy–swaddled pot. She pushed the mug into the other woman's hand. "Don't mind my germs."

"I won't." Seeker pressed the warm, rough-glazed surface against her cheek. The tea smelled of summertime, haymaking and warm winds. "I came to see how you were doing."

Carel shrugged, settling one hip on the edge of the desk. "Strange. Ian—your son, yes?—visited this morning. He told me I could spend months here for every hour going by in the real world. And that I was welcome to stay as long as I liked. He told me more about the politics too. And I'm cramming history."

Ian. Ian stands at the Queen's right hand now. It struck Seeker that she did not know the man her own son had become. *One of us will be the betrayer. He looks seventeen.*

But he is many times that, in the years of Faerie.

"What do you think?" Seeker sipped her tea.

Carel shrugged and gestured around the room, fingers splayed and sweeping. "How can you refuse an offer like that? Look at this place. It's . . ."

"Magic."

"Yes. And then there's that dark-haired singer."

"Cairbre? I thought you liked girls."

"I do. I didn't mean like that. I mean, I could learn something from a musician like that." Her eyes danced. "And Morgan wants to teach me magic."

"Don't forget the ballads," Seeker said, and her geasa wouldn't let her say anything more. She cupped both hands around the mug and swirled, watching the brown fluid sparkle.

"I won't." Her dark eyes met Seeker's, and she chewed her lip. "I dream things now," the Merlin said. "I hear voices."

"Voices?"

"A voice? The Dragon's voice. It's full of . . ."

"Riddles."

"That too," Carel said. "And instructions. I have a lot to learn. I need all the help I can get."

"Seduced by Faerie already, Merlin the Magician?"

"Not everyone who comes to a lover's bed is seduced. Some do it of desire, some are paid cold cash—"

"—some come of their own free will?" Seeker tipped her head, dismissing *that*.

"—some may have agendas of their own, or serve masters who do." Carel's eyes met Seeker's, and Seeker understood as plainly as she understood anything that this was a warning too.

"It's all a chess game," Seeker replied.

The Merlin grinned. "Some prefer poker, you know. Will you tell me about the Dragon Princes?"

Seeker bit her tongue. "Have you heard of Hermann the Cheruscan?"

"Arminius. The German rebel."

"Yes. He was a Dragon Prince. Called Sigurd in the songs. Two thousand years ago, he was the sacrifice. And after him, Arthur Pendragon. Harold Godwinson. Vlad Dracula."

"An . . . interesting list of names." Carel flipped a page of an open book back and forth with her fingertips. "What do they have in common?"

Seeker watched the Merlin carefully, and said, "As with everything *otherwise*, there's more than one story about them: where they come from, what they are. What purpose they serve."

"But?"

They shared a smile. "I always liked Robin's version the best. Better than Morgan's or Cairbre the bard's. Robin says the Dragon Princes come every five hundred years or so. That the first, the Yellow Emperor, Huang Di, cut a deal with the Dragon on behalf of the oppressed, that those enslaved could never be held forever."

"Pretty story."

"No," Seeker said. "It's not. Like all deals with the Dragon, there is a price. Twice in a millennium, a Dragon Prince is born. He is born to death and glory, to madness, to loss, and to eventual sacrifice. If he fails—if he will not serve the debt he is born into in blood—then he pays the price Harold Godwinson paid."

"He was . . ."

"The last English king of England. Elevated to that rank by the deathbed choice of his immediate predecessor Edward, called the Confessor.

"He faced immediate challenges on two fronts: from the Norman William the Bastard, later called William the Conqueror, and from the bloody warlord Harald Hardrada of Norway, whose invasion was supported by Godwinson's brother Tostig."

"His brother?" Carel closed the book she was toying with and frowned. "Nice family."

"Wait for it," Seeker replied. "Godwinson met the Norse at Stamford Bridge on September twenty-fifth, 1066, and was there victorious despite the machinations of his own family. He and his battle-weary men were at their meat on September twenty-eighth, so the ballads record, and so Robin assures me is true, when word came that William the Bastard had landed.

"Godwinson brought his exhausted men nearly three hundred miles in seven days, reaching London on October fifth. They met William's men in battle at Hastings, beside an ancient apple tree, under the banner of the white dragon of England, and it is recorded that they held the field against archers and superior forces 'until the stars shone in the sky.' "

"You mean the Norman conquest."

"Harold failed. Yes. But. If his men had not been weary with traveling the length of England and back to fight Harold's own brother and a foreign lord, who can say what might have happened? As it was—well, sources vary. But Robin says it took three knights and an archer to hack Harold to death on the blood-soaked earth of England's most famous battlefield." Seeker breathed in, sipped the tea, and breathed out again. "Thus the death of a Dragon Prince."

Carel watched intently, her fingers folded under her chin. "You should have been a lecturer."

"I was a TA, actually. And now you're going to ask me what Harold's death had to do with anything."

Carel smiled and said, "So, tell me, Seeker. What did Harold's death have to do with anything?"

"Harold did not spill blood for the Dragon at Stamford Bridge. He was a failed Dragon Prince."

"Blood." Carel said it calmly, but she also swallowed hard when she said it.

"Do I need to tell you about the others?"

"Briefly, I think. What happens when they succeed?"

"They exist to overthrow conquerors. They're warlord and sacrifice in one. There was Hermann, or Sigurd the Dragon Slayer. The dragon he slew was the Roman army; he was a German who served Rome under the name Arminius, and was said to be the finest general of the Western empire.

"But Arminius turned his back on the legion and became once again

Hermann the Cheruscan. He gathered the warring tribes of Germany and organized them in defense of that land. At Teutoburger Wald—despite Hermann's betrayal by his own father-in-law, a rival warlord named Segestes—Hermann so badly humiliated the Roman commander Varus that Varus committed suicide. Then Hermann sacrificed prisoners to Wotan on altars and gallows, until the wood dripped with bodies like ripe, taut apples abandoned to windfall and rot.

"Segestes pleaded with Rome for protection, and gave his daughter, Hermann's pregnant wife, into Roman captivity. There Hermann's son was born, and there he died. Hermann himself drove the Romans from Germanic lands, and died at the hands of his own blood relatives on the field of battle."

Carel had leaned back against the desk, her hip propped, her arms crossed. "Betrayed by a brother?"

"You know," Seeker said, "I'm not sure. But are you beginning to sense a trend?"

"What about Vlad Tsepesh?"

"It was the Germans who called him that. *His* name was Dracula. And you can figure out what *he* sacrificed."

"I've read about the Ottoman Empire. They weren't nice."

"They taught Dracula everything he knew, apparently," Seeker said. "You know Vlad and his brother Radu were held by the Turks as hostages for I can't remember how many years?"

"No," Carel said. "I didn't know that. And Vlad was a Dragon Prince?"

"Maybe the most successful of the lot. Certainly the most enthusiastic. He came to the crown under siege by the Turks and oppressed by Hungarian overlords, killed a lot of people in the most awful ways imaginable, and"—Seeker saluted with her mug—"is remembered as a national hero of Romania, a man who kept his country free in a time of conquest. And who was betrayed and eventually assassinated by that same brother Radu's command."

"Another brother."

"Sometimes it's a son," Seeker said. "Or a wife, or a sister. Or all of those at once."

Carel stilled. "Arthur," she breathed. "*There's* a fairy tale."

"Most likely."

"Can you be a fairy tale and also a Dragon Prince?"

"You can apparently be a whole goddamned bushel basket of fairy tales. It's required. We're all fairy tales together. There is, in fact, nothing to prove Arthur was real. Ard Ri or general, Christian or Pagan, even his name is the subject of scholarly dissent. If he even existed, as some will say he never did."

"I can hear the *but* hanging up there like a great big water balloon," Carel said.

"But I know where Arthur lies. I've combed my fingers through his hair and I've seen the Gwragedd Annwn come down in the moonlight to bathe him and straighten his head on the pillow. I know that his story is true, as are all stories that last that long."

"But he wasn't real."

"Now he was," Seeker said, and handed Carel back the mug. "More?"

Carel poured, watching her hands. "So there's always a sacrifice."

"Always. Or he fails."

"And he fights for the underdog."

"So to speak." Seeker took the cup back and sipped. "The Dragon must be fed. And when the Dragon has supped enough, the final morsel to satiate her is the life of her Prince. Earth the dark mother devours both lover and child."

"My Dragon."

"Your Dragon," Seeker said, harshly. "What you serve."

Carel pushed herself from her perch. She hooked her thumbs in her waistband, eyes cast down at the floor, and paced three or four steps before stopping and turning to stare at Seeker. "We're fucked."

"We're fucked," Seeker confirmed. "Welcome to fairy tales. Have a nice day. Canapé?"

Carel stared at her for a three-count and then burst out laughing, hands pressed to her stomach, whooping and wheezing.

"Well," Carel said, when she had wiped her eyes, "you did say you weren't going to lie."

"Freedom paid in chaos," Seeker said.

"And the sacrifices?"

"Dragons like innocent blood," Seeker said. "Arminius sacrificed camp followers and beardless boys among the Roman soldiers. Dracula tore the breasts and bellies of women with iron pinchers. And Harold refused."

"And Arthur?"

"Children," Seeker said. "Like Herod before him. A generation of baby boys."

"And that's what lies before me? As a . . . servant of your Dragon."

"Not mine. But yes. You. And the father of my son."

A long silence stretched between them, and Seeker thought she wasn't fooling herself when she called it understanding. "I'm here if you need me. I hope . . ." She hesitated, set the mug on the desk. "I hope we'll be friends."

"I know we will," Carel said, and then took a deep breath and leaned forward, as if about to say something else.

Seeker cocked her head, waiting.

The Merlin shook her head. "I need all the friends I can get." She gestured to the book on the desk, and the next words came out an uncomfortable tangle. "Ian said the man I — I drew a sword on? — was the Dragon Prince. That I marked him."

"You're the Merlin," Seeker answered, quietly.

"It seems like a dream, now . . . is that your husband?"

"I'm not married," Seeker said. She reached for the mug, her fingers brushing Carel's hip. The Merlin slid sideways on the desk to give her room. "But he's Ian's father, yes."

"You're not together anymore, then?"

Seeker shook her hair, wet, cold coils moving against her neck. "My job doesn't lend itself to long-term relationships."

"That's a pity."

Is she flirting with me? Carel's dark eyes sparkled. Seeker gestured with the mug. "Sometimes." *She is.*

Something dark and chill moved under Seeker's breastbone — an ancient bleak webwork of magic and compulsion. *I know how to bind her.*

The way to tame a wild thing is not to pursue it, but to make it pursue you. That is the way the Merlins have always been brought to heel. She's a mortal, and can be bound to Faerie by mortal rules, not fey ones . . .

. . . which means she must consent to it.

And that it's better if she never knows she's bound.

And how does one obtain a Merlin's consent? Why, the same way Nimue gained Ambrosius'. The same way Tam Lin gained Janet's, and the Queen of Faerie gained Thomas the Rhymer's.

With a symbol.

With a kiss.

And with the knowledge of how to *do* it came the tightening of Seeker's binding, and the need to see it *done*. Seeker put the tea on the desk and stepped back. "I have things I must accomplish," she said. "Will I see you at dinner?"

"I'd like that," Carel said, and showed her to the door.

Keith found the Queen unattended in her retiring-room, the door propped open to permit the draft that brought him her scent. He took it for a sign. The Mebd was not one to go warded about with courtiers and men-at-arms in her own palace, and Keith knew from old experience that she was open to those who might make so bold as to approach—if they were willing to risk the barbs of her intellect to do it.

He stood in the doorway and watched her head bent over her embroidery hoop, the gray light from the window catching on the white veil over her hair and the silver sliver of her needle dragging violet silk. He did not speak, but stood and thought about the itching wound under the bandage on his neck, waiting for his presence to command her attention. She would have noticed him before he ever came in sight, as he had followed the trace of her scent. At last she looked up, the corners of her eyes crimping, and tucked the needle through the fabric stretched over her hoop.

"Your Highness," she said unexpectedly, and came to her feet gracefully as a length of cloth drawn on a string. "You honor the Daoine Sidhe with your presence, Dragon Prince."

He sighed and pushed the door shut with his heel as he came into the room. "Not you too, Your Majesty."

"Me too?" Polite whimsy, but the look she gave him through her lashes was wryly amused and most unqueenlike. She turned to face him, the folds of her gown falling perfect as flutes on a column, and drifted across the narrow room to stand beside him.

" 'Dragon Prince,' " he quoted, mockingly. "I am Prince of nothing, yet; my father lives, and there are wolves between me and the head of the pack. And I have never wished to be Wolf-Sire. What if I refuse the purple, Your Majesty? What if I refuse to make the sacrifice?"

"Then, like Harold, you fall." Ruthlessly cool, her eyes shifting toward a green as deep and opaque as the sea. "To be the Dragon Prince, you must be warlord of something—the pack will do—and you must spill the blood demanded. Do you suppose everyone who is a King wants to be one?"

"It's how all good fairy tales end," Keith answered, bitterly. The Mebd blinked, lifting her long white skirts in her long white hands.

"Not all," she said. "What seek you of me, Keith MacNeill? Elaine has taken my bargaining chip from me; she has permitted you your son—"

He drew a breath. She was almost as tall as he, and the way she angled her chin up slightly to meet his eyes was more imperious than any downward glance. "And you've claimed him so firmly that if I answer this so-called destiny, Ian will stand as the pack's Sire's son and as the heir to the Daoine Sidhe. You've bound us together one way or another. Unless I refuse to lead."

"In which case we all pay for your weakness. Yes. I've often wondered"—she smoothed her skirts, as if considering—"why is it that the pack's Sire must have a son? If the leadership is not passed by primogeniture."

"The young wolves are the future of the pack," Keith said, watching her eyes. "What's a leader with no future to protect?"

Her eyes gave nothing away, not even a flicker to show if his barb had struck. "Ah."

"So you've got your wish to ally the wolves and the Fae," he continued. "Unless I refuse. And you know I cannot. And I must kill a cousin to be Prince. I do not see what advantage any of this offers the pack, Your Majesty."

"Advantage remains to be determined when the cards are played out," she said. "What is it that *you* want? In trade for your more willing cooperation?"

"That you can give me? Elaine's freedom." He fisted his hands on the cloth of his trousers.

"I will not give you that, but your son is my heir, and that cannot be taken back. It is possible and more than possible that when I pass my bindings to him I will not pass that one."

"Then Elaine dies with you."

"Knots can be cut. Do you love her, Dragon Prince?"

It was the last question he had expected. It struck him almost dumb. He nodded, finally, recollecting himself, and glanced down at his boots. "We do not take it back, when we love."

"Even when you've betrayed your love so carelessly? Never mind" — she interrupted herself — "what is it like?"

"What is it like to be chosen?"

"What is it like to love?"

"Ah." He stepped back until he felt the boards of the door against his spine. "It's not like anything," he answered, and then clarified. "I think it's a choice."

"Most don't seem to think so."

"Most are not wolves."

She nodded judiciously, moving away to pour wine. She offered it to him with her own hands. "A choice to love? Or a choice to keep loving?"

"A choice to keep your soul," he answered. "I know the Fae believe that a thing with no soul cannot love, and a thing with no heart can feel no loyalty. I think instead that if one has a soul, one *must* love." He smiled. "And hope. One must hope, or one is dead."

Her lips twitched at the irony in his tone. "And what do you hope for? With your doom marked on your throat like the bite of a wolf?"

He tried to pin her on a glance, but she slid free with a tilt of her head and a smile—acknowledging the effort, dismissing the effect. "If I am a Dragon Prince," he answered, "then I am already as good as dead. So hope should not matter to me, should it?"

"But it does."

"Yes," he admitted. "It does."

Chapter Twelve

Seeker leaned on figured stone in the shadows of an archway and pressed the palms of her hands to her face. The flesh was still warm from the heat of the tea mug. She shivered nonetheless. *The Faerie host needs humans among it for games of hurling and for fighting,* she remembered. *But Ian's not human. No more human than I.*

No more human than Tam Lin.

I wish I knew my son well enough to know what he was up to. But there are ballads about that too, aren't there? "William my son, where will you go? For your father will kill you when he comes to know . . ."

"Damn it to Hell," she muttered, and braced herself against the wall, fingering through the shadows of the Mebd's palace for a glimpse of her son.

Some rooms were warded against her. One such was the Mebd's bedchamber, and another was her study. The rooms of both Cairbre and Cliodhna were spelled so that she could not see in. Warded, as Seeker warded her own rooms when she wished privacy. Carel's were not, but the Merlin was bent over her desk, reading, and sometimes glancing dreamily at the window or the wall. Ian's was not — but she did not find him there. Seeker cracked her shoulders, stretched, and sought farther afield. Something brushed the edge of her awareness again. She frowned, remembering a similar sensation from the night before. *Kadiska? Here?* Possible.

But then Seeker did find her son, caught a glimpse of his face where the interplay of light and darkness outlined long eyelashes on a tender cheek, and shadows curled in the blue-black hollows of his hair . . . and in the long, dark hair of the girl in his arms, hair which draped over his shoulder to mingle with the black velvet of his cape.

They stood in a niche behind an arras, and if the tapestry had not been disarrayed, no light would have crept in to cast a shadow for Seeker's use. The young woman's face was pressed into the curve of Ian's shoulder. He bent over her, and Seeker felt a tingling shiver of guilty memory as his lips moved against the girl's ear, murmuring something that was more breath than words, then trailing kisses down the side of her neck. She laughed and lifted her head, and Seeker blinked and banged her skull on the archway. The girl was Hope, her loden-green eyes shining with delight as she looked up at her smiling suitor. "I've a lesson," she said. "I'll see you after dinner." And she slipped out of his arms and let her fingers trail down his cheek before she pushed the tapestry aside and danced away.

Ian blushed when, a minute or two after also leaving the hiding place, he saw Seeker coming toward him along the cross-corridor. "Hello," she said. "I was looking for you."

He smiled at her, watching her eyes very carefully. She wondered if she was projecting her own misgiving onto him. His face seemed calm under the faint reddening of his cheeks, his skin as fair as his father's. Seeker felt a fist knotted in the fabric of her heart when she looked at him: the high cheekbones, the porcelain-fine, angled tips of his ears showing through the tangled black curls. *He looks like an Elf-knight.* The gold links of his belt rustled as he shifted from one foot to the other, his father's gesture. *He is.*

"Mother," he said, waving her into step beside him. "Wet hair and barefoot, roaming the halls. You'll catch your death."

"I'm accustomed to the cold." He moved like a young wolf, cocky and confident, his expression impassive. "Has the Mebd been good to you?"

"Like a mother. If she were distant and manipulative."

She hissed; he turned. "I didn't mean it that way."

"Of course not." Seeker forced a smile. "She named you her heir. She must trust you very much."

"I've given her no reason not to. You're not about to enlist me in some conspiracy against her, are you? Because I . . . you, and my father. I've only just gotten you back." Was that worry? She couldn't quite tell, but he stopped walking and turned to face her, lifting his shoulders and chest. "But she's been kind to me. As kind as she can be. Given what she is."

"Heartless as Arthur?"

"She's got a heart," Ian answered, with a funny little laugh. "No soul, but all the heart and heartbreak in the world." His dark curls bobbed as he shook his head. "Mother."

"Yes?"

"What did Arthur do that was so terrible?"

"Oh." She put a hand on his shoulder, stroked the soft cloth of his doublet. *If he were blond, he'd look like Hamlet — the young Prince all in black.* "Why is he bound? There's a similar legend about Vlad Dracula, you know. That he'll come back when Romania needs him."

"I hope I don't live to see that," Ian answered, his right hand dropping to the hilt of his sword. An unconscious gesture, and so automatic it told Seeker volumes about how long he'd worn the blade. *The Mebd has been raising him to this role.* "But Arthur didn't do anything like what Vlad did."

"No." Seeker pulled a tangled handful of damp hair out of her face and tugged it back. "Arthur tried to kill his son."

"Did kill his son."

"Earlier. When Mordred was a newborn babe. Arthur . . . Ian, Merlin Ambrosius told Arthur that his son and Morgan's would be the downfall of Britain and the death of the King. Arthur had already earned Morgan's enmity — whether over politics or over the death of her lover, the legends aren't plain. You could ask her. You might even get a straight answer."

He smiled through lowered lashes. "You're dodging the question."

"Morgan hid her son from him. So he had all the male babies in Cornwall taken from their mothers."

"Ah," Ian said, as if to keep her from saying more.

"And," she finished, pitiless, "set adrift on the sea, Ian. Abandoned.

To drown." *If he's to be a King*, she thought, *let him learn what kinghood costs.* "And they did."

"And that's why he sleeps in Faerie now? In payment for that crime?" His voice didn't quaver. His green eyes were bright with curiosity.

"No," Seeker told him, turning away. "That sacrifice fed the Dragon, you see. It was expected of him. It was the price for Britain's salvation. He sleeps in Faerie now because someone thought they had a use for him."

Jane Andraste took one look at Matthew as he stumbled in the door and ordered him into the bathtub. He went, stripping off his sweater and shirt, and tossed them at the hamper in the hall and missed. Jane, following, stopped him with a hand on his back, a brushing touch that nevertheless made him hiss. "You fell," she said. "You should go to the emergency room."

"I'll be fine," he said, turning to face her. She lifted her chin to look him in the eye. He smiled. "We'll need to set wards on the apartment I was in tonight—"

"You stopped her." Relief, and Jane's eyes seemed to catch more light. She stepped away. "You might have bruised a kidney."

"I'll be *fine*," he insisted, and shut the door so he could strip off his jeans in privacy—even though her interest was about as intimate as a physical therapist's. "She'll be back if we don't ward them, now that she's found them. It's a baby, big family in a little apartment. You know how it is."

"I'll see to it," Jane answered, voice muffled by the door.

Matthew slid the shower door back in a slot that needed oiling, regretting the abruptness of the gesture as he bent painfully to adjust the water. *"Bath,"* she said. "You'll regret it if you don't. I'll fix you a drink."

Her footsteps clicked as she walked away; he dumped shampoo into the tub to make bubbles in self-defense. He knew perfectly well he had no chance at all of keeping her out of the bathroom once he was in the water, but at least the doors were frosted glass. He was in the tub, steaming water and foam lapping at his belly, when she brought him iced grapefruit juice thinned with vodka, along with a half-dozen ibuprofen tablets, which she fed to him two at a time. "Ice when you get out of the tub," she said. "Heating pad tomorrow."

"Yes, Mom." He gulped grapefruit juice, cold enough that the alcohol didn't sting any more than the acid would account for. "Medicinal purposes, right? This isn't mine."

"I have a flask in my purse," she said, flipping the toilet seat down and sitting on the lid, crossed ankles precise under her tailored skirt. She'd kicked her shoes off, and a run was starting over one pedicured toenail.

"Don't get pulled over."

"I never," she said, offended, "drink and drive. Which is why you're drinking my vodka and I'm not, because I have to be back in Albany for nine a.m."

"Ouch. Sorry, rough night to call you down here."

She leaned forward enough to pat him on a soapy shoulder, carefully averting her eyes. The sallow bathroom light turned her hair from iron-and-silver to pewter, and cast haggard shadows down her cheeks. "It's all right. I'll send a team to take care of the warding and guarding on your Faerie child—"

"Not mine," he said. "I'm pretty sure of that. The family's probably a social services candidate, given the neighborhood—"

"That makes it easier."

He shifted in the water to give her the empty glass back, suddenly dizzy with heat, alcohol, and the realization that he hadn't eaten in almost twelve hours. "Jane—"

"No passing out in the tub. I did pick up Chinese, but I don't think you're quite cooked yet."

"Not yet." He slid down in the water, his muscles starting to unknot. "How bad *does* my back look?"

"It's hard to tell under the ink," she answered, leaning back and closing her eyes, holding his glass cradled in interlaced fingers. "You're going to have one heck of a bruise."

"Could be worse." The vodka was making him giddy, and maybe a little brave. "Jane, have you ever seen a unicorn?"

She coughed, abruptly bolt upright and stiff. "A unicorn? I've

glimpsed one, once or twice. I wouldn't try to touch one, personally."
She grinned. "Chastity was never a virtue of mine, if it doesn't horrify
you to hear an old lady say so."

"I saw one today," he said, his fingers curling with the memory of its
warmth. "I—" He looked up. She was leaning forward, elbows on her
knees, intent as a carrion bird. He shivered, despite the heat of the tub.
"In Central Park."

"Did it notice you?"

"It just looked at me," he lied, and changed the subject quickly. "It
was the Unseelie Seeker tonight."

"If it had been Elaine," Jane said in a too-even voice as she stood, "I
would have assumed you would have mentioned it. Is your robe in the
bedroom? You should eat something, I think, and lie down."

"It's in my closet," he said, and she left his glass on the back of the
toilet and walked out of the bathroom.

"On the left-hand side?"

"Mm. Yes. Jane, she said something about Kelly tonight."

"Something you hadn't heard before?"

"She wanted to know if I had the same tattoos," Matthew said, as
Jane poked her head back through the door. "Why would she want to
know that?"

The archmage chewed her lower lip. "To unsettle you? Do you need
a hand out of the tub?"

"I can manage," Matthew said, bracing himself to endure the pain.
"You should—"

"—go warm dinner back up," she agreed. "Yes. Do you want coffee
with that?"

"With *Chinese*?"

Seeker stumbled on the age-smoothed flags of the vaulted corridor, too
tired to lift her foot properly as she rounded the corner. Fire surged the
length of her shin; she toppled against the wall and nursed her stubbed
toe, tears stinging her eyes. A few steps confirmed that it was broken.

At least she could walk on it. And there wasn't much to do for a broken toe except live with it. "Gharne," she muttered.

He was there as if he had always been, dark body warm and soft as suede as he coiled around her neck, rubbing a poison-arrow head against her cheek. "Mistress? Problems?"

"Nothing," she said. She let one hand slide along the wall as she fumbled toward her chambers, somehow got the door open and began fighting with the buttons on her top. Gharne lifted into the air as she gave up on the closures and ripped the shirt over her head, his claws leaving tiny pinpricks behind. As she bent to struggle with the trousers, she noticed that the tub was gone and the floor had been mopped. "Lock the door, Gharne."

He sailed that way, moving like a flying squirrel: weightless, wings unbeating. "You need more rest, mistress."

"I'm going to sleep for a week." Her hair was still wet and tangled as she bent over the bed. Her fingers traced an impression in the neatly tucked bedspread. She wondered how long Whiskey had waited for her. "Don't let anyone wake me unless the world is ending."

"Do you mean that literally?" He slithered between Seeker and the bed and peeled back the covers. She already shivered, a cool draft leaching any lingering warmth from the room. The fire had burned cold.

"Use your judgment," she answered, and let Gharne pull the blankets over her.

Seeker awakened an indeterminate time later in the gray darkness of Annwn. At the edge of her sleep, she thought she heard small, scratchy voices distorted by echoes, but she couldn't make out the words. She opened her eyes on the charred, upside-down silhouette of Gharne perched vulturelike on the headboard, his serpentine neck pulled comfortably between furled wings. She rolled over and propped herself on her elbows, and the perspective righted itself. "When is it?"

"Tomorrow, very early."

"Oh, damn." She sat up, head throbbing with the effects of too much sleep on top of not enough, her toe aching in protest. "Has anyone come?"

"The Kelpie," Gharne said in mild disdain. "The werewolf, and the Mebd's pet—along with that last mortal you stole."

Nobody I wanted to talk to. And that's only half a lie.

"And the Merlin," Gharne continued. "She said not to worry about dinner."

"Damn!" Seeker reached for a robe and stood, the oakleaf-dagged hem fluttering around her ankles. Someone had kindled a fire during the night, so the room was slightly warmer.

Gharne coaxed her to ring for breakfast; brownies brought it when her back was turned, and she never saw them. After jasmine tea and pastry Seeker's headache receded to a tolerable, grasping pressure. The mist had rolled in, but there was no lightening beyond the heavy velvet drapes. Seeker pushed herself to her feet and winced; the nail bed of her toe was purple, the whole thing swollen and sharply painful. She limped to the windows and leaned against the frowning green man carven between them, her left hand splayed over his face as if caressing the muzzle of a friendly dog. In the tangerine light, her olive skin seemed not very different from the golden stone. The pattern of oak on her dressing gown made her feel almost an extension of the carving.

"Gharne," she said after a short while, "do you know any stories of people who could talk to animals?"

"Other than Taliesin and Merlin Ambrosius, you mean?" She thought he was smiling, a mouthful of rose-thorn teeth white against the velvet blackness of his hide.

Seeker clapped her other hand to her forehead. "I'm stupid," she said.

Gharne hopped up on the rust-colored cushions of the window seat. The panes separating Seeker and her familiar from the garden were contained in Gothic arches, clear glass set in filigree of that same golden stone. "Overworked," he answered. "You drank of the well under the hazel tree, same as they did. What's so surprising about being able to talk to animals?" He shook out his wings into her silence. "Where are we going now?"

"To visit a dead man and his sister." She let her hand fall from the green man's cheek and went to dress. Seeker wasn't sure what moved her, but she pulled stout gray trousers and a green tunic with a braided belt out of the cabinet, adding a silver-bladed knife at her hip. She winced as she pulled a boot on over her throbbing toe. "I look like I think I'm Robin Hood," she said wryly, standing before the mirror, twisting her hair back.

Gharne circled her head twice, inertia-less as a shadow, and moved toward the door. He slid through the heavy wood a moment before Seeker closed her hand on the cool irregular amethyst of the knob and pulled it open. He paced her down the palace's endless vining corridors to the garden and outside, into tangled mist and breaking darkness. Wisteria hung heavy over the portico, scenting damp air, and Seeker limped down a white gravel path, her ankles brushed by ferns uncurling as if for spring among others brown and crumbling.

The fog hung thick. She found her way through the moss-dripping boulders, into a narrow crevice and across a lacquered bridge as the first true light of day penetrated the overcast. She felt as if she moved through layers of milky crystal, translucent and illuminated—but the fog burned off by the time she came to the pavilion housing Arthur's bier. She saw its pale struts clearly against the darkness of the open, parklike wood beyond. Something moved on the edge of it: a silhouette, a stag white as a chalk cut, watching her. Then he tossed his head and vanished into the beech trees and ironwood.

Seeker's eyes followed the dozen points on the white hart's antlers; she paused midstep. It was a problem she hadn't considered. The Sluagh—the Wild Hunt—rode no more . . . had not ridden since the Prometheus Club and their minions bound Faerie in iron and oak and copper, in railways, roadways, the spent cartridges of a hundred wars that laid chains across the earth.

In the New World, the greatest wreaking of the Promethean Age had been completed at the moment when a golden spike joined the Union Pacific and the Central Pacific railroads. In Asia, along the course of the Trans-Siberian, across the width of Africa, skirmishes were fought and battles raged. The fey folk witched weather to blizzard and drought, sent the furious ghost-lions of Tsavo and angered the mortal warriors and spirits of the American Southwest, killed workers by the hundreds along the railroad routes. Faerie had magic, and wrath.

Men had iron. John Henry, Paul Bunyan: the folk heroes of the industrial age wielded axes and hammers. Men had once met Faerie on

Faerie's terms: with wits, with music, with Names and knotted hair and riddles told in the dark of the moon.

But men had iron.

Men prevailed.

What mystery there was stepped sideways, slipped elsewhere, ceased to be seen. And was soon enough forgotten, for the lives of men are short. Very short indeed.

And the worst of what was bound was the Sluagh: the Host of the Unquiet Dead, the shades of evil men who rode and fought forever—the hunt that rode at the back of the Horned God, and slew whatever it touched, and slew whatever it saw, and could neither be evaded or appeased. The Sluagh killed like the Elf-stroke, only not so quick and painlessly. Humans still remembered the rides of the Sluagh as plague years, like the unholy darkness that fell over Europe from 1347 to 1350, laying bony hands on Kings and paupers—or like the smallpox in the Americas, the reeking years of death that swept the continent far in advance of Lewis and Clark.

The Host of the Unquiet Dead *could* rise from uneasy slumber and stalk with the thunder again: the Wild Hunt, the Riders on the Storm. If that was the weapon the Mebd intended to use, if Faerie shook off Promethean chains . . .

Seeker shook her head and put her foot down, frowning like a cat. Gharne settled on the rocks with a hiss. "What are you waiting for, mistress?"

"I don't know." She limped forward and climbed three white stone steps into the open pavilion, leaving Gharne behind. Under the eight-cornered roof, the smell of roses lingered. Seeker crossed the floor to the high bier where the sleeping Ard Ri lay, his broad hands crossed over the hilt of a sword that was not his. The Gwragedd Annwn had been and gone; his uncut hair was neatly ordered, the tips blonder than the root. Slow breaths stirred his tidy, gray-shot red beard. *I wonder why they trim the beard and not the hair*, Seeker thought. She reached out and laid her right hand on Arthur's, leaning close to study his face, placid as a sleeping child's.

"What are you dreaming of, Your Majesty?" His breath smelled sweet when it brushed her cheek. There was a fine line between his brows. "I half hope it's nightmares."

And half hope it's not. She shook her head and pulled her hand back, letting it trail down the length of his blade. "What will it take to awaken you? A threat to Britain, they say. Then shouldn't you have been there at Hastings, at Coventry, my lord?" *I'm talking to a dead man. A miraculously preserved corpse. It's glamourie and nothing more. Smell the roses? Odor of sanctity. Smell of sainthood.*

"But you were no saint, were you, my lord?" Seeker yanked her hand back as she carelessly nicked her thumb on the mirror-bright edge of the bronze sword. She examined it and sucked the wound, tasting metal. "Is what I've done so much worse than your own deeds? I think not. I cannot think so."

The ancient warlord breathed in, breathed out, did not stir. She straightened the sword in his grip; her sudden movement had disarrayed it. "So if not Britain, what is it? What can awaken you? Dammit—" Blood welled, and she sucked it off again. The wound stung. "*Dammit.* If I'm Lancelot's granddaughter, Lancelot who did and did not exist . . . I owe you something, don't I? It's not so much that Gwenhwyfar was unfaithful. What woman can resist an Elf-knight, after all?"

Seeker paced back and forth, covering the few short steps from bench to bier and back again. She forgot to favor her foot, her bootheels clattering on the stone. Reminded of Whiskey, she shivered and stopped, stood still with her head cocked as if listening. No sound followed, and she addressed the sleeping king again. "How all the stories contradict themselves. How can you be such a bloody enigma, man? Worse than Robin of Locksley, worse than anybody this side of . . . Joshua ben Joseph. There are *records*, for crying out loud. I can tell you Boadicea's dress size. So how can you be such a cipher? Such a myth."

She leaned over his bower, ran her fingers through the raw, ruddy gold of his hair. "You existed, you did not exist, you were a dozen men with a dozen names, and none of them Arthur. Arthur, the Bear of Britain. You were a warlord, you were a general, you were Ard Ri, a High King. Roman, Saxon, Welsh. From Yorkshire or from Scotland.

Your wife betrayed you with your son, with a rival warlord, with your bravest knight. Your sister is a fey witch, she's a priestess, she's an avatar of the goddess. . . . You had another sister, Anne—a twin, or younger—or you had only yourself and Morgan. Of all of them, all your family and all your kin, the only one who never betrayed you was your foster-brother. Who is remembered now as a braggart and a fool, although that is not how the oldest tales of Cei the Strong, Horsemaster of Camelot, would paint him."

She breathed in, breathed out, bit down on a sigh. "And let's not even get into Gawain, Agravaine, Gareth, and Gaheris. And you're supposed to wake up and save us? When? How, and from what, Dragon Prince?"

Her head snapped up, her bound hair bobbing on her shoulder. "Morgan's tapestry," she said out loud. "The witch never does anything without a reason. A white stag and a black . . ." Knuckles whitened on the edge of the bier. "Surely not the Sluagh. The white stag is the mark of Kings, and the black stag is Cernunnos."

And Cernunnos leads the Hunt. Seeker shivered, and felt her way backward to the bench. *Is that what Arthur's for? The Wild Hunt? Ah, no. Let that stay chained. Please, for the love of everything holy.*

But it wouldn't be beyond him. Arthur, King of Britain . . .

. . . wouldn't be beyond any of the Dragon Princes—the ones who lived long enough to meet their destinies, anyway. Numbly, Seeker stood, and came back a third time to the sleeping King. His lips were slightly parted, his eyelashes bright against the pale weathered skin of his cheek. *Sleeping Beauty,* she thought. *Snow White.*

And impulsively, Seeker leaned down and kissed Arthur Pendragon once, wetly, on the mouth. She tasted roses, pungent as the Merlin's tea, and she tasted her own bittersweet blood, and the fainter sweetness of the sleeping man's saliva. Her tongue slipped into his mouth, and her left hand knocked the slender crown askew; she kissed him with enough force to open his warm, pliant lips and press his slack head back against the feather pillow. His unchanging breath stroked her face. She pulled back a moment later, only a little, to see that his expression had not altered.

"Damn you, Arthur. Wake up, damn you, and do this for me. I can't do it alone." Seeker bit her upper lip and thumped one hand on the edge of the bier. "Dammit. Arthur Pendragon. I need you." *You are a thousand stories, Ard Ri. And all your stories end the same.*

I cannot bear this alone.

I cannot bear this at all.

He never stirred, though she stared at him for long minutes, counting the rise and fall of his chest. And then she smoothed his hair carefully, straightened his crown and his clothing, and left him as she had found him, a frown between his eyes and a trace of enigma bending his smile.

Chapter Thirteen

The Leannan Sidhe was like a gossamer doll. The outlines of Cliodhna's bones showed through skin as translucent as her gown, as translucent as the fog, and her hand on Keith's arm was cool to the touch, like wax. He didn't look at her when she said his name, falling into step beside him on the gravel path. "Your Highness?" she tried again.

"A bit premature, isn't that, my lady?"

She smiled. Needle teeth in his peripheral vision; he didn't turn. "Are you waiting to be crowned?"

"I have no intention of being crowned," Keith answered. He shook her arm off and moved faster, unease prickling the hair on his neck. "All I'm needed for is a figurehead. There is no reason why Fyodor Stephanovich cannot lead the pack—"

"You know what happens when a Dragon Prince refuses the crown."

"Is it anything like what happens when he refuses the sacrifice?" Keith stopped and turned his back to a yew hedge, folding his arms and squaring his shoulders forbiddingly.

Cliodhna stopped well back, taking the hint. She let her own hand hang gracefully against her thighs, raising her chin so the tendrils of her hair that had come loose from her chignon slid across collarbones like wings. "Far worse," she said. "In the past, it has been fate that decided the advance of a Prince, and the men who are sons of the Dragon are not often the sort without ambition . . ."

"I have ambition," Keith answered, when she had let the silence linger too long. "I am simply not the sort who is willing to kill to get it. Especially not to kill a wolf like the Russian wolf."

"So it's the blood that worries you? Keith MacNeill—" She smiled. "Blood is your destiny, my Prince."

"*Your* Prince is the Cat Anna, Cliodhna. Do not taunt me with titles." He scrubbed his hands against his trousers. The tape on his bandaged throat tugged his skin when he glanced down. "In fact, do not taunt me at all. What do you want?"

A tilt of her head invited him to continue walking beside her. He settled himself more firmly on his heels, and she awarded him the point with a faint sigh and a smile. "Add me to the parade of those seeking an alliance, then, Keith. Is that straightforward enough for your wolvish sensibilities?"

"I have that offer from the Mebd already," he said, a chill of premonition stroking his shoulders as if a shadow fell across him. *Like a bone to be chewed.*

"Not like mine," Cliodhna said, and reached up to pull the pins from her hair. It came down over her shoulders in a tumble of black as lusterless as dusty velvet. "The Mebd wishes your influence. And if you are to be a warlord, you must have an army. And if you are to be a Prince, you must have a throne."

"You'll tell me the Cat Anna would come to me as chattel, with no vow of the pack's aid against the Magi *or* the Daoine Sidhe? The Mebd has offered me fealty. What if I accept both?"

She reached out and pressed the jeweled hairpins into his palm, combing her fingers through her hair so that it fell in smoother waves. "I say you nay," she said, with a seashell curve of her lips that showed the edge of those fatal teeth. "I say that if you come to us, my Prince, you will have no need to shed the blood of any wolf to become Prince of the pack. That the armies of the Unseelie host will be yours to command, and you will be our warlord and our Prince in truth as well as courtesy."

Her scent peaked; she held his gaze steadily, daring him to look away. And he did, down at his shoes and the coils of mist that made them seem so different, the premonition crystallizing into prophecy. "This is a marriage proposal."

"Aye, my Prince. Your freedom from blood debt in exchange for your hand for my Queen."

Keith swallowed hard, trying to choke down the all-too-vivid memory of a closing door. At the offer held out to him as if on a gilt salver. At the spectre of hope, of the possibility of preserving Fyodor Stephanovich's life along with his own. The Dragon Prince must rule, and he must make the sacrifice.

Prince. Nowhere does it say Prince of what.

But.

The Unseelie Fae.

"I'll think on it," Keith said, and gave back her jewels.

"Come back to my rooms," Cliodhna said. "I will show you the documents, so your decision may be more informed."

Gharne flew down to Seeker's shoulder and began preening her hair as she emerged from the pavilion.

"I saw the werewolf," he said.

"Here?" Seeker's foot throbbed. The path to Morgan's cottage led through the woods, and Seeker walked toward them.

"With the Leannan Sidhe. The vampire muse."

"Cliodhna." Seeker pressed both hands to her forehead but didn't stop walking. The pain was returning. "Politics," she swore. She ran her hand down Gharne's warm, buttery-soft neck. "I'll ask him about it later. Gharne, follow them for me?"

"Your wish is my command," he answered, and slithered free of her neck, falling into flight. Seeker watched him go. She wanted to walk through the mist-swirled open spaces under the trees and crunch leaf litter under her feet. But she also wanted to find Morgan in time to weasel a better breakfast out of the sorceress—assuming Morgan didn't throw her out on her ear.

She reached through shadows to see if she was observed, pausing so distraction wouldn't trip her down a well. She saw nothing, and sought the dappled shadows under the trees. A moment later, she stepped out

of the rose-scented shade along the north wall of Morgan's cottage and
into watery daylight. Somewhere in the forest a woodpecker sang of
beetled wood; Seeker chuckled at the bird's single-mindedness.

She paused with a hand raised beside the open door, ready to knock,
but—"Come in," Morgan called over the rustle and *thwack* of the loom.
She never looked up.

Seeker stepped across the threshold, waving a greeting to Connla
and Evèr, whose plumed tails murmured on the mat. She stood in silence for a moment, watching Morgan work. A forest glade took shape
under the sorceress' fingers, delicate knotwork showing the outline of a
silver unicorn peering through a fall of tripartite leaves: poison ivy, and
the edge of the unicorn's horn was bright with a rusty stain. Morgan
glanced up and caught the expression on Seeker's face.

"People forget," she said softly, "what the myths were for. I used my
own hair for the bloodstains. Do you like it?"

Seeker nodded and came the last few steps into the room. "Caledfwlch. Where is it?"

Morgan threw back her head, startled into laughter. Cinnamon-
colored strands cascaded over her shoulders. She set her shuttle aside
and stood, dusting off the front of her skirt, still laughing. "Clever girl.
How did you know?"

"You told me you collected swords from vanquished knights."

"Not vanquished, not precisely. But I might be able to lay hands on
this thing," she said. "For a price."

"Don't you owe me something for everything you've concealed from
me . . . Grandmother?"

Morgan stepped between her dogs to swing the kettle over the fire.
"What of the things I've given you?"

Seeker shrugged. "I thought that favor was to your sister."

"I don't do favors for my sisters," Morgan replied. The familiar scent
of her herbs rose from the box beside the fire as she measured. "Have
you broken your fast, Elaine?"

"I could eat," Seeker answered, wondering why she didn't feel the
need to fight the name today. "I need the sword."

"For Ian?"

"For Keith." Seeker pulled the bench out from the wall a few inches and sat down on it. "Or maybe for Arthur. I'm not sure. I'm not sure what happens next."

"War," Morgan said, and walked away from the fireplace. She sliced bread on the table and brought it back to the fire, toasted it while the water boiled and spread it with honey. "Come sit at the table and eat, and we'll talk about swords."

"Swords and dragons." The tea smelled sweeter today, or maybe it was the honey. Seeker took the smooth-grained wooden plate that Morgan handed her.

"You'll bind him, all right." Morgan looked down into her mug as if reading the tea leaves, or perhaps the reflection in the steaming surface. "It's what you're for, and it only matters if you do it witting or in heedlessness. One way, you can accomplish great good, or great evil. Or both—the two often go hand in hand. The other way, you will find only failure: for Keith, for yourself, for your son."

"I want . . ." Seeker took a bite of mealy bread and washed it down with tea. "I want to do what's best. Avert the war, maybe. I want Faerie to exist." It felt strange in her mouth when she said it, but she knew the words were true. "But mortal men . . . my family, Morgan. I had friends."

"I had lovers," Morgan answered. "I had a husband, and I had sons. I had a brother. Don't you understand yet?"

"No," Seeker said, but honesty wouldn't let her leave it there. "I don't want to."

"Learn," the witch said brutally, and stood. "You can have a sword for the taking, but the price is this, Elaine Andraste. One answer, to one question. Whenever and wherever I choose."

"Done," Seeker said, and stuffed the rest of her bread into her mouth. Her fingers were sticky; she dipped them in her tea and rubbed them clean before swallowing the rest.

"Hmph," Morgan grunted. "You make a deal too quickly, girl. But done is done." She turned away, and came back a moment later with the leaf-bladed Celtic sword that she had let Seeker hold before. Seeker put out her hand and hesitated. She glanced over at Evèr and Connla. The male seemed to be dozing, but Seeker swore Evèr winked at her, a doggy grin.

Seeker shook her head and let her hand fall. "No." She turned and walked to the wall, to the tapestry of the white and black harts running as if teamed. "This," she said, her hand hovering alongside the plain-hilted sword in a sheath covered in worn embroidery. "That's Caled-fwlch."

"Excalibur," Morgan said, leaving the other sword beside the empty mugs. "A sword beaten from the iron in a falling star, a meteorite. Do you suppose it's true?"

"All iron comes from stars," Seeker replied, her hand still not quite brushing the hilt of the blade. "It's the last element they can burn before they go nova. Iron's the skeletons of stars, and it's what makes our blood red. I was going to be an astronomer. Ironic, isn't it?" She thought of the tapestry, of the white hart, of the unicorn.

"This one fell farther than most," Morgan said, and took it down from the mud-chinked wall. She slid it from its sheath and let the edge taste air.

The blade was dark and shiny with oil. There was no trace of rust on it, and the edge glittered in the firelight like a shaft of sunlight falling through clouds. Seeker held her breath as Morgan thrust the blade out to her, hilt first. "Well, take it. You bought it."

Seeker shook her head. "Arthur was cautioned to remember," she said, "that the sheath was more valuable than the sword. And you won that away from him first."

Morgan smiled, a sly downward glance, and weighed the limp tapestried sheath on the palm of her hand. "I did, didn't I?" She looked up and tossed her hair over her shoulder. Strands caught on ivory cotton. "Clever girl. Go, then. Take them both. And may the Devil's own luck go with you."

It was the last mow of the season, and Matthew was a city boy at heart. Curved blades effortlessly turned yellowing meadow into a soft greensward that clung to the curves of the hill like a knit dress to a beautiful woman's hip; the sight lightened his heart and his step. The

topnote of cut grass, a clean, organic scent, came to him through the cattle fences as he passed a harvested field and ascended Horsebarn Hill,
pressing a fist against the pain low by his spine.

A road girdled the hill like a belt. Below it and behind him on one
side lay the campus where Carel Bierce worked. On the hill's other
flank, a small broad valley led down to a marsh with a stream running
through it, the grassy bottom dotted with grazing geldings and mares.
Matthew leaned forward, accustomed to walking but not accustomed to
climbing, his calves shaking, wincing with the effort so soon after his
encounter with the Unseelie Seeker. *Work it or it'll stiffen.* It was small
comfort.

A cluster of trees graced the peak of the hill, a few clapboard-sided
houses among them, and as Matthew came over the ridge he could see
a figure so diminished with distance he could have covered her outline
with his pinky nail.

Jane waited for him beside a tangle of brambles: wild roses and black
raspberries, both past their season, and the whole weighted down with
the strangling branches of bittersweet. Scarlet berries and their papery
vermilion casings scattered the dirt road under her hikers; she had broken some branches loose and was twining them into a wreath sized like
a crown, her head bent down and her silver-black hair breathtaking
under the sunlit blue of the autumn sky. She raised her eyes as Matthew
tromped up, fists doubled in the pockets of his camouflage jacket, hair
blowing across his face. "How's your back?"

"It hurts," he admitted. "But not as badly as I expected. What are you
making?"

"A crown for the Summer King." Wryly, and then she raised her
hands to place it on his head. It slipped askew, his straight heavy hair
giving no purchase, and he reached up and steadied it left-handed.

"I've never been crowned before." Matthew tucked his fingers
against his palm and slid his hand back into the warmth of the jacket.
Small twigs prickled Matthew's scalp through his hair; he could smell
the acrid scent of the berries. Starlings and sparrows quarreled over the
ones remaining in the bushes. "I don't suppose it grants me any special
powers?"

"Alas." Jane rubbed cold-chapped hands together and shoved them into the pockets of her coat, lifting her chin to gaze down the hill past barns and fences, to the woods and river bottom below. She was dressed immaculately, even here.

She probably irons her jeans. Matthew's lips twitched, but he kept them closed against the chuckle. "Here?" he asked.

Jane nodded, scuffing the ground with a boot. "This is the place. Or one of them, I should say."

"I only managed to follow the Merlin as far as the bottom of the hill," Matthew reminded. "The moonlight was too bright to cross all that open space without her spotting me."

"Yes," Jane answered, jerking her head at the rosebushes. She crouched and laid her palm flat on the ground as if feeling for a heartbeat. "But this is where the thorn trees are. And yes . . ." She smiled and looked up at Matthew, who grimaced as he titled his head and the wreath slipped down over his eye.

He dropped to one knee beside her. "Yes?"

"You did well." She fumbled in the pocket of her tan suede jacket and came up with a handspan-long iron spike and a red-handled pocketknife.

"Now what?"

"Now we bind the mound. Give me your hand, Matthew." She opened the knife and balanced the spike against her knee.

Matthew looked at her, his eyebrows drawing together as he frowned. "That's a knife in your hand, Jane."

She grinned up at him. " 'Scared of a little fire, Scarecrow?' I need enough blood to wet the metal. Just a prick."

Matthew kept his hands folded in his pockets. "Are you calling me a prick?"

"Perish the thought. Here." She folded the knife open and held it out to him, handle first. "Make the cut yourself."

He took the knife, red plastic handle slightly sticky from the heat of her palm, and eyed it dubiously. "What do we hope to accomplish with this?"

"Blood and iron," she said, polishing the iron spike on her spotless

blue jeans. "We spike the Faerie mounds, weaken the connection between our world and theirs. Enough times, enough passageways—"

"And we'll cut them loose. What about the children, then?"

"I think we'll weaken them enough to go kick their asses first, and
then go in and get the changelings. Are you going to bleed for us or not,
Matthew?"

He weighed the knife in his palm, used the heel of his hand to push
the ridiculous, flopping wreath back up on his head, and stroked the
blade across his thumb. "Blood."

"Just a little. Then I'll seal the spike into the hill."

"Hmmm." But he set the rounded point of the blade against his skin
and drew it toward his wrist, slicing rather than pressing. Skin cuts better than it punctures. "Very well," he said, hiding the pain as shiny dark
fluid welled around the blade. "There. Just a little, then," Matthew said,
holding the railroad spike out to Jane. The shallow cut on his palm, bi-
secting the mound of Mars, was already crusting. "Enough blood, archmage?"

"Blood enough," Jane said, and set the tip of the spike against the
root of the white oak they crouched beneath. "There's a mallet in my
pack," she said, gesturing to a bag he hadn't noticed, tossed on a pile of
leaves. "Hand it to me."

When she struck the first blow, Matthew felt the earth under his feet
shiver, as if the tree were curling its roots deep down, like the fingers of
a man in pain.

Seeker watched from the shadows, Gharne draped across her feet,
heavy as a hunting dog, but the door to Cliodhna's chamber stayed in-
exorably closed. "I suppose it's too much to hope that he climbed out the
window?" Seeker's physical self was curled on a divan in a small niche
library down the corridor from the Unseelie emissary's room, the heavy
weight of a bronze-and-copper-hilted sword depending from her belt at
an angle, the tip of its scabbard resting on the floor. She held an ignored
book in one hand. The other lay against the sheath, but she couldn't feel
the burn of cold iron through it.

Gharne mumbled something, but didn't lift his head. Seeker wiggled her boot under his jaw. She'd taped her toe, and the pain had subsided to twinges and aches. "Gharne, would you find the Kelpie for me?"

He sighed. "If I had known you would be this much trouble, I never would have tried to eat you all those years ago."

"Pity," Seeker said. "I would have missed the company. Come find me once you know what he's about. I suspect there won't be much rest for either of us from here on in."

He rose into the air and passed through the nearest wall. Seeker thought she heard a brownie chambermaid shout in surprise as he glided through the corridor beyond. A few minutes later, her *otherwise* eyes showed her the door of Cliodhna's room opening, and a tired-eyed Keith came out. "I'll think on it," he said back into the room.

The Leannan Sidhe stood framed in the doorway, backlit from the windows behind her, clad in a different but equally diaphanous robe. Seeker flinched at the casual way she laid a hand on Keith's arm before he turned away. "Think hard."

He nodded, the corners of his mouth turning down. Rooms away, Seeker thought about stepping through the shadows, taking his arm and dragging him away from the fey, soul-killing muse. The Leannan Sidhe pressed against his arm, but he kept his gaze on her eyes. Seeker sighed in relief, and remembered Whiskey, and cursed herself. And then she caressed the smooth-worn ancient pommel of the sword called Excalibur, and shook her head. She still trusted him. Foolish, reckless, and possibly stupid. But she trusted Keith MacNeill, Dragon Prince, a man doomed to bloodstained life and a bloodier death.

He extricated himself from the Leannan Sidhe and prowled in the other direction. She thought of intercepting him, stepping from the shadows to catch his sleeve, but she was more interested, suddenly, in what he might do. A cat-shadow stretched on the floor behind her and she forced a breath that came out like a hiss. Her footsteps silent, she left the library and paced the hall, following the corridor away from Cliodhna's room until she came to a cross-passage.

She turned left, parallel to Keith and a few dozen yards behind, letting *otherwise* sight tell her where he was. He paused by the door to Seeker's room, but she did not permit her stride to falter, even when he raised his hand to knock. Other Fae were in the corridor, so Seeker kept her expression distant and aloof, suitable to the Queen's servant. The Queen's grandniece. One or two of them looked askance at the sword, but none showed recognition, or any aversion to the presence of cold iron.

I bet that would change if I drew it, Seeker thought. Not too far away, Keith lowered his hand before it could touch the door panel and continued on his way. He turned down a side corridor, counting doors, and this time he didn't pause before he raised his hand and rapped sharply. *Carel's door,* Seeker thought, as the Merlin opened it and blinked up at the werewolf.

"Hello," he said mildly. "You nearly cut my head off. I thought we should talk, if you were feeling better."

"By all means," she said. "Come in. I suppose I owe you an apology, but you did leave bloody handprints on my clothes."

"I'm told to expect that," he said, as Carel grasped the heavy door behind him. Seeker stepped into a dark corner of the corridor and out of the tapestry-shadowed wall behind Keith.

"Boo."

Carel jumped, the door slipping from her fingers to close with a bang. Keith spun, half-crouched and reaching for the collar of his shirt as if he meant to tear it off. And then rocked backward, a strained laugh sliding out of his mouth. "I'm glad you're here," he said.

Carel leaned on the doorknob. "You walked out of the wall."

"She does that," Keith replied. "She's a Seeker. A shadowmaster." He was looking at her, looking into her eyes. *The way he did the Leannan Sidhe,* Seeker thought, but he hadn't been smiling faintly when he looked at the Unseelie woman. *He likes to see me using my power. Who would have thought of that?*

And then came a voice that was not the voice of her conscience. A vast, old voice that touched her nerves like honey and acid. *He loves you, Elaine Andraste. You are the mother of his son.*

Mist?

"She wants us," Keith said, breaking the settled silence. "She wants us now."

Seeker nodded, and Carel glanced between them, shaking her head so slightly it could have been a tremble. "Where?"

"Put your boots on. Follow me."

Carel studied Seeker's face as she had earlier studied the pages of her book; Seeker kept her expression serene. And when Carel nodded and crouched to fish around in the wardrobe, Seeker reached out, as if unconsciously, and squeezed Keith's hand.

He didn't react for a moment, and then, slowly, he squeezed back. Carel sat down on the edge of the bed; Seeker caught Keith's eye and smiled slightly before she stepped away, kneeling to help the Merlin lace her boots.

Heartsick, Seeker led her charges from the palace and down the river to that shallow ravine at the base of the down. Distances were strange in Faerie, and it could have taken an hour or a day to walk it. The path led them through a butterfly-filled wood, over a moss-covered log laid across the stream — seeming first to be there, to be not, to be nothing but the blade of a sword laid edgewise — and, at the last, left them hopping from rock to rock like children.

"If I didn't know better," Carel said when they paused for breath, "I'd think things changed here from moment to moment."

"They do," Seeker answered. "That's one of the reasons why it's so easy to get lost." She caught herself humming and frowned. "There, under the vines. That's where we're going."

"It looks like a cave."

"A bit more than a cave," Keith interjected. "Well, we'll see soon enough." The strain in his voice drew Seeker's attention. His face was paler even than usual and it wasn't only from the grayness of the light; a fine layer of sweat shimmered on his forehead. He rubbed his hands together as if they hurt.

Carel noticed too. "What's wrong?"

He blinked. "Don't you feel it?"

"No."

He shrugged. "It kind of . . . aches . . . to be here. Let's get it over with." He slogged forward, his boots sucking in the streambank muck, and lifted the vines hanging over the cave mouth. Carel followed without a word and Seeker brought up the rear, still fondling the hilt of the sword at her hip. The cool, deadly weight comforted her.

Keith led them through the tunnels in darkness, Seeker guiding Carel with one hand on her shoulder so that the Merlin would not fall. Warm and humid air coiled about them: tasting, reckoning, remembering. "Mist?" Carel said again, softly.

Words failed. "You'll see."

The glow greeted them before they came in sight of the Dragon's lair. Keith stumbled. Seeker stepped around Carel, owlsight serving her now that the darkness was imperfect, and gripped his forearm. He leaned on her like a drunken man, fevered through the cloth of his shirt. Carel's footsteps came close behind, echoing, and the Merlin must now be able to see them as silhouettes against the crimson glow lighting the fog. *I'm not supposed to be here.* But she had to be. She tasted a droplet of sweat when Keith shook his head like a wet dog, staggering; she held him up by main strength.

The heat was dizzying; she didn't remember it being so bad. Carel grabbed Keith's other elbow. "Is this normal?"

Seeker shook her head, wondering if Carel could even see the gesture in the red-lit darkness. "I don't know. It's been five hundred years since the last time."

"The last time? Dracula? Oh. Hell."

"Yes."

"Blood," Keith said, clearly. And then they rounded the corner into the searing brightness of the tunnel overlooking Mist's chamber.

Keith went to his knees. Seeker bent over him. "Get up, get up!" Dragging at his arm. "Get up, dammit!"

Carel let go of his left hand. He pushed at the vine-traced floor feebly. "It wasn't this bad in the dream."

"This is it," Seeker said. "She's chosen. You're it. Refuse, show weakness, and she eats you, or worse, casts you out to fail. So let's do this thing."

And then Mist's massive, shifting laughter boomed through the cavern, and her great opalescent eye blinked lazily in the opening of the tunnel—*occluding* the opening of the tunnel. "Indeed, Elaine Andraste,

Seeker of the Daoine Sidhe," the Dragon whispered. "Let us do this thing. Come unto me."

"It hurts," Keith said.

"So does being born," the Dragon answered. "Carel Bierce, Merlin and musician, scientist and seer. Clever of you, my lady, to study so deeply the secrets of the earth. Did you never suspect that the very bones of the earth lay under your skin? No? Come unto me."

The Merlin moved forward, not shuffling but striding crisply, moving as if under the force of a command. Her footsteps carried her to where the passageway widened to cavern, almost within touching distance of the boulderlike head, before she stopped and put one hand out to brace herself against the wall. Seeker squinted her eyes to hurting, trying to look at Carel's form stark against the black-bright glare of the Dragon. "No," the Merlin said, quite clearly, and slammed her fist into the wall. "No. I'm not a puppet. I don't care what you are. I'm not a puppet."

Mist reared back, a violent hiss spraying droplets of flame from red-lipped nostrils. Wings unfurled the width of her echoing chamber and hot gold hailed from scrabbling talons. "Who are you to deny me?"

"Merlin," Carel said, her head swaying dangerously. "And born to master you. So don't give me any shit, Mist. You may live in my head, but I live in yours too, and this initiation is going where I say it goes. I don't know what you got away with before, but I am not going to let you be pushing me around."

Seeker's fingers felt numb at the ends of her hands. Somehow, she kept her hold on Keith's arm and helped him get one hand and one foot down and force himself to his feet. Blood streamed down his face from his nose, from the corners of his eyes. He spat blood on the stones and it sizzled there. His hands left red smears on Seeker's green tunic as she led him forward, into the gale of Mist's dark, chaotic laughter.

"And you, Dragon Prince?" Her head ducked, darted like a hungry pike, showed a smile fanged in stalactites—impossibly fast for something her size. "Do you deny me too?"

He shook his head. "She's the will," he said, waving a bloodstained hand at Carel. "I'm the hand, I guess." He stepped away from Seeker, although she held the hem of his shirt as if she could prevent his going. "You've got me looking the part. Blood and more blood. Is that all there is?"

"Blood makes the grass grow," Mist hissed, her forked tongue a lightning bolt caressing Keith's bloody face to leave a streak behind. He didn't flinch any more than he had when Carel leveled the sword at his throat. "Choose your battle well, *drighten*. Choose well your sacrifice. Choose your betrayer."

Keith opened his mouth, and Seeker—shivering in fear, her hand tight on the hilt of Caledfwlch—Seeker stepped in front of him. He dropped a hand on her shoulder, as if to push her aside, and Carel turned back to them with eyes, opal-bright as Mist's, wide in shock. "Damn you, Dragon," Seeker said, shrugging Keith's hand away. "No. He's mine. Father of my son, and I claim him. You cannot have him."

"I cannot?" The Dragon winked, amused. "Father of your son, you say, and it is a rightful claim. And how will you stop him from carrying out his destiny, when he was born to stride the earth as the Dragon does, to bring me the blood that is rightfully mine?"

"I can't." Seeker shook her head. Carel smiled farther down the corridor, her teeth dazzling white in the gloom, a low laugh bubbling in her throat. "I can't, because he'll do what the stories demand. Spirals, it's all spirals, and I know it."

The Dragon lowered her head. "Will you marry him?"

"I will." *Unless the Mebd countermands it.*

A long silence, as if Mist considered. "It is not enough. I'll not be subject. Your claim is fair, but my claim is older, and written on the stone the world was forged upon."

Seeker smiled then, and unsheathed the sword. "I have a second reason." Mist lunged at her, the great head narrowing as it drove into the passageway. Carel squealed, throwing herself against the wall, her hands spread flat as the Dragon's muzzle hammered past like a freight train a finger's breadth away. Seeker laughed, and didn't step aside; Caledfwlch felt light as a bee sting in her hand and it was Mist who drew back, blood running like magma down a slash from the top of one nostril diagonally across her face to split her lip.

The Dragon hissed, spraying blood like smoking jewels into the tunnel. "Caledfwlch. Two reasons," she said. "I'll have that sword for my horde in a moment, though."

"I think not," Seeker answered. *Keith. Carel. Forgive me.* "I gave you two reasons."

"Have you the third?"

Morgan, I hope I'm guessing right about what you gave me, all those years ago. Four things you told me never to forget, no matter what, and I remembered them all.

"Yes," Seeker said, and—too softly for Keith or Carel to hear over the rasp of the monster's breathing—Named the Mother of Dragons to her face. "Maat." *Thank you, Morgan.*

And slowly, slow as a glacier retreating, slow as stone worn down by water, Mist nodded her acquiescence to that Name and, folding her wings, lay down upon her bed of gold. Seeker sheathed Caledfwlch and turned her back on the Dragon, dropping to one knee before Keith. She unhooked the blade from her braided belt and held it up to him, hilt first.

"Your Majesty. This is yours now."

He took it, bemused, and drew the blade a handspan from the sheath, watching it glitter in the dragonlight. "Marry me?" he said over its edge.

"So it seems."

"Did you bind her?" A toss of his head over his shoulder, and Seeker shook her head.

"No. She can't be bound that way. I—I proved myself, I think. I wasn't supposed to be here. It was supposed to be you and Carel . . ."

Keith nodded. He looked down, swallowed, wiped blood from his face and tested the edge of his sword on a thumbnail. "You changed the equation."

"I don't know what I did," she admitted, struggling to her feet. "But I never want to have to do anything like it again."

"This is only the beginning." Carel's voice, soft with the certainty of prophecy. "There is blood upon blood to come."

——ᴇ Chapter Fourteen

Keith walked Seeker to her room. She stopped him with a raised palm, turning to look at him as she touched the cool stone of her doorknob. "You can't trust me," she said.

"I know." He arched his eyebrow and smiled out of the left side of his mouth. She bit her lip against the pain. "Do you think that ever stopped Arthur from loving Guenevere?"

"Arthur didn't exist."

"Now he does." He reached out and brushed a strand of hair that had escaped her hasty braid away from her cheek, tucking it carefully behind her ear. His fingers lingered. "And if I can't trust you . . . well, whose fault is that, but mine?"

She didn't have an answer for that. Didn't have an answer when he tilted her chin up and looked her in the eye. "If I were going to get over you, Elaine, I would have done it by now."

"Do you think Janet ever got mad at the balladeer?"

"Janet won," he reminded her, and kissed her on the mouth before she could say anything more. He pressed her against the door and nuzzled the side of her throat, holding her face cupped gently between his hands. " 'She'll shape me in your arms, my love / to a woodland beast sae wild,' " he sang under his breath.

"But hold me fast and fear me not," she thought, *"the father to your child." What is it with men singing me "Tam Lin"?* She put a hand on his chest, ready to push him away. She thought about the sulfur-tinted breath of

dragons, and the seaweed smell of the Kelpie. *At least tonight you can have the fantasy.* She pushed him back enough to catch her breath, although it took all the concentration she could muster. "When's the full moon, Keith?"

"Three weeks," he said. "Waning from full, now. You used to know."

"I used to be somebody you could turn your back on."

"I'll take my chances," he said. "I'll steal you back from the Faeries. Like Orfeo. 'What shall I give you for your play? / Pray, let me take my lady away.' "

"You were the one who gave me to the damned Faeries in the first place. After you realized I was a changeling. When I didn't know a thing about it. Because you didn't want to watch me grow old and die, remember?"

"I remember," he said. "I live with it."

I'll lie to you, Keith, she wanted to say. *I'll use it against you. I'll wrap you around my fingers and I'll make you serve the wishes of my Queen. Even if she pretends to bend a knee to you. Even if she names you sovereign.* But the geasa commanded, and with a sigh, she surrendered to it and twined her fingers in his hair. "We all know those songs."

"We hear them sung enough." He whispered against her skin, "You're not Guenevere. And I'm not Arthur. Unlock the damned door, Elaine."

We're doomed one way or the other, she thought, and did as she was told.

Matthew twisted the iron ring on his wedding finger and folded his arms over his chest, waiting. The earth under his shoulders was cool, soothing to his still-sore lower back, new-mown grass tickling the nape of his neck, the ground soft when he pressed his shoulders into the hollow. "Set the ward and watch it," Jane had said.

And he could have watched from one of the fast-food joints that ringed the campus—a little island of suburban consumerism in the midst of a rural society of dairy farms and hardware stores ranged along state highways—but the sun was warm and the sky was blue. He'd entertained himself by wandering the campus, reading the plaques screwed into the bark of various botanical specimens and the tidy signs posted beside the geological ones, and had finally settled down here. Surely the Merlin would return before too much longer. He'd checked her class schedule, and her first section of the week was at one that afternoon.

She didn't seem the sort to abandon her students, although Matthew admitted that first impressions were misleading. And he was himself absent from Monday classes currently—*A college education will do no one any good if the world ends while we are engaged in the classroom,* though that did nothing to assuage his guilt—but still. He thought she'd be along. And so he closed his eyes and attuned his senses to the iron spike linked to his blood that he and Jane had driven into Horsebarn Hill.

Power ran thickly here, and many things clustered around it, huddling close. Matthew felt them moving, tracking them by their ripples like trout beneath a stream. He opened his eyes as he sat up, distracted momentarily by the vermilion-and-brown flicker of a cardinal shedding its summer plumage for winter. Someone coughed behind him, and Matthew shook his head and sighed. "I suppose you won't believe I let you get the drop on me intentionally?"

Carel's voice had an amused burr. "You can pretend I believe that, if it makes you feel better."

"It might." He rolled forward in one smooth motion, finding his feet, the heels of his boots leaving indentations in the greensward. "Take a lot of chemicals to make a lawn this green."

"Or a lot of bullshit," Carel answered, pushing her braids behind her ear. She carried the same suede backpack, but today she wore faded blue jeans and a velour turtleneck with a patchwork vest unbuttoned over it. Always the gypsy colors and swing of fabric. "Here in academia, we have both. I take it you were looking for me?"

"Indubitably. You have a class. May I walk with you?" He laid a hand on her elbow; she shrugged, but didn't shake it off.

"You're here to persuade me again."

"I was going to ask how you slipped past my ward without me feeling it, when you came back from Faerie. But if you wish to be persuaded . . ." Matthew shrugged in his turn. "You know what the Fae are. You know what the Fae do. What more do you need?"

"And the Prometheus Club is innocent in its power?"

"I never said that. But we're trying to protect—" His bruises reminded him of exactly what it was he meant to protect.

"Have you ever been married, Matthew?" Unexpected and abrupt. She finally looked up at him as she said it, her expression arch and concentrated.

". . . um? No." He shook his head, then pushed escaping locks of hair out of his eyes. "I haven't been married."

"Neither have I," she said, her sternness melting into a conspiratorial grin as she stepped onto the path. "But a friend told me that in a good marriage, nobody wins."

Matthew frowned, nibbling his thumbnail, noticing she'd sidestepped his question about the wards quite neatly. "I'm not sure I understand what you mean."

"A marriage is a state of dynamic tension. It works as long as nobody gets the upper hand and keeps it." She leaned forward as they came up the hill toward Beach Hall, walking faster, digging in. She wore black Chinese slippers that made leaflike scuffing sounds on the cement of the sidewalk.

"And?" The tall Gothic doors of the big gray building opened and closed as students passed through them. Carel paused at the base of the stairs; Matthew hesitated one step up, turning back so he could see her face. "And, Carel?"

"And you're in danger of winning," she said, and walked up the stairs. He turned to pace her; she pinned him at the door to the hall with a single level glance.

She is the sorcerer, and this is her tower. I cannot pass within without passing into her power. He stopped, his boot just shy of the threshold, blocking the door that the Merlin held open while students continued to pass through the other side. "This isn't a partnership," he said. "The Fae are parasites. They have the morality of a tapeworm."

"A medieval man might have said they have the morality of a wolf," Carel answered, something resonant in her voice. "Rapacious and cunning, and taking what they wish when they wish it, unless they can be made to fear. But *we* know more of wolves than that cold shepherd watching his flock, do we not?"

"It's hardly the same thing—"

"One cannot have safety without eliminating risk," the Merlin answered. "Sheep are pretty dull, Matthew. Is your sympathy with the lion or with the lamb?"

That drew him up short. "Can it be with both?"

She smiled, and tilted her head to one side, speaking over her shoulder as she let the door swing closed between them. "When the lamb must die for the lion to live? That, Matthew Magus, is what I am trying to find out."

Seeker lay awake in the light of a single candle, her awareness flitting from shadow to shadow *otherwise* through the darkened palace. Keith's arm lay across her waist, his breathing heavy and even against her neck. She smelled the blood from his wound and tears stung her unblinking eyes, while she riffled shadows like a pack of cards. She wasn't sure what she sought, and the palace wasn't silent at night, or even restful; a whole nocturnal kingdom sprang to life when the candles were doused and the curtains drawn.

From shadow to shadow she followed the sound of music: a great standing harp, played softly; a falling rill of notes like water, sad and slow; and a woman's voice. *Hope*, she thought, picking out the words. " 'Fain would I be / in my ain country. . . .' "

Half knowing what she would see, Seeker peered through shadows and found the room where the apprentice bard sat, clad only in the long rippled tumble of her own midnight hair, a lone candle burning beside her. Ian lay propped on his belly just a few feet away, once-crisp white sheets tangling his legs, watching her play.

Candlelight played across his shoulders, muscled with sword practice, and the hard little dimples on the back of his arms . . . and the fine white scars that laced his skin here and there. He stood and crossed the room to his lover, picked up her hair in both hands and rubbed his face along the length while she sang to him and smiled.

Ian covered Hope's hands with his own and stilled them on the strings—covered her lips with his own and hushed her voice before he led her back to the bed. Seeker closed her eyes and let shadows fall before her like the velvet draperies concealing the Mebd's throne.

She pressed her face against Keith's shoulder. Distantly, to her surprise, she heard a rumble of thunder. He murmured in his sleep, or perhaps it was a growl, and pulled her into the curve of his body. She closed her eyes and listened to the sound of his breathing, felt the warmth of his breath stirring her hair. He woke before sunrise and kissed her, seeming surprised to find her awake.

"Leaving me?"

"In a little. Not because I want to," he murmured, and tasted her shoulder. "But it might be better if people thought they could play us off against each other. We need every advantage we can get."

"Keith . . ." He was warm, and he smelled of sweat and faintly of brimstone and cold rain.

His hand cupped her breast; he brushed the backs of his fingers down her jaw, across her lips, as if feeling her breath when she spoke. "I'd forgotten how soft your skin was," he said.

"You keep talking like we're in this together."

"If not us, then who?"

She couldn't sleep after he left, either. Instead, she wrapped the belt of her dressing gown tight, poured herself a glass of whiskey—pretending it was late at night and not early in the morning—and tossed another log on the embers of the fire before settling against the soft brocade of her wing chair to watch the flames consume it. Oak, this time, to burn pale and long. Her feet were not quite warm through when a scratching at the window roused her.

She stood and set her glass aside, picking her way across the room to push the draperies back. Rain streaked the glass and doused the dark shape beyond it, and she wondered. She swung the window open.

"When was the last time it rained in Faerie?" Whiskey asked her. "Come with me and feel it on your skin."

She leaned out the casement and let the rain fall on the back of her neck, cold as a Kelpie's heart. "Uisgebaugh. Out on such a night," she said.

"You smell of whiskey," he said. "There's something poetic in that." He leaned forward, as if to kiss her face.

"Stop."

And he stopped, frozen in place as if pinned. "Does he know you're using him?"

"Yes," she said. "As surely as Tam Lin used Janet. She got what she wanted in the end, though, didn't she?"

"She got what she deserved." He made a dismissive gesture with one shovel-sized hand, the silver on his thumb glittering wet in the darkness. "Your werewolf might have claim enough on you to break the binding. But he's not strong enough, is he? Not as strong as the Mebd."

"He's the Dragon Prince. If not him, who is?"

"You are," Whiskey said. "I am. But I'm Tuatha de Danaan. Full-Fae, and not only am I bound to you . . . but only someone with a soul could lay claim of love on you."

"Alas," she said, mocking. "One less reason to free you."

"One more," he said. "I'd make a better ally than I do a slave, my lady."

"An ally like Cliodhna. I don't need those."

"Come out into the rain."

"Come into your power, you mean."

"Careless woman. No, I'm saving that for if I need it. I'd rather have my freedom given than take it."

"Why?" Something rose up in her, unbidden. A memory. *You go to judgment with what you are born with and what you have earned, less what you have given away.* "It's worth something to you, freedom given rather than taken at the price of my life. It's worth something rare, isn't it?"

He snorted, blowing raindrops from his lip. "It is," he said unwillingly.

She looked him in the eye. "What?" she demanded.

He shook coarse dark hair and pawed the earth. "The tithe," he answered, the words dragged from him by the force of her command. "Free me, of your own will, and I cannot be chosen."

"Is that a danger?"

"Lady," he said, "your own father went to pay that toll. A willing sacrifice is worth more than one unwilling. But still. Have you not asked your-self why so few of the full-Fae remain, and why so few of their children?"

"The palace stands all but empty," she said. "Isn't there a way out of it? If it's destroying Faerie?"

"The bargain was made long ago," he answered. "It was meant to protect us, when the new religion came and the old gods were under at-tack. Mac Llyr chose to live under the overlordship of Hell rather than face destruction at the hands of the angels. His own sister went to pay that tithe." Rain dripped down his face. The light was growing—still dim, but growing. "We chose a lesser place that was still a place. And there is a way out of it. The Mebd could go, and Àine with her. My fa-ther's heirs."

"It's happening now. The Magi, the iron and steel."

"They'll drive Hell out as well," he said. "The Devil is out of fashion."

"The Dragon Prince comes to protect those under threat of conquest and destruction. He's here for us. For this war."

Whiskey snorted.

"I'll free you. You have my word on it. I'll free you. After the war."

"You could die in the war, mistress."

"So could we all."

He nodded, then, considering. "Is your word good?"

"You've my oath."

"I may still kill you if I can."

"I'll chance it," she said, and moved to close the window.

He stopped her with a hand on her arm, thumb pressing the wet silk of her robe against her arm. "Come out into the rain. Ride with me. There was thunder, earlier."

"I'm to be married."

"So you are," he said, "and you'll need me more than ever, then." And he took her hand and drew her down from the window, and up onto his back, and so away through the garden and the parklands beyond at a canter and then at a wild, wild run.

Keith returned home through the thorn-tree path. He wasn't surprised to find Fionnghuala at the MacNeill house; he'd stopped at her cottage on his way home, and there weren't many other places she might be at teatime. He *was* surprised to find her sitting by the fieldstone hearth in the parlor with Fyodor Stephanovich, Eremei Fyodorovich, and Vanya—with no sign of Eoghan, although his scent was fresh in the house. "Father?" Keith said by way of announcing himself.

"Upstairs," Fionnghuala answered, standing to greet him and smoothing her skirts with a shake.

Vanya leaned against the hearth behind her. He straightened but did not step forward, his hands folded tidily over powerful forearms. "He was tired," Vanya said, his voice making the euphemism an obvious politeness.

He is dying, you mean. Someone nudged Keith's elbow: the young wolf Eremei Fyodorovich, pressing a whiskey into his hand. He held it up to the light curiously and smiled. "Thank you, Younger Brother."

"You're welcome," the young wolf said, and withdrew. Fyodor himself stayed silent, sprawled in a chair too low for his long legs, his strange eyes watchful over hollow cheeks. Assessing his son's manners, Keith thought. Assessing the competition.

There was a message in Fyodor playing host through Eremei. And Keith answered that communication when he set the glass down untasted on the side table. Caledfwlch dragged at his belt, and he knew every eye in the room stole glances at it.

"You're wounded, brother," Fyodor said, rising out of his chair like a stream of smoke. "You smell of blood."

"Aye," Keith answered, turning his gaze from the black wolf to Vanya, trying to put his question into his eyes. Vanya tipped his head toward Fyodor, the obvious answer. *Try him. I cannot speak for my cousin in this.*

Damn, Keith thought, as Fionnghuala rubbed her hands together and glanced about the room, obviously at a loss to follow the conversation. "Gentlemen?"

"There are complications," Keith said, meeting Fyodor's gaze and showing his teeth in a smile that was also a warning. He picked the offered glass up off the side table again, lacing his fingers around it. "We need to speak, Fyodor Stephanovich. More even than we did before."

"I do not wish to kill you," Fyodor said. He kept his hands low, palms pressed against his thighs, his pointed chin tucked tight to cover the softness of his throat. "It's very near."

"Yes," Keith answered. "And I meant—" He shook his head, raised his glass, and knocked Fyodor's whiskey down. "I meant to step aside, Fyodor Stephanovich. But the situation has changed."

Something—Keith's scent, the brittleness in his voice—must have alerted the other wolves in the room. Fionnghuala knotted her hands in the folds of the skirt she'd carefully smoothed over her knees.

"Meaning you will no longer stand aside?" Vanya, gently, moving forward to refill Keith's glass and return it to his hand. Offerings, younger wolf to elder: the powerful sting of the whiskey's scent brought tears to Keith's eyes.

"Meaning I no longer can," Keith said, and made sure he had Fyodor's gaze before he continued. The black wolf waited, his lanky form relaxed. "Fyodor Stephanovich, have you heard of a thing called the Dragon Prince?"

A slow, painstakingly precise nod.

"It seems I am he," Keith continued, "and the consequences if I do not claim my princedom are too heavy to contemplate."

The fire popped sharply in the quiet that followed. "How do you know?" Vanya, of course, after a speaking glance from Eremei that obviously urged the question on him.

"The Dragon told me," Keith answered, and leaned his head back helplessly. "There's more. Fyodor—" He was interrupted as Fionnghuala cleared her throat.

"Gentlemen?"

"You're confused, madam?" Fyodor, with a toothy human smile, turned his attention on her.

She shook back the waves of her hair. "No. Not precisely. But wondering if Eoghan should be present for this discussion."

"No," Keith said, flatly enough that he startled himself. "My father has . . . ideas. And I'd prefer to settle this through compromise if possible. Tell me you won't fight me, Fyodor." Coldness filled Keith's belly; he tried to put the urgency into his voice, into his eyes.

"I can make no promises," the black wolf said, scrubbing a hand across his curls. "But I can listen to your arguments. You said there were complications, however. And that is only one."

Sharp. "Yes, there's more. The Mebd has named my son her heir, and so the pack is involved whether we choose to be or not. And this is the year of the teind to Hell, and there is no telling who may be sent."

"Hell," Fionnghuala said, the note in her voice stark enough that Vanya put a hand on her elbow to steady her. "That's still going on?"

"Still?" Despite himself, the surprise got out to color Keith's voice. "Nuala, you cannot be old enough to remember—"

"On the contrary," she said. "I've seen Hell my own self, and lived to tell the tale."

"So have I," Fyodor put in, turning away. His slouched, narrow shoulders rose and fell as he fixed himself a drink. "I'm not sure how it signifies."

"Because you are speaking metaphorically," she said, with dignity. "And I am not. Because I was Fionnghuala mac Llyr, of the Tuatha de Danaan like the Mebd and her sister Queens who are the daughters of my brother Manannan. And I was the first tithe who went to serve the Morningstar, when the deal was cut, fifteen hundred years ago."

Keith turned, just turned and stared at her. "Nuala?"

"Surely," she said, "you did not think the name of a strange American could be an accident."

He shook his head. "You served in Hell and came back out?"

"Some are permitted to leave," she said with a shrug. "Once they've broken and been put to use."

"Broken?" Just the word felt sharp-edged on his tongue, as he tried not to picture what she meant.

"Everyone breaks." She came to Keith and lifted his whiskey from his hand, downing it like a man. She smiled into the empty glass. "Now, that brings back memories." Then she looked up, looked from Keith to Fyodor to Vanya, her clear gaze settling at last on Eremei. The young wolf watched his elders in obvious, utter confusion. Keith could not look away from his face, which was, he suspected, what Fionnghuala had intended.

"So," she said. "Tell us, Dragon Prince. Who is Faerie's enemy, that wolf and Fae and Hell must all strive together to defeat them?"

"Remember what I told you about the Prometheus Club?"

"Ah, yes. I have been gone for some little time, haven't I? But that begs the question"—a tilt of her head fanned her hair across her neck—"what happens next?"

Keith coughed into his hand. "I take Fyodor to Annwn, if he's amenable. And you as well, Nuala, if you like—"

"I've seen it," she said dryly, turning her gaze on Fyodor. "And yourself, Fyodor Stephanovich?"

The black wolf smiled. "Why not?" he said. "Since Nuala tells me I haven't *actually* seen Hell."

Seeker trailed ribbons of laughter through the rain as the white stallion stretched himself to a bone-shuddering run, sweat-and-rain-wet hide rough against her thighs when her robe slid higher. His pounding hoof-beats echoed until they came up a rise to a horizon of water glistening black as oil under groping fingers of light. "Rain and sunlight," Seeker said. "Weather."

The Kelpie whickered, pawing the emerald bank, turning up rich earth and clots of sod. "Something's changing," he said.

Seeker untangled cold-cramped fingers from the wiry strands of his mane and slid down his foam-white shoulder. The rain plastered her robe to her body and her hair to her neck. She shivered hard, gritting her teeth so they wouldn't chatter, and leaned against the stallion's steaming side for warmth. He fell away like water under her hand, and she startled, ready for a fight—but instead of a threat, Whiskey in human form stood from a crouch and put his arm around her shoulders. "You should take your robe off," he said. "You're chilled with the wet."

"Then dry me." His hand went to the collar of her robe; she knocked it away. "Don't you think of anything else?"

"Have you known a lot of studhorses?" He stepped back and made a gesture as if smoothing cloth over her body; the water vanished off her skin. "I can't do much for the stains."

She turned away from him and strolled along the arched bank of the loch. "I'm sure there's a brownie at the palace who can." The light moved in narrow bands over the water, reminding her of hands stroking a face. "Why did you come for me this morning?"

She watched his face from the corner of her vision: noticed the clever lie, almost felt his frustration when he could not force it past his lips. Knew that frustration as her own. "I was lonely," he said. "There was no one to share the rain with."

A simple statement. It struck her with unaccountable sorrow. She swallowed and stooped to pick a pebble out of the turf. "What about Kadiska?"

He grinned, showing her his even white teeth. "Surely you didn't imagine she and I were friends."

"Well acquainted." She couldn't keep the bitterness from her voice. The rock in her hand was white, flat, glossy, like a chip of chalk or bone. She weighed it in her palm for a moment and spun it into the loch. It didn't skip.

"You did tell me to distract her."

"I did."

"You're jealous."

"Don't be ridiculous." His grin widened, and she struck him across the face. "Bastard."

The blow turned his head. He blinked and raised a hand to his cheek, shaking his head. "I serve my lady's pleasure," he said. "But if you didn't like the attention, you could order me to stop."

Seeker pulled back to slap him again and stopped. She bit her cheek, blood salty and sweet on her tongue. "I just came from another man's bed, Uisgebaugh. What do you take me for?"

"The Queen of all Faerie," he said, the smile falling off his face. "Or soon to be. And a lonely Queen was she. And to be precise, it was your own bed, and no one else's."

"There's a song about you, little treachery," Seeker said. She spat blood on the grass. " 'Whiskey, You're the Devil.' Where's Gharne?"

The water-horse brayed laughter. "I left your familiar in the Caribbean. I imagine he'll find his way back fairly soon. Once he realizes I slipped away from him. I'm hard to track, mistress mine, for all he was clever. You're still shivering."

She wrapped her hands over her arms. "It's no matter."

"Ah," he said. He tugged her stiff body close and warmed her against his chest. "You want to run away."

"Only if I can take Keith and Ian with me." She sighed and let him hold her, shaking her head slightly from side to side. "I had some wild idea that if I could wake Arthur up, he could take Keith's place."

"You know that wouldn't happen, mistress."

"I know. And I couldn't wake him anyway."

"May I speak freely?"

She remembered a command not to speak of Keith in her presence. "As you will."

Soft, whickering laughter against her ear. "What are you going to do, my lady, when your lover's hands are red with the blood of innocents? When he goes to feed his Dragon? What will you do then?"

"Try not to watch," she said. "Whiskey. Are you trying to become my friend?"

"Not in the slightest," he answered, with no sign that he fought the compulsion of the question. "But I need you strong, my lady. I guard your heartbeat as my own."

"Why do you pursue me so?"

He paused and thought about it. "My lady Seeker. Seduction is what I do. It is what I am. Young women are my rightful prey, the sadder the better."

"And you so sad and alone yourself."

"It is," he said, "what it is. You can command me away from you with a word. But you haven't yet."

"No, I haven't, have I? I wonder why that is."

Whiskey started to speak and then paused, as if realizing her phrasing did not compel him to answer. She cocked her head at him and gestured him to continue. He sighed and spread his hands. "You want to hurt him," he said. "But you haven't quite the courage to do it. You want vengeance and you need him, and you need his attention. You're furious. Furious at him and at yourself. And I'm an easy thing to hurt yourself against."

"Better pain than that . . . numbness, again." Her eyes dropped. "There's blood under your fingernails."

"There usually is, my lady." He turned from her, staring out over the black water of the loch. The torn clouds sealed like a wound overhead. He squatted on the unkempt turf and let fingers the color of the rippling water trail through it.

"What do you think of Hope? And Ian, my son?"

"I think you cannot trust them, and they should not trust each other. I think as well that Hope's a weather-witch, and strong enough so her power now and again jostles even the Mebd's control."

"I can't trust them. Or Keith, or you, or the Mebd, or Morgan, or Àine. I can't trust Robin and I can't trust Carel and I can't trust Mist. I sure as hell can't trust myself."

"Ah," he whispered, dipping his fingers in the loch once more as the clouds closed for good. "You begin to understand."

"Whiskey," she said, suddenly curious, watching the beads of water sparkle and then go dim upon his skin. "Surely you found it hard to trick people into thinking you were anything but Fae, three or four hundred years ago, looking like that?"

"I didn't," he said, straightening. "I didn't look like this." When he glanced back up his skin was pale and his features fine under a shock of straight black hair, his Caribbean eyes less startling in contrast. "Not in Ireland, anyway. But I don't like this skin. It's pasty."

The petulant tone startled Seeker to laughter. "For a monster, you persist in being strangely charming."

His broad shoulders twitched, as if shaking off a fly. "I'm a monster, all right," he answered. "Any human shape I wear is just a guise. But the line between monsters and gods is a fine one, isn't it?"

She watched him stand and stalk away. He stopped perhaps ten feet down the bank, and from behind she watched the texture of his skin and hair change back, the broad shoulders grow a little more slender. "I could bid you to hunt no more. What would happen then?"

"I would starve," he said. "Eventually. And the seas would go unrevenged. How like a human."

"Oh?"

He snorted in disgust. "Wolves and foxes, hawks and bears. They eat the same things your people like to eat, the rabbits and the deer. They might be a threat to your obscene fat flocks of sheep and sharp-hooved cattle. Poison them, trap them. Hunt them with dogs you've bred into monsters, mockeries of dogs so gigantic their hearts fail after a few short years of running blood through their enormous bodies. Vilify and fear them, give them evil names. The animals that serve man are blessed, and those that serve their own autonomy are evil? I think not. A wolf is just a wolf, my lady. Innocent."

"You kill because you like to," she growled, coming up on her toes. "Don't compare yourself to a wolf."

"The only difference between me and a wolf," he answered, striding back to her, leaning down into her face, "is what we hunt, and how we hunt it. Don't deceive yourself that your lover has never tasted blood, or that he felt no joy when he ran the prey to earth. Or that your son is innocent of such things, either."

She grabbed his shirt collar. "Who are you to judge human morality?"

"Honest," he answered. "And without the pious illusion that my needs are somehow moral and those of the rest of the world are not. Like your Wolf-prince. Like the Dragon and her servants through the years. Arthur was more moral than Mordred—how? I do what I do to preserve my own, and if there's blood on my hands to the elbow, so mote it be. My lady."

"That's . . ." . . . *wrong.* "How does it make you any different from the human Magi? Any better than the other side of the war?"

He caressed her cheek with a wide-open palm, his thumb in the notch under her lip. She jerked her head back. "It doesn't," he said. "Except your mortals do what they were going to do anyway, and then cloak their actions in the justification of right and wrong because they cannot face the truth."

Her skin tingled where he touched her. She leaned into him and shouted. "You can save the nature-red-in-tooth-and-claw speech. We're *supposed* to be better than that."

"You lot seem to say that often." The smug, condescending smile. "Does it make you feel *better*? Will it make you feel better when your

lover slaughters mortals by the thousands? Do you suppose it comforted Dracula's wife when she threw herself from the tower, that her
husband had done what he had done to protect his people? Or John
Hunyadi of Hungary, for that matter, when that selfsame Dracula paid
suit to Hunyadi's daughter, even from captivity? Do you suppose
Harold died comforted, knowing he had refused a course of savagery
and *failed*?"

Her robe fluttering about her, she struck him. Backhand, with a doubled fist, and then kicked him when he staggered, first in the belly and
then, when he went to one knee, in the chest. She thought he would at-
tack her, or shift back to his horse form to absorb the blows. Instead he
knelt, the wet grass staining his trousers, and raised his chin. Seeker
slammed her elbow into his forehead and her knee into his throat, kicking him again until he wrapped both arms around her knees and tripped
her backward onto the greensward.

"It feels good, doesn't it?" he whispered, and nuzzled the hem of her
robe aside, baring the length of her thigh. "Go ahead and hit me. I don't
mind."

Chapter Fifteen

Matthew was very tired, but his hands hurt even more than his back did, and so he kept on walking. The warning wasn't the pulling, sweet sharpness that heralded a Seeker, however, so he walked instead of running: boots scuffing on gray pavement past the red neon sign of the movie theater on Forty-second, through the clamor of advertisements, to the crossroads of the world. *And isn't it interesting that we keep coming back here*, he thought, remembering Patience.

Times Square barely dimmed in sunlight. Stacked LED screens shone over hustling crowds, traffic a constant chromed shine on Matthew's left. Enough people to vanish among, a fine thaumaturgic hook to hang a pass-unseen on. He stepped around a bootleg tape dealer and followed his pain.

He spotted his quarry half a block away, loitering but not obviously, a sleek black head rising over the crowd. People turned to look as Murchaud passed, even with a glamourie dulling his unholy beauty. Some of them obviously wondered if they should be recognizing a celebrity.

The Duke of Hell made direct for Matthew, limping only slightly, his face impassive.

Matthew had some idea what it must have cost him to hide his pain in the presence of that much iron. "Come on. Let's go to the park. Assuming it was me you wished to speak to."

"Who else would come to investigate?" Murchaud said mildly, and fell into step beside him. "I hope you don't mind walking." He gestured rather helplessly at a passing taxi.

Matthew laughed. "I walk a lot. I like my exercise."

"I can see that."

Matthew felt the appreciative glance. He deflected it with a turn of his hand. "I'm afraid you're not my type, Murchaud."

A chuckle. "How do you know?" Met by silence, and Murchaud took it with equanimity. "I wanted to speak with you alone."

"Do you stand against your brothers because they sent you to Hell, Murchaud?"

"No," Murchaud answered. "I went to Hell willing, in another's place. I speak for the Morningstar to Jane Andraste because it amuses the Morningstar to have it so, and he doesn't think a few tens of hundreds of Magi should go . . . unliaisoned."

Matthew dragged his hands out of his pockets. It was too much; the pain was breaking his concentration, and he needed every drop. He pulled his rings off one by one and weighed them in his palm, eyes tearing in relief. "Ah."

"Would it were so simple for me," Murchaud said, clubbed hair bobbing over his collar as he turned to watch a groundlit El Camino lowrider purr past. "Aren't you going to ask me what Hell is like, Matthew Magus?" A very tired voice, without the lilt Matthew expected.

"I was going to ask why no one came after you, like Tam Lin."

The Duke of Hell broke stride at that, but recovered quickly. "Those who had the power did not care for the risk," he said quietly. "And the one who cared for the risk had long ago surrendered whatever the Morningstar would have liked of him." A long pause, and the jocular tone returned. "It's just as well you didn't ask about Hell. For I would have answered you thus: 'This is Hell, nor am I out of it.' "

Matthew slipped his rings into his pocket and answered, " 'Hell hath no limits, nor is circumscribed in one self place, for where we are is Hell, And where Hell is there must we ever be.' I teach that play."

"I know." Murchaud grinned, sideways slyness. "And may I say that it amuses the author greatly."

"How—" He struck his forehead. "You're pulling my leg, of course."

"I must be." Dry as gin, matching Matthew's stride effortlessly. "You'd never expect to find a poet in Hell."

"You're very charming."

"I work at it."

"What do you want?"

"I want to know why you serve Prometheus, lad." Deadpan, and deadly smooth in the delivery.

"Because . . ." He paused. It was not a question that would brook an easy answer. "Because Prometheus will care for my brother, if anything happens to me. Because they're the road I have to a little revenge, for what the Faeries did to Kelly. And the only means I have of seeing it never happens again."

"Hmmph." And then silence. Murchaud glanced back over his shoulder, threading through the crowd without effort even when he paid no attention at all. "Pity we've left the crossroads."

"Why is that?"

He stopped, and Matthew stopped a step farther, turning to face him. Murchaud's pale blue eyes caught and reflected the orange-and-crimson glow of billboards and LEDs. For a moment, Matthew could have fooled himself it was flickering flames, but he stretched his hands, working relief through aching fingers, and refused to look back down.

"Because," Murchaud said, "I could do the same in exchange for your soul, and it would prove less costly in the long run." He glanced down, and started walking again.

Matthew stared after, then hurried to catch him. "I thought Hell and Prometheus were allied, Your Grace."

"*Hell* and Prometheus are," he said, archly.

Seeker stepped through shadows, leaving Whiskey by the black water's edge. "Weak," she cursed herself, kicking the grass-stained rags of her robe into the corner. The window still stood open, a cold draft filling the room. Although some sprite or brownie had banked it, the fire had burned down. She rang for water, trying not to think too hard about it, and while she waited she wrapped the counterpane around her shoulders and kindled a new fire.

Once the flames stood tall, she threw the robe upon them. Wet silk scorched and stung her nostrils, smoking hard until she adjusted the flue. Her whiskey still sat on the table by the fireside chair; by the time she remembered it, a bath had been brought, and she locked the door, left the window open, and stood sipping liquor and glaring at the steaming water.

She finished her drink, but she still stood cradling the empty glass after she dropped the comforter on the floor. "Dammit!" Seeker whirled and hurled the glass into the fireplace. She felt no better when it shattered.

She straightened and tossed her hair back. "Whiskey, stay the hell out of my bedroom today. Do you hear me?" There was no answer. She hadn't expected one.

No rose petals this time: just clean hot water in a footed wooden tub. She groaned as she slid down into it; her body felt beaten, as bruised and abraded as Whiskey's had been when she left him. The memory nauseated her, but so did the touch of the steaming water. *At least you didn't let him fuck you.* She dug splinters of grass and earth from under her fingernails. *It doesn't count if he doesn't put it in you? Oh, so we're back in high school, then? I guess we are, at that. Well, it won't happen again.* She drew her knees up and shivered. *No matter how good he can make your body feel.*

Yes, he's had a lot of practice. A little hors d'oeuvre before he eats them in a nonmetaphorical sense. Devil! Her stomach clenched on emptiness.

The water grew cold before Seeker felt she'd scrubbed enough. She toweled herself roughly, examined the bruises along her knuckles and the heels of her hands, and dressed for luncheon. *Best if people don't forget I exist.* But she didn't believe it.

She took herself down to the galleried, glass-ceilinged hall in a sweep of petticoats and steely brocade, listening to the clatter of her bootheels on the stone. She entered through the back door and appropriated Peaseblossom's place at the high table beside Cairbre. The Mebd's antique councilor could sit in *her* old chair if he didn't care to contest her for pride of place. *I should have been playing politics years ago, instead of sulking like a whipped child between assignments.* On the far end of the table, Carel winked at her, and Seeker smiled back. Keith was nowhere to be seen and neither was the Mebd.

"Good afternoon, mother." Ian leaned over her shoulder and kissed her cheek, a hand laid lightly on her arm. "Her Majesty would like to speak to you at your convenience. After lunch, I believe." He lowered his voice. "She's closeted with dusty old Peaseblossom and the Unseelie emissary just now."

"I was hoping we could dine together tonight," Seeker said, covering his hand with her own.

"I'll cancel my engagements," he answered with a grin that seemed curiously cool. "Nice choice of chair, mother."

Something felt strange under her fingertips; his skin was cool and taut, and she couldn't feel the blood moving under it. "Your hands are cold."

"So is the hall. The wine will heat them soon enough."

She returned his smile as warmly as she could. "I think the trouble's going to get deeper before we find a way through, but it's a start at a solution. What do you think?"

"I think I'm heir to them both, so it doesn't matter much which one bends a knee to which, but my father has a better chance of reining in Àine than the Mebd has." His hair glowed almost blue in the lamplight, and the calculation in his eyes chilled her. And then his frown eased, and he shrugged, all boy again. "I'm thinking I'd rather not wind up married to any of my great-great aunts for the sake of politics, either."

"There's a girl, then?" Just to see what he would say.

"Mother!" He blushed. "Maybe. But I can't marry where I want even if I wanted to, if that makes any sense, so there's no use dwelling on it."

"Ah."

Cairbre, pretending not to hear the conversation, passed Seeker a plate. She poked at the meat with her knife, surprised to discover she had an appetite.

Ian flagged the server down to bring her wine. " 'Love where you may, and marry where you must,' " he quoted wryly.

"A family tradition."

"Apparently." He kissed her cheek. "I should sit down so people can eat." She smiled after him, Whiskey's words about blood and hunters an unease at the bottom of her mind.

"A fine lad," Cairbre said in her ear. "You must be proud."

"Extremely," she answered. Ian took his chair and sipped his wine, and the low hum of conversation in the hall dropped as the diners fell upon their food. "Do you have any children?"

"Alas," he said. "Have you given any thought to the future between these two kingdoms, Seeker?"

"We need each other," she said. With the rustle of many-colored cloth, the bard Cairbre nodded. She caught the motion from candle-shadows, just as she saw Ian catch Hope's eye across the width of the hall and smile. A thousand tiny movements, a thousand significant gestures. As useless in its complexity as the murmur of voices filling the room.

"We do." The bard's rich baritone. "Despite what the Unseelie are. I've been talking to your Merlin, Seeker. She's a scholar as well as a Mage."

"I know." Seeker tasted her dinner. Hunger wet her mouth and she set about dismembering the slice of roast on her plate. "You planned to have me sit here, didn't you?"

"Just a little come-hither," Cairbre admitted. His long fingers flickered as he spoke. A narrow band of pale scar circled the base of each one. "I hope you don't mind."

"Not at all." She reached for the bread, and Cairbre passed her the butter without being asked. "That was quite a performance the other night, master bard."

" 'Greensleeves'? Amazing. A mortal, and so young. That voice, and that audacity: I'd have made a bard of her such as the world had never seen, if I'd had her from nine or ten." And then Cairbre seemed to realize what he was saying. "If she wasn't on another path already, of course."

"Ah." Red wine stung her palate. She forced a smile and spoke between bites. "I'm interested to hear what has the Daoine bard standing back-to-back with the Unseelie court, if you don't mind. And what use he thinks he might get out of such as I."

Cairbre rubbed a hand across his chin. "Not back-to-back. Shoulder to shoulder, perhaps." He held up his hands, licking a drip of gravy from his nail. His fingers were strong, tendons visible along the sides. Seeker reached out and touched the ridges of scar because his gesture seemed an invitation.

The scars were raised like beads of solder; they felt shiny-slick and hard under her fingertips. "You're showing me these wounds for a reason, harper."

"I had an experience with Prometheans," Cairbre said. "I was bound seven years before I won free. I wore"—his lips thinned, and he dropped his hands upon the tabletop—"iron rings on my fingers."

Seeker flinched, lowering her gaze to her plate. She imagined for a moment she could feel the ache of that iron in her bones, up her arms to the elbow, deep in her shoulders like the pain of a dislocated joint. She remembered the ponytailed Mage grabbing her hand, remembered the iron winding his own fingers. Proof against Faerie magics. *Bold bastards.* The scars on Cairbre's hands looked like old, deep burns. She shuddered. "Why didn't they kill you?"

"I expect it was an experiment." He picked up his spoon and tasted the soup cooling before him. "As you can probably understand, I will do what needs to be done to eradicate them. Cliodhna indicates her Queen will too." An eloquent gesture, not quite a shrug.

"And what does she want with me?"

"Alliances. You move in powerful circles, and you carry the blood of Queens. You have the ear of Morgan and of the Mebd, and the service of one of the most powerful of the wild Fae. A Tuatha de Danaan. Not to mention your own post and position." Cairbre rested a hand on her arm. The calluses on his fingertips caught on the nap of her sleeve. "And your links to Keith MacNeill and to his son."

"Links," she snorted. "What a charming way to put it. So I've made myself a valuable commodity."

"That's not all it is." He shook his head, straight dark hair swinging against his shoulders. Seeker liked the way his face rearranged itself around the corners of his smile. His eyes were dark over the line of his beard. "It's a matter of, who do you want to be turning your back to when the war comes?"

"Not *if*."

He rubbed his hands together against a chill she didn't feel. "It's already here, to speak precisely. We've been slow in marshaling our forces." Cairbre poured more wine, and Seeker realized she had finished hers. "My fault as much as anything. Something I'll start to remedy tonight. We're past the time for love songs."

"War songs?"

"Well, it won't be 'Bury me under yon rose tree,' I can promise you that." He stuffed a folded slice of roast into his mouth, wiped his cropped black beard with his hand, and pushed his chair back. He walked around the short end and crossed before the table, bowing to Ian as he passed. Cairbre reached up over the table, one toe on a little step, and caught Carel's fingers in his own. Seeker leaned forward to watch the drama between the roasts and goblets and twining arrangements of flowers and ivy.

Cairbre smiled at the Merlin and kissed her fingers, making a flamboyant little gesture of it. "My lady," he said in a carrying voice, "if you've finished your meal, will you come and play with me? We had only a taste of your music, and it has left us hungry for more."

Carel said something too softly for Seeker to catch over the murmur of voices in the shadows.

"Then bring your wine," the bard replied, which sent laughter rippling and rebounding the length of the hall.

Carel must have nodded, although Seeker couldn't see it through the gathering, because he released her hand and she stood, taking her goblet. She sparkled, clad in honey-and-orange-streaked velvet that dripped with carnelian meshwork, and she took his hand again at the foot of the dais and let him lead her to the corner of the hall where a hammer dulcimer stood shrouded in a pall of black cloth.

Seeker blinked, the draped outline a reminder. She pushed her chair back and started to stand, but the courtier beside her laid a hand on her arm. "One song," he said. "They'll talk of this night a thousand years from now."

"If any of us live that long." She sat back down, frowning, the need to act tugging like a fishhook in her lip. Despite it, she folded her hands around the stem of her goblet, watching with the rest of the murmuring crowd as the Merlin and the bard uncovered the instruments. Carel sat behind the dulcimer, and Cairbre pulled a low bench close and settled a guitar over his knee. He didn't speak. He turned his head, shared a glance with the Merlin, and nodded a moment before she struck the strings.

The peals of the dulcimer struck through Seeker like ice crystals, and what Cairbre sang was not the martial ballad she anticipated. His voice was velvet stroked up the inside of Seeker's arm at the same moment that it was a razor honed bloodlessly sharp, parting skin. A lament as still and cold as a rain freezing in the trees, and Carel's voice came in to support his on the chorus like stars coming out in the perfect blackness of a midwinter night. Seeker didn't know the song, which surprised her, and after it drifted closed in softness and grief, she couldn't remember a word, although her eyes burned and her pulse beat against the skin of her throat. She realized she was on her feet, like half the hall. Like Ian, who stared down from his place near the center of the table, his knuckles white on wood.

Carel struck one last peal from her instrument. It echoed into the silence of the hall like a crystal goblet struck with a knife, and the hush was complete.

Cairbre stood up from his chair a moment before the spell would have been broken by applause. "Let's have a drummer!" His deep voice boomed from the broad-beamed rafters. "Let's have a piper! Summon my student! Push back the tables! Let us have dancing, an it pleases my ladies and lords!" He faced the high table, and Ian smiled and raised his hand, comfortable and in control in his spotless black and slender golden circlet.

"See?" the courtier said into Seeker's ear.

She nodded and tugged her wrist out of his grip. "I expected 'Johnny Cope,'" she admitted, and turned and slipped behind the arras, and away.

Gangling Fyodor Stephanovich charged up the hill like water flowing down it; Keith, toiling behind, had to admire his enthusiasm. Keith was fit, but the length of Fyodor's stride defeated him. Shins aching, he resigned his dignity and broke into a trot, scurvygrass tugging his boots, dotted with scraggly, fading asters and campion.

A moment later, Fyodor crested the ridge and paused, glancing back over his shoulder as Keith drew up. "Where do we go from here?" he asked, and followed the line of Keith's pointing finger. "A hedge?"

"Burnet rose and hawthorn," Keith said, leading the black wolf up the continued rise to a peak. "Thorns are the gate to underhill," he said. "Are you carrying iron?"

"A knife," Fyodor answered, and unclipped the sheath from his belt. "I was careful in my clothes."

"Keep it," Keith said. "Keep it sheathed, but it can't hurt to have a bit of iron to hand."

"How do we get in?" Fyodor's eyebrows rose in amused arches, his fingers curling through the sunlight as he spread his hands wide. Keith thought he read some kind of trouble in the black wolf's expression, nonetheless.

"Here as elsewhere, it's polite to knock." Keith suited action to words. He kept his left hand on Caledfwlch's hilt, just for the reassurance of the sword's heavy presence.

Fyodor's calm certainty as the black mouth in the hill yawned before them would have been a disappointment, if Keith hadn't picked his sharp, worried scent off the sea breeze. "After you, Younger Brother," he said, graciously.

Fyodor was too proud to glance back, but he drew himself up before he moved forward, and Keith knew the gesture was intended to remind the black wolf to courage. "Onward and inward," he muttered, as cold darkness closed around them, the movement of the stones as silent as the movement of air.

"'Further up and farther in,'" Keith answered, and grinned. "No Heaven here, alas. Just the Westlands—there."

Three steps forward was all it took to bear them into the light. Fyodor blinked, raising a hand to touch his hair as the sweet spring-scented wind curled through it. He craned his long awkward neck, rolling onto the balls of his feet, and Keith indulged himself for a moment in just watching the worry and wonder chase each other across Fyodor's face, followed by a strange, dark recognition. Fyodor Stephanovich closed his eyes. "You never said why, Keith."

"Call it a wild impulse," Keith said, turning his head to get the lay of the land. It never did look the same way twice. Today they had come out at the head of a sloped ravine that formed a scalloped corridor between stark ranks of treeless hills. Indirect light lay across it like a golden rind, slanted through the overcast, and Fyodor began to unbutton his shirt, movements jerky as a marionette. "Younger Brother?"

"This is not a place for being human in," Fyodor answered, heel-toeing out of his boots while folding his shirt into smooth thirds. His scent was like glass, and Keith almost whined in received anxiety. "I come here as a wolf or I do not come."

"This place is something to you."

Fyodor stepped out of his trousers and turned, his eyes open wide enough that Keith could see that they were gray as seaglass. "Babi Yar," he said. "It looks like Babi Yar."

"The massacre," Keith said, being old enough to remember. Not that such things could ever really be forgotten. He tugged his shirt out of the waistband of his trousers.

"It was more than a massacre," Fyodor Stephanovich said. "The executions at the ravine went on for months. SS Special Squad Four A: I remember very well. Later, they said thirty-three thousand Soviet citizens died there, gypsies and Ukrainian Jews and the miscellaneous others."

"They?" Keith asked. Fyodor would not look at him, but Keith would be damned if he would risk this heartbeat of honesty to intemperate demands.

"I think it was more," Fyodor said. He crouched on the green grass with the flats of his palms spread wide, but he did not change. Instead he looked down the ravine, shivering. "They took our coats and walked us to the edge of the cliff. They shot us in the head, one at a time."

"Us," Keith said, unable to restrain himself in the face of Fyodor's lingering silence.

"Thirty thousand died at Babi Yar, and I was one of them. An SS bullet of lead and steel won't kill a Ukrainian wolf."

Keith stacked his clothes next to Fyodor's and laid Caledfwlch on the grass, where he could grasp the sheath in his mouth after he changed. "We'll come back and dress after we look," he said. "You'll see this isn't Babi Yar."

"Isn't it?" The black wolf shrugged. "Isn't this the place where stories are true?"

"Is Babi Yar a story?"

"It is now. One of Russia's greatest poets wrote a poem about it. About how there was no gravestone there."

"Yevtushenko."

That drew a surprised look, those expressive brows rising high.

Keith shrugged. "It's supposed to have changed the Soviet Union's national perceptions of the victims."

"You've read it."

"Only in translation." Keith could not shake the sensation that Fyodor's look was a balance, weighing him.

"Pity. You should learn Russian, then. Come along, Elder Brother. It is time to run."

Seeker didn't need to step *otherwise* to come to the Mebd's throne room. The passageway behind the arras led from the dais of the one to that of the other, and beyond. This room was smaller than the hall, but not much. Gray light fell through faceted windows on the west side, lying in tall swathes on the blue-and-green-tiled floor. Seeker paused with one hand on the tapestry before she stepped from behind it, unsettled, letting her own eyes and those of the shadows survey the room.

She stepped past the gilded chair that sat at the edge of the dais, letting her hand trail over ornate scrollwork before she grasped the thick gold rope that hung against the wall. It looked like a bellpull, but when she drew it down, the heavy green burned-velvet curtains behind the chair slid apart, whispering on the tile, revealing a tall shape veiled in still more velvet, velvet so red it seemed black in the failing light. What it covered had the general outline of a peaked dining room chair under a sheet, but the top stood eight feet high.

Seeker stood staring at the thing for a long moment: the shrouded throne of the Mebd of the Daoine Sidhe, used only on state occasions and never uncovered. She caught her breath, listening to the faint tones of fiddle and drum drifting through the passageway. And then she reached out left-handed and fingered the cloth where the hand of some-one seated in the embrace of the throne would rest, expecting softness and the feather-feeling of the pile against her skin.

The cloth was harsh to the touch, as if something sticky bound the fibers. When she leaned closer, relying on the sense of smell inherited from her cat-shadow, the rusty smell of old blood filled her nostrils. *Why is the Queen's throne soaked in blood?* Raising her head again, Seeker could see the outlines of stains, duller than the sienna sheen of the unmarked cloth. They almost looked like sweat stains, dried sticky-thick where arms, back, thighs, buttocks would press. Seeker laid her hand on the velvet and tugged at it, almost yelped when something snagged, sank into her palm and bit. She clapped it to her mouth and tasted blood, fresh blood: her own. Something yellow-white and hooked like a tooth poked through the dark cloth.

The gouge across her palm was superficial. She glanced at it, and reached back out to the edge of the velvet pall, more carefully this time, keeping her eye on the shadows.

"That's forbidden, isn't it?"

Seeker didn't jump. She was already turning when Kadiska strolled up to her, bare feet patting the tile. " 'Everything not forbidden is com-pulsory,' " she quoted. "I thought you were skulking about."

"Unkind words . . ." Kadiska's necklaces jingled faintly as she leaned forward and reached out, turning over Seeker's injured hand. "That looks like it hurts."

"Not much. And I've never been *told* not to look."

"Taking refuge in technicalities?" Kadiska's shadow swayed long on the floor, cutting across a wan rectangle of window-light.

"You picked an interesting time to come out of the shadows."

"You knew I was watching you."

Seeker smiled and shrugged noncommittally. "On orders?"

"Somewhat." Kadiska let go of Seeker's hand. Blood freckled the tiles at their feet. "Are you going to look?"

"Of course. Are you going to help?"

"It could strike us blind, you realize. There's a wild magic in some of these things." But her brows were arched, and a sly look slid from the corner of her eye.

Seeker brushed Kadiska with her elbow. "Chicken?"

The Unseelie Seeker laughed and laid one hand on the stiff dark fabric, the turn of her body like the sway of a rope. "Ready."

Together, they lifted the cloth. It snagged on something sharp; Seeker tugged gently, mindful of the edges, her own bright blood soaking into the rusty stains. They worked the heavy edge up and bundled it back, enough to reveal what lay beneath, yellow-white and jumbled together.

"Bones," Kadiska said.

"No." Seeker walked around the throne and—carefully, delicately, as if handling broken glass—reached across the arms and pulled the pall back farther, lifting it off the jagged edges that threatened to slice her skin. "Horns."

Seeker backed away slowly, stopping only when the Mebd's chair of estate caught her in the small of the back. It screeched a half-inch across the tile; she winced as Kadiska shot her a sour look. Under the pall, the throne was a jumble of lance-pointed ivory, curves and arcs interconnected like the finest filigree, every inch covered with intricate spiral carvings. The whole gleamed softly in the filtered light, except where old blood stained the spear-tipped points with rust. Seeker felt the room should have been full of silence, but she heard a distant fiddle climbing up a jig like a child tumbling up stairs, laughing.

"Antlers, rather," Seeker corrected herself, and, edging back, reached out to lay her bloody right hand against the smooth warm material of the throne. "Dear—" She stopped herself before she said the painful name of the Divine, some corner of her mind amused that she'd forgotten herself enough to even think of it.

Kadiska rubbed one hand across the curving row of scars on her breast. She touched a curved antler point, drew back a finger dripping red. "It's an implement of torture. How could it not have killed her?"

"Magic," Seeker answered.

"Who could sit in such a thing?"

"The Mebd has done it," she answered glibly, and then she swallowed bitterness and swore. "Oh, sweet hellfire. Ian."

Kadiska blinked at her, not understanding at first. And then she laid a hand—the one that wasn't bleeding—on Seeker's arm and squeezed. The silence, broken by the distant strains of a reel—flute and that joyous fiddle again—cloyed. "It may be a long time hence," Kadiska managed at last.

Seeker nodded. "I have to go back to the dance," she said. "I'll be missed otherwise. Help me cover this up."

Chapter Sixteen

eeker came back to the great hall through the carved, heavy
blackwood doors at the far end. Although it was still only
midafternoon, Cairbre's impromptu party seemed a success. By
the wall, the bard struck sparks from his fiddle; they scattered, hissing,
to the green-and-rose-checkered marble floor. Hope stood behind him,
fingers flying over the silver branch of her flute. Carel had left the dulcimer. Seeker scanned the crowd for her and found her dancing with
the Kelpie, who guided her in the unfamiliar steps while she laughed
and held her skirts high in her left hand, watching his feet.

Ian. He sat on the steps beside the Mebd's chair, leaning back against
the baroquely carven and gilded base. Her pale fingers moved idly
through the glossy darkness of his hair. Seeker shivered at the relaxed
pleasure in his face, seeing again the bloodstained ivory throne. *Of course
she can't bind him,* she realized. *He has to outlive her.*

But most of us won't. She felt a kind of sick relief in that. *At least I'll never
have to see him sit in that . . . thing.* Seeker walked forward, keeping to the
edge of the hall so as not to interfere with the dancers. Cairbre caught
her eye and winked as she passed; Hope might have, but she was leaning into the music, elbows up and eyes closed. Seeker saw the Mebd
glance down at her and then steal a look at Ian.

Otherwise, she saw Whiskey coming before he reached out gently and
laid a hand on her arm. "Dance with me, mistress?"

Seeker's right hand still stung, although the bleeding had stopped.

Whiskey let his hand slide down to her wrist, lifted it, and turned it over.

"I can smell the blood," he said, and kissed the wound as if he kissed the open palm of her hand. His tongue rasped skin, slick and rough, and she shivered again—for new reasons.

"I hate you," she whispered.

"Such a human passion. I thought you were delightful."

"You provoked me on purpose."

He smiled. She saw no trace of her violence on his face.

"I like a woman with the will to fight. Shall we dance?"

She let him lead her out into the midst of the dancers, the white linen and ivory brocade of his shirt and doublet like a slash of snow on the wildflower riot of colors. "You're wearing shoes," she said, surprised. Low black boots covered his feet, soft suede falling in folds around the ivory silk of his hose.

"A doublet looks odd without hose," he said. "And hose are awkward without boots." They stepped into line as a pavane began, the slick floor hard under her soft-soled shoes, his hand warm as he raised hers high. Her skirts chafed her legs, starched gray cloth rustling against the tile. Whiskey danced well, surprising her, leading her forward in the pace, dip and sway. Their hands parted and linked as the moving columns bore them apart and brought them back together, a stately and decorous few feet separate. Seeker felt her face burning and wondered if the blush showed.

She examined Whiskey through the arch of their arms. His eyes stayed forward, face impassive; she studied the weight of his lower lip, plump with a faint frown. She almost stumbled, and returned her focus belatedly to the dance even as it ended and Whiskey swept a cold, mocking bow, precise as ice sculpture in his softly shining white. Seeker matched him with a curtsey, hand raised high and her head bowed and tilted, her own gown gray as drawn steel among the tumult of greens and blues and rose-petal colors worn by the Fae. Whiskey straightened, that frown still bending his lip, and released her hand. "Remember this," he said, and stepped back into the laughing crowd.

"Whiskey—"

"Seeker."

Seeker turned to the Merlin's touch on her sleeve. Carel's autumn-colored robe hung in folds from her shoulders, soft pleats bending around her breasts and hips like the curve of a caress. "Care to scandalize the room? Cairbre promises a waltz, which seems to be his idea of modern dancing."

Whiskey, you sly son of a bitch. But seduction was his stock-in-trade, after all.

As if led on a rope, Seeker turned to Carel and took her hand. Her movements were smooth, assured as Whiskey's had been—and almost involuntary. A stranger in her own body, she smiled. "For him, it was invented practically yesterday. And two women dancing won't be as much of a scandal as you might wish," she said. "The rules have always been different in Faerie." She tucked a braid behind her ear. "You know I'm charged with your seduction."

"Again, you assume I am innocent," the Merlin said and laughed. "Have I no agenda of my own? Is it still seduction, when aid is given willingly?"

I guess it happens now, Seeker thought, and surrendered to her geasa, taking the Merlin into her arms. *It never rains but it pours.* She giggled inwardly, a sound that would have been tight and shrill if allowed past her lips. *If it ever rains at all.* She remembered cold droplets of water brushing her face, cold lips brushing her skin. *I can't do this. I can't do this.*

I don't have any choice in the world. The Merlin smelled of peppermint and lavender, this time. Nothing like Whiskey. Nothing like Keith. *I wish the Mebd had torn my heart out, as she threatened Tam Lin. Give me a heart of stone; if I must be Fae, let me be Fae, and no more of this death by inches.* The music swelled up around Seeker. Carel led, a little awkwardly, and Seeker closed her eyes so she wouldn't have to see the faces of her family, her friends, her Queen or her servant. *No more.*

But she'd pretended that, hadn't she?—almost thought she had become what was demanded of her, become what she needed to be to survive in the loveless lands. Jealousy, rage, fear, possessiveness, desperation. A distant and elemental sort of joy. Those things, she was sure, surged in the breasts of the Kelpie, of the Mebd. But love? Compassion?

Maybe Morgan can feel them. But how I wish, myself, that I could not. The music was crisp, sharp, bittersweet, and Cairbre gave it a touch of a reel under the stately rhythm of the waltz. The Seeker of the Daoine Sidhe turned her head, nuzzled warm braids and cool twisted beads aside, kissed the silk-soft neck of the legended magician. Through stiff silk and lace and folds of petal-thick velvet, she felt Carel's body press against her, heard a whispered hum on the other woman's breath.

Through *otherwise* eyes, Seeker saw Fae looking—or very carefully not looking, as the case might be: saw Cairbre frown as he bent backward, lifting the bow and the fiddle high; saw Kadiska in the shadows, silent as a coiled and waiting snake, shake back her hair and wink through half a bittersweet smile; Whiskey's hair-tossing headshake as he stole a look around the shoulder of a lady to whom he paid court, and Ian's casual glance and dismissal.

Oh, Seeker thought. *Oh, oh, oh.* And tasted salt and the faint oily flavor of moisturizer, Carel's ever-changing scent filling her senses with the aroma of lilac now. The Merlin leading her, the geasa moving her, Seeker danced in the arms of the one she was ordered to bind and betray, unable to taste the tears burning her eyes. Carel tossed her braids aside, nudged Seeker's cheek with her nose, and gently, gently, gently caught Seeker's lower lip between teeth like a tightly knotted strand of pearls. And then the Merlin smiled wistfully and said, "Shall we give them what they expect, my friend? Or merely something to talk about, for now?"

They say that what the Faeries touch cannot be trusted. Soap bubbles and glamourie, deception and dis-ease. There was so little truth in that, and so much.

Seeker leaned against the wall, one glass of wine more than she should have had inside her and another one in her hand, and watched the Faeries dance. The Mebd had left, with Ian. Carel had gone back to the musicians. Seeker could still taste the sweetness of the Merlin's saliva and the nibbling caress of her lips, and she swirled tart, tannic wine over her tongue to drive the taste away.

Seeker snorted into her goblet. Carel smiled along the wall at her, and

Seeker's lips curved in an answering smile whether she willed it or not. *Bind the Merlin and bind the Dragon.*

Bind her any way you can.

Ah, but Ian said the Mebd wanted to see me. Maybe I can get away with that.

Experimentally, Seeker finished her wine and set the glass aside, just as the musicians finished a slip-jig and moved into a more martial tune. "Ah," she said under her breath. "So 'Johnny Cope' it is."

She let her bootheels rattle on the stones, pivoting on one foot to walk beside the wall, heading for the black wooden doors at the bottom of the hall. Hope handed off her flute and fell into step a few feet behind Seeker, hurrying. "I've a meeting with the Queen," Seeker told her, lengthening her stride.

"I need your help," Hope said softly, catching up. "Five minutes. Just five."

"All right." Seeker didn't slow, but she glanced at the earnest girl. "Follow me." She pushed the door open, old wood waxed smooth against the palm of her hand, the panel heavy but perfectly balanced. Her footsteps sounded decisive, and she wrinkled her nose at the irony of that.

Can I trust her any further than I can trust him? What the Faeries touch . . . She turned and caught the broad flared tippet on Hope's sleeve, pulling her to one side and into a small room off the hall: little more than a niche behind the stairwell, but outfitted with a window and a short pair of benches. Seeker dropped the girl's cuff and shook her own skirts wide before she sat, leaning against the polished stones, turning her face to the misted glass.

The gardens beyond seemed brighter under the overcast, the colors more saturated than in sunlight. Seeker let the side of her face fall against the cold window, breathing the cooler air beside the glass, and watched as Hope spread out her dress and settled herself opposite, humming a little air of warding to keep their conversation private.

"I'm pregnant," Hope said, without preamble. "Did you know about Ian and me?"

"Yes," Seeker answered, everything she'd thought of saying dying. "Does he know?"

"Not yet. Tonight." Her tongue protruded between her lips, like a child's in concentration. "I needed to tell you something first. Look."

Hope gestured out the window, and Seeker followed the line of the girl's wrist, leading her arm. *The Mebd has had her in deportment lessons . . .* which was not so surprising. Not as surprising as the way the clouds boiled and tore, a thin ragged slit letting a glimpse of sunlight through, a single beam that tumbled to earth, struck a rainbow along the way like a spark from flint, and then vanished. Seeker caught her breath. *I thought so.*

"You did more last night."

Hope coughed, concealing her mouth with the cupped palm of her hand. A sheen of sweat, fine as the silk she wore, covered her forehead. "It's easier when I'm . . . emotional. Sometimes, then, it's not so easy to control. And it's been better, I think, since . . ."

"If it's a boy," Seeker said, "pretty soon you'll start to smell things. Hear things. He will make you alert. Give you a taste of his senses. That will go away when the baby is born."

"And if it's a girl?"

"She won't be a werewolf," Seeker answered. "Only the boys. Only the men." Her heart caught in her throat. *She'll just be of my blood, and Morgan's. And the Mebd's.*

And Uisgebaugh, an inner voice reminded her. *Did you forget that he's your great-uncle?*

The rules are different. For gods.

And for you? What rules apply to you, Elaine Andraste? What did the Kelpie say?

She answered herself without irony. *You do what you were going to do anyway, and then cloak your actions in the justification of right and wrong because you cannot face the truth.* Hope's hand rested over her belly.

"I need you."

"You said that." Seeker leaned forward and put her hand over Hope's, as if she expected to feel something. Of course, it was far too early. "He can't marry you."

A dismissive gesture of the young girl's hand. "What's a marriage worth?"

"Whatever you pay for it," Seeker answered dryly, and Hope gave her a tight little smile and squeezed her hand.

"Seeker. I want to win him free."

Something flared in Seeker's breath. Something white and hot, eye-wateringly bright. She thought about the throne of twisted antlers, the flaking taint of blood. "He's not bound. Not tangled in her hair. He can't be . . . or he couldn't survive to *be* the Mebd's heir."

Hope shook her head. "She has his heart."

"He cares for her."

"No." She hummed a bar of music: *"If I had known, if I had known, Tam Lin . . ."*

" 'I would have taken your heart,' " Seeker finished, speaking rather than singing, her voice hollow and soft in her own ears, " 'and put in its place a stone.' Oh. Oh, Hope."

"Yes," the girl said, misunderstanding. "She's made him Fae. She's taken his heart away. She has it in a box, and she feeds it little drops of blood, and while she has it there, he can love me but he cannot give me loyalty."

"And if he cannot, you cannot win him free."

Hope smiled. "Can we be friends?"

"Yes," Seeker answered. *Grandchild.* "I think we can."

The two women sat in silence until jingling footfalls and a calling voice disturbed them. "Seeker?" The Puck's voice, and Seeker stood and stepped out of the little niche to face him.

"Robin. Is your mistress looking for me?"

"Aye," he said, holding up his hand.

Seeker sighed and took his long fingers carefully. "I don't know why she doesn't just say my name and summon me," she said.

"It wouldn't be polite." He led her through the weirdly woven passageways of the palace. "She's in the garden." Before Seeker could ask further, he opened a glass door of jewel-colored panes and gestured her outside. She'd never stood on this particular patio before; raised up over the lilies and iris of the morning garden and paved in white stone with airy railings, it gave the impression of a low balcony.

Robin drew the door closed behind her; it clicked as it latched. The Mebd, clad in robes as white as the marble under her feet, a veil of down-white lace covering her hair, did not turn toward Seeker. Rather, the Queen stood straight and serene, her hands resting on an alabaster railing carven of stone so fine that even the filtered light made its translucence glow. A sweep of stairs began beside her, leading down, and a young wolf lay across the landing.

He rose when Seeker emerged from the doorway and paced toward her, toenails clicking, and then his wet nose touched cold on her hand. She stroked his head, his fur cool between her fingers. *Oh, Ian.* Somewhere a thrush sang, and the light breeze made the lilies nod and shoulder one another.

He raised eyes to her that glittered like peridot, let his tail sweep on a graceful curve, and turned and trotted down the stairs. "Greetings, Seeker," the Mebd said. Seeker started to curtsey, but the Queen's gaze remained fixed on the flowers below, so instead Seeker came up beside her and set her hands on the railing too. Seeker studied the Mebd's bone-china profile through the fall of lace stroking the Queen's cheek, and found it as flawless as a slightly smiling mask. As always.

"Your Majesty."

"You gave MacNeill something."

"Yes."

An angled look, a slow flutter of the Queen's long eyelashes behind the veil. "I'd rather," she said, and Seeker could tell that she phrased it carefully as a suggestion and not a command, "that he not learn more about that blade or its sheath than absolutely necessary."

"I understand," she answered. And then the Mebd turned to face Seeker fully, and it seemed the cold railing fell away from Seeker's hands and the earth shifted under her slippers.

Except for a few strands woven into the fine braided circlet which held the Mebd's golden waterfall of hair back from her face, that hair tumbled unbound and combed smooth upon her shoulders. "Do you understand that too?"

"Your Majesty . . ."

"Hush. Yes?"

"Yes."

The Mebd's mask never shifted. She touched the single intricate braid remaining. "This is not the first time I have taken this precaution. Although it proved unwarranted before. Still, there are a few who have need to know this thing. You are one. You will not speak of it. I will rebraid my hair tonight. But I will tie no knots."

Seeker nodded, feeling the pull of the compulsion on her skin. "Do you think you can get away with this?"

"They're accustomed to obedience," the Mebd said with a slight widening of her smile. "I am willing to risk your life, because I know I cannot trust you, else, and I have need of you. Your heart lies with the mortal men, though your family and interests lie with us, but you will learn the truth of it. Daoine and Unseelie, Elaine. Mortal and Fae. Each is less without the other. But I will not risk the lives of the Daoine Sidhe any more than I must. Or pay any prices higher than the ones I pay already."

Seeker thought the mask slipped for a moment, slipped and then settled back into place again. *Flawless. And cold.* She wondered if there were scars, white as ice on that skin white as snow, covering the fey Queen's neck and back, her thighs and arms. The Mebd looked down, studying the way Seeker's skirts brushed the pale stone. "Pay, Your Majesty?"

"Paid," she said, and that was all. Whatever emotion stirred behind her eyes faded and fled; she straightened and squared her shoulders as one shouldering a pack, tossing her sun-colored hair behind her shoulders. "Paid, and paid, and paid. Now go. I imagine someone must be waiting for you."

And so the Seeker returned to her rooms.

I wonder how Nimue felt, when she bound Merlin Ambrosius under the hill through the power of his love for her. I wonder if it was anything like this. Seeker unfolded her hands and let her fingers trail over the edge of her vanity, smudging idle letters in the wax protecting the ancient wood. Candles and oil lamps warmed the chamber with a flickering glow, making the figures in the wall hangings dance. *Did she wait for him like this? Knowing he would come to her? Knowing he had no choice?*

Maybe Ian's right, and it's all destiny we can't escape.

Except she chose. And made you understand that she knew what she was choosing.

Seeker closed her eyes. *Bind the Merlin.* No latitude. Only the command. Her pacing footsteps carried her from the window to the wall and back again, alongside the drawn curtains of the bed. *I didn't expect to like the Merlin.*

She fiddled with a candle on her desk, swirling the wax inside the thick amber pillar; her fingers dented the heat-softened sides before she forced herself to set it down. *The Mebd has freed her servants. Almost all of her servants. And I'm bound to hold that secret too.*

In the back of Seeker's mind, a laughing Mist unfurled wings like the leading edge of a thunderstorm. The old Dragon's earthquake voice rasped and grated in her memory: *"These are the older rules, and even the Mebd must abide them — that in life one may be bound or bought, but in the end you go to judgment naked, clad only in what you were born with and what you have earned, lessened only by what you have sold or given away. That which is taken by force, for good or for ill, goes unconsidered."*

When the time comes, she recollected, *remember this conversation.*

"Is it time?" She pulled her favorite chair to the fire and settled into it, stilled her jiggling toe by an act of concentration. "Mist, I wish I knew what you were talking about. At least Whiskey I understand." *Not that I particularly want to.* Seeker shook her head. She'd had no appetite for the supper that the court was attending, as much an organic continuation of Cairbre's carefully machined "impromptu" party as it was a formal meal. Instead she waited — poorly — wearing a path in the rug, a random, fussing circuit around her bedchamber while half her attention remained scattered through the shadows, castlewide. *I need to be cold for this,* she thought. *Cold and clean. Go away, and let the geas do as it will with me.* She closed her eyes. *I can't help it. There's no blame.*

No blame.

No, that's not true, is it? She was standing again, her hand tracing the bas-relief of the green man's mane of oakleaves beside the window. The glass was cold against her cheek, and outside the night was thick with stars and a crescent moon she could have sunk her heart on like a hook.

Keith had said, *"Once you would have known that."*

A moon like a horse's hoofprint.

There's blame, all right. All the blame in the world. Plenty of blame to go around. Whiskey knows it. And the Mebd knows it too. And Mist. I could — She felt after it. Felt the chill of the oblivion, the machinelike automation that had held her twenty-five years. It was still there, restful as the sleep that comes at the end of the long icy struggle in the black, sucking water. *I could go back. Slip back. Lie back and drown.*

I hurt less then.

Absently, she picked at the scab on the palm of her hand where the throne had bitten. *Arthur too. Dracula, Hermann.*

They were heroes, though. Seeker winced as she pulled too hard and blood welled up. She pressed her hand to her mouth, tasting blood, remembering the lingering way Whiskey had licked it from her palm. *And Morgan,* Seeker thought, in resignation and realization. *She's got her share of the blame too.*

But that was what it was to be Morgan le Fey. You did what you had to do. You sent one son to die on the battlefield, and you sent another, still living, to Hell. You waited and watched and pulled the threads. You bound and enslaved and manipulated and twisted. You spilled blood like wine upon the ground, and you paid the piper, and you paid the toll.

And you never got to say *It wasn't my fault.*

Seeker closed her eyes, but the eyes in the shadows beyond her door stayed open: wakeful, watchful. *That's what Mist meant.* She could take her own damnation in both hands. Claim it. Claim her own treachery, and know what it was she chose to do, and why. Because to deny it, to pass the blame . . .

The Mebd could bind Seeker. But she couldn't take her soul. And she couldn't take her name. Those were hers to keep, or to give away.

Or to destroy.

The window glass was as cold as the ice welling inside of her. As cold as the cold place in the center of her where the Mebd's sorrowing, merciless china smile had come to rest, divulging nothing, grieving endlessly. *"I'll take your heart / and make your heart / a stone."* Seeker shook her hair back. She mouthed Gharne's name, but didn't give it breath. She imagined the little demon was hiding, embarrassed as a cat that Whiskey had caught him.

"I could," she whispered instead, meaning, *I could crawl back into the darkness and never come out. Following orders. Don't think, don't ever think of what they mean. Be like the Mebd, cold-cast, porcelain and perfect. Above the pain. Look culpability in the eye and smile right back at it.*

And then the memory of Mist's chuckle, and Whiskey's knowing glance. *Remember. Remember.* Morgan. *I had a lover. I had a brother. I had a son. Remember.*

"Oh, fuck," she said. "All right. All right. Damn you all, all ready all right."

She turned to greet the knock on the door a moment before it fell, the shadows already telling her who was there. Bearing a bottle of wine and a pair of long-stemmed glasses, and a tentative expression. *Carel.*

"Fuck." Seeker raked one hand through her hair. "All right. I'll do it. Eyes wide open and Devil take the hindmost."

She opened the door gently—so gently.

"I"—Carel held up the bottle—"thought we should talk."

"No," Seeker answered. She took Carel by the wrist and drew the Merlin into the room, and into her arms, and into a darkness that the candles couldn't begin to disperse.

Seeker's lips moved against the other woman's throat. "Is this what you wanted, Carel? Is this your choice?"

"I don't think you're right," the Merlin said, as the door swung shut behind them, "but I don't want to live in a world without you. But it is only an alliance I offer, and not my soul. You can't have the Dragon."

"The Mebd will kill me," Seeker said bitterly, smiling, and took the glasses from the Merlin's hand. The Merlin touched her wrist. "If all stories are true, that must mean that stories can be changed."

Two wolves arrived at Morgan's cottage as the sun was going down, and Morgan met them at the door with steaming wine and clothes fit for a Faerie Queen's court. Keith didn't ask how she'd known. It never paid to admit mystification where Morgan le Fey was concerned. "We're expected, I take it?"

"My most royal sister is planning an announcement," she said, gliding barefoot across the slate-tiled, rush-strewn floor of her cottage as Keith belted the black iron spatha over borrowed wool. "You'll want to be there."

"Morgan." He heard his own exasperation. Morgan graced him with a smile that seemed assembled of bent rose petals. *Butter wouldn't melt,* Keith thought, and said, "Is there anything you *don't* do out of spite?"

The smile grew, spawning dimples. "Spite has very little to do with any of it, Dragon Prince."

She carried herself differently in skirts, more proudly, with a conscious sway to her hips: as if they reminded her of older times. The brocaded hem brushed the floor as she stood on one foot to slide her slippers on, her unbraided hair falling around her face like draped silk. Not surprising, after all: he knew wearing the short-sword made him stand straighter too.

Fyodor slouched against one of the peeled doorposts, long fingers laced over lean biceps, vastly amused by the charcoal-gray Edwardian suit and rose-red cravat that Morgan had dressed him in. "Fata Morgana," he said, when she turned back to the wolves, draping her hair behind her shoulder. "The witches in my childhood stories are very different, my lady."

"Baba Yaga has a cauldron also."

"Do you fly in yours?" Fyodor straightened away from the doorframe as she came toward him, and bowed over her hand with courtly Old World grace.

"Sometimes." Keith was surprised that she blushed when the black wolf's lips touched her fingers. "But mostly I make stew. Shall we visit my sister's court?"

Fyodor's larynx dipped as he swallowed. His scent sharpened with interest. *Now there's a complication,* Keith thought, and shook his head. *Well, it doesn't hurt me to have him interested in Annwn, now does it? Hush up and use what you're given, wolf.*

Morgan whistled her dogs and shut the door behind her guests. Her raven fluttered down from the rooftop to join them as they climbed the low slope to the wood's edge, the red dog and the gray dog casting left and right. The bird had a twisted wing; Keith noticed when it settled in a beech beside the path.

"Your bird is hurt," Fyodor said, and Keith wasn't sure if his attention had been drawn by Keith's, or if he'd noticed on his own.

Spear-shaped yellow leaves fell around them as they came into the wood. Morgan caught one in her hand and turned it toward the sky to examine it. A little sunlight came through the clouds and the branches, illuminating the brown-edged nibbles between the veins until they shone like glowing eyes. "He came to me because of it," she said, letting the leaf fall. Her smile was very white, and she offered it to Keith rather than Fyodor.

Keith leaned forward as the slope increased, his left hand guiding Caledfwlch's blade. They passed through the woods with magical quickness, crossing a broad, shallow stream on a bridge that Keith had never seen before. The boards creaked under his feet, and frogs splashed along the banks. For a moment he thought he heard something large shift beneath the silvered boards, but Morgan never broke stride and he and Fyodor paced her heels as if teamed. The wolfhounds rustled leaves and pushed through bushes; the crow cawed once, sharply, still flitting from branch to branch.

They came out of the wood in less time than Keith would have imagined possible, at the top of the long hill overlooking the Mebd's palace and the sea. Breakers combed the sand far below; Keith was certain at least one of them showed patches of white and dark that weren't merely seafoam and sea wrack buried in the glassy gray-green depths of the water. He looked away, preferring the view of the palace, gold spires gleaming softly in the watery overcast light. "Well, Younger Brother?"

"Amazing," Fyodor said, when Keith and Morgan had held their silence for a little while. He raised his head, scenting the breeze, picking out the scents of ocean and palace and wood. "I had thought it would be . . ."

"Less like a castle in a fairy tale?" Morgan offered.

Fyodor shook his head, curls bouncing like springs. "*More* like a fairy tale. Less *real*."

"Wait until you meet who lives there," Morgan said, and led them down the hillside, wolfhounds bouncing at her heels.

Fyodor Stephanovich is taking his introduction to Annwn shockingly well, Keith thought as they crossed the courtyard past the fountain and came up the low steps to the main doors. *But then, people — and wolves — are more likely to surprise you with pragmatism than with panic.* The black wolf did crane his neck a little as they entered the great hall, which was currently empty of Fae. The broad-paned glass ceiling showed overcast now, but when night fell the clouds would tear off as they always did, and the starlight would fall through.

"And where is the mother of your son?" Fyodor asked, picking his feet up precisely so his borrowed boots would not scuff in the herbs strewn across the patterned stone.

"Around somewhere," Keith answered, dropping his hand to tousle the ears of Morgan's gray dog. She leaned against his hip with a breathy sigh. "We should meet the Queen."

"We should," Morgan said. "If she will see us." The witch clapped her hands together, a hollow report that echoed back from the vaulted roof. "Otherwise, we will entertain ourselves until dinner is served, I imagine."

The patter of bare feet answered Morgan's summons. Rather than the page girl, Keith watched Fyodor's reaction, enjoying how the black wolf's scent peaked to surprise and then curiosity at the sight of a child garbed in ragged velvet castoffs three sizes too large for her. A child, more intriguingly, with a hare's powerful legs and long ears laid close to her neck among the hair. She had antlers too, three-pointed tines like a young stag's; they almost overbalanced her when she curtseyed. "Your Highness?" she said, her gray eyes downcast.

"Monkshood," Morgan said, earning a shy smile. "Canst say where I might find the Queen?"

A moment passed, Keith watching Fyodor's idle contemplation of the surroundings, and then the page returned and led them to the retiring-room where the Mebd sat by the window, at her sewing. "A Wolf-prince and the Dragon Prince," she said, tilting her head back to examine Fyodor without rising from her chair. "You're dressed well, at least." A disdainful glance leveled at Morgan, which could have been playful and could have been in deadly earnest. "And then there's thee: sackcloth and ashes do not besuit our dignity, sister."

Keith wasn't sure if that was the royal *our* or the collective one, but he nonetheless filed the comment for further consideration. "Your Majesty," Keith said, when Morgan did not step forward. "May I present Fyodor Stephanovich. I ask, madam, that you set your case before him."

The Mebd shrugged, but she stood and set her embroidery hoop aside. "My case?" she said, tilting her head back to look the black wolf in the eye. Morgan laid her hand on Keith's elbow; he didn't bother to shake it off, but he saw no need for the reminder. " 'Tis not so much a case, my lord wolf, as an inevitability. We will combine to survive, or we will face destruction. The alliances are shifting; I see an opportunity for Faerie to win free of Hell, and in so doing to soften the wrath of the Prometheans. Your brother wolf"—she nodded to Keith, her long neck inclining—"is a gift to us, an indication that the time is ripe."

Fyodor's slow smile showed long ivory teeth and curved crow's-tracks down his leathery cheeks. "Yes," he said. "Doomed Princes, ancient unbreakable patterns: it's all very dramatic, I'm sure. But what's the truth behind it, Your Majesty?"

She paced in a circle, regarding him, her train sweeping the rug. Keith stepped back against the wall, Morgan beside him, and kept himself out of the way.

"The truth behind it is, we do what we must," she said, making a dimple. "It's not so much a matter of prophecy or of portents as of geasa, and of the relationship between predator and prey." Delicate fingers brushed Fyodor's sleeve. "Surely a wolf can understand a kinship such as that."

Morgan leaned her shoulder on Keith's as they slouched against the paneling, her arms crossed as if in imitation of his own. Keith managed shallow breaths through his nose, the scent of Fyodor's curiosity and the Mebd's craft sharp in the little room, overpowering the tang of rosemary that hung around Morgan.

"A wolf can understand plain speaking," Fyodor said, cocking his head. Keith stopped himself as he was about to step out from the wall to cover the other wolf's flank: instinct of the pack, and he knew now why Morgan kept so close. "Tell me, Mebd of the Faeries, to what use would you put my pack?"

My pack, Keith thought, amused that he couldn't deny it. Fyodor should have been the Dragon Prince.

"You should ask the red wolf what purpose he'd put the Daoine Sidhe to," she said, coyly. "Since it's to him we'll pledge our troth—"

"A troth already given Hell," Keith said. "You'd see me break you from that treaty—"

"Aye," the Mebd admitted. "For your son's sake, and my heir's. And break the bondage the Prometheans have placed over us as well—"

"Why the wolves?" Fyodor, still quiet, his accented voice like crumbling chocolate.

"Wolves need not fear iron," Morgan said, when it became apparent that the Mebd would not answer. "Prometheus is armed against the Fae. There is little they can do to harm the pack, unless they were to learn in advance of your assistance."

"Our assistance is not promised," Fyodor said, with a sideways glance at Keith. Keith offered him his toothiest, least reassuring smile. "And the pack is less than it was."

"Faerie is not what it was either." The Mebd turned her arm over to show him the inside of her wrist. She drew her sleeve up and showed him pale and livid scars that marked her alabaster skin. "The Queen is the land," she said, and Keith thought she came as close to pleading as he had ever heard a Faerie come. "Surely you've heard that. The Prometheans leech us, Fyodor Stephanovich, with chains of iron and blood and witching woods, and it's only by feeding Annwn on our own heart's blood that we have kept any strength at all. You know what will befall when we are conquered. You *know*, wolf of the Ukraine."

He nodded and stepped away from the Queen, lowering his eyes, looking down. "*Da*, yes. The humans are proud of their Alexandrian solutions—"

"Genocide," she said calmly. "It will be a slaughter, Fyodor Stephanovich."

He nodded—"I have seen it done"—and his voice, so calm, might have been a blunt knife peeling Keith's skin back. *This is the wolf the pack needs. Not me.* "And what will it be if the wolves come to fight with you and Faerie conquers the mortal realm, Your Majesty? Will all strictures be burst and the Fae rule again as childlike gods over men?"

"We have no interest in ruling them."

"No," Morgan said, her eyes on the Mebd's, sparing a glance for neither wolf. "The Fae wish merely to reign. Never rule. But you will prey upon them."

The Mebd smiled, and lifted one shoulder and let it fall. Fyodor shook his head, and this time he looked at Keith, who was suddenly aware of his own tongue-tied silence. "And is not the Dragon Prince born to be betrayed by one of his own consanguineous line?"

"He is," Morgan said.

"I'm prepared," Keith answered.

Fyodor smiled. "Then who is to say that your betrayer will not be a brother wolf? Will you kill me if I oppose you to the end of the challenge, Keith MacNeill? If I fight you for your chance to stand as Sire to the pack?"

Keith opened his mouth to answer, to say *Yes, I'll fight. For Ian and his future if nothing else*—but the thoughts went spiky and dangerous, and wouldn't quite permit themselves to be shaped into words.

"Stay for dinner," the Mebd said, moving into the line of sight between Keith and Fyodor, looking from one to the other. "Stay with us. We'll announce your betrothal tonight, my lord Prince. Do you suppose tomorrow is too soon to marry?"

Chapter Seventeen

I an found Seeker at breakfast and sat beside her, chair scraping and skipping across the tiles as he dragged it closer. He picked up a plate and piled it with steaming rolls. Seeker pushed her meal around aimlessly.

"Did you forget me?"

She looked up and frowned. "For . . . oh. Dinner. Ian, I'm so sorry. . . ."

He shook his head, skin glimmering like ivory. A faint flush colored his cheeks like the sunward side of peaches. "It's all right. I imagine the conversation with Her Majesty upset you. And I had a long talk with Hope." He busied himself tearing a roll open, the sharp nails on his thumbs pressing through the crust and releasing the fragrance of fresh-baked wheat. He spread honey and butter over the ragged crumb.

The smell made Seeker's stomach clench, and she leaned back. "Hope?"

He looked up at her, serious. "She and I are lovers, mother." He pressed the halves of the roll together. Dripping butter and honey, they slipped and stuck. "She's with child."

Seeker bit her tongue on the easy response. "I'm going to be a grand-mother."

"Yes." He smiled and tore a piece from the roll, tucking it into his mouth. "I told father last night." A rolling shrug, and he set the rest of the bread down, pouring tea for himself. "Pity you missed dinner. There was quite the little drama. I think I'll have a chair moved up here for you, so you can sit by me. Instead of tormenting poor Peaseblossom."

"It's good for him to have his cage rattled once in a while. What sort of a drama?" She pushed her plate away; food was hopeless. She pulled her mug closer instead, so she could cradle the warmth in her palms.

"The Mebd set the date of your marriage."

This time, she did choke. "When?" she asked, the glare she directed at him heating her own face more than his.

"Tonight," he answered, with apparent unconcern. "See what happens when you don't pay attention?"

"That seems a little . . . arbitrary." She swallowed tea too hot. It burned the back of her throat, but she refused to splutter. "Sudden, even."

"Well, Her Majesty is nothing if not arbitrary. She pressed the issue. Something about my legitimacy."

Carel didn't mention it last night. Seeker closed her eyes on that memory. *Because she thought I already knew. Was coming to ask what it meant, and is savvy enough to notice that the marriages bandied hereabouts are chiefly political.* "Perfect," Seeker answered. "I don't suppose she has a dress picked out?"

"Probably," Ian answered, starting on his second roll. "I've been thinking about the enemy."

"Cold word, that."

He nodded, but it was dismissal disguised as agreement. "Arbitrary," he said, a chuckle coloring the word. "Cold. Have you forgotten where you are, mother?"

"No," she said. "I'd never assume anything Fae confused itself too much with morality."

"Good." No irony shaded his voice. "You need to eat, you know." He pushed his own plate at her. "Break bread with me."

Unwillingly, she took bread he had buttered already and spread with honey, holding it in her fingers, unable to raise it to her lips. "What have you been thinking, then?"

"I saw a black stag in the wood."

She dabbed a finger in honey, licked it off. The sweetness sickened her. "I saw a white one. Milk-white, with a rack like an emperor's crown." *Like that bloody throne in the other room.*

"Cernunnos."

"Oh, no. Ian, no." The bread scattered crumbs.

"I'm a hunter and a Prince, mother. Fae and mortal both. I know. . . . The Mebd taught me the Names."

She held up her hand, but his voice, soft and assured, rolled over that fragile barrier. "I could ride with them. I could call them up—the Sluagh, the Hosts of the Unquiet Dead."

"No." She shook her head, kept shaking it, unable to stop. "Not that."

"Are you afraid for me, mother?" He took her hand in his cold one and covered it with his other pale palm.

"You're talking about unleashing the Wild Hunt."

"Well," he said quietly, "it would be awfully hard for the enemy to pretend there was no magic in the world then, wouldn't it? Besides . . . the sacrifice. I thought it would be better. . . ."

Her thoughts took on a terrible slowness, thick and clear as the honey still cloying her tongue. "That's too much," she said. "Too much blood. Too much. And it's your father's responsibility. Dammit. His blood to shed, not yours. Not *yours*, do you hear me?"

He looked up at her, blinked. She realized she was standing. That she had been shouting, and every eye in the hall was on her, and that her hands were clenched to whiteness over Ian's. She drew her shoulders back and bit off a breath, did not turn to survey the room. Gave his fingers an extra squeeze before she jerked her hands away. "Not yours," she hissed, and stalked from the hall.

It was raining on Manhattan, a steady biting precipitation that splattered Matthew's windshield with fat gray drops and left tire-dragging puddles in the hollow places on the road. The rain would be the end of autumn's colors; golden-red and auburn leaves would clot the gutters near the park by morning, stripped from the branches as if by brushing hands. October was passing quickly, and he was no closer to convincing Carel Bierce to give the Prometheus Club another chance.

Matthew parked the car in a lucky space that he'd been manipulating chance and reading portents in favor of for almost two blocks, opened the door, and stepped over a White Castle burger wrapper snagged on a sewer grating in the flooded gutter. He flipped the hood of his sweatshirt up. A middle-aged woman caught sight of his tattooed wrists and put the breadth of the sidewalk between them. Matthew sighed resignation.

Prometheus would have sent a car, of course. But he didn't want to rely on them. Not for this.

Not at all. *I should have worn a suit,* he thought, but the constrained symbolism would have been more harm than help on a personal level, even if it did disguise him as a responsible member of society as far as the hospital staff were concerned. Instead, he zipped his camouflage jacket over the heather-gray hoodie and stuffed honestly chilled hands in his pockets, glad it was the rain and not Faerie treachery, for once.

Autumn was sliding into winter, and sometimes he didn't think it could happen quickly enough.

A hunched but unhurried stride carried him across the puddled sidewalk; he passed through revolving doors and stood dripping in the dim, luxurious lobby as his eyes adjusted. A crisp young person in ivory and blue manned the desk. Matthew dragged his hands out of his pockets and walked forward, fortifying himself with two deep breaths of filtered air.

"Hello," he said, when the young woman with the carefully pinned cap looked up. "I'm Dr. Szczegielniak. I'm here to see my brother, Kelly Szczegielniak. He's coming home with me."

Kelly stayed quiet as Matthew lifted him out of the car and into the wheelchair. Another time, he might just have carried his brother across the garage to the apartment building's elevator—Kelly was frail enough that it was just as easy to keep him up, once he was lifted, as it was to open out the chair—but Matthew's back was still complaining from his fall.

The elevator climbed; Matthew found himself smoothing Kelly's thinning hair and forced his fingers to rest on the slightly sticky handles of the wheelchair and curl into the black plastic grooves. Kelly made a sound like a nervous dog, huddling into himself, but calmed when Matthew relented and rested a hand on his shoulder. "Hang tough, Kell. It'll be fun. Like old times."

And hopefully he won't try to climb over the caregiver while I'm at the college. Of course, the caregiver that Jane had arranged was a Promethean, which made all the difference, but . . . *Oh, admit it, Szczegielniak. You're afraid to bring your brother home.*

The apartment door opened as Matthew wheeled Kelly up to it, dull tan hallway carpeting giving way to the gunmetal-blue and gray-green variegated wall-to-wall carpeting he'd installed himself, unwilling to live with the complex's seventies' industrial shag. Kelly curled into the vinyl of the chairback as Jane framed herself in the door, the smell of chicken stock and cooking vegetables drifting onto the corridor air. Matthew patted his brother's hair again, and wheeled him into the apartment. "Jane, are you everyone's mom?"

"Soup's on," she said, nudging her discarded shoes out of the wheelchair's path with a stocking-clad toe. "And I only mom the deserving. Can he handle hot food?"

Matthew shook his head. "If I can't get enough of the soup down him, there's a case of Ensure in the trunk of the car. But I wouldn't will that on my worst enemy."

"How bad could it possibly be?" Jane closed the door crisply and engaged both locks and the security latch.

Kelly had raised his head and was craning his neck to examine the room. Matthew's tastes ran to the eclectic, and bookshelves. His computer desk, in the corner, could have docked the *Lusitania*. Matthew checked to make sure his brother's seat belt was fastened, and crouched to unlace his own boots. "They gave me butter pecan."

Jane, for all her dignity, mimed gagging like a teenager. "For the love of God, Matthew. Just put an egg in his whiskey, or let the man starve in peace."

He followed her into the kitchen, pushing his brother before him, and seated Kelly at the edge of the table. Jane waved him away with a glance when he would have gone to assist her in spooning soup into bowls. "I've been thinking of moving," he said, settling down on a white-oak Danish chair. "Out of the city. After . . ."

"After the ritual?" She half filled the first bowl and slid it into Matthew's freezer to cool. "You're edging up on asking me why I asked you to bring Kelly home."

"I was considering coming at it directly, actually." But he smiled, and when she turned to him, Jane grinned. "All right, what are you plotting?"

"It's more what the Faeries plotted for us," she said, and set the bowl she was filling on the edge of the sink. "Take off your jacket, Matthew. Give me your hand."

Unhesitating, he did, and she unbuttoned his right shirt cuff and pushed the blue-and-white broadcloth up to his elbow. She laid his forearm on the table and unwound the rain-dampened blanket he'd draped over Kelly's shoulders to reveal a sweatered left arm. She pushed the sweater up as well, Kelly passive under her touch, his head twisted to one side as he hummed under his breath. Matthew knotted his hands into fists, watching the veins move over the tendons, and willed himself to stay still as Jane nudged Kelly's arm against his.

"The ink?" He forced himself to look at the way the black, sharply delineated lines on his own skin echoed the livid indigo of Kelly's. "It didn't protect him," Matthew said. "It won't protect me."

"No," Jane said, leaning back and exchanging a motherly expression for a brittle, determined smile. "But it brought him back to us alive. And has given us a link to Faerie that we can use to bring the Westlands to us. More or less."

Matthew considered, moving his arm just far enough that it didn't touch Kelly's skin, although he could feel the brush of hairs on fine hairs. "It would be better if we were twins," he said, when a crash of breaking glass from the street reminded him that he should be speaking.

"We will use what opportunity gives us," Jane said. Matthew looked sidelong at his brother, and couldn't look for long; Kelly had drifted off, his eyes drooping to slits, a thin line of saliva drooling down his chin. "You know what I'm going to tell you."

"Yes," he said, fiddling with his rings. "Someone always has to sacrifice something to make magic that large work. I can't believe you expect this of me, Jane."

She shook her head, her hand on his shoulder as he rolled down his sleeve. "I expect you'll do what you have to do, Matthew. I have faith in your commitment. And of all of us, I think you and I have the most to lose."

A few moments' thought before he could bear to nod, but he did, words sticking in his throat like burrs. "Yes," he managed eventually. "We have both got something to lose, haven't we? Tell me it's worth it, Jane—"

"It's worth it," she said, the ring of certainty in every word, and then she brought him a bowl of soup he couldn't eat. "Tomorrow," she said, "I think you should make one more attempt to contact the Merlin."

"It's falling apart, Gharne." White gravel scattering before her, Seeker stomped along the hardened path. Her familiar floated alongside, matching pace. "I thought—I don't know what I thought. Everything's crumbling, and I don't know what to do."

"It's been crumbling for a thousand years, mistress. Empires rise and fall. Languages die and peoples go extinct."

"It's different when it's your children."

"Why?"

She stopped on the path and dug her toe into the gravel, looking down. Her hair fell into her eyes and she smoothed it out of the way. "It just is."

"Right." His tone was mocking, but he came to rest on her shoulder, nuzzling her ear. "I notice you've given up the conceit of being the innocent victim."

"A victim is a victim. I can't afford to be that. And innocence . . . well." She shrugged and looked up. The white roof of Arthur's pavilion showed over the roses. She licked her lips as her gaze settled on it, and a black-beaked raven took flight from its peak. She heard other footsteps on the gravel, beyond the hedge and rosebushes, and reached through shadows to see Keith speaking with a black-haired man. It was a temptation to eavesdrop on Keith and his raggle-taggle Wolf-prince. It might even be a duty. *I cannot trust him. I cannot be trusted.*

And yet she hesitated, twisting her hands together. It would be the Fae thing to do. The Mebd, Whiskey, Robin—even Hope—would not hesitate to use their power so.

And it would be the human thing to do, to trust even if trust seemed foolhardy. Seeker reached up to scratch the softness behind Gharne's ear and kept walking. "He's supposed to come in our hour of need."

"Someone's hour of need, anyway." Gharne settled his wings warm over her shoulders. "But you don't know how to wake him."

She pushed her hair back with her hand. Her fingers tangled in Gharne's braid, and she unsnagged them abruptly. *I wish I could get this mess cut.*

She stopped, contemplating that, and worried her lip between her teeth. "Gharne?"

"Yes?"

"Get Keith for me. Tell him to bring his sword. And leave his friend behind." She shrugged the protesting familiar off her shoulder and walked forward, eyes fixed on the roofline of the pavilion. Keith was sitting on the steps when she came from among the fall of yellow roses.

Caledfwlch leaned against the rail and Keith's long legs stretched out. He stood as Seeker approached. "You always liked this place. The Mebd's arranged us a state wedding."

"I heard." She couldn't meet his eyes. Her own stung. "Keith. I—"

"Don't." He shook his head. "I don't want to talk about it. We can't have normal expectations of each other anymore."

It wasn't what she anticipated, and it wasn't what she wanted, but she nodded. He put a hand on her elbow to guide her up the steps. She smiled. "I do love you."

"I know." He gave her arm a squeeze before letting his hand fall. "Every time I come here, I find myself wanting to say, 'He looks so real!' As if he were a wax doll."

"He's about as much use as one," Seeker commented dryly. "May I borrow your sword?"

"Useful or not," Keith said, "I can't have you lopping his head off."

"Ah. I didn't mean to. Keith . . ."

"Yes?"

"Ian came to talk to me. About the baby. And—" She forestalled Keith with a raised hand when he leaned forward, a smile cracking his face. "He told me he thought of a way to deal with the Magi."

Her tone carried the message. "I'd rather not know."

"But you have to know," she said, pitiless. "He says he knows how to summon the Hunt."

"Jesus Christ!" Seeker flinched, covering her ears. Keith, instantly concerned, took her wrists in his hands. "I'm sorry. Oh, no." He stroked her cheek before he backed away. "So you think Arthur is an alternative?"

"I—Keith, you're many things. You're not a general."

"I know. Fyodor Stephanovich is, however."

"Who is Fyodor Stephanovich?"

"My rival," Keith said bitterly, leaning back on the alabaster rail. "The wolf who should be Prince of the pack. The wolf, in point of fact, that Mist once asked me if I would follow, were he the Dragon Prince."

"And would you?" Seeker caught herself nibbling her lip and forced herself to stop. Instead, she pulled a single yellow rose from the bush and shredded its velvet petals, wet gilt marking her fingertips.

"In a heartbeat."

"And will he follow you?"

He wouldn't look up from his careful perusal of his nails. "That remains to be seen. It should be his, Elaine. He was made for it—"

"But you were born to it."

"Can a man be born into the wrong role in life?" He turned to track the flight of a raven—the same one? another?—across the cinder-colored clouds. "Sometimes I wonder if you would have been happy if I had not found you."

Seeker pressed her fist against her chest to ease the pain. "Kadiska probably would have stolen me away to serve the Cat Anna," she attempted. She reached out and brushed her fingertips down his arm. "And then there would be no Ian—"

He swallowed hard. "Our son. He'd unleash something like that?"

Like a bee drawn back by the scent of honey, he returned to the thought. "I've heard stories."

"Get Cairbre to tell you." Seeker breathed deeply, taking in the scent of roses that surrounded the sleeping King. "When they ride, they destroy whatever falls in their path. Hamlets. Villages. Towns. Entire civilizations."

"I'd like Faerie to survive this," Keith said. "But not at that price. If they're awakened, can they be put down again?"

Seeker shrugged. "If I'd been chained for a few hundred years, I might wake up a tad cranky. They were put down once."

"Mist was chained under the earth too."

"Exactly. Now may I have Caledfwlch? Please?"

He drew the short, dark spatha out of its sheath and offered it to Seeker. She palmed the leather-wrapped hilt and felt the thing's weight in her hand. When she looked up again, he regarded her, something that wasn't a smile folding the corners of his eyes. "What are you going to do with that?"

Seeker grinned into the blade. It didn't reflect her smile. "I'm going to cut the King's hair," she said, and walked toward the bower where Arthur lay.

"Wait." Keith laid a hand on her shoulder. She turned toward him, frowning. "Elaine."

Her lips thinned. She started to shake her head, until he brushed the sword to one side and palmed her cheek, holding her gaze. "Is this just a political marriage?"

"We're going to get killed," she answered. "Or you are."

"So I'm selfish," he said. "If I were dying of cancer, would you still marry me?"

"If you were dying of *cancer* . . ." She sucked her lip, letting her voice trail off. "I wouldn't know what you're going to do. What I'm going to do."

"So life sucks. So what." His mouth twitched. "We do the good we can do on the way to the gallows. Tell me something."

"Yes?"

"How are our geasa, how is our wyrd, any different from that of any man who struggles and is probably defeated and dies, except that ours is more manifest?" He sighed, full-chested, and scratched at his beard. "Will you feel better if I promise not to trust you?"

She closed her eyes and shook her head. "Keith, it's not fair to you."

"Crappy excuse," he answered. "It'll be harder on you. I get to die messily. And probably young. Now, if you want to spare yourself the pain . . ."

"I can't be faithful. I can't be anything."

"I'm not making any promises," he said, and bent to kiss her. "Why do we have to talk about this?"

She permitted the kiss but couldn't bring herself to soften into it. "What's the alternative? Ignore it?"

"Why not? Live in the moment. We wouldn't be the only ones ever to do so."

Live like wolves. Why not, indeed? Seeker nodded, feeling edgy and brittle. "I see." She drew away from him, turned, and looked down at the sleeping King. Caledfwlch's tip dug a careless furrow in the floor stones; she lifted it, swearing.

"What's your plan?"

"Just a hunch. Did you ever stop to wonder why the Gwragedd Annwn trim his beard, but never cut his hair? Lift him, please."

Keith removed the bronze blade from Arthur's chest and took him by the shoulders, pulling the sleeping King into his arms. Seeker reached up and combed her fingers through Arthur's waist-long hair, feeling the frayed ends frizzy against her palm. She lifted Caledfwlch and braced it against the edge of the bier, pulling Arthur's smooth locks into a rough ponytail.

Keith supported him like a sleeping child, too big to carry. "Watch the sword," he cautioned.

"Well, don't drop him on it."

The werewolf rolled his eyes. "Heaven forefend."

The strands seemed hard as wire. The point of the blade bit into stone, but she had to saw the ruddy gold of Arthur's hair back and forth across the black iron blade, and still it resisted. Frustrated, she yanked harder; Keith held Arthur's head steady, knocking his golden circlet to the floor.

One by one, strands parted, curling away from the blade. Seeker stepped back, Caledfwlch cold in her right hand, Arthur's hair clutched like a flagging banner in her left. The sleeping King shuddered, and Keith laid him down. "Poor bastard." He reached to smooth the ragged edges of hair from Arthur's face.

A hand latched onto the werewolf's wrist before even Seeker could have reacted, and Arthur's eyes opened as if on springs. "Cei," he said, in a voice that gave no hint of his long sleep. "Shake me no more. I've had the strangest dream."

And then he blinked, sat up, and released Keith's wrist. "I beg your pardon, sir. My sight was blurred, and you're not who I took you for. What is this tongue I'm speaking?"

"Fae," Seeker said. She dropped a curtsey, ridiculous in trousers. "Ard Ri. Welcome back from your rest."

Arthur's eye lit on the sword in her hand. "I was dying," he said with the air of one remembering. He swung his legs over the edge of the bier. "Bedwyr said he'd give that blade back to the Faeries."

"He did," Keith answered. He extended his hand and helped the Ard Ri to his feet. "You slept. You did not die. Morgan and her sisters brought you here, Your Majesty, and it is some fifteen hundred years since you shut your eyes. You're in Annwn, where you have slumbered while the world went on without you."

We should have told him that while he was still sitting down, Seeker thought. Arthur staggered, and Keith caught him. Seeker stepped back to keep the blade out of the way.

"Fifteen —*hundred*." His eyes were the blue of cornflowers, and he was of a height with Keith. "Is there still a Britain?"

Keith nodded.

"Good," Arthur said softly. "Then I'm not King anymore. By the grace of God."

"No," Keith answered, his fingers whitening on Arthur's wrist as

Seeker flinched and looked quickly away. "I am. A King of sorts, though not of England. And I need your help, Ard Ri."

"Yes," Arthur said. "I imagine."

Arthur regained his strength quickly on the walk back to the palace. He shied from the blade at Keith's hip after Seeker returned it, but seemed otherwise steady, occasionally running his hands through his tattered hair with a wry little frown. "Gwenhwyfar?" he asked Seeker as they came within sight of the castle, in a voice without hope.

"Only you," she answered, letting him lean on her arm.

"How did she die?"

"In a convent, the legends say. Old and not alone."

"That is . . . good. What of Lance?"

She stopped in her tracks and turned to meet his eyes. "Arthur." She shook her head. "Dead in battle. All gone but for you. And Morgan."

The King licked his lips, and then he turned his head and spat. "Morgan. And where has she been for fifteen hundreds of years? Still fancying herself a Queen?"

"No," Seeker said, watching Keith's back as the werewolf strode ahead. "But you should know she's my grandmother. And my father's sire was Lancelot." She felt the old King stiffen against her grip. She didn't turn to look at his face.

The scent of Elaine's concern blew from her in tatters on every breeze, but that wasn't the chief source of the worry stiffening across Keith's shoulders as he walked. That honor went to the raw, rank scent of hidden fear that dripped from Arthur like cold sweat, provoking Keith's hackles to rise even in human shape. If he'd been a wolf, his ears would have been pinned against his skull. He jumped when Arthur spoke:

"Do you hear the Dragon?" The King's voice was level as frozen water.

That's what an Ard Ri should sound like. Even when he's shaking in his boots. "Not recently," Keith answered.

"It's because I stood up to her," Elaine said. "She won't interfere now, the way she would have."

"Are you certain of that?" Keith glanced back.

Elaine's weight shifted as Arthur straightened, standing upright under his own power now. "No," Elaine said. "And what are you certain of?"

He stopped completely and turned to face her, frowning, though he couldn't keep the twinkle out of his eye. He could feel it there, beating its wings below the surface; it broke free quickly and turned itself into a grin. "I've missed that."

And as if Arthur of Britain were not standing beside her, she blushed and said, "So have I."

Arthur held his peace, and without another word they found their way to the Mebd's retiring-room, where the door was again propped open. The Queen looked up as they paused in the doorway, and Keith laid a hand on Arthur's elbow, honestly concerned the King might pivot on his heel and bolt.

"Welcome," the Mebd said, standing and laying her sewing aside. If she were surprised, it vanished under her porcelain mask. "Welcome, Arthur of Britain. And you, Seeker of the Daoine Sidhe. And you, Dragon Prince. We greet you all."

"Your Majesty," Arthur said, and went down on one knee before her. Elaine curtseyed more slowly, and Keith stood his ground. "I am Arthur of Britain no longer, or so I am told."

"But it matters what you were as much as what you are." The Queen smiled and gestured Elaine to her feet. "Seeker," she said. "There are clothes and servants in your quarters. You must go and make ready for your wedding. Dragon Prince, you as well."

Keith glanced sideways at Arthur. "Ard Ri—"

"Arthur," Arthur said, without taking his eyes from the Mebd. "I've had enough of the other. It's all right, Dragon Prince. Her Majesty and I have things to discuss."

Elaine surprised Keith when she pressed him back against the wall in the corridor and kissed him hard, a little catch in her breathing as if something hurt her. "Tonight," he said, checking the hang of the short-sword at his hip.

"Tonight," she agreed, and turned away so fast it almost looked like flight.

Keith closed his lips over a promise he couldn't have kept, and went to find a page to tell him where he was supposed to report to be groomed and dressed. *From pack wolf to show dog,* he thought, as young Wolfsbane showed him to the chamber that had been reserved for his use. There were servants already within, and Keith braced himself to be fussed over, but the first words out of the pixie valet's mouth were, "A messenger came for you, Your Highness."

"A messenger?" Stupidly, shrugging out of his borrowed jacket. "And do you know where to find Fyodor Stephanovich?"

"He is with the messenger—"

"Send for them." Sharper than he meant it to be. He drew a breath. "Please."

"As you wish."

They had him down to his trousers and barefoot by the time the door opened again, and it was only a few moments. Keith spent the time counting fragile breaths, knowing before he caught the mingled scents from the hall who would enter the room at Fyodor's side. Knowing what the message would be.

"Elder Brother," Ivan Ilyich said, holding the door for Fyodor as he came in.

"Vanya. Welcome." The darkness in the blond wolf's eyes confirmed his panic; perversely, his roiling gut settled once he knew. "It's my father."

"Come soon," was all he answered.

"I am to be married in a very few hours, Vanya." A struggle to keep his voice level. "Will he last the night?"

"At least. But not much longer."

"Ah." Keith looked from Vanya's bright azure eyes to Fyodor's that glittered like cleaved rock. "So it begins."

"So it ends," Fyodor answered, crossing the room to close one skeletal hand on Keith's bicep. He squeezed in sympathy. As Keith met the other wolf's gaze, they shared a silent nod.

"Go on ahead," Keith said, drawing a breath, breaking his first promise already. "Go. Take my son. I'll be there."

"Elder Brother—" Vanya began, from the doorway.

Fyodor cut him off with a gesture. "As you say. Congratulations on your wedding, Keith MacNeill."

"Thank you," Keith said, and spread his arms so the sprites and brownies could finish undressing him.

Chapter Eighteen

A small army of maids and ladies lay in wait for Seeker when she returned to her chambers. They bathed her and dressed her in layers of underthings, corsets and garters, all of them meant to be seen. In private, at least. The Mebd had indeed chosen a dress for her: neither white, ivory, nor Seeker's habitual gray, but an emerald-green watered moiré silk jeweled in gold thread, amethyst and tourmaline across the low-necked bodice and down the peacock length of the cathedral train.

Seeker suffered her hair to be oiled and dressed, diamonds pinned through it and pearls shining against its darkness like moons seen through a mist. The maids' brushes made her face as perfect as the Mebd's, if golden rather than porcelain, and the gown weighed on her; its violet-silk-lined Queen sleeves and ruched skirts were heavy as stones piled on her chest. *This isn't how I thought I'd marry.*

A tap fell on the door as the last emerald button of the portrait collar was fastened at the nape of her neck. Seeker startled as if someone had kicked the door of her stall.

"Come in!" Her voice stayed steady. Even commanding. *Wonder of wonders.*

But composure fled when the door to her chamber opened and Whiskey came into the room, impeccable in a white tie and tails. He smiled and swept a bow, a silver horsehead cane in his right hand and a spray of blossoms in his left. "I see Her Majesty forgot your corsage, mistress," he said, as the ladies and maids withdrew out of earshot, one or two of them shooting him nervous glances. He extended the blossoms to her: a spray of tiny violet orchids, each no bigger than the diamonds in her hair, with an emerald pin to fix them.

"How did you know the colors?" It was the first thing she thought, and she regretted the words as she said them.

"I've seen the dress," he answered, with a satisfied smile. "If I may pin you?" He winked at the double entendre.

Seeker restrained herself from smacking her forehead; it would have destroyed a half hour's paint. "You may."

He handed her his cane and the flowers, retaining the pin. Long, warm fingers slid under the low neckline of her gown, protecting her from the stabbing tip. "It wouldn't do," he said, securing the orchids over her bosom, "to spill blood on the silk. Even if the color is dark."

"What is that supposed to mean?"

He winked, and his fingers slid a little. She struggled not to gasp, but she couldn't hide the shiver. "Nothing," he answered. "Careful. You might tumble right out of that gown, my lady. Despite your corset."

"Your hand, Whiskey."

"Yes, mistress." He smiled and stepped back. "I suppose I shouldn't ask for the honor of giving the bride away?"

She wished she could pivot on the ball of her foot and stride away, but the corset set her spine and the train drew her shoulders up stiff, and she would have had to march on a sweeping curve to manage a turn. "Arthur is doing it," she told him. "The Mebd asked him."

"Ah, well. Then I will see you at the feast, I hope." He reclaimed his cane and turned away, then hesitated with one hand on the door. "And perhaps claim a dance or two." Flawless, he bowed and left before she could answer.

Arthur awaited Seeker among the tapestries outside the throne room. He turned to her as she came through torchlight, flanked by her attendants. Though his gray-blue eyes gave away nothing, she saw the way his chest rose and his breath caught as he looked her over. "Were you fair instead of dark," he said, "would swear I knew you, Queen Elaine."

"Not Queen yet," she answered.

"Soon enough to deserve the courtesy." He took her arm, sliding his hand under the floor-brushing sweep of the Queen sleeves. "I've only seen the like of these once before."

"They weren't in fashion yet when you . . . entered your slumber," Seeker told him. "Where would you have seen them?"

"On a Fae maiden's gown," he said, turning too-bright eyes away. "The music is starting. Is your train arranged, my lady?"

"My lord," she answered with a nod, wondering at his reaction. "Let us do this thing."

Brownies, strong beyond their size, swung open the relief-carven doors, and Arthur in his cochineal and royal purple led Seeker over the sea-blue, sea-green tiles into the Mebd's throne room. He tightened his grip on her arm when she shuddered and might have stumbled, sneaking her a wry little grin. "You're white," he whispered. "Fear not. 'Tis a pleasant sort of torment, marriage. In its way."

Seeker nodded, but her eyes were fixed on Keith, who wore green and gold to complement her gown. He turned to watch her enter, his hair very bright against all that verdigris. Not as bright as the red, red robes swathing the Mebd, however: robes as red as the pall over the throne upon which she sat, her body seeming relaxed and at ease. Seeker winced at the sight, feeling the gouge on her palm sting as if fresh. She let the corset hold her straight and didn't limp on her taped, aching toe.

The wedding itself passed in a blur. Seeker couldn't remember the vows she spoke, or the ones Keith answered, or anything except the susurrus of the Mebd's voice as she administered them without rising from her throne. When it was done, Seeker felt his lips brush hers and couldn't bring herself to close her eyes. The ring on her finger was a broad red-gold band paved with emeralds; it felt even heavier than the gown.

A handmaid lifted her train. Keith took her arm and helped her descend the steps. She searched the crowd with flickering eyes, restraining with an iron will the urge to turn her head. "Have you seen Ian?"

"Before the wedding," he whispered, bending toward her. "I sent him on an errand."

"Away from our *wedding*?" The guests stood, applauding as they passed, turning like so many clockwork follies.

"I'm leaving after the toast," he said, and she realized that the lines around his eyes and mouth were more than the worries of a marriage that wasn't as he had envisioned.

"Keith, what's going on? Where did you send Ian?"

Her voice was low, for his ears only, and he answered the same way: "My father is dying. I'd have left already, but I wasn't going to leave you at the altar."

"I'll come with you," she offered. "I just need time to change. Or something—" Arthur caught her eye, and offered her a half-bow with his applause as they passed. Seeker smiled in return, noticing that he was flanked by Cairbre on one side and Cliodhna on the other. "—to hack the train off with."

"Elaine," he said. "No. I'm sorry. It's only for the pack."

"You and your fucking macho werewolf society," she hissed.

"Sorry." He even sounded sorry. "Elaine. My *father*."

"I didn't get to go home when mine died." They were at the door and walking down the hallway now, to more applause; brownies and bogies lined the walls, clapping and cheering. And Whiskey, standing last before the doorway to the great hall.

"You'd prefer not to see this. Trust me. Besides, you'll have to hostess the feast in my absence."

Something rose up in Seeker, a sort of icy precision that seemed to flow up the channel of her spine. "Go." *I'm a Queen now. Although I'm sure the Mebd wouldn't put up with this.* And then she thought of the Queen's impassive face as she leaned on her throne and felt her cheeks blanch.

You've misjudged her. It was an odd thing, a voice that might have been someone else's, speaking as if in Seeker's ear. *You've misjudged it all.* Someone brought wine in glasses, and she and Keith drank the toast.

Keith took his leave with a kiss, and the Mebd came up beside Seeker as she watched him walk out of the hall, still clad in his wedding green. "Congratulations," the Mebd said in her ear. "Have you seen the Merlin?"

Seeker finished the wine that was left in her glass, set it down and picked up her husband's, shaking her head in answer to the question. Carel had not been at the wedding. "I want my son's heart back," she said, frowning around the goblet's crystal rim.

"It was that or his soul," the Mebd said softly. "I've kept it fed. You peered under the pall on my throne."

"So?"

"So if I hadn't taken one or the other, he would not survive sitting on it, kinswoman. And the throne must be fed as well. It's something of what has kept Annwn alive." The Queen inclined her head to Seeker and turned away.

"Scian," Seeker said after her, softly.

The Mebd halted, one foot in midair. She set her slipper down gently on the rose-and-green marble of the floor and turned, her placid face half-smiling. "She taught you all the Names, didn't she? All of Manannan mac Llyr's children."

"No," Seeker answered. "She didn't tell me her own."

"No," the Mebd answered, braids swaying like ears of wheat under her veil and her crown. "She wouldn't." The Queen nodded slightly in acknowledgment, turned once more, and drifted away like a ship cutting water.

Seeker never knew how she made it through dinner, or out of her gown and into her nightdress, except that many hands helped her. Those same servants would have put her to bed, after, but she threw them out and built up her fire and sat drinking tea with brandy and staring into the flames, gnawing her thumbnail until she tasted blood. Someone had taken the jewel-toned orchids from her gown, trimmed the stems, and set them in a water glass on the mantel, and every so often her eyes rose to it and then sheered away.

"I told you you would need me more, after the wedding."

"I didn't summon you, Whiskey," she answered without turning her head.

"You didn't bid me stay away, either," the Kelpie answered from the doorway. He shut the door as silently as he had opened it and threw the latch behind. "You look lonely, my lady."

She stood, letting her teacup clatter on the table. "And you're just the man to help me with that, I suppose?"

"I'm not a man." But he came to her, smiling, to lay a hand on her shoulder. "I thought you wouldn't say no to company."

The crystal-hard clarity that had infected her earlier didn't shift. She found herself frowning, meeting Whiskey's blue eyes and his companionable smile. "I thought about what you said to me by the loch," she said, taking his hand in her own. "I was thinking that I might understand you better if I were full-Fae."

"I might understand you better if I had a soul." He shrugged. "But I doubt it. And we don't need to understand each other. If anything, mistress, you need to understand the Magi."

"I understand what I need to," she said bitterly. "Prometheus. What more do I need to know?" She thought of Matthew and shook her head. "Fire or godhood, what does it matter what you're stealing?" She ran her thumb along the broad silver band around his. "There's a limit to how much iron that silver can protect you from, water-horse."

"I know," he said. He kissed her on the mouth and she didn't have the energy to push him away. "There's a limit to how long a mortal can bear to be alone." His teeth touched her neck, her ear. His breath was hot as acid on her flesh.

"I know," she answered, leaning into his embrace. "I need to be stronger, Whiskey. And I need to be free of the Mebd." *Lile,* she thought. *Scian. Maat. Damn you and your riddles, Morgan. I think I finally understand.*

"Make your King stronger," he offered, long fingers brushing her cheek. "Strong as his love for you."

She looked at him with something that didn't feel like pity. "Have you ever loved anything, Uisgebaugh?"

"I have no soul," he answered.

"No," she said, "but you have a heart. Ian can feel love; he can't feel the pain of betrayal, though. The Mebd is soulless, and you are, and there's no love in either one of you. But you can hold fast to something, can't you?"

"Fast indeed."

"Can you hate?"

"I've never needed to." A gesture with an open hand, moon-silver glittering.

"I've been thinking about bondage, you know." Almost hating herself: wishing she could hate herself. Wanting one last taste of hatred, before the end. She saw the startled expression cross his face, alert like a horse prick-eared after a lump of sugar.

He didn't speak, just stood. Expectant.

Hopeful.

"Will you accept a gift of me, Uisgebaugh?" Ritual words. She thought of a braid in the Mebd's golden hair, and smiled a lie.

"Yes," he said softly, and she trembled, and thought of the throne. *Nothing with a heart could sit on that and live. And Ian will never sit on that thing.*

The blood of Manannan mac Llyr.

You go to judgment . . . less what you have given away. All right, Mist. Maat. I understand now. "I am Elaine Elizabeth Andraste MacNeill," she said. "And I give unto you my soul, Uisgebaugh. My soul and my Name, and all that entails."

He gasped in pain. Gasped and cringed, and then fell to his knees, his face twisted in torment. He screamed into his fists, and then he folded like a broken doll.

The wind from one door opening closes another.

I knelt beside my milk-white steed and cradled his shaking body in my arms, feeling curiously light and contented. I smiled and stroked his hair while he wept. "All's fair in love and war," I whispered. "I wish I could say I was sorry, Uisgebaugh. It hurts rather badly, doesn't it?"

He nodded against my nightgown; before he was done with weeping I stood him up and I took him to my bower.

It was good to be less than alone.

Chapter Nineteen

"You tricked me," Whiskey said against my neck, sometime before sunrise. "You tricked me."

"Poetic, isn't it?" I let one finger stroke his shoulders, gentling a sensitive horse. His flesh shuddered as if he flicked away a fly. "The question, my dear, is have I made you less of a monster, or more."

"More," he whispered, sounding small but never hesitating. "Is this what you felt? Mistress? This hurt?"

"More or less."

"Take it back."

Everything was numb except the tips of my fingers where they touched him. I was numb. I should have hurt. Should have screamed myself raw as meat, as Whiskey had when I gave him my soul and my name. Instead, I felt hollow: curious milkweed husk with the silk and seeds blown wide by autumn.

An absence. An amputation: the absence of love. The absence of compassion. I don't mean to suggest that there was no more pain. But the pain no longer distracted me.

Already, I could see the advantages.

"I feel like a dragon," I said to Whiskey, wondering.

"You feel like a Queen," he answered, moving in my arms. "Take it back. I don't want it."

"Neither do I," I lied. "I don't need it anymore." *"Alas, my love. You do me wrong, to cast me off discourteously. . . ."*

"If I had known. If I had known, Tam Lin. . . ."

Oh, yes. It's not the old songs, only. *"As you are now, so once were we."*
I knew.

I knew why the Mebd had stood before her chair and wept, wept like a woman left utterly alone in the world, with the weight of the world upon her. Wept the cold, silent tears of a creature that could not know love, and could not know hope, but could know fear and loyalty and passion and a kind of cold battlefield courage.

Such a creature she was. And now so was I.

"It hurts," he said.

"I know." I stroked his hair one last time and he started to cry again. "It's going to hurt." Irritated by my own pity, I pushed him away, slid from under the covers and stood. The cold light brewing beyond the window drew me. I leaned against the leaded panes and smiled.

"Gharne."

My familiar slid through the gold stone of the wall and curled on the window seat, smug as a cat. "Mistress."

"Take care of Whiskey, please. I have errands to attend."

My familiar preened his wing talons dismissively. "As you wish it. Where are you going?"

"To visit my lover."

He cocked his head to one side, eye smoldering under the browridges. Whiskey's sobs became silence. "Which one?"

"Hah." Naked, I turned my back on the window and summoned a servant to help me dress. While she selected my clothes and laid them out, I searched shadows through the castle, and elsewhere. Through those shadows I heard music, and it drew my attention down the broad golden corridors of the palace, leading me at last to the doorway of the Mebd's quarters. The shadows opened themselves to me, willing, much to my surprise. I realized something else as well.

Kadiska. The Mebd could have walled her without the palace as easily as Àine has walled me out of the Unseelie courts.

In the Queen's chambers, Hope sat over her harp singing softly, old songs and the new, while Cairbre filled cups by the wall and the Mebd sat beside a low enameled table. Beside her rested Morgan, in blue jeans and a charcoal sweater. Arthur Pendragon leaned against the wall, as far from the red-haired sorceress as the size of the room permitted.

"We're all family here," Morgan was saying. "More or less." She gestured to Arthur. "I wish you would believe me, brother."

"I still remember the cloak," he answered quietly. "And how you weaseled Caliburn's scabbard away from me before Camlann."

She smiled. "Ancient days." Her fingers flickered out and back: dismissal. "We're on the same side now."

"You expect me to fight on behalf of the Fae courts." He shook his head. "Sorcerers. And murderers of innocents."

"Stealers of infants?" Morgan countered, her smile that much wider.

Arthur blanched. "Aye." He took the cup that Cairbre handed him, and quaffed it in a mouthful.

"You wouldn't have survived that spear thrust, scabbard or no scabbard," Morgan replied, as Hope finished the "Fairy Reel" and began to sing an old American song. "After fifteen centuries, Artus. A little faith."

The King shook his head while I laced the collar of my blouse. "What about Elaine? You're still selling *your* children into bondage. Sister."

"Yes," Morgan said. "*About* that 'child Elaine' . . ."

I glanced over my shoulder at Whiskey and frowned. And then I stepped through the shadows into the Mebd's sitting room, appearing beside her chair. ". . . she's listening," I finished for Morgan, bending to kiss my grandmother on the cheek: a dry kiss, the brush of butterflies.

She glanced at me and then raised her hand to her lips, her eyes wild. "Elaine. Oh, you haven't."

"For Ian," I said against her hair. "Blood of my blood." Morgan le Fey closed her eyes, and I moved away, claiming the center of the room.

Arthur's eyes followed me as the Mebd set her glass aside and stood. "Queen Elaine," they said in unison, and then Arthur laughed and stepped forward, extending a powerful hand. "You seem more Fae than I remember."

"I am more Fae than I was," I answered, and kissed Arthur and then Cairbre, a red-bearded cheek and a black. "Have the night's counsels been kind to you?"

"Aye." The Mebd examined me. "Such courage, kinswoman."

"It was nothing," I lied again. "We'll speak later. About Ian. And other things."

"Yes," she answered. "We will speak of those things." She tucked a braid behind her ear, and I frowned at the tug. Unfair, that giving away my Name had not broken the binding on it. I had hoped—

"Good," I said. I smiled at Arthur. "My lord. My husband has left me to arrange things while he attends his family." *Husband.* The word tasted strange. "Will you be our general?"

"When is the war?" he answered, as Cairbre handed him another cup and brought me one.

"Good man," Morgan murmured.

I smiled. "As soon as we find it. We'll have to hunt them where they den. Mebd?"

"Elaine."

"Where have you hidden Faerie's heart?"

Hope plucked a false note on her harp, and the rill of music fell silent. *"Mother, tell my baby sister not to do the things I've done."*

The Mebd laughed, delighted, her head thrown back and her pale pink lips parted like blossoming rose petals. "You tell me, clever lass. How did you know?"

"Morgan, may I ask you a question first?"

"Of course."

How could I not have seen this sooner? "The white hart is the symbol of the King."

"Yes. That's not a question."

"It isn't, is it?" I felt the strange lightness take me again. "What's the black hart, Morgan?"

She grinned and tipped her glass. "The symbol of the King."

It stopped me short. I looked from Morgan to her brother, and then around the room from sister to sister, and then to the bards. I blinked. Arthur took a step forward, feeling for a sword he wasn't wearing. "You fucking bitches," I said, not bothering to hide the awe in my voice. "Faerie's heart. You put it in the throne. That's why there's no weather in Annwn."

"No love," Arthur said. "No passion."

"No storms," the Mebd answered. "No sunshine. No sleet, no rain, no hail, no thunder. But a heart needs blood to live, in a body or in a box."

The music had stopped, and Hope stood and came forth. "What am I?" she asked quietly, one hand pressed to her stomacher.

"The future." And there was something in the Mebd's smile that silenced Hope, and me. And then she looked at me, the age-old Queen of the Daoine Sidhe, and smiled a smile even older than she was. "There's only one goddess, Elaine."

"Fuck," I said, even if it wasn't my Name anymore. "But there are a thousand memories of Her."

"And a thousand shadows."

The Mebd seemed ready to burst with delight. "And each of us reflects her somehow. 'I see it crimson,' " she quoted. " 'I see it red.' You know what we're for, don't you?"

"We?"

"Leaders," the Queen of the Faeries said, but when I shook my head Morgan answered, smiling and toying with her cup.

"Elaine," she said sadly, "when you go to judgment, blood to the shoulder . . . Elaine, smile. And get thee to Hell with dignity, remembering those who go before that same judgment with no defense, save the honor they pledged in your care."

"You're telling me that what we're doing is wrong."

"No more wrong than what they're doing," Arthur answered with a smile made bitter by the lines between his eyes. "But holy things have no mercy for the choices of the battlefield."

"The evil that exists to oppose other evils? It seems to me I've read that somewhere." The wine tasted tannic and sweet, full-bodied. I wanted more.

"Somebody has to take the blame," Cairbre said. "Better to do it knowing."

The Mebd folded long white fingers in her lap. "Better," she agreed, "to choose your Hell." Her eyes met mine, green and violet all at once, like light shining through three-color jade. "There's another issue we haven't considered."

"What issue is that?"

"Hell," the pale Queen said. "Hell. And the tithe."

"You're going to worry about that now?"

The Mebd shrugged. "There's a way out, of course. There always has been."

Cairbre snorted. "*If* we dared to take it, and leave ourselves unprotected from the wrath of Heaven."

"How is Hell protecting us now?" The Mebd's voice rose as the sound of the harp fell away. "What more do we have to fear than what has already befallen? Bound into an otherworld, powerless, painted ever further from the corners of reality?"

"Will you pay it?" Arthur came away from the wall. "Will Àine? Both of you would have to go."

"She could be made to," the Mebd answered, turning her ring. She looked down. "No," she contradicted herself. "I could not make her go willing into Hell. I presume too much."

Hope caught my eye before she stood, and I already knew what she was going to say. "We deserve everything the Magi have done. They do it to protect themselves."

"So we lie down and let them?"

Hope managed half a breath, no more. "No. But we're predators. We have been. Do we whine because the sheep have grown fangs?" She seemed strange to me, sharp and fragile as a glass dagger.

"No," the Mebd replied. "So if it's blood to the shoulders, as Morgan says, then blood let it be. If Àine came to Hell with me, we could pay off the teind once and for all. But she won't, so judge me as you will—and I'll stand to that statement."

"I don't worry about judgment anymore," I said, thinking of Tam Lin, looking at Arthur. "Judgment, or pity."

The Mebd smiled on me. "Excellent. Tell me who shall I pity in your stead?"

"Nobody," I answered, and turned away. "I've got a Merlin to talk to. Call me if things get interesting."

❈   ❈   ❈

At the university, I knocked on the door of Carel's office. It seemed polite, and her frown when she looked up told me I wasn't precisely welcome. "How was the wedding?"

"We missed you." I pulled out a chair and sat across from her. "Care
to go for a walk?"

"No, I . . ." Her hesitation ended when I smiled. "All right. I could use
the break. Publish or perish." She shoved ineffectually at the pile of high-
lighted papers on her desk and stood. She wore a button-down corduroy
shirt today, and blue jeans and boots. "Midterms. Almost Halloween."

"Halloween?" It's easy to lose track of time in the human world.
"Hallow's Eve. Next week?" *The tithe.*

Carel gestured out the window, getting her coat. "Week from tomorrow. Notice the leaves?" She shook her head.

"I thought you'd chosen," I said, trying to make my voice easy and
my smile warm. "We need you."

"I know." She led me down the broad stairs with their traction strips
and through the double doors of the building.

I studied her stiff back, the way her braids bounced as she walked.
"You're angry at me about the marriage."

"You're going to tell me it's only political."

"That would be bullshit."

"I know that too." She stopped and looked at me under the shade of
a stand of white pine; her eyes gleamed dark and bright. "Oh, hell," she
said. "Hell. 'God help the troubadour.' "

"Yes." I knew. "Crisis of faith?"

"I chose." She closed her eyes. "I stand by my choice. But I didn't tell
you what I chose, did I? You just assumed."

There was nothing I could say to that, and so I nodded.

"We're groping toward something, but I don't know if it's darkness
or light. Mist tells me things. I serve her. But I cannot trust her."

"You can," I answered, looking into her black opal eyes, knowing it
was true. "You can trust her to be Mist. Darkness *and* light."

"That would suggest to me that I am on both sides," Carel said. "We
are all the Dragon's children, Seeker."

I breathed in hard. "What did Kadiska tell you?"

That startled her. She looked up, blinked, and shook her braids so the beads rattled. "She told me you'd use me and discard me. Trick me into betraying my own kind for the power of Faerie, and lock me away for safekeeping when you were done."

"All true," I answered. "Unless you can stop me."

"I see." She turned away from me, looking out over the goose-dotted waters of Mirror Lake to the little island at its center, a riot of maple leaves, the green of conifers, and birch trees white as upthrust bones. "Why is Mist chained, Seeker?"

"Chained?" I blinked. "Bound, yes—as far as I know, by the rules she set herself."

Beads clattered. "There's a chain half-buried under the coins. Iron chain, I think. You never noticed?"

"I've only been there twice," I answered. "How close can you get to something like that?"

The question had been rhetorical but she answered anyway. "As close as it takes. Would you like to go sit in the tree?"

The Merlin took me by the hand and led me up the bank toward Old Man Willow. I expected him to rustle his branches, welcoming, but there was no response. "Hallow's Eve," I said. "That's it, I expect. I didn't know it was coming so fast."

"Halloween's on the new moon this year," Carel said. "I hope that means the students will be decently behaved. For a change." She put a foot on the stairstep root and was hoisting herself into the willow's branches when a voice interrupted.

"What a beautiful day for a walk."

A familiar voice. And an unwelcome one.

The rain had come up from New York City and swept the leaves from Connecticut sugar maples as well: a classic nor'easter. It was easy to pick the two women out among the branches of the willow; Matthew came up the slope, panting lightly from running in steel-toed boots, and forced himself to slow to a walk as he came in under the branches. His bruised back protested, but it was healing. "Merlin," he said. "Elaine. Fancy meeting you two ladies here."

He rubbed his hands together, easing the ache of his rings. The Seeker was pulling her shadows around her, cat-claws that were just material enough to scratch showing at her fingertips: no subtlety this time. Ready to fight. Light glazed Matthew's spectacles for a moment. He stepped sideways, seeking a shadow.

"I rather imagine you planned it that way," Elaine purred, silky-cold. She had height from the tree if she decided to pounce, but he didn't think she would. Unlike the Unseelie Seeker, Elaine was . . . ambivalent, he judged.

"You imagine right." He extended his right hand to Carel, iron rings dull against pale skin. "My lady Merlin. I've come to speak with you one last time."

"In Faerie you're given three chances," Elaine said, tucking a braid behind her ear.

Matthew looked up, surprised, and met her flat, reflective eyes, and wondered how he had thought her easily swayed. "In magic as well."

"Matthew Magus," Carel interrupted, gripping his hand as he reached up into the tree, fire opal glittering in silver on her thumb. "I know you—"

"A little, at least."

"Would you truly stand by for genocide?"

Matthew stepped back, retrieving his hand. "It's not genocide, and I've told Elaine as much. It's not even retribution. All we plan is self-defense."

"All *you* plan," Elaine said. "What about your masters?" The Merlin half crouched in the tree behind Seeker, and Carel's hand on Elaine's shoulder silenced her. Matthew squirreled that bit of information away. The power dynamic had changed.

Matthew glanced down and tugged his glasses off, unzipping his camouflage jacket in a calculated display of confidence to polish the lenses on his shirt. "I can make you human, Seeker. Take the Fae taint out of your blood and make you mortal again. And there's a place for you both in Prometheus. We take care of our own." He wondered if he kept the betrayal out of his own voice when he said it. *Kelly.*

And wasn't it the Fae who broke and bent him? And is being dead better than being what he is, Matthew Magus?

Perhaps. Perhaps.

He risked a glance up. Carel's hand was still tight on the Seeker's elbow. The Seeker's mouth worked. "Human."

Matthew slid his glasses back up his nose. Carel flashed him a smile at the gesture. "It won't work on full-Fae. But we have been experimenting. We have ways." And he spread his hands wide, showing Seeker the iron rings on his fingers. Waiting for the realization to touch her eyes.

"Hellfire," she whispered, and looked at Carel. "Experimenting. Cairbre." Then she looked back at Matthew, gray-green eyes wide, her long neck arched like an angry swan's. "How do you justify that, Matthew Magus?"

"Justify?"

"Torture—"

"How does Faerie justify death and kidnapping and trickery and rape and crippling, Elaine? How do they justify you?"

"Survival," she said, and Matthew nodded.

"Likewise. And how do you justify it?"

Elaine edged forward, twisting her hands together, ready to hop from the tree. Matthew stuffed his own in his pockets to hide the trembling and the pain. Carel turned aslant and dropped her hand from Elaine's shoulder to the bark of the tree that cupped them as if in a giant palm.

"I don't justify it," Elaine said, at the same moment Carel leaned forward to ask, "What have you done to my tree, Matthew?"

"Your tree? The willow?"

She nodded. "He's asleep."

"And likely to stay that way." Matthew shrugged, hunkering down himself to rest his ass on the heels of his shoes. He picked idly at a flaked bit of bark in the grass, looking down at his hands rather than up at the women in the tree.

" 'Tonight it is good Halloween,' " Carel quoted. " 'The Faerie court will ride.' What happens on Hallow's Eve, Matthew?"

"Halloween's not for a week," he answered, pulling the strength of iron around him. The Seeker's shadowy clawtips worried yellow furrows in the willow's much-scarred bark.

"Come back to humanity." And even Matthew could hear the plea in his own voice. Elaine's fingers twitched deep into the tree, and it never shuddered. Matthew imagined that she was visualizing tearing his throat from ear to ear. "Like everything else Fae, the tree will be bound. But it will be unharmed. No genocide. I promise you. And you, Carel—"

She collected and gathered herself; he interrupted, talking fast. "You're one of us. You have friends, family, students. How do you justify what will happen to them if Faerie wins?"

"What will happen to them if Faerie wins?"

"Ask her Queen," Matthew said. "Ask the Unseelie Queen. We'll never be safe again."

The Merlin disengaged herself from Elaine and the tree as neatly as a gymnast sliding to the ground. "I don't justify magic, Matthew Magus, or claim its price is not too high. But neither am I certain that *safe* is all that healthy. Besides, who says somebody has to win?"

Matthew's smile creased into a frown. "What do you mean?"

"A greenhouse is not a garden," the Merlin answered, and now Elaine slid out of the tree behind her, her boots soundless on the bare damp earth. "And a garden is not a jungle, mortal Mage." She seemed larger, darker, as if the shadow of vast wings had fallen over her. She glanced up at Elaine, the breeze bringing Matthew the odor of incense that hung on her hair, and she grinned like a wolf. "Of course, if the Seeker wishes to accept your offer—"

A garden is not a jungle. Matthew's tongue seemed swollen. "I'm willing to accept the cost," he said. "I wouldn't let my child wander in a jungle." *And this is one more way to save Kelly's sorry life a little while longer, isn't it?*

The shadowy wings seemed to flicker and settle against Carel's back. She tilted her head, watching him out of one enormous eye.

"Come home, Elaine," Matthew said. "Leave the monsters under the bed where they belong."

The Seeker of the Daoine Sidhe closed her eyes. "And what happens to the past? To the evidence? You won't need industrial smelters to dispose of the bodies of the Fae . . ."

"I don't understand," he said. He reached out to take Elaine's wrist in his hand, as he had one other time. She shivered like a deer. His fingertips brushed her flesh.

"Bhopal," Seeker said, shaking her head, covering his fingers with her own. "Nagasaki. Wounded Knee. Diamond mines in South America. The coolie labor that built your chains across North America, Promethean."

"You're going to hold me accountable for that?"

"You hold me accountable for whatever broke your heart." She smiled and freed her hands from his, touched his face as if in benediction.

"Don't pretend you love Faerie."

"I don't," she said. "I hate it. But my family lives there, and I'll defend it to my last breath. And another thing. You need better monsters than yourselves, Matthew Magus."

She interrupted herself, looking down in surprise as if confirming that iron still clinched Matthew's fingers. "The rings don't hurt. Carel—"

"All's fair in love and war," the Merlin said, one hand on the bark of the somnolent willow. Matthew met her eyes, and her eyes looked through him. "And Matthew Magus has touched a unicorn. Haven't you, Mage?"

"How did you know that?"

The Merlin smiled, the Dragon smiling through her. "It's in your eyes. He can't hurt you, Elaine. Now go home, Matthew Magus, and decide if you really do want to die with your hammer in your hand."

Chapter Twenty

The pack had assembled.

Wolves and men, yellow eyes and green and blue turned with Keith as he walked the length of the main hall, Caledfwlch tapping his thigh like a metronome's wand. Eoghan lay by the fireplace on a pallet, and Keith had to walk past every wolf in the hall to get there. It could not have been more quiet, but their concern smelled like muttered conversation. Fewer than a hundred had come, and that more than half the pack. *How did there come to be so few of us?*

How did we come to be so few?

He knew the name of almost every wolf; the ones he did not he presumed were Russian, by the kinship of their scent to Fyodor's or to Vanya's. Fyodor and Vanya—and Eremei, and Ian—clustered near Eoghan. *I wish Morag were here.*

But she could not be, of course.

Such things were only for the pack.

Vanya crouched closest to Eoghan, although as Keith hunkered down beside them he could see his father had turned his face away from the cup of water the blond wolf was coaxing him with. *Old bigot,* he thought affectionately, and reached out to take Eoghan's hand in his own. "Father, I have come."

"And about time it is, you daft bastard," Eoghan replied, turning to look Keith in the eye. He squeezed, and there was still strength in the grip, but the bones in his hand felt as if they were in danger of poking through. "I thought I'd have to get on with the dying without you."

"I had to get married," Keith said, and showed his father the golden band. "How do you like your grandson, Sire?"

The dry laugh was strong too. Eoghan wouldn't show weakness. Couldn't. But there was a particular little hitch in it that spoke of pain, and Keith could tell the old wolf collected himself so his breathlessness wouldn't show. *How did it happen so fast?*

"I like him well enough, for a cub with the look of his mother," Eoghan said.

Keith smiled to hear him sound so much like himself, and then steeled himself for the question he knew he had to ask. "Father, do you think it's time?"

"While I can still walk," Eoghan answered, using Keith's hand to pull himself up. "Spare me the ignominy of dying in my own bed. What's the sky like, son?"

"Full of stars," Keith answered. *Wolves do not weep.* "A mild night for a journey."

"Pity," Eoghan replied. "A little cold would send things quicker. Tell your son about me, lad. Now help me off with my pajamas."

Keith's hands trembled as he undid the buttons on Eoghan's top. His father lay passive before him and permitted the touch, his skin already cool; Keith bowed his head, breathing deeply. He was surprised by a warm presence at either shoulder when he looked back up. Ian squatted at his left hand, cool eyes acute and long-fingered hands deft as a surgeon's as he helped undress his grandfather, and on Keith's right hand Vanya leaned a little closer, steadying him with his warmth. Keith looked up, seeking Fyodor's eyes, but the Russian wolf leaned back on his heels, arms crossed, watching the pack. *Claiming the pack.* Keith understood the body language well enough, and as he gathered his father into his arms he couldn't be bothered to care.

"Are you strong enough?"

"I will be," Eoghan said, and made his change.

The wolf Keith lifted in his arms might have been a bundle of dry-rotted twigs wrapped in a moth-eaten blanket, for all he weighed. He'd been a black-hackled tawny thing once, and now he was gray to the ears. Vanya moved back. Ian fell into step beside Keith, and Keith didn't shake him off as he should have. Rather they walked side by side to the doorway, Eoghan nuzzled against Keith's neck. Ian rushed ahead to get the door, and then turned back to watch Keith's progress, his green eyes more curious than fearful. But then, he'd never had the chance to know Eoghan.

And he didn't know what happened next.

Keith crouched to set his father carefully on his feet. The old wolf swayed, lean as a coyote, and then limped forward. He looked back over his shoulder at Keith, who reached out to take Ian's hand when Ian would have gone to him.

Keith shook his head. "From this point onward you go alone, Prince of the pack."

Eoghan whined once, not eagerly but not in fear.

Keith gestured him onward. "Go on, father. Go home."

The old wolf shook himself once, from nose to tail tip. Staggered. Caught himself before he could fall, though it cost him evident pain. And went out into the night alone.

Long seconds—Keith counted them, three or four—and then every wolf and every man in the room threw back his head and let his throat swell on a resonant, ringing howl.

Ian rubbed the back of a hand across his mouth. "You just let him go like that?"

No, Keith thought. "It's what he wants, lad," he said roughly. "Shut the door."

"But—" Ian glanced back out into the blackness. "What do we do now?"

"We get drunk," Keith answered. "And when he's dead, we go and bring the body back—Ian?"

"Father," Ian said, as something detached itself from the darkness and came through the unclosed door to light on his hand. A bird, a raven. Heavy enough that it dipped his fist inches toward the floor. "It's got a message—"

Keith's sword bumped his leg as he turned. "Who is it for?" *And what kind of raven flies at night?*

"For me," Ian said, a dark line between his eyes as he glanced back up. "It is from the Mebd. I am summoned home."

Keith swallowed and laid a hand on his son's black-clad shoulder. "I can't come with you. I have to see this out." And pretended it didn't sting at all when Ian shrugged and looked up at him, cold and fey again.

"It's all right," Ian said. "From here I go alone too, it seems."

We were barely back in the palace when Cairbre came and parted me from the Merlin, dragging her off to some private consultation. I stood in the hallway for a moment after, at a loss, and thought of returning to my rooms . . .

. . . where Whiskey was no doubt waiting for me.

Perhaps not that. And then I thought, *No*. I owed him what I owed him. And if his grief discomforted me, so much the better. I owed him . . . I owed him what Morgan had explained. Absolution, and to carry his guilt and his sin as my own.

Mortal, I would have feared that choice.

Mortal, I never would have made it.

The palace was completely quiet as I wandered its translucent corridors, even more so than its usual haunted emptiness. Having come from the mortal world, only slowly did I realize how strangely bright it was growing within the walls—and not until I opened the door to my chamber and stepped inside did I realize the reason why.

Whiskey stood silhouetted before the diamond-paned windows, sunlight streaming past him to play with the dust motes hanging in the air. Gharne was curled on the window ledge like a watchful feline, his wings folded tidily against his shoulders. They were watching the sun rise over the morning garden.

"Hope?" I said without thinking. Whiskey turned his cheek to me, regarding me sidelong in that manner of his.

"The Mebd," he said. "She's blooded the throne. Ian is King, and the silence is broken. The heart of Faerie beats again."

"Blooded the . . ."

He came toward me, raised his hand, took my shoulders, drew me to the window. "Listen," he said.

Silence. Outside, birds sang among the lilies and the roses. And then, close by, shattering, almost painful in its brightness and depth, the tolling of a single enormous bell. It banged against my diaphragm, knocked the breath out of my lungs. I would have fallen to my knees if Whiskey hadn't caught my elbow and dragged me upright. *"Dead!?"*

"Dead," he affirmed. I felt for my pulse. It thundered in my wrist. I looked up at him in question, and he shook his head as if in punctuation to the sudden tap on the door.

"Come," I called automatically, and Robin pushed the unlatched door open and came inside.

He fumbled toward us, toward the window, as if blinded by the diamonds falling from his eyes to ring on the golden flagstones, rustle on the thick-laid carpets that he crossed. He shoved something into my hand, his ears drooping, and sagged against my arm.

My fingers closed on it automatically, whatever it might be. It felt smooth and warm and itchy, like a cord, and I held it up into the sunlight to examine it. It *was* a cord. A braid, more precisely, golden as wheatstraw and bound at both ends with golden wire and topaz. "She's gone," the Puck said, unnecessarily, as I stared at the thing in my hand. He might as well have handed me a snake for all I knew what to do with it.

"Oh, my," I said. And then fear like a talon closed on my heart. "Ian. The throne. Whiskey, come." I moved toward the door, the tolling of that bell calling the iron in my blood.

"Wait!" Puck's hand, sharp on my sleeve. "There's more. She said to bring you Ian's heart. I knew where it was kept."

"Was." One word, a tooth of ice.

Puck closed his eyes. "Gone," he said. "Gone from the vault as if it had never been, and a single candle to light its place. A candle I last saw in the Mebd's own hand, Your Majesty."

"Robin," I said with a sigh, leaning back on my heels to consider. "Call me Elaine. Or *my lady* if you have to."

"Yes, Your . . . my lady." He shook his head. "I don't know what it means," he said. "But Prince . . . King Ian is gone as well. And Hope. And from the stables, two black horses."

Whiskey snorted, his head thrown back and his eyes rimmed all around with white. Silver rang on the floor. "*Truly* black?"

"Yes," Robin said, miserable, and sat down on the floor with his head in his hands. "He's been talking about the Hunt, my lady, but no one thought he'd unleash it."

"Thousands," I said, hearing the sound of my teeth grinding together. "Perhaps millions of mortals, dead. They've been chained too long. I can't . . . and his heart. Oh, hell. It has to have been Kadiska."

"Yes," Whiskey said. "Kadiska, and Cliodhna. It's been a project of some time for them."

"You *knew*?" Gharne's hood flared, eyes bright slits.

He let his head hang down. "You never asked."

And he never would have volunteered it, until I gave him a conscience. I remembered him eyeing the Leannan Sidhe at the ball and closed my eyes, and sighed. "I'm an idiot."

"I'm very old," he answered, and put his arms around my shoulders. "She meant to trade you the heart for your betrayal. I told her it would work, possibly even be enough to despite your geasa."

"My son's heart. The Fae are . . . devious."

"So are you."

Why didn't I think to ask him before?

Because he had you distracted fending off seductions, silly cow. "All right." I shook myself, peeled fingernails from my palms. "We're going after Ian. Why would Hope go with him?"

"She loves him," Whiskey said. "And she hates mortal men."

"So do you."

"No," Whiskey said. "I eat them." And pawed my floor with a dinner-plate hoof, feathers flowing black as wind-torn storm clouds, shaking out a white, white mane as he swelled and changed and grew. "Get on."

I did, and as his silver-clad hooves rang on the floor, I dragged Puck up in front of me and kneed my grieving stallion forward. I had to duck the doorframe; Gharne sailed through it, flanking us, and Whiskey kept to a rolling canter while I knotted the Mebd's gold-wound braid around my left wrist, where it made a shining bracelet. I would wear it, I decided, as a reminder of sacrifice, and that things are not always as de-fined as they may seem.

"Do you know where to go?" I shouted in Robin's wind-ruffled ear. He squinted between his knobby black fingers.

"I imagine he's gone where the binding was laid," Robin answered, leaning over Whiskey's neck as I ducked another doorframe. The white stallion clattered out into the sunlit courtyard, shaking out his mane, gathering himself for a leap.

"Then no water where we're going, Whiskey," I said. He bunched himself and then soared on an arc like a breaking wave, the power of three thousand miles of ocean behind it. He hit the reflecting pool in the front garden dead center; Robin shouted, bubbling, as we went under.

We broke water into clean air and bright sun in the North Atlantic, tasting the salt of seawater that is more than salt and more than blood. "Then I'll get you as close as I may," Whiskey answered, and I felt him gather himself beneath me again, a ship winged in white sails bellying the wind, a wave wreathed in white froth cresting on the sand. "Hold on tightly. You'll not have seen this before."

He cut water to a standing foam on either side, while Robin at first hid his eyes in Whiskey's mane and then peered around, thrilled at the sensation of speed. Gharne flitted overhead, graying the light that fell through his wings. I bit my lip in fear, but there was nothing to do but hold on and will Whiskey to ever-greater speed. "Gharne," I shouted, the words ripped from my lips by the teeth of the wind, "find Keith for me. Tell him what has happened."

"Mistress," the gliding shadow answered, and banked northward and was gone.

Not too much later, Whiskey hauled himself up the bank of some-thing that wouldn't have been dignified with the name *river* anywhere but in the American West. A puddle. A creek, a rivulet, a wash. Sage crushed under his hooves. Mesquite stung my nostrils. He blew air heavily, head hanging almost into the dust. "Whiskey?"

"Tired," he said. "No matter. Which way, mistress?"

I showed him with a shift of my weight, my hand on his neck. "Should that have tired you so?" I could have come here faster, but I needed

Whiskey. And Robin couldn't hurt. Ian would have to do it the hard way—overland in Annwn, where distances are deceptive, and then parting the veils to the world beyond—under hill and out where the thorn trees grow.

"None of us are what we once were," Robin answered for the water-horse, sitting very still and small astride Whiskey's withers, his black hands knotted in the white froth of mane.

"True," I said, which seemed a terribly inadequate answer—and all the answer needed, nonetheless. Whiskey just snorted and lengthened his stride: stumbling walk to jarring trot, jarring trot to weary canter. "Brave thing," I murmured in his ear as his hooves pounded the water-less soil. Every impact rattled through him like a hammerblow.

Silver shoes or not, this was not easy.

The sun fell swiftly, becoming a red and corpulent thing low on the horizon, crimson light outlining dun-colored hills and lending texture to the rutted hardpan. Whiskey, stumbling at every fourth or fifth stride, staggered to a halt and almost went to his knees. I slid off his shoulder in an undignified hurry, dragging Robin with me. "They're not here yet," Whiskey said, gagging and spraddle-legged.

"They could have been and gone." Robin leaned on the stallion's heaving flank, a sort of wincing crouch demonstrating the pain in the little Fae's bandy legs.

"No," Whiskey answered, cool water flowing from his hide, streaking the clotted dust, wetting the hardpan. "We would have felt the bindings break."

"Are we sure it will be here?" I reached up and draped an arm over his withers, feeling the heat rising from his skin. "One of the other railroads? Something else?"

"This was the golden spike," Whiskey answered.

I almost heard the ghost of a coyote's laugh. "Then we wait," I answered. "Maybe they'll come with the moon."

"Maybe they will," Whiskey said, and dropped into the mud.

I felt him fall away under my leaning arm, straight down, like an imploded building. I knelt beside him, sliming the knees of my trousers. His hooves were cracked, bleeding at the tender frog. I felt a cold sort of pity as I touched the watery blood. "Whiskey, you're injured."

"There is no water here," he answered. "T'will heal. It would have been worse without the shoes, mistress. A little rest, and I'll be right as rain." He chuckled at his own joke.

"Mmmm." I pulled shadows up around us as the sun finished in a swirl of bittersweet colors and stars simmered against the indigo sky. The Milky Way spread overhead; I could make out Betelgeuse and Bellatrix, gaudy epaulets on the broad shoulders of the Hunter. Giant red stars, full of iron. The same sort of stars that, a few million or billion years before, might have been the source of the iron in my blood, the iron tainting seawater and the red earth of Utah and Nevada and Arizona. *I wanted to be an astronomer.*

The thought didn't even sting. I felt no loss, no sorrow—except the sorrow of wanting to feel that loss.

It is very dark in the desert at night.

I settled in the mud beside Whiskey and Robin, and composed myself to wait. *Kadiska has Ian's heart.* Yes, and I would be on her heels as soon as I'd stopped my son from unleashing the worst thing I could imagine. *Child, you cannot do this thing.*

But he could.

And he would.

I leaned back against Whiskey's flank and looked at the stars— serene and uncomplicated, and not the trace of a cloud to hide them. The water-horse breathed easier; he'd let his hide and the earth grow dry. Robin dozed against my shoulder, and I breathed a sigh into air rapidly blooming with desert chill. There might even be dew, later, and that would help Whiskey.

I had time to think, watching the stars, leaning against my stallion. I fingered the golden bracelet binding my wrist, feeling the slick convolutions of the braid. *I wonder if the Unseelie are allied with Prometheus. It would explain a lot. Like how Matthew knows as much as he knows.*

And how does Matthew know as much as he knows, anyway?

The hair in the bracelet tickled and itched. I sucked silently on my teeth, finding and naming stars. Betelgeuse and Bellatrix. Sadalmelik and Aldebaran. Rigel and Alcyone and Menkar and Castor. Such strange and lovely names: strange and lovely as the names of things in Faerie.

There is a power in the naming of things.

Scian, Lile, Maat.

Fomalhaut, Achernar, Menkalinan. Sirius, Suhail, and Saiph.

I smiled in the darkness, knowing what Morgan had done. Knowing what Morgan had given me, and what she had made of me. Knowing something that I had never told another soul, except the Mebd, because she had demanded it of me. And Ian, when Ian was too small to understand what he heard, much less remember it. Not Keith, and not Robin.

My weapon.

My only son's Name.

Keith dragged his gaze from the closing door and turned back to the room, to the assembled wolves and men. "And now we must choose as well." He let his gaze wander over the members of the pack, but none of them would meet his gaze—until he reached Fyodor, who stood with both hands folded behind the small of his back and would not look down.

A rustle—nothing so concrete as a murmur, but merely the restless shifting of feet and hands—swept the hall. Keith laced his fingers together as well, and breathed out, and breathed back in again. "Fyodor Stephanovich," he said. "It seems we must discuss the leadership of the pack."

"What discussion remains?" Fyodor came the length of the parquet floor with a strange, diffident sort of confidence. Vanya and Eremei flanked Fyodor, one on either side, but Keith stood alone, tilting his head back slightly to look Fyodor in the eye. It was only with an effort that Keith managed to keep his hand off Caledfwlch's hilt, his fists unknotted at his sides. "Is there anything left to us but decision?"

Keith tilted his head and rubbed at his throat, watching the other wolf's eyes. Vanya and Eremei had stopped a few steps back, lending support without intended intimidation. "No," he said. "I suppose there isn't. Come, Fyodor Stephanovich. Let us drink together before we must make war."

But the black wolf laid a hand on his shoulder when Keith would have walked past him, taking a firm grip on the sleeve. "I do not understand why you must fight to claim the pack." His voice was low enough that Keith suspected Vanya and Eremei heard it, though no one else.

Keith's mouth twitched. "Because it suits the Dragon. Because I'm born to be a sacrifice, Younger Brother: a sort of a Summer King. I don't know if your Slavic fatalism has room for the Celtic concept of geasa. . . ."

"Hmm." Fyodor bit the knuckle on his thumb. "They're not so different, you know."

"Yes. I did not think so." Keith smiled, feeling a bit of that fatalism himself, and Fyodor smiled back, bitterly. "It's not so much a fate or a destiny as a . . . a doom, a wyrd. A condition that must be fulfilled, and avoiding it will only see it met in an unexpected way. So I must become a Prince of something. And I must fill the role of the Dragon Prince."

"Yes, you must," said another voice: a woman's voice. A voice that should not enter among them now, in a time and place that was meant for wolves of the pack. Her scent followed a moment after, sharp and sweet with the tang of the sea.

"Nuala," Keith said. "You cannot be here."

"The King is dead. Long live the King. Now is not the time for wolves to fight their brothers, brother wolves."

Fyodor had not looked away from Keith. Now he did, but glanced at Vanya rather than Fionnghuala. "Ivan Ilyich," he said. "What do you know of this?"

Vanya shrugged and spread his broad hands wide, forelock falling into his eyes as he tilted his head, allowing a quirk of smile. "I know very little," he answered, as if it were a great admission. "But I suspect a great deal. My lady Nuala—"

"—can speak for herself," she said tartly. "The Prince of the pack is gone ahead, and the Mebd of the Daoine Sidhe—"

"The Mebd is dead?" He'd taken a half step forward, he realized, but only when the susurrus of conversation rose into a buzz. "But Ian—"

"Aye, was summoned home. Make of it what you will, Keith MacNeill. It does not signify. What is significant is that it is time for brother wolves to compromise."

Fyodor folded his arms, his attention on Keith so strongly that Keith could almost see pricked ears. "I will not stand for a war that sees the humans face . . . a holocaust."

"Though they'd stop at nothing to eradicate the pack, if they knew it existed?"

The Russian wolf shook off Nuala's question like so much rain. "What was your quaint Americanism? It does not signify."

Vanya coughed lightly into his hand. "If the Prince of the pack is the Ard Ri of Faerie"—suggestively, one eyebrow rising—"then the war could end as he decreed it. Assuming the war did end as we wish it to."

Keith glanced from Vanya to Nuala. "You're suggesting something too clever for me to follow, I fear. And you still aren't supposed to be here, you know." But he managed it with a twist of a smile this time.

Fionnghuala lifted her curtain of harsh gray hair with her fingers and brushed it away from the sharp bones of her face. "Now, Keith, are you suggesting I might be plotting something? And I'll have you know my kind were old in Britain when yours were still hiding from dire wolves in the wood that stretched from the Atlantic Ocean to the steppes. We come and go where we wish, *go n-ithe an cat thú is go n-ithe an diabhal an cat.*"

Fyodor cleared his throat. "I do not speak that language."

"She said, 'May the cat eat you and the Devil eat the cat,' " Keith translated. "I think my lady is a little put out with us, brother."

Before Fyodor could answer, Fionnghuala turned her head to the side and spat on the parquet, her throat working in cords. Keith laughed out loud in sudden delight at her gesture, biting it back when she rounded on him, hands on her hips. "Aye, and you'll kill this your brother over a damned tradition? I'd think two smart wolves could find a better way between them. The traditions of the pack are well and good, boys, but not when they blind you to solutions, or have you lining up to die because it's the way things have always been done."

She flashed, glorious, her hair tumbled back and the bridge of her nose sharp as a dragon-backed ridge, and Keith dropped his gaze to the floor and shook his head, hair falling in his eyes. "Talk to him," he said, angling a nod toward Fyodor. "The last thing I want to do is fight this man."

He was startled by Fyodor's warm hand on his shoulder. "It's genocide I can't permit, Elder Brother," the black wolf said, without looking at him. "That's why I have to fight you."

Keith turned, careful not to dislodge Fyodor's hand, and reached out and placed his own hand on Fyodor's shoulder. "Nobody wants genocide."

"But you're prepared to pursue it."

Silence, and Keith knew the whole room was watching, waiting, leaning into the quiet as if leaning on a wall. "Fyodor Stephanovich," he said, "I give you my word as a wolf that neither humans nor Fae will meet such a fate at my hands. And I will do everything in my power to prevent such occurrence."

"Your office demands blood, my brother."

Keith could smell the emotions swirling behind Fyodor's impassive voice, the richness of fear and sorrow like old thick blood, the determination and the bright sharp steel of need and fear. He breathed it deep and nodded. "It demands blood," he answered. "Rivers of blood. The blood of innocents. But it doesn't demand *all* the blood. And I can promise you, not a drop more than I have to shed. Ever."

Fyodor held his gaze. Held it while the ranks of the pack shifted restlessly, while Fionnghuala folded and unfolded her white hands and Vanya took silent, watchful Eremei by the elbow and led him a few yards away.

And then the black wolf sighed and shook his head, and muttered, *"Kroviy e bolshye kroviy."* And then with great, implacable dignity, he reached up and unbuttoned the collar of his shirt, tilted his head back, and offered Keith his throat.

Chapter Twenty-One

Robin drowsed against my knee like a child. The beads and baubles in his long ears and hanging from his motley glittered faintly in the waning moonlight. A wild, sleepless sorrow hovered inside my chest. I had known I would lose love. I had not realized it would take hope and faith with it. But then Ian, heartless, could still feel love. What he could not feel was loyalty, or the kind of reckless courage that makes a moral judgment, drives one into a hopeless fight and still draws the line that there are things one does not do.

Things like the Wild Hunt. Something even the Mebd thought better bound. But perhaps I was too quick to assign blame to heartlessness. Humans have their hearts. Humans have their souls. And look at the abominations they achieve.

"There's no way to win this," I said, mostly to myself.

Whiskey snorted, warm breath tickling the inside of my ear. "Wars are not winnable," he said, softly enough not to disturb the Puck. "The object has always been to lose less than the other fellow, mistress, and take enough to show profit."

I would have answered, but a rattle of gravel and the sound of low voices buried under hoof-clatter stilled me. I jiggled my knee under Robin's head, and his knobby fingers convulsed on my trousers as his eyelids cracked apart. He sat up, and I pushed fingers into my matted hair and then pulled them out again, defeated by crusts of salt and knots like hairy-legged spiders.

I stood, not shivering in the desert chill; Whiskey let us get clear before he heaved to his feet, still limping. His tail flicked, his ears pinned back above the coarse tangle of his forelock. I gripped his mane in my right hand and cat-leapt onto his back, though the earth was so dry it sounded hollow when he put one hoof down, and then another. He snorted a platinum-blue plume in the moonlight.

"Robin?"

"Ready. Aye," the Puck said, stepping close enough to Whiskey's side to rest his hand on my boot. "It's a strange and heady thing to be free, Queen Elaine, isn't it?"

"I wouldn't know," I said, and touched Whiskey with my heel as two riders appeared on slender Fae horses, black in the light that etched each furry sage leaf and broom-twig branch of Indian tea in silver and dun: all the colors of the shadows and highlights on a coyote's fur. A hoarse call, an old woman's irate croaking, parted the night on my left side, a flurry of black wings bearing it. My first thought was Gharne, but I heard wingbeats. A blur of feathers and jet-button eyes: Morgan's raven.

No blade and no reins, no saddle. The heads of the silhouetted steeds and their riders came up at the bells of thunder cracking from Whiskey's hooves. The raven laughed beside me, his wings impossibly broad, sheltering me as the figure who must have been Hope raised her hands and clapped them over her head, an answering peal to the roll of Whiskey's onslaught.

A wind sprang up, no moisture in it but a pall of stinging dust, and black clouds slammed over the stars like the lid of a stone coffin sliding shut. Whiskey's mane lashed my face, and he put his head down into the wind, bunching his haunches and driving himself up the hill. Robin had been left behind. Lightning forked down the sky, a river in reverse, once and again, and again, lighting Hope's face and her hair streaming out like a tangled banner behind her.

"Ian!" The raven circled overhead, impossibly large. Storm crow, battle raven. Lightning glittered between the feathers of his wings, forking the roiling black clouds, sheeting from horizon to horizon, an endless staccato strobing. My stallion sidestepped, single-footed, and I felt my hair stand on end as a clap of thunder I felt *inside* rang my ears, rattled my skull like the clapper in the bell. Blue light—electric blue now, not pewtery moonlight—rippled the edges of the bird's dark wings. Coronas of lightning limned each feather, extended in thunderbird radiance from horizon to horizon. Hope dropped her hands and stared, and then raised one fist and made a pulling, ripping gesture. The veils of lightning arced and rippled, the smell of burning plastic bitter in my nostrils, the earth scorched black by the curtains of fire dropping from the raven's wings, around me.

The storm ripped my son's name from my lips. I drew a breath more sand than wind and roared his name again as Whiskey careered toward him. *"IAN!"*

Hissing through the dry air, the rain came in fat drops, burning like a baptism.

Ian had a sword out, upraised; he half-lowered it when lightning revealed my face. Whiskey would have checked at that but I touched him forward, clutching his mane in my left hand, my right holding my wind-tattered snarls away from my eyes. The lightning shattered, fluttered. I couldn't hear my own voice as the black bird spread wings as broad as the torn clouds writhing overhead. Whiskey's hooves splattered mud now, rivulets and viscid clumps, and a mortal steed would have slithered and gone down badly, shattered bone amid the terrible betrayed screaming of horses. Even the Kelpie struggled and slipped, just shy of the ridge-top, but Weyland's shoes held, and—fighting the footing, fighting for balance, strengthened by the rain—Whiskey gained the crest of the hill in a rush and a stumble that brought us between the coal-black, rain-wet horses.

Morgan's bird overshot the hilltop as Whiskey sat on his haunches. I clutched his mane, slipping, not at all certain how I hung on. *"She's pulled him down beside her,"* I thought, inanely. *"She's let the bridle fall."*

"Ian, don't do it! Don't do it!" The bird passed over and the storm went with him like a counterpane ripped back from a bed. He wasn't a raven anymore, but something huge and old as the faint coyote laughter still ringing in the fading thunder.

Ian's left arm was bared to the shoulder, the sleeve of his shirt hanging in wet rags, and as I watched he gentled his wild-eyed mount with the pressure of his thighs. He laid the edge of the forte of his sword against the inside of his arm. "Mother," my son said coldly, as blood, red as rowanberries, welled over the wet pale skin of his hand, "get out of the way."

I let go of Whiskey's mane and raised my hands to the wilderness of my hair, turning my back on the girl, catching Ian's glittering green eyes with my own. "By my hand and my heart," I replied, "by the name of your soul . . ."

Hope shouted and spurred her gelding into Whiskey's shoulder, her thin hands sharp on my wrists as she dragged them down. "No! Fuck you! No!"

Whiskey reared, pulling her out of the saddle. She held me tight, and without stirrups I had no chance. We fell hard in the mud between horses, black hooves and red blood raining down around us. Hope's gelding sank white teeth into Whiskey's neck, and a silver-shod hoof replied across the gelding's shoulder, bone and blood sickening against a hide like rippling night.

I twisted to land on top of her, sensible enough not to put my full weight on the elbow I drove into her diaphragm.

Hope's horse screamed as Whiskey slammed into him again. I covered my head with my arms as he leapt us, hoof glancing off my shoulder like a blow with a sword, and took the hill at a skidding run I couldn't bear to watch. Hope rolled over and puked into the mud. Over the screams of the horses, I heard Ian's voice still rising in the unnatural calm after the unnatural storm, naming Names I had never heard, and some I knew. Names of gods, it must be, and Names of Fae, and Names of men. Blood ran down his arm, dripped black in the moonlight from his fingers, stained the blade of the sword, which he raised now, ready to plunge it into the waiting bosom of the earth. I saw his fingers tighten, saw him lean forward, ready to throw himself down over the shoulder of his horse. Something ran behind me—footsteps splashing and slipping, garbled swearing. *Robin. He'll never get up the hill in time.*

Maybe I can get in between the sword and the ground.

It would probably kill me. It might not even stop the blade from severing the binding.

I was dragging myself to my feet when Whiskey whirled on planted forelimbs and lashed out behind, muzzle brushing the earth, silver-shod black hooves fracturing the last sad remnants of the moonlight. Ian shied away from the blow; it would have taken him high in the chest. Instead I heard bone crunch and shatter, and the flat tensile crack of the sword blade.

Ian's horse shied. Ian fell, keening like a broken-backed rabbit. Hope kicked the inside of my knee and I went down too, mud in my mouth, fire across my shoulder and a crunching sound as I tried to get the leg under me. Wet earth tasted of desert and smelled of dog. I expected a knife in the kidney, a knife between the shoulders.

Whiskey snorted and began to turn. Ian clutched his arm and did not rise. *If you can't stand, roll,* I thought, and pushed myself over just in time to see Hope looming over me, brown as a mud goddess . . . and to see Puck tackle her at waist level and spin her down into the slime.

"Mistress." Whiskey, his voice urgent and low.

Whining with the pain of it, I blinked mud away and shoved myself to my knees. Over my shoulder, the vast white movement that was Whiskey drew my attention, and I turned as best I could.

Ian had retrieved the broken stump of his sword in his left hand, and Whiskey pinned that hand to the earth with a hoof as big as the boy's head. Robin's scuffle ended with a thump, and I heard Robin groan and curse, and sounds as if he pushed himself to his feet.

"Ian," I said. "Swear to me you will not try this again."

"Mother," he said, pain making the edges of his voice glitter, "I will do what I must do. Faerie is mine to protect. I am the heir to the throne of the Daoine Sidhe."

You are her King, I thought, but thought of the bright edges of that throne and didn't give it voice. "Very well," I said, and—my right shoulder twisting under my skin like a knife when I raised my hands—I teased loose a mud-clotted, salt-clotted lock of my hair, and began again.

"By my hand and my heart, by the name of your soul," I whispered, feeling like every word had barbs. I'd named him after Keith's grandfather. And my father. "By this lock of my hair, I know you to me."

And because I'd wanted him to have a Name no Fae would ever guess, I'd named him for the very first star I'd ever known the name of. A star that was in the sky, that night in summer when he was born. Behind me, Hope and Robin were silent. I wondered if the girl was conscious.

"Ian Patrick Rasalgethi Andraste MacNeill."

Ian whimpered. Whiskey snorted, and lifted his hoof, and turned his black-daubed face to look at me. "He needs a chirurgeon," the waterhorse said, his ears pinned back. He lifted a mud-caked hoof. "Silver. The wounds will not heal of themselves. And you need a doctor as well."

"Get him up," I answered, trying and failing to rise. "We're going home." I put my hand down in the mud and pushed harder, but my elbow wouldn't lock and my knee wouldn't bend, and I thought I was going to wind up face down in the mud until Robin came and picked me up, his strange hands unusually gentle.

Kelly was fascinated and frustrated by the flickering images on the television set. He was unresponsive to Matthew, even when Matthew fed and cleaned him, but he'd sit for hours hunched close to the screen, pressing his fingers against the picture tube as if he expected his hand to melt through the glass and become part of the magical world on the other side.

Matthew couldn't bear to watch, and he couldn't look away. He made his brother as comfortable as possible, grateful for and resentful of the caretaker that Prometheus had arranged so he would not miss work, and he pretended, almost, that Kelly was not there. He kept his routine with a scrupulousness that bordered on denial. His apartment was cleaner than it had ever been. He contemplated tearing out the harvest-gold countertops and replacing them with something modern and glossy.

And he waited for Jane, who checked in via e-mail and brief meant-to-be-reassuring phone calls, and never gave him the information he wanted, quite. It was too much time to think, and Matthew went from restlessness to insomnia very quickly. He strained a muscle in his neck, which kept him out of the weight room, and when he tried to run all he could think of was Kelly, huddled under blankets although the apartment was not cold. The inactivity made him worse, more restless and more unhappy.

On Devil's Night Jane called from the lobby to warn him she was coming up.

Appropriate, Matthew thought, slipping the security latch. She was alone, dressed impeccably in a dark plum suit that walked the line between conservative and couture. Her shoes matched her bag and her hair was braided in a careful crown upon her head. Pearl earrings stood in stark contrast to the twisted iron torc that rode her throat, matte black roundelles flanking the notch of her collarbone.

She smiled. "Are you ready to travel?" she asked. "I've brought the car."

Matthew folded his arms. He blocked the doorway with his body. "I'm not sure I can do this, Jane—"

"Matthew." Calm and certain, as she raised her eyes to him. "Let me in."

"I can't—" he said, but he stepped aside, obeying. "I can't." He locked the door behind her and put his back against it, breathing deeply, cold all down his spine.

"I ask nothing of you I am not willing to give myself," she said, walking across the stippled rug toward Kelly. "Nothing I will not give myself."

"Elaine—" He shook his head and cleared his throat. "She's in a position to make a decision. Kelly is *not*."

"What do you say, Kelly?" She leaned down beside him and stroked his hair out of his eyes. He ignored the touch, his fingers leaving greasy lines across the television screen. Jane looked up at Matthew, who had not moved from his place against the door. "Kelly went willingly, Matthew. He chose what he chose. He would have died fifteen years ago if it weren't for the link between you and him."

"A very convenient link," he said. One Jane had suggested and paid for, in point of fact.

"That doesn't change the fact that he went with the Fae, and that he wants to go back. Don't you, Kelly?"

He didn't look up. He was humming softly to himself.

Jane smoothed his hair again and continued. "Elaine was stolen away, and I'm still willing to sacrifice her if I must." She turned then, and looked up at Matthew. "Another thing you should know: do not trust Murchaud if you see him, after tonight. The Morningstar tends to play both sides against the middle; chaos is his aim, and I think we've gotten as much help out of him as we're likely to without paying the piper. And Murchaud's own loyalties are . . . erratic."

"I see. Is that a subtle way of telling me he's in revolt against Hell? There's a certain poetic irony there."

"Isn't there?" She smiled. "Get the door, Matthew. It wouldn't do for us to be late."

A limousine brought them uptown to the Prometheans' penthouse, Jane taking stewardship of Kelly's wheelchair throughout. Matthew kept his hands in his pockets, relieved to be released of the duty and itching with shame over that relief. Kelly seemed to doze in the car, and he didn't awaken when Matthew lifted him again in the heated underground garage and settled him—a bundle of twigs in an armload of blankets—back into the wheelchair after Jane unfolded it.

Palpable silence clogged the elevator as they ascended. Kelly moved slightly in his sleep, blinking into what passed for wakefulness. He turned his head from side to side, examining the interior of the elevator, and then slumped back against his chair. "What does the ritual entail?" Matthew asked, as much to fill the silence as because he wanted to know.

"The sacrifice must be in Times Square," she said. "At midnight, and it must be performed by no man's hand. We've summoned an avatar to accept it, so that won't be a problem."

"So what are we doing here?" The penthouse indicator lit; the door dinged open. Jane wheeled Kelly forward and Matthew trotted to keep up.

"Tapping into the power we've raised," she said. "Laying the web of deceptions that will let us do what we have to do in the middle of New York City without being noticed or arrested. Tightening the final knots in the net before we cast it."

"Dotting the i's and crossing the t's."

"Exactly." Jane said.

Matthew was unprepared for the swell of applause that greeted them as they passed from the antechamber into the workroom. Even Kelly reacted to it, studying the lines of cheering Prometheans with intensity. Matthew, shivering, lowered his hand to Kelly's shoulder. "Don't worry, Kell," he said, aware that he was talking to himself as much as to his brother. "It will all be over soon."

I ordered Ian to confine himself to his chamber and sent a chirurgeon to set his broken arm, while Robin escorted Hope back to her quarters. I relaxed into steam, hot water to my chin, and wondered if the Mebd knew what she was doing when she swore fealty to Keith. If she knew the position it would put me in.

Of course she did. Scrubbing peanut sauce–colored mud from the creases of my elbows, I rolled the thought like rolling beach-worn glass across my palm. She had told me her agenda the last time we spoke. Not just the Magi, but Hell as well. The Mebd meant to see us sovereign. I couldn't imagine what else she'd think to buy by her death.

She'd known a way out of the teind, and didn't think the Cat Anna would be willing to pay the price, so she'd chosen instead to blood the throne. Chilly phrase, that. *Blooding the throne.* Like blooding a blade. It made me think of tempering, Damascus steel plunged smoking into the heart of a slave . . .

. . . which made me think of Caledfwlch.

I plunged my face into the water and scrubbed soapy hands across my skin. The water grew brown; silt and sand gritted between my buttocks and the bottom of the tub. I stood when the knock came on the door, filthy water sheeting from my body, and wrapped myself in a bath sheet. "Come in."

The handle turned, candlelight flickering violet on knobby amethyst. Bright eyes peered around the edge of the door, and a thin arm fringed in velvet rags and coins appeared. "Lady?"

"Robin. Come in." I stepped over the high rim of the bath, favoring my knee, wondering what it would take to get central plumbing and a hot tub in Annwn. *I should look into that.*

The Puck slipped in and shut the door behind. "His Majesty is here."

"His . . . Oh. Keith. Is he coming to see me?"

"I told him you were indisposed. He requests your presence as soon as is convenient, my lady. He's gone to see Prince Ian."

I riffled shadowy images, spying on my husband and son without a second thought, only stopping once I found Hope curled thoughtful beside her window. Keith could handle Ian as he wished. I had business with the girl.

"And . . ." Robin let his voice trail off.

"And?" I knew what Robin would tell me before he shaped the words. I saw their bright eyes, their laughing grins. Human, all of them, in deference to the waning moon — but there was no way any of them could be mistaken for anything but wolves.

"He brought the pack."

Chapter Twenty-Two

lean and garbed, I sat upright in a carven-backed chair while
Puck wound a strand of silver-gray pearls through my plait. He
stroked the last strand into place and placed a kiss on the top of
my head. "You're worn out," he said. "Those are some nasty bruises."

"I bet you have a few of your own," I answered. He helped me cover
them with makeup and glamourie, and dusted my shoulders with per-
fumed powder. "Planning to wrap me up in a bow?"

"I think not," he said soberly. "My lady, I think I know what you're
planning."

"Good, because I don't." I placed my hands on the warm, weighty
arms of the chair and pushed myself to my feet. Fortunately or not, the
injured knee was on the same side as the broken toe. I had one good foot
for standing on. The gown Robin had chosen wasn't mine; it was green
and silver, with heavy panels of lace and brocade as soft as brushed cotton. Elsewhere, Keith's conversation with our son continued mostly futile, and predictable. Hope had not glanced away from her window.

The breath I drew tasted cold and chill. *I could go now,* I thought, *and
sit on the throne.* With the thought came the conviction, and a distant sort
of fear. "Robin," I said, making my face a mask, "Find K—my lord husband for me, please? I believe he will be in the Prince's chamber. And
have him meet me in the throne room."

"Yes, my lady," he answered, and I garbed myself in a placid smile
and took myself before the court.

The hallways seemed different. No, not the hallways. The very stone of the flags and walls itself seemed . . . more solid, and yet more translucent. The stones hushed my footsteps instead of ringing with them, and yet the sun from without shone through them, golden as the walls. Torches guttered and cast dancing shadows here and there, a confusion of greater and lesser lights, for there was really no darkness in any corner now. The moving air through the corridors was heavy with the scents of lily and rose, the rot-sweet aroma of honeysuckle and jasmine, the lighter crispness of an early summer day. There was an electric smell too, as if a thunderstorm crackled just over the horizon.

Hope. Morgan must still be holding her in check. I wondered how long she could manage. I pushed open the carving-gnarled doors to the Mebd's throne room and entered across the azurite-and-malachite tesserae, admitting of no limp for all it pained me. Here my bootheels clicked softly, and that same breeze ruffled the velvet draped alongside the windows, letting shafts of sun dapple the floor—and move across the bier laid in the center of the hall, and the figures gathered around it, low voices whispering across the echoing hall as little more than the sound of the surf. The whole gave the impression of a cool forest glade: the pillars between arched windows like tree trunks, the frescoed vaults overhead and the sunlight flickering through the translucent places in the burned-velvet draperies as if it fell through wind-stirred leaves.

She's not just given Faerie back the heart she locked away in that throne. She's given her own strength into it.

Gone as a sacrifice. A sacred Queen.

A goddess, even an old and forgotten one, standing the sacrifice a mortal once would have. That's a powerful offering.

I hope it is enough.

There were some half-dozen mourners, and each of them looked up as I came closer. *Of course.* I hadn't even paused to think on it; I frowned in irritation at my own shortsightedness and went to join Cairbre and Cliodhna, Arthur and Morgan with her black bird on her shoulder, Whiskey and Keith, and Carel, who was the first to turn to me and step forward, still wearing the clothes I'd brought her back to Faerie in, a maroon sweater I knew as the product of Morgan's needles pulled over her jeans.

The Merlin grasped my forearm when I hesitated and tugged me toward the rest, but she didn't say anything. Cairbre's eyes were a challenge when they found my face. "Queen Elaine," he said in complicated tones, "I understand you've placed your son under a compulsion."

I let the smile touch my mouth but not my eyes, brushing past him to stand beside the Mebd's alabaster bier. I almost chuckled when I recognized it. I'd last seen it in a pavilion in the garden, the resting place of another King.

Arthur bowed over my hand as I came up beside him. Keith laid a hand on my shoulder as well, and I gave him as reassuring a glance as I could. "I understand," he muttered, and I remembered what I had said to Robin. On my other side, Arthur, King of Britain, squeezed my hand.

I bent over the body of the Queen.

She lay shrouded in an emerald wrapper, her face pale within its folds. I couldn't see her hair. Her hands were crossed over her bosom, the right one pierced in two places by narrow wounds, washed white and bloodless before the body had been bound. I didn't want to see the rest of her.

I never understood her. Never gave much thought, I realized, to anybody's pain but my own. I leaned closer to Keith, and murmured by his chin, "The funeral? How are you?"

"I won," he answered.

I brushed his mouth with my fingertips. "I'm glad you're back. I hear you brought the pack with you. How many?"

"Twenty dozen or so. All of us."

"That's all of you?" I almost forgot to keep my voice low.

"We were never many. And that's two more than you might have got."

"All are welcome." I laid my hand over the Mebd's hand. It felt like wax, and I drew mine back, the chill seeping into my bones. Morgan had drawn away from the crowd and stood close beside the dais, where the terrible throne still stood under its pall of rust-colored velvet.

"Queen Elaine," Cairbre said again, from across the bier. "I demand an explanation of why you have done what you have done to your son. Do you intend to usurp his throne?" I heard the rattle of Whiskey's silver on the stone behind them, and I knew he meant them to hear it as well.

Arthur rocked on his toes. He and Keith made a comforting pressure at either shoulder, and I could read support in the glance they passed. I stepped back, away from the bier, from the body, out from between them. "Actually, master bard," I said, "I mean to do exactly that. He's unfit to rule, and I'll detail why in private if you like."

Keith pinned me on a look. I swallowed hard and gathered myself. It was easier than I had imagined to draw up a veil of imperious attitude and smile. I imagined myself taller, imagined myself angry, and pulled the subtlest glamour I could around me. I let the darkness and the cold within show in my eyes.

I pushed past Arthur Pendragon, and Arthur Pendragon got the hell out of my way. I came around the bier smoothly, feeling electricity flowing up my calves, my thighs, with every step. The pain lingered, but I did not show it. Energy pooled at the base of my spine, pushed upward, as if the palace itself fed me. *The Mebd*, I thought. *Her doing.*

I rounded on Cairbre, and he fell back too—two steps, three, swept to one side as if by a wave. Whiskey gave ground too, and I strode between them and up the broad, shallow steps of the dais where a Queen awaited.

I thought Morgan might reach out and catch my hand to stop me. Instead, she moved aside, her hair running like water over the blackness of her gown. The gouge in the palm of my hand ached, and I closed my eyes, thinking of the bloodless wounds piercing the Mebd's white skin. I reached out and grasped the edge of the velvet pall.

"Elaine," Morgan said into my ear. I looked over at her. Her eyes were identical to the eyes of the raven.

"Were you ever Queen of Cornwall and Gore, Stormcrow?" I asked. "I mean, really."

She chuckled. "That too," she said. "At least, I was, now. So say the stories."

"I see."

Thunder rattled the roof. Morgan le Fey raised her eyes to the frescoed ceiling and shrugged. "She's strong."

And then a silence, which I did not fill.

"Yes, I see that you do understand," Morgan said, a Queen in every gesture. " 'I see it crimson. I see it red.' " She smiled, the echo of my own, and stepped away, unblinking as her raven.

A hand fell on my shoulder. I turned to it and was stopped by the panorama of the throne room spread before me. Every eye in the room followed the train of my gown up the stairs. Every eye in the room saw Cliodhna's white, white fingers, sharp nails crimson as wet berries, catch my sleeve, saw me turn about and duck my head to speak into her ear. "What is it?"

"Ian's heart," she murmured. Her breath was cool and moist as the skin of worms—fat, healthy night crawlers, the kind that turn up in plow furrows on dewy mornings. "I'll sell it to you."

"For what?" My voice fell so low I couldn't hear my words, but she did. "Fealty to your Queen?"

"Aye," she answered, and I leaned back just a little and smiled. She smelled of clotted blood: iron and salt. I thought about iron, and salt, and bindings and chains.

I shook my head. "You let her know I'll be coming to take it," I answered, and turned away from Cliodhna and raised my hands in a sudden, sharp jerk and then brought them down hard, as if shaking out a blanket. The pall snapped up, bellied over trapped air, and when I snatched it aside it slid, rippling heavily, sliding on a breath of air from the open windows, the discolored patches stiff and dark.

The throne shone, knife-tipped, mellow ivory between the crusted traces of the old Queen's blood. My mouth worked as I examined it, seeing how I could sit among those spines so that they would only mutilate and not slay me—how the arched curves of antlers would support my weight.

I heard first a gasp, and then silence. And then a tremendous, elastic crash as the stag-carven doors burst open, and I turned to face what came clattering into the throne room over the precious, intricate tiling: a brace of harts, one black as a raven's glistening wing, the other white as the dead Queen's skin. They trotted the length of the chamber as if teamed, cloven hoofbeats echoing. I almost thought Arthur or Keith would step before them, but Whiskey put hands on the two Kings and held them, though Keith's fist clenched on Caledfwlch's leather-bound bronze hilt.

I descended the dais to face the stags as they went to their knees before me, one and then the other. "Hail, Elaine Andraste," said the white one. "Hail, Keith MacNeill," said the black. Their racks were magnificent; I had to peer through the forest of antlers—fourteen points each, at least—to see Keith walking forward, still holding the hilt of his ancient sword.

He came up beside me.

"You're wearing the sheath," I murmured to him, having an idea what happened next.

"Excalibur's sheath? I am," he said. "Why?"

"It's blessed by the goddess of war," I answered, taking his hand to hold him steady. He looked down on the kneeling stags in wonder. "Morrigan. The Lady of Crows. You'll never bleed to death while you're wearing it."

"Oh," he said, and the black stag lurched to its feet and ran him through. A moment later, the white did the same for me.

Beyond magic, the trick to going unnoticed is to look like you belong. And magic always works the better when it's assisted with symbolism and a little subterfuge. So Matthew waited with his brother and five other Prometheans in early-morning darkness, watching the streetlights shine through the red-and-white banners of the TKTS booth on Forty-seventh and Seventh. He was wearing a reflective safety vest and a blue Con Ed hard hat and doing his best to look like part of the scenery.

At least he could pass for rough trade. *Or one of the Village People.* They'd had to settle for giving Jane the white supervisor's hard hat, and there was nothing to be done about Kelly except weave the pass-unseen spell so tightly that light barely got through, and trust the eyes of passersby to skip away from something unexpected in the midst of the usual scenery.

"What do we do now?" Matthew asked, leaning close to Jane as he nudged a sawhorse striped with reflective tape into more perfect alignment around the manhole they'd appropriated.

"We wait for the summoned creature, the symbol of the relationship between Faerie and our world, to appear," she said. "Our spell will bring it to us."

"And then?"

She looked up at him sadly, reaching to push a few yellow strands of hair behind his ear as a panel truck rattled past, belching and swaying like a drunk. "Your ponytail's coming undone."

She didn't need to say the answer. He knew it. *And then it accepts the sacrifice, and then the bridge is built.* He handed her his hard hat and pulled his ponytail holder loose with a thumbnail, slicked the escaping lock into the rest, and twisted the elastic back into place. He'd tugged the hair unevenly, making furrows and ridges like a poorly plowed field, but it would serve. Jane reached up and set his hard hat on his head, tilting it playfully. "Here we are at the crossroads," she said.

"Where you go to sell your soul," Matthew answered, with a sideways glance at Kelly. He knew she meant to chivy him out of his black mood. It wasn't working.

"But this is the crossroads of the world—"

"So it's the world's soul we're selling?" He tried a grin to soften it, knew he failed when she glanced down.

"You're wearing your shirt inside out," she said.

As the Merlin had once mockingly asked him if he would. "It never hurts to take precautions. You're wearing iron tonight."

"I am."

"What's that?" One of the older Prometheans, a banker with a midtown branch, reached out to lay a hand on Jane's forearm. Matthew heard it a moment later: a peal like the chime of a glass bell, distant and muted under traffic noise. Jane's head came up, graceful on her long, fine neck, and she turned at the precise moment that Matthew did.

The unicorn had paused on the other side of the street, beyond the sawhorses, tossing its sea-white mane. Lights gleamed red and green along the blued steel arc of its horn. It stamped a cloven hoof again, snorting, shadowy nostrils seashell-delicate in its refined muzzle.

"Oh," Matthew said, the palms of his hands tingling with a sensation like desire. Jane and the others drew away. Jane's hand was insistent on his sleeve, pulling him away from Kelly's chair. He went as if she held his controls, shuffling a little, craning his head to look back at his brother. "Kell—"

Jane shifted her grip, closed a hand entirely around his wrist. Her hands were cold, her fingers like ice. Matthew shook his head and frowned. A taxicab backfired, rolling between the Magi and the unicorn, oblivious to both, its off-duty light glowing. Matthew had the oddest sensation that the unicorn was waiting for the WALK signal.

The light went red. The unicorn started forward. Kelly stood out of his wheelchair.

"Kelly—" Matthew shook Jane's hand off his wrist and turned back, wondering if she would follow him. He didn't want to risk her. But he couldn't walk away. He wasn't the sort who walked away.

Kelly tottered forward on the ruined stumps of his feet. Blankets tumbled about him, tugged at his ankles, slipped away. He never looked at Matthew, just shuffled toward the unicorn as the unicorn trotted to meet him, the staccato of its hooves increasing in speed.

Matthew ran.

When it reached the middle of the crosswalk, the unicorn lowered its head, accelerating.

Matthew stepped between Kelly and the unicorn.

At first he thought it had missed him, that the blade-spiraled horn had skimmed past both him and Kelly. He thought the staggering blow that struck the center of his chest was the unicorn's shoulder, its hoof. It knocked him against Kelly and he expected to tumble to the ground. But—*Not so fast, Matthew Magus*—the mocking voice of his own common sense—and when he looked down there was the unicorn, eyes calm as forests and a rivulet of his own thick blood twining down the scrolled gutter of the horn, trickling from the base across the white, white brow, beading on the forelock like hawthorn berries on snow. He tried to breathe in, raised his hands to push the unicorn's head away, cradled its cheeks as he had once before—

The pain came in on a rush. The air did not.

There were hands on his waist, a heavy weight against his back . . . a movement as swift and sure as the lunge that had run him through, and he was on his knees, the unicorn five feet away in the crosswalk, blood dripping off its incredibly long lashes and making it blink. Something fell against Matthew's back, a sharper jolt of pain. *I'm certainly taking my own sweet time about dying,* he thought.

And then hands were pulling the rag-doll weight he refused to identify as Kelly off his back, hands were rolling him over. Bright worried eyes hovered over his face. He blinked at the brilliance of them, rolling his head to the side. "Don't move, Matthew." Jane's voice, and hands unbuckling his reflective vest, stripping open his blood-soaked, inside-out shirt. Fingers pressing his skin, followed first by a startled gasp and then a comprehending chuckle. Cold air prickled goose pimples on wet flesh. "Well, I'll be damned," the archmage said, and tugged him until he was sitting up. "Not a mark on you, Matthew Magus."

"Kelly?" It surprised him that his own voice came out a clear, resonant tenor and not a thready pain-choked whine.

"No," Jane said. "It ran you both through. Are you sure you were never Secret Service, Matthew?" A blatant attempt to provoke a laugh, but he pushed against her hands and got his feet under him and tugged the rags of his shirt closed across his chest. "It's over, Matthew," she said, and caught his chin when he would have turned to see Kelly's body.

He wanted to tell her that it could only be worse to imagine what it might have looked like, a crumpled rag discarded on the street, but she grasped his cheeks like a unicorn's and made him look into her eyes. "We did it," she said. "Can't you feel it? We've made our bridge, and there are still other children to be saved."

"There aren't any children left." Matthew rubbed the back of his left hand with his iron-ringed right thumb. He raised his eyes and looked at the changing lights, at the weirdly angled buildings, at the awnings and the marquees and the red and white and golden lights. "At least, not any innocents."

"There's you," she said, and touched his cheek. "Not everyone can survive being run through by a unicorn's horn. There's a reason they sent virgins to decoy them, of old."

"I'll be sure to tell the boys at the gym," he said. He turned his back on her. The unicorn had vanished as if it had never been, leaving only a disarrayed row of reflective sawhorses. "I'm sure they'll get a laugh out of that."

Keith had not known any pain like it. His vision went white before it went red, and through the agony he closed his hand on Elaine's, as if he could force strength into her. The black hart's antlers parted cloth and flesh, piercing him — breast and belly, arms and thighs — like the closing door of an iron maiden. Elaine didn't scream, didn't so much as whimper, and Keith held his breath thinking he could at least match her courage.

He couldn't. But he couldn't draw a breath to scream, either, so what passed his lips was the high-pitched whine of mortal agony, a sound not distinguishably human, or animal: the resonance of pain. In the dumb, enfolding silence, the sound echoed. As his vision cleared, he saw Kings and Queens and nobles all stand, as transfixed as he and Elaine.

The stags held them up forever, an eternal *now* while Keith swore suns rose and set and the moon slid over the sky a half-dozen times. Keith's breath made a funny bubbling sound in his throat; the air was rank and moist with the smell of blood. Rivulets of scarlet coiled down the black stag's antlers, threaded his ears and the silken, corded muscle of his massive neck. *This is what the Mebd felt before she died. And worse. This is what she felt every time she sat on that throne.*

This is what Elaine will —

Don't think about it. Just don't think about it, wolf.

And he knew the truth, that Elaine would not have survived it had she been whole, and that Keith would not have survived it if he were anything but a wolf.

The black stag stepped back, and Morgan caught Keith before he measured his length on the stones. Whiskey must have cushioned Elaine's fall, but he didn't see. Instead he saw . . .

. . . everything.

Annwn cast out before him like a map unscrolled with a snap of the wrists, ragged edges and *Here be Dragons* and great swatches of sepia ink and watercolor blues and greens. He saw a river of blood, high hills, deep vales, and a ring of sacred trees around the well by a Fae smith's anvil. Greens so green they looked ink-wet in the sunshine, and rich black earth like crumbled charcoal. And then it reached into him, sun and shadow, soil and water, heights and valleys—reached into him, and took hold of the beat of his heart, and the pulse of his blood, and enfolded him like the caul a marked child is born under. He heard ringing—rhythmic, measured, a sound like the beating of a smith's hammer. *Down, down, down.*

The King is the land. The land is the King.

He heard the voices then—small voices. The voices of the earth: of the worms and grubs and the smaller things that keep the soil alive and nourish what grows there. *Look, look here,* the voices said. *Look at this darkness under the grass. Look at this blood staining the soil.* Something stung deep under his breastbone, a pain like the bubble in his side from running too long. Something. A dart, a hook. Something that lanced into him and locked, dragging him upright though Morgan tried to fold him in her arms and keep him down.

A dark and glistening span, dripping red as rust, but it wasn't rust that dripped from the cold iron bars and braces, the black twisted vines of a thing that spanned . . .

Blood-slick, it twisted even as it jabbed into his heart, and the heart of Annwn, which were the same. And he couldn't have put into words, precisely, what it was that it spanned, although he felt the presence and the pressure of the Magi raising it, locking it like a barbed fishhook into the flesh and bone of the Westlands. A bridge. A blade. A sword thrust.

He opened his eyes, struggling against Morgan's grip until she released him, her hand still resting on the nape of his neck. He turned his head to see his wife.

Arthur knelt over Elaine, holding her hands. The ancient warlord said her name and touched her breast with a fingertip. "Elaine. Healed as if it never was."

Keith looked down at his own breast. Not quite, he saw. Perfect white scars showed through the rents in his shirt.

"Arthur," Elaine said. "The Merlin and I were followed when we came into Faerie. The Magi are here. They're building . . ." She paused to find the name, while Keith himself fought to get breath into his lungs. "They're building a bridge. Something to lock Annwn into the mortal realms. Take the pack. Take the forces of the Daoine."

Arthur stroked his beard judiciously. "Where must I go?"

"Bring me a map," Keith said, pushing Morgan aside to sit up as well. "Wait, never mind. I can show you. Come on."

He rolled to his knees and then his feet. "We ride to war."

"Keith." Elaine's voice, sweet and empty as the toll of a bell, cool as a blade.

He closed his eyes. *Too much, they ask too much.* "Elaine. Don't ask to come with us."

"No," she answered. That damned Kelpie stood beside her, quivering with eagerness. Someone was missing: Cliodhna. Elaine spoke on. "I have another task."

"What's that?" Arthur asked.

Morgan's jaw tensed. Keith stepped between them and his wife, reaching to touch Elaine's sleeve. Silent understanding: all he could give her now.

"Ian's heart," Elaine said. "I told the Unseelie bitch that I was coming for it." And then she kissed him, once, and turned and took her leave.

—= Chapter Twenty-Three

The hallway outside Hope's room was full with music: skeins and skirls of it, the dance of bow across fiddle. Three guards stood beside her door, armored Elf-knights bending together in low conversation. I wouldn't have trusted the task to common men-at-arms. There was glamourie in Hope's music, and the power to bring a heart to trials and tears.

I wished I had time to stand at the gates and watch Keith ride out at the head of the army. I wished I were riding with him as Morgan and Carel rode. They would observe, at least, and lend such power as they could. The first blood of much blood.

I wondered what the Magi had sacrificed to cloak their eldritch bridge in so much gore.

The Elf-knights stood aside for me, and I spoke to the eldest in low tones, asking him to ride out with the others and meet the enemy laying siege upon our borders. He nodded and took his brother knights with him when he went, a little spark of respect or possibly fear in his eyes. I stood for a moment watching billowing cloaks and listening to jingling spurs as they made haste down the corridor. *There's more to it than being called Queen.*

I shook my head, cold air seeping through the holes in my ragged gown and my plait moving like a serpent against my spine. Then I squared my shoulders and pushed open the door, entering the presence of the mother of my grandchild-yet-to-be. She ignored me when I gestured her final guard to follow the others. I watched her for a moment: standing before her window with her fiddle under her chin, a perfect statue with her rippled dark hair hanging loose and long. Her lashes lay like tear-smudges across her cheeks as she made the music dip and weave. *"And oh, their hearts were weary,"* she played. Then she finished her song and turned to me, laying the fiddle aside.

"Your Majesty." Cold, but not as cold as the Fae are. "You intend to keep me prisoner?"

"No," I answered, refusing to show the ice pick of pain locking my knee. "I'm here to take your parole."

In other days, I could have laughed at the perfect round O her mouth made. She found her voice after a moment. "Ian?"

"He's recovering. The knights are riding out, Hope. War's on us, and I need to be able to trust you."

"I see." She studied the window. "My loyalty is to him."

"Damn you, girl." There wasn't any force behind what I said; it just came out tired. "Don't you understand? He can't have both his heart and the throne. It's one or the other."

"One or the . . . what do you mean?"

"The throne would kill him. The Mebd meant to force me to choose. Because she knew nothing but a threat to Ian would make me do what I've done."

She turned back to me, painfully lovely. Painfully young. *She loves him.* I suppose it's never easy, for any mother. I had been cheated of Ian for so long. I would have thought that would make it easier to let him go, but it didn't. "You're usurping his place. You've chained him."

I smiled and jerked the pearls out of my hair. There was a comb on her vanity, and I took it up. She watched while I worked the old braids out of my hair. One, and then another—my shadow ghosts, my ancient familiars. Whiskey and Gharne. Ian. The loose strands felt strange as they floated around my face. "In case anything happens to me," I said to the mirror. My golden bracelet shifted on my wrist, prickling.

Hope watched, and said nothing.

"I'm going to get Ian's heart back now. It's chancy, what I have to do, and if I don't return, he's King. It'll be your duty to be his conscience and his compassion. Do you understand?"

"No." But the lie was in her eyes. "This isn't fair."

"You're starting to understand." The garden was bright beyond the windows, and clouds sailed and broke in the sky. "I've asked Morgan to lift the magics that were keeping your gifts in check. You'll have your storms."

"You must love him very much."

"No," I said. "I can't love him at all." A cold tear itched in the corner of my eye. I blinked it back. "Go to him," I said. "Stay with him if you can. It may destroy you; it will certainly hurt." A milk-white stallion, patched with black, cantered along the path among the lilies. He stopped below Hope's window and tossed his mane, snorting. I flung the casement wide.

"Mistress," Whiskey said, until he saw my hair flying in the breeze and whickered, his ears pricked.

"Call me Elaine." I stepped onto Hope's low balcony. "I won't constrain you to go where I must go. But I would as soon not go alone."

"It will be as you wish it," he answered, and came up beside the banister, so I could step from its broad stone surface to his back. The wind in my hair felt alien as he leapt into a gallop, headed west.

Whiskey's ears flicked back to catch my voice as he ran. I sighed before I spoke. "I thought it would be Halloween."

"Well," he answered. "You were right, if only barely. And more, this is just the overture. But the veils between this world and that are thinning and when they're thinnest is when they'll strike."

"Tonight. At the dark of the moon. When Keith is weakest." I thought of Harold Godwinson and his frantic charge from one end of England to the other.

"Aye." He slowed to a canter as we came to the crusted banks of the river of blood that flowed between the Mebd's lands—my lands—and those of the Cat Anna. "And we not knowing how many of them there are, or where lie their strengths."

"No," I said. The blood was hot against my skin as Whiskey plunged, swimming strongly. "But I mean to make Àine tell me." *Scian, Lile.* "I don't want to destroy the humans, Uisgebaugh."

"It's us or them," he replied. "They know that. It's how they've managed to bind us and break us, these past few hundred years. Their steel has wounded the earth too deeply for us to do more than cling to the edges of memory now."

Clean water washed the dripping blood from his flanks, was less successful with my skirts. "Why is the iron in blood and earth no problem for you, Whiskey?"

He snorted and shook the high crest of his neck. "Why doesn't it trouble you? Forged iron, forged steel. A weapon is only a weapon with a will behind it, and a chain is only a chain when someone holds the key."

"Ah." And it always *was* forged iron, in the stories. *Iron, cold iron.* "It's not just a weapon," I said. *Telescopes and scalpels and printing presses.* "I was human once."

"So you were." He stood for a moment, poised and silent.

"Were I still . . ." I didn't know how to finish the sentence. " 'Nature red in tooth and claw,' " I said at last, helpless to explain.

"Aye," he answered. "And Faerie and the world are brutal and arbitrary by their nature, and man is the thing opposed to that chaos. Where one prevails the other must suffer."

I opened my mouth, and shut it. *I've chosen my side,* I almost said, but something stopped the words at my lips. "Must it? Are there games no one loses?"

His ears flickered in an equine shrug. "I cannot say, now, in the cold light of conscience, that any vengeance wreaked on me is unwarranted."

"But still you choose Faerie."

A shudder ran the length of his barrel and he shifted under my weight. "I am what I am." There wasn't any apology in it, but there was a sorrow I hadn't heard from him before. It reminded me of someone.

It reminded me of Morgan.

"Whiskey," I said softly. "You sound like a grown-up."

He snorted and pawed the earth. I could hear the iron growing through the soil, see the green grass dying at the root. "There are sins on both sides," he muttered.

"Oh, hell," I said. "John Henry couldn't have done it without a hammer, you know. But you were right about one thing."

"What's that, Elaine?"

"I do have a tendency not to want to face the consequences of my choices. I'll try to do a little better at that."

I expected . . . sympathy, or something. What I got was pure, unadulterated Uisgebaugh. "You'll have to do better. You're among the heroes now. The choices you make, you make for all of us." Before I could frame an answer, he plunged forward, shifting to a hard run once again.

My knee wouldn't absorb the punch of his stride, to ride over the jouncing. I sat on my ass and took it.

The Cat Anna's palace was stark white stone, fantastic gables and crenellations, gaily bedighted in banners of a thousand colors. Most interesting to me was the one granted nearly equal dignity with Àine's own banner: plain vermilion silk, tattered at the edge to resemble flames—the banner of an emissary of the Prince of Hell.

"Good," I murmured into Whiskey's backward-flicked ear.

"Good?"

"Two birds with one stone." I patted him on the shoulder and slid down his side, my ornate and tattered skirts stiff with my own blood and the blood from the river. I thought of the source of that blood, and shivered. We'd put it to a high tide soon, or die in the attempt.

And that's what Keith is for. Shedding blood.

The thought would have clenched my stomach hard, not very long ago at all. Now I examined it with a sort of cold, alienated regret. *We are what we are. No. We're what we make of what we're given. The Dragon said as much.*

"And did you think you'd be rid of me that easily?" A shadow detached itself from the roof of the gatehouse, gliding weightlessly down to settle on Whiskey's withers.

"Gharne. I . . ." Self-consciously, I reached out and pushed loose strands of hair behind my ear. The emeralds set in my wedding band caught a few strands. *Keith. Be safe.*

Whatever it costs.

"You should have discussed it with me," he said, and hopped to my shoulder. "But that's all right. As long as I have your word you'll come get me back if anything bad happens."

"Of course."

Whiskey shifted and shrank. He tilted his head and picked an imaginary spot from his white silk velvet sleeve. "Are you going to dress in glamours?"

"No," I said, smoothing the raggle-taggle brocade. "I look as I intend." The sweep of cloth left dull red brushmarks on the pale stones as I passed over them and made my way to the gates. They stood open, guarded, and the Elf on the right lowered his halberd to block my path.

"State your business, my . . . lady," he said.

I frowned, and crossed my arms over my chest. "I am Queen Elaine of the Daoine Sidhe," I said, as Gharne mantled behind my head, flaring a cobra-hood, not troubling himself to hiss. "We require an audience with the Cat Anna."

"I will send a page." His voice stayed level, while his expression commented on the ruin of my gown.

"She will see me," I said, "if she wishes Annwn to endure another year. Now let me pass." I moved to brush past him. His companion stepped into my way, and Whiskey was moving forward to shatter the Elf's halberd when a lynxlike cough interrupted.

Kadiska coiled into the doorway, a hood of shadow flaring behind her to match the one Gharne made over me. Tiny golden bells tinkled along the seams of crimson trousers as the Unseelie Seeker came to me. "Seeker," she said through filed teeth. "I am glad to see you've finally come to visit me at home. Let her pass."—that last aside to the guardians.

"Call me Elaine," I said, and walked across the bone-white flagstones to take her hands. She kissed the air by my cheek, her tight little smile including Whiskey and Gharne. The shadow behind her melded with Gharne's outline, fused and then tugged apart again as she leaned back. I felt his talons prickle my shoulder like a cat's small claws.

"You've untangled your hair," she said softly, leading me within the curtain walls and the bailey.

"I'm not Seeker anymore." My spine was stiff under the weight of ruined brocade. "I want Ian's heart back."

"I am sorry about that," she said.

I let my shoulders rise and fall and kept my face impassive. "I know,"
I answered, pleased that my voice never wavered. "I would be too.
What can you tell me about . . ." Whiskey snorted softly as I angled my
eyes toward the orange-red banner that snapped overhead on a breeze
warmer than it had any right to be. ". . . the emissary?"

"One of the dukes, I think. I've been away." She gestured helplessly
with the hand that didn't rest on my sleeve. "You know where."

"I'd thought to find your Queen in collusion with Heaven."

"They sent a Voice."

"And?"

"And? Àine closed the gates in his face. Ninefold wings and all.
She does have some pride. You know who she was, once. Which of
the sisters."

"No. But I can guess."

"They called her Caillech. The Lady of Cats. The Queen of Sor-
ceresses."

Whiskey angled his head down at me, his blue eye rimmed in white.
"Tuatha de Danaan," he said. "My father was born of the union of the
earth and the sea."

"Children of Dana. I haven't forgotten. Nor have I forgotten who
Dana is."

Kadiska's hand slipped off my sleeve. I wondered if her fingers felt as
numb as mine. "Who Dana is? The mother goddess."

"Yes," I answered, and opened my hands like butterflies. "And more.
The Tuatha de Danaan, the old gods who followed their own rules before the new gods came. They're her sons and daughters. Dana is the
mountain and the chasm. And moreover, Dana is the Dragon."

I almost felt the earth shiver under my feet, heard the rattle of a distant chain. How ridiculous, to think iron could hold something like that,
unless it chose to be bound.

Whiskey shied, silver ringing on the flagstones, bare footsteps taking
on the echo of hoofbeats. "And you're her granddaughter too," he

pointed out. He moved a step closer, as if to shield me with his body, and the gesture scored my heart; he was never meant for such things as caring, and I could see the realization in his face, of how he'd fallen, gentled, from what he was. *"Alas, my love, you do me wrong. . . ."*

I blinked and laid a hand on his arm, noticing the blood under my fingernails with amusement. "That's what it's about, isn't it? She won't choose one set of children over the others. We have to work it out on our own."

"Like any good mother," Whiskey answered, "she will offer advice."

"We'll kill each other."

"Then she'll start over, as she has a dozen times before." It was a smooth voice, androgynous and cultured, unexpected. I didn't turn. "She is what she is, after all." A hesitation as suspicion blossomed in my heart. *The emissary. The speaker for the Prince of Hell.*

"Hail, Queen Elaine," the voice continued, smooth and seemly. "Eleanor, Helen, Ygraine. A queenly name. Your mother chose well. I could wish I had seen you before today."

"Good afternoon." If I had had a soul it would have quailed. "They told me you went as the tithe, and went willing."

"Yes," he said, and I turned to regard him, Murchaud, son of Lancelot.

He was shining dark, and exceeding fair: beautiful and awful, his long hands pale as bones against the red velvet of his coat. He had, I thought, Morgan's hands: strong-fingered, capable. His hair shone blue-black in ringlets and a ruddy light gleamed behind the windows of his eyes, as clear as water running over stones. It would have been amazing, indeed, if my mother could have resisted him. If any woman could.

Except for greener eyes, Ian favored him. *"What is yonder mountain high, where evil winds do blow?"*

"Was it very terrible?"

"Hell?" He smiled. "Yes, it was very terrible. Your mother yet lives, Elaine. A dutiful daughter would visit her."

"Do *you* visit her?" It came out cold, and I was pleased. *My father is the son of Morgan le Fey and Lancelot du Lac. My father is an Elf-knight. I* thought of the ballad of brave Isobel, and the seven King's daughters. *My father is a Duke of Hell.*

"When my duties permit," he answered. Whiskey moved between us when my father came to take my arm, and I was grateful. I couldn't have borne the fever of that touch. "I've come to take you to the Queen. And speak a moment, truth be told." He hummed a bar of music, and for a moment I was only relieved that it wasn't "Tam Lin."

"She wept for you, you know."

"Possibly," he answered. "Whom stand I accused of wounding?"

"The Mebd wept for you when the Merlin sang her 'Greensleeves.' " I heard Whiskey breathing in the silence—deep, slow, measured breaths.

"A tithe doesn't count unless you place some value on it. But you are only in part correct. Come along, Your Majesty. The Cat Anna awaits you."

They flanked me on either side, Kadiska and Whiskey, with Murchaud leading the way. My father was slim and straight, broad-shouldered, wearing his oiled jet hair in a gleaming club at the nape of his neck. His boots made scarcely any sound at all upon the flag-stones, and fey sunlight sparkled on the rubies in the scabbard of his sword. It made me feel strange inside to look at him. Strange, and sad, and . . . fey.

My father is a Duke of Hell.

I'd never wondered what became of those tithed to Hell. I'd assumed that they were tortured, enslaved . . . and yet here he was, splendid in crimson and scarlet and a deep orange like bittersweet berries on the vine. The doorman opened the main portal for us, and we swept in past him. My skirt rasped on the stone, still leaving marks like a drybrush dragged across paper. Somewhere, a piper played a lighthearted air, at odds with the graveyard hush lying over Àine's palace. The interior doors were high and ornate, wrought, I thought, of ivory. There was no doorman here, although a quartet of guards stood watch, and Murchaud pushed the right-hand door open with the fingertips of his gloved left hand.

In a room as white as Whiskey's hide, the Cat Anna stood before a simple throne of hammered silver cushioned in white silk like the draperies that blew beside windows paned in clear and ruby glass. They cast a shifting rose-dappled light upon a floor of pale, green-veined marble. She acknowledged our entrance, a gracious nod catching light on her coiled and braided dark hair. She wore a diaphanous gown not unlike the one I'd seen her in when last we spoke, when she caught my sleeve on the steps of the dais.

Whiskey stamped one foot in the silence, and I laid a hand on his arm to steady him, feeling his skin shudder. *This one, I should have seen coming. You keep forgetting you're living in a Faerie tale, Elaine.* "Cliodhna."

"Elaine." She smiled and swept down the stainless white stairs, silver bells jangling on her ermine slippers. Kadiska and my father looked like spots of smoking blood against all that white, stepping away as the Queen came toward us. "I apologize for the subterfuge."

Whiskey's eyes were wild. I squeezed his arm once and stepped away, blood flaking from the rags of my dress. Schooling my expression to one the Mebd might have worn—not unlike the one the Cat Anna wore herself—I went to meet her as an equal. "I haven't come to bargain," I said.

She dipped her head and dropped what might have been the first increment of a curtsey. "I wish to speak of alliances. With you, and with Duke Murchaud."

"There will be no alliances." The strength of the land flowed through me like a green current, even here in this Snow Queen's palace. I thought of Dylan Thomas, suddenly: a poet kissed by the Faerie muse if ever one was. I wondered if he had seen Cliodhna the Leannan Sidhe—or someone like her—plainly before he died, or only through the vapors of his bottles.

Oh, we still prey on men. And what do we give in return?

The light from the windows fell across Àine's alabaster profile like the glow from a fire. She turned and winked at me, her eyes liquid and lovely as a doe's. "We still need each other," she said.

"You have something of mine. I mean to have it back."

We give them poetry.

She was just opening her mouth when my father interrupted. "There are old bargains to be kept. A new Queen—or King—of the Daoine does not abrogate the treaties signed long ago."

"The treaties, father, that cost you your freedom? Whose stead did you go in? Who would she have commanded to the tithe in your place?"

He didn't answer. The Cat Anna reached out and trailed one cold, clawed hand down his sleeve, her talons glistening like mother-of-pearl. Her lips were lacquered red as the rubies woven through her hair like frozen blood, and diamonds set in platinum glittered in her ears and on her wrists and at her throat, cold as a frost-hardened dew. "Those treaties have kept us alive for many a long cold year," she said, spreading hands white as lilies. "The Snow Queen, the Summer Queen, and the Queen of Air and Darkness too, for all she won't claim her throne."

"And all of you scared and shaking? I don't think so. And I won't live like that, or ask my children to."

"You have no choice, Elaine."

"Father"—understanding, suddenly, why the word *mother* sounded so strange on Ian's tongue—"I have the only choice any of us can make. Do you know how the debt can be paid?"

He took a breath and looked at me, and I saw red light flicker behind the coolness of his gaze. "There's a sacrifice that would do it." I saw him holding that breath, saw it swelling in his throat.

"Father."

He shook his head. "I'm sorry. *'Blood is the god of war's rich livery.'* I am not permitted to say more."

"Never mind," I said. "My predecessor told me." The Cat Anna's pearl-white talons dug through the sleeve of my gown, piercing my flesh. More red welled to stain the green-and-silver cloth, and I glanced at her in irritation.

"If you want Ian's heart back, you'll do what's wise."

Kadiska hissed, and Gharne reared up over my shoulders and hissed right back. "Right now," I said, "Keith's forces—all the wolves of the pack—and the Daoine are on their way to do battle. The Magi have a grip on Annwn, and they won't let it go. They mean to anchor us to the mortal world and finish out the bindings they began so many years ago.

And where are your men, Àine? Where are the forces of the Morningstar, father?"

"Renew the treaty," he said, with a twist of his mouth that I recognized in the mirror. It told me he was lying, and I knew by the look in his eyes that he intended me to know. "And he will send them. The bill is all but due."

"Rebels are as rebels do," I replied. "Funny how these bright new kingdoms always turn into bureaucracies and empires, and repeat the sins of the Kings of old under different names."

"They do call him the Prince of Lies."

"He's playing both ends against the middle, isn't he?"

"It's what he does," my father said, and I knew by the strained look on his face that he fought a geas to say that much. "His goals are—what they are. And he has hoped these long years to find a way to regain the attention of his Creator, who has turned His face away from the Morningstar and all he does."

I felt Whiskey beside me, comforting and powerful, a massive, irascible presence. "You're telling me that the Devil is misbehaving to get the attention of the Divine? Like a sulky child, Murchaud?"

And my father tilted his head and twisted his lip into the second cousin of a smile, nodding as he sighed.

"What if I gave him the Queens?"

The Cat Anna snarled and ripped my arm from elbow to wrist, pulling me off balance so my hurt knee gave way. Air rippled as Gharne launched himself from my shoulder. I heard Kadiska squeal when he hit her, but I couldn't turn to look; I staggered, trying not to fall, and went down as my knee failed in a white light of pain. My father moved, stepping back, stepping away—and Whiskey saw it and moved toward Àine, blocking her swipe at my face with a massive forearm, whickering as her talons opened red gullies in his flesh. He closed his other hand into a fist as I fell back onto ice-hard flags. I gagged, my diaphragm spasming, and drew a painful breath.

Adding insult to injury, the broken toe twinged.

My unbraided hair fell into my face. Whiskey struck Àine across the face, his shout rising up to a whinny as she too fell back on the stones.

My father folded his hands, and Gharne and Kadiska rolled on the floor, a blur of crimson on black, and jangling bells. I pushed myself up on one elbow and raked my fingers through coarse dark locks.

It had been nice while it lasted.

Uisgebaugh pinned his half sister and held her down on the stone while I spat blood and recited the binding, closing my eyes so that I couldn't see the bright tears tracking his cheeks. *Uisgebaugh. Maat.* Morgan gave me the names, knowing how they would be used. Knowing, along with the Mebd, what I would use them for.

Scian, Lile, Maat, Uisgebaugh. "Lile," I whispered. She was strong. Powerful, and ancient, and a Queen. And I was fresh from my initiation on the horns of a stag, and with the lifeblood of Annwn, the Mebd's dying gift, running through my veins like coursing, clean springwater.

The Queen of the Unseelie Fae went limp, and fell against the floor. Gharne squeaked.

"Àine, tell your Seeker to quit fighting. Whiskey, you may let her up now."

Murchaud came forward to offer me his hand, and I ignored it. Red ran through my fingers, dripping to the white, white stone. It fascinated me. I smeared it in bloody handprints and spatters as I forced myself to my knees and then my feet. I might have been walking on nails from the pain in my leg. Whiskey held me up.

"Father." I lifted my chin to look in his eyes. "Tell the Morningstar that Annwn will aid him. That we will pay him one last tithe, once the battle is done. And that in return we are quit of our debt to him, and the prices paid, and the protectorate is ended."

He smiled tightly, and didn't spare a glance for the cursing Queen who still knelt on the floor. "He won't be happy."

"I don't give a *shit* if he's happy," I answered, and turned away. Gharne launched himself toward me, wobbling in flight, one wing beating crookedly. He settled on my shoulder with a hiss. Kadiska looked better, but not much; he'd gouged her face and breasts and her blood too was puddled on the stone. "Kadiska."

"Mistress." Smoothly and as if she meant it.

"Once you're free of the Cat Anna," I asked her, "do you want a job?"
A thud, as Whiskey did something I didn't observe to silence the Queen.

"Yes," Kadiska said, slowly rising.

"It means more blood."

She shrugged. I squared my shoulders and swallowed hard, shaking with reaction. "Excellent." Gharne rubbed his petal-soft cheek against my face. "Bring me the heart of my son."

Within the palace gates, the Puck brought Keith a blood-bay stud to ride, a dish-nosed, fine-boned animal big enough to be a cart horse if it weren't for the grace of his lines. He looked like a red horse who'd splashed through a pot of ink. Keith eyed him uncertainly for a moment, but the horse sniffed his proffered hand like a gentleman and ducked his head to be rubbed across the poll. "Fine fellow," Keith said. "What's his name?"

Robin Goodfellow coughed. "Petunia."

"Petunia? You're pulling my leg," Keith said, but the big horse's ears flickered and he lipped Keith's jacket. Keith scratched his nose. Crowd noise outside the gates told him his army was gathering. He heard the distant resonance of Arthur's horn, and shook his head, keeping his hands gentle for the horse's sake. "I am not for eating, Petunia."

"He says neither is he," Robin translated.

Keith couldn't tell if he was joking.

The horse whuffed. Keith accepted the reins and walked to the near side. Once he was in the saddle, he remembered more than he expected to, his body settling comfortably into the leather. "Just like falling off a bicycle." Somebody had already gotten the stirrups right.

Fyodor came from upwind, making no pretense of hiding his scent. Eremei accompanied him like a figurine cast from the same mold, and Ian—released by Elaine's decree—sulked between them. Keith smiled; the boy had a lot of growing up to do. He was spoiled, stubborn, and unaccustomed to living with the consequences of his actions. *But that changes today.*

"Younger Brothers," he greeted them.

Fyodor tilted his head in slight deference. Eremei's obeisance was more direct, and Ian acknowledged Keith's words only with a chin-lifted stare. His sling shone white against the velvet blackness of his doublet. "I could have made this unnecessary," he said.

"I'll pay my own prices," Keith said, his voice harsher than he intended. "I want your parole, Ian."

Ian ground the sole of his boot against the ground, but to his credit he didn't scowl as much as he obviously would have liked to. "What would you like me to promise?"

"To follow my orders, and comport yourself as befits a wolf of the pack."

The boy sighed, fingering the golden collar that flashed behind the open neck of his shirt. "You have my word, father."

"Sire," Eremei corrected gently, much to Keith's surprise. He laid a hand on Ian's shoulder and squeezed; Ian gave him a wry sideways look.

"Sire," Ian echoed. "Am I to stay confined to my rooms?"

"No," Keith said, looking into Fyodor's eyes when he spoke. "You'll ride to war with the pack, as is your place. Go and fetch a sword. Your woman is bringing your mount."

Carel and Hope didn't appear until Morgan did. They'd gotten the Merlin up on the back of a docile bay mare, where she clung as if she'd be happier with training wheels, and Hope led one black gelding and rode another. Puck excused himself and brought horses for Fyodor and Eremei, and Vanya arrived a few moments later on a muddy chestnut. No one spoke.

Ian rejoined them within the half hour, Cairbre in tow. A suspicious expression twisted the bard's thick lips, but he held his peace as he swung into the saddle and unlimbered his lute.

Keith's bay never budged through the delay, except to shift his weight from one hoof to another every few moments. "Well," Keith said, glancing around the party.

"That's it but for the army," Eremei said. Keith gave him a tight smile. At least somebody's sense of humor was intact.

Arthur's horn sounded once more. "Come on," Keith said. "We ride."

Arthur had arranged the muster into a pageant, and Keith, at first reluctant, now began to comprehend the Pendragon's intent. Arthur had lined up the Daoine Sidhe along the road leading through the gates of the palace, three and four deep, centaurs and man-headed bulls and bull-headed men, pixies and sprites and creatures that were such random assemblages of parts that Keith could not begin to describe them, or guess what they might be called. And they cheered as he passed.

It was a strange sensation, like being surfed along on the crest of a wave. He straightened his spine, lifted his chin, and let the reins fall slack. Petunia needed no encouragement to arch his neck and prance, even though his name made Keith bite his lip to keep a suitably stern and kingly expression.

The army peeled off to follow them, four abreast, as they rode forward. There were more Fae than Keith had expected. Arthur must have sent beaters into every hill and dale of the Daoine Sidhe's holdings.

Or perhaps they turned up for the funeral. He stifled another smirk as Arthur fell in alongside on a chestnut even redder than Keith's bay. "You've stripped the garrison."

"If we lose, there will be no one left to hold the fort," Arthur answered, staring straight ahead.

"Don't worry," Keith said, turning his head as the curve of the road offered him a good view of the train of the army stretched out behind them like a long, glittering tail. "If we lose, there won't be a fort to come back to."

Arthur grunted. On Keith's other side, Morgan laughed low in her throat. "Just remember," she said. "Even when the world ends, you still have to get up and plow the next morning."

They stopped to eat and to rest the horses several times before they found themselves at the base of a down Keith remembered from his waking dream. The scent of blood and rust hung thickly on the air, almost thready, making the horses paw and sweat. Whatever magic the hart had left in Keith told him only an hour or two had passed in the mortal realm, however, and that the ritual had completed its mischief. "This won't be pretty."

As they crested the hill, Arthur's chestnut shied, gentled only by his rider's confident hand. Petunia, though steadier, stopped stock-still on the rise and refused to move for long moments, until he had satisfied himself of the terrain.

Even the memories could not adequately prepare Keith for the reality of the massive helix of black steel that pierced the meadowland below, a blue-edged auger screwed into the earth below like God's own seed drill. He'd expected troops, mortal men, guns and soldiers, but the vast black span stood there, alone and utterly unconcerned.

It pinched his breast, pain like a racing heart. "Well," he said, glancing from Arthur to Fyodor to Ian, and settling finally on Vanya, "it seems they've brought us the war."

"How do we fight that, Sire?" The wolf's eyes already held the answer before Keith spoke. *We don't.*

My new sense of the land showed me the place we were going: a shallow bowl of meadow bordered on one side by the flank of a rolling hill and on the other by a wood of beeches. The fabric of Annwn was worn as thin, here, as an old man's handkerchief, and the tang of iron filled the air. A trembling heartbeat shuddered my ribs. It wasn't mine; it came from the carven cinnabar box tucked into my sash, a box warmed from within to a heat like blood.

I had expected the tense-drawn waiting before battle, perhaps punctuated by cheers when I rode in with the Unseelie at my back. They were a fearsome sight: Jack-in-Irons, headless and bearing an axe, towering in clanking chains over the rest; Elf-knights on black-horned and antlered steeds that breathed flame from charred nostrils; green women and redcaps and all the varied boggarts and unkind sprites of the darkest Fae. Kadiska was back in the ranks somewhere; I'd forced Àine to release her from her binding, and provoked the Queen's second challenge doing it. The Unseelie made a looming shadow over the greensward behind me . . . and still were not so many as I could have wished.

Sobering, to see again how Faerie had fallen.

I had hoped for a cheer, but it wasn't a cheer that greeted us. Rather, the cry of steel on silver was audible even beyond the top of the rise. I leaned forward on Whiskey's neck as his long strides carried us over the gentle ridge and into sight of the war, away from the broad-shouldered figure in black armor who had ridden beside me. I'd changed my gown for trousers and a chain hauberk, and I had a silver sword I hadn't the faintest idea how to use strapped to the saddle that Whiskey had grudgingly accepted.

A strange sort of battlefield stretched before us—Whiskey, me, and the Unseelie warriors—as we crested the shallow hill and paused for a moment, reviewing the scene. The black earth looked boiled, sod torn as if harrowed. Out of it, blacker still, a twisted grapevine of gnarled iron ascended, arching back and away over the blasted beech copse. I remembered whispering green leaves—saw the memory of them in my mind—and tasted sickness. There were no Magi defenders on the iron bridge. Instead Daoine Sidhe hammered at its base, the ponderous roots sunk deep into the living soil, while the rest of the army spread out around the vale. We must have startled scouts ahead of us; a party was already riding up the hill. I pictured Keith's outriders flushing under Whiskey's hooves like a bevy of game birds and smiled. At least my lord husband was alert enough to post a rearguard. Or, more likely, Arthur had been.

The bridge of iron hurt like a knife sunk in my side, like poison spreading through the earth. I felt it as a bruise, and I wondered how long the Mebd had endured the like: the subtle taint of the Magi's influence. I imagined their bindings must lie on Mist like a prisoner's shackles. It made my bones cold to think of it. *Why doesn't she cast them off?*

But I knew the answer. She wasn't ready to start over yet, and Mist's ways of doing things were either very subtle—or involved the overthrow of mountains. I scrubbed my hands together, the scarred-over gouge in my palm itching. My right arm stiffened under the bandages.

Keith rode at the head of the group coming up the hill, mounted on a blood-bay destrier with a mane and tail black as sloes. I was surprised to see, beside him, Ian sullen-browed on his true-black, and Hope on hers as well. Carel looked uncomfortable on a mahogany bay, Morgan splendid on a dappled palfrey with her raven on her pommel and her wolfhounds by the stirrup. *"First came by the black steed. Then came by the brown. . . ."* And then there was Arthur, as far from Morgan as he could ride. The old King was mounted on a red, red chestnut, a fey warhorse bright as a dragon on a banner, whose braided mane, luxuriant feathers, and high-footed gait put Arabians to shame.

"Then Tam Lin on a bluid-red steed, and he'll ride neist the Queen."

Except Arthur's not Tam Lin. I found myself looking at Ian and bit the inside of my cheeks. *Janet won.* My father's ambiguous smile swam in front of my eyes. *And the Mebd did not. Or did she?*

That bridge. Like a halberd, a gaff. A boar-spear spiking my side. But with it, surrounding it, filling my heart like a song, the power and the strength of Annwn. I nudged Whiskey down the far side of the rise, and came among them like Death on my pale horse. Kadiska heeled her mount forward as well and broke from the press of the army. We left the black-armored general of the Unseelie beside his standard-bearer, who bore a blood-colored banner. Kadiska carried a standard too; the flag of the Unseelie snapped above her as she shifted her gelding into a canter, the pole braced in her stirrup, and over that bone-white pennant . . .

I heard Arthur laughing first, before the rest of them realized what they were looking at. The peals of his voice rose over the ringing of the hammers and the chisels, soft silver and bronze, even ensorcelled, blunting on the iron bars. Ian roused himself enough to curse. Hope gave him a startled look, and I couldn't help the smile. I looked over my shoulder and—despite everything, despite the pain and the despair and the promise of sorrow and the beat of my son's unhomed heart against my ribs—I felt the laughter bubbling up in me, as well.

The heralds would blazon it: *Or, a dragon passant regardant gules:* On a field of saffron, gold like the gold of her hoard, gold as the gold of the sun, a dragon red as all that endless sea of blood—walking forward, and looking back.

I'd had the banner sewn in haste while the Unseelie host was arming, and the harried seamstresses had made her a bit cross-eyed. So Arthur laughed, and threw back his head, hair chopped too short to braid bouncing under his helm.

A woman's voice first took up the chant. "Pendragon!" Once, twice. The third time I heard two voices. By the fourth repetition a dozen, and by the fifth every voice on the hill was uplifted, Daoine, Unseelie and those who were not quite any of those. *"Pendragon! Pendragon! Pendragon!"* The chant rattled the earth under the horses' hooves. Whiskey pricked up his ears, arching his neck, knowing himself displayed.

And Arthur looked at his sister, who had been the first to cry approval of the banner, and his laughter fell away. Tears shone on his cheeks and soaked his auburn beard. Morgan met his eyes and fell silent, but I saw the way her lip pinched between her teeth. I shifted in the saddle; my knee was bound tight to bear my weight in the stirrup, but it didn't help the pain.

"More a crooked dragon, brothers and sisters," the Pendragon called, once the cheering died enough that he might be heard. "And appropriate to the cause," he said more softly, reining his chestnut closer. The warhorse was bigger than Whiskey; he flattened his ears at my mount. Whiskey eyed him calmly, ears pricked, amused exasperation in every line.

"Look at the other side," I answered in as low a tone, and gestured Kadiska to rein her mount around. A renewed roar burst from the armies below, for on the left side of the banner was the stylized silhouette of a wolf, its pose identical to the dragon's. Arthur cheered with the rest, and then he reached out and grasped my forearm, curbing his restless stallion. I winced as his grip pressed blood into my bandages. Whiskey stood like a rock. "What is this army you've brought us, Elaine? Things out of Hell?"

"Only one," I answered. "And he's here on his own reconnaissance. The rest are Dark Fae and suchlike."

"Only . . . what are you talking about?"

"You'll want to meet him," I said, tugging my arm away, and gesturing to the visored paladin in lacquered black who rode at the head of the army.

"A black knight."

"Lancelot's and Morgan's son," I answered, and kicked Whiskey harder than I had to, riding toward my husband, my Merlin, and my son, leaving Arthur wondering behind me on a horse sidling and dancing at his rider's sudden tension.

"Take your soul back," Whiskey muttered for only me to hear as we crossed the space between groups of Faerie and Kings. "I cannot bear what you burden me with."

"Maybe after the war," I said. *Isn't Whiskey more worthy of protection than Ian is?* The thought shamed me, because I knew it was true. I liked Uisgebaugh better than I did my own son. Meanwhile, Kadiska reined in her mare a discreet distance away and planted the standards.

Keith greeted me with open arms, although Whiskey flinched away from the contact, skittish as a Thoroughbred. He forgave me for the thump to his ribs; I felt him forcing himself to stand when Keith reined his stallion over and squeezed my shoulders. Carel glanced over and glanced away, braids swinging and clinking. She sat her bay mare as if a rod had been sewn up the spine of her coat, watching Morgan ride up the hill to where Arthur faced Murchaud, and Murchaud slowly lifted the visor of his helm. Ian wouldn't look at me, but Hope slid me a smile that the Prince didn't see.

"No luck bringing it down?"

"Nothing," Keith said. "We try sorcery next."

"Their magic is more rooted in the world than ours is. Ours is glamourie and illusion. It's cold and deceptive. Theirs has . . . death and life and all that human passion behind it."

"We have Carel."

My gaze turned to her. She still looked away, watching as Morgan slid down from her horse and drew her black-haired son out of his saddle and into her arms. Watching them, I wondered what Mordred had looked like. He must have had red hair, or fair at any rate, and those striking pale eyes. I glanced at Ian and caught him staring at me. "That's your grandfather Murchaud," I told my son. "You won't have met him before."

Ian's mouth opened, his tongue very red behind lips that seemed bloodless. He closed it again and drew harder on the reins than I liked to see, urging the horse uphill after Morgan and Arthur. Hope glanced at me again. I jerked my head after Ian, and she nodded and went, riding like her ribs hurt.

I didn't feel too bad about it.

"I bound the Cat Anna," I said to Keith when we were more or less alone; Carel remained carefully out of earshot. "There's been no re-sistance?"

"None," he answered. "But if we can't break this thing loose, it will . . ." His face twisted. "I can feel it, Elaine."

"Like a spreading bruise."

He shoved sweat-stiff curls off his forehead, and I touched his other hand where it rested on the pommel, easy on the reins. I felt Whiskey tense, but he hid it well, lowering his head to crop the grass. Keith sighed and shifted, but didn't pull away. "How do you know?"

The pain in him might have been my own. "We're King and Queen," I answered. "I'm going to talk to Carel. Be good."

"If you can't be good, be careful." An old, old joke. I was surprised he remembered it.

Whiskey raised his head and shook his mane out. It was a mess of tangles and snarled seaweed, bladder wrack and kelp and less identifi-able things. I wondered if he'd let me curry it again. He struck the earth with a hoof and water bubbled from the perfect imprint of his shoe in the turf, cold and clear as if from a fountain. Keith's blood-bay stallion watched suspiciously, then lowered his head on slack reins and drank.

The water-horse whickered and something clicked in my head. *Uis-gebaugh, bless you for trying to make me look smart.*

"Weyland," I said. "He can't refuse a commission. Any commission. It's part of his bond. Summon him here and pay him in silver, and have him rip the damned thing down. They'll come to defend it then."

"And we'll be waiting."

I shook my head. "You'll be waiting. You and Arthur. And Carel, probably."

"Where will you be?"

I closed my eyes, feeling that cold inside. "Times Square, I imagine." I looked up the hill at Jack-in-Irons, a hulking, shaggy shape that smelled of rot even from a few hundred yards. Sunlight glittered on the hanging blade of his axe.

"Elaine, what are you suggesting?"

Whiskey was calm and solid under me, one ear back and one ear for-ward, his breath coming in time with the beat of Ian's heart. "If they want a war," I said, "we'll bring them a war. I've cut you a deal with Hell and the Unseelie, Keith. I'm afraid you're going to have to live with it."

"Do I get to know the prices?"

"I'll pay them on my own. Consider it a wedding gift and don't ask." I couldn't meet his gaze. *I have everything I ever wanted. Keith, Ian, my freedom. Love. Respect. Power.*

It tasted like ashes and iron in my mouth, an electric feeling as if I bit down on tinfoil. "I need to talk to Carel." Whiskey moved away before I could rein him, pulling my hand out of my husband's. I felt Keith looking after me as we went to stand beside the Merlin.

Carel didn't ride well. Her bay mare tugged at the bit, uncomfortable, and I wondered if she had ever been on a horse before. But she didn't quite sit like a sack of potatoes; there was hope for her yet. She turned, frowning, as I rode up beside her. "I haven't any right to be upset with you," she said.

"But you are anyway."

"Yes." She sighed. "The boon the Mebd granted me for my song. Do you remember it?"

"Yes. I'll honor it, of course."

"It's already used," the Merlin answered. She gestured with a fine-nailed hand to the braided bracelet around my wrist, below the edge of the hauberk. "I asked her to cut that out of her hair, before she sat down on the throne and died."

"You—" It rocked me in my saddle. I clutched the pommel and tried to remember how to breathe. "She was going to kill me?" And then the next layer sank in. "You were with her?"

A very simple answer. "Yes."

It changed everything. Changed my thought. The Mebd hadn't trusted me at all. Had intended my death, and Whiskey's, and that death was part of her plan. Ian, heartless and motherless, but linked to Hope. Keith, faced with the destruction Ian would have wrought. Keith might have killed Ian.

But the mortal world would have fallen in flames.

"Was she really so ruthless?"

"She honored her word to me," Carel said with a shrug. A little condemnation, and she knew it when she said it. She narrowed her farseeing eyes.

"She meant to make Faerie supreme again, and was willing to pay in her own blood to get it. Her own blood and grief." *This is what I am now,* I thought. *This is what I've become.*

"That is what she was born to do," Whiskey said, his voice like coffin nails. "And, Elaine . . ." He dipped his head as Carel looked at him, and looked at me. "You are stronger than she. Stronger than Morgan. I don't think she knew what Morgan taught you. And it was the Mebd who taught Ian the Names of the Hunt."

"Do you know them? The Names?"

"Yes." His tail stung my calf.

Carel coughed. "Whatever was meant to happen no longer matters. What matters now is what did happen, and what will."

"Worried you backed the wrong horse?"

"The Dragon doesn't take sides."

"No. But she is a side all on her own, and you serve her." I wasn't sure myself what I meant. "And I begin to think I serve her too," I said. "She moved me on the board easily enough."

Carel nodded. We watched Keith ride down the hill, to tell the chiselers to stop chiseling. Kadiska rode beside him, bearing the banners again, and the Unseelie streamed down as well, out of ranks and now simply walking to join the camp. Arthur and Morgan and Murchaud must have finished their parley. I thought about the harsh texture of Carel's braids, the coolness of the glass beads woven into them. "I took advantage of you," she said, after a long silence.

"And I, you." Forced by honesty to answer. "I'll never bind you into a tree, Merlin Magician, or lock you into a cave."

"Never say never."

"Mist trusted my decisions." The air felt clear and complex as I breathed it in, warmed by the sunlight and chilled by the not-too-distant sea. "And you saved my life."

Carel chuckled. "Didn't I? I won't say I'm not jealous."

"Of Keith?"

"Among other things." She shrugged, and I saw her close her eyes.

"Wouldn't you expect the Dragonborn to be a ruthless thing?" A reaching gesture with her hand, toward Keith and the rest, fingers spread. She smelled of bittersweet chocolate and nutmeg. "Or the Dragon Prince, for that matter?"

"Thank you. For my life." Whiskey shifted under me. I knotted a hand in his mane.

She turned and studied my face, her eyes glistening. "Mist will let us destroy ourselves, if that's what it takes," I said. "And if the mortals go too far, she'll shrug them off like a too-small coat. Legends and mythologies, races and civilizations come and go. The Dragon remains."

There was a little silence, as we watched the people move along the length of the slope. "So here it is," I said, to break it. "I mean to take the battle to them. They've made their own mythology, but ours is not gone yet."

"Most of them can't even see into this world anymore. That presents a problem, if you mean to demonstrate magic."

Hoofbeats: horses approaching at a trot. I glanced over my shoulder and saw Arthur riding toward us, so much a part of his horse that he seemed a centaur. Morgan was beside him, and Ian. Behind them, I saw Hope coming down the hill with Murchaud, as if in search of Keith. "Hail, my ladies," Arthur said, smiling. He drew rein. "What are we discussing?"

"Morgan," I said, "you know mortal magics. Can you make them felt, these days, in the mortal realm?"

She looked down and ran her fingers through the tarnished strands of her dapple's mane. "Once," she said. "No longer. The old sciences are tied up in metal and technology now. The Dragon is bound."

"Fuck." It had seemed like a brilliant plan for a few short moments. Prove to the mortals that Hell and Faerie exist. There was power in that, and it would do less damage than Ian's plan to unleash the Hunt and simply *kill* as many mortals as possible.

Whiskey snorted and stamped. "I can make myself felt," he said. "And Hope can."

"It won't be enough. Freak storms and flash floods. Those can be explained away."

"Yes, they can," Carel said. "Along with earthquakes, volcanoes, and anything I could muster through Mist. She's chained by proxy and by symbol, but it binds her as surely as the laws she wrote for the rest of us. There's no magic in the real world while she's bound."

"I saw a unicorn in Central Park once," I said. "No one noticed her. And then there's the willows . . . the last one I knew who would still look up and talk seems to have drifted off into treeness now. Faerie's become all but transparent. I guess that means there's nothing to it but to ride to war."

Arthur closed his eyes then, briefly. He opened them again and looked at Morgan. She read something in his face I didn't know him well enough to see. "Artus. No."

"Pendragon. Two Dragon Princes at once? Unprecedented."

"So is a female Merlin," Morgan answered. "Times change."

"They do indeed." He took his helm from under his arm and lifted it onto his head. "There's been one sacrifice already."

Morgan looked ready to argue. Arthur silenced her with a gesture. I wished I knew what they fought about. "Queen Elaine. I'll need my sword back. If you would speak to your husband?"

"Need your sword back? Caledfwlch? What for?"

Arthur Pendragon chuckled, and stroked the neck of his bloodred horse. "I'm going to save a Dragon."

Chapter Twenty-Four

I knelt in the green grass, watching Weyland Smith limp around the massive base of the black iron bridge, sucking his teeth, naked and carrying an iron hammer. He stopped every so often and knocked with the hammer on one of the branching roots of the structure: sometimes a light tap, sometimes a double-handed, back-arched blow.

Cold, wet earth cloyed around the fingers of my left hand, which burrowed in the soil like blind, seeking worms. Moisture soaked through the knees of my trousers, and my chain mail hung on my body thick and fluid and heavy. The prickle of tiny claws touched my right forefinger; I held the sparrow close to my lips as I whispered in its ear. A fine-etched tawny-and-gray head I could have worn as a pendant turned from side to side, eyes dark as black garnets catching the light. The delicate bird studied my face for a moment longer, after I whispered, "Spread the word to your brothers, little friend. Go. . . ." And then feathertips brushed my nose and eyebrows and tiny talons left ephemeral prints in my skin, and a weight so slight it wasn't a weight at all ascended into the sky.

Caledfwlch was a heavier weight across my back, in the plain new scabbard I'd brought to go with my own borrowed silver sword—the one that Keith now carried. "I won't be needing the scabbard," Arthur had said, irony dark in his eyes before he turned to go off among the ruined beeches with his sister and her son. I didn't wish to know what they spoke of. I'd give him the sword when he returned.

I was half-surprised Keith had trusted me with it. But then, he'd seemed half-relieved to see it go. Ian stood over my left shoulder, his eyes following Weyland as the crippled old smith examined his task. "Contracted and paid for," I heard Weyland mutter. "There's got to be a way to get it done."

Ian sighed. "This never would have happened if you'd let me call up the Hunt, mother."

"Over my dead body," I answered, and meant every word. Ian's heart still beat against my side, strangely like the struggles of a kicking baby. I put the thought away. "One thing you'll need to learn to be King is that every action bears a moral responsibility." *I should get Whiskey to explain this to him.* "Every choice is a burden."

"I know that."

"No," I said, standing up and smearing dark earth off my fingers onto my tabard. I lifted my hauberk and fumbled in my sash, drawing forth the lidded cinnabar box, not much bigger than a pack of tarot cards. It was a beautiful thing, the lacquer-red lid carven with coiling dragons and cherry blossoms. It trembled in my hand as I held it up, or perhaps it was my hand that trembled. "Ian."

"I'm to be King," he said. "To sit on the throne would kill me, if I had a mortal heart. The Mebd said so."

"You'll take it," I said. "You're Keith's heir as well as mine. And you're a wolf. No mere chair can kill you."

"I say no. I should be King of the Daoine. And who are you to gainsay me, who gave your soul away?"

I laughed. "When your child is born, Ian MacNeill, you ask me that question again. If you need to."

"You cannot make me do this."

"Oh," I said, "that's where you're wrong, my beloved. My son." I took a step forward and opened the box.

The heart within it glistened like a ruby on its bed of pearl-white satin. It pulsed a steady beat that fluttered with tension or fear.

"Mother."

"It's for your own good," I said, and picked Ian's heart up in my hand, letting the red-and-black box fall upon the grass. "Open your shirt."

Light leaked between my fingers like drops of blood. Ian looked around for intervention, but he was used to following orders, and used to obeying a Queen. I felt someone watching me — Keith? Carel? It didn't matter.

"It will make Hope happy," I said. I had the sudden wild thought that I was holding a bird in my fist, and that if I opened my fingers it would fly up, cardinal-red against the cobalt of the sky.

He startled and paused, tugging his shirt open over the smooth pale expanse of his chest. He looked so terribly young, a slender boy with a boy's narrow shoulders and his father's green, green eyes. "Do you think so?"

I laid my hand on his chest, opened my fingers, and pushed.

I felt no resistance. One moment the heart was in my hand, red and hot and pulsating. The next my palm lay flat against the cool skin of Ian's breast, a pink flush of warmth tingling beneath it, spreading rapidly throughout him. He never even closed his eyes, but his hands came up and wrapped loosely around my wrist.

"I don't feel any different," he said, and then he sat down on the grass and started to cry in silence. He gave my wrist a tug to bring me down on the grass beside him. I sat uncomfortably, half of the box under my hip, and didn't care. I sat there in the grass while Hope came running toward us, holding my son's hand, looking up at the shadow of the great iron spiral across the cloudless sky of Annwn.

Keith left Petunia's reins looped lightly over the branch of one of the birch trees. He stood in the tawny, translucent leaf-litter and waited for his father-in-law to join him. Murchaud didn't bother to tie his winged, fanged black steed. He simply stroked its nose and left it where it stood, the reins knotted around the pommel. Keith was surprised that his own mount seemed singularly unimpressed by the hellbeast. Whatever it looked like, it must have smelled like a horse.

The two men fell into step among the dark and the silvery boles, the rustle of beech leaves counterpoint to each stride. Keith knew he was being outwaited, and didn't intend to be the first to speak, but Murchaud had the patience of a cat to go with his pale, cunning eyes. At last,

Keith sighed and gave in. "You wished to speak with me, my lord duke?"

"Please," Murchaud said. "Call me by my name. We are related by matrimony after all, and it is a rare enough pleasure to hear my name spoken." A pause, which Keith did not fill. "You know I was the husband of the former Queen?"

"And yet she sent you to the teind."

"No," Murchaud said, studying his flawlessly manicured nails. "I had a lover. She sent my lover. But he had had dealings with the Morningstar in the past, and I could not permit that one to claim him again."

"He?"

"Does that surprise you, Sir Wolf?"

Keith looked him up and down, considering. "I don't hold it against you, if that's what you mean. So she sent your lover to Hell out of jealousy?"

"Nay," Murchaud said, shaking his head. "Out of need. He is a poet. He was a favorite of hers."

". . . Cairbre?"

That drew a short bark of a laugh. "Cairbre's former student. A stolen poet, a mortal man."

"And what became of him, after you went to Hell in his place? He did not come to the crossroads to pull you down?"

"No." Murchaud gave over his perusal of his fingernails and let his hands drop to his sides. The sleeves of the surcote he wore over his black chain hauberk fell to cover them. "He followed me." An expressive shrug. "But it is different to be a guest in Hell rather than a captive. So I should say that I *have* a lover, not that I *had* one . . ."

Keith turned to stare at the iron spiral laddering into the sky, and could not keep the coldness from his tone. "You have many lovers, it seems."

"I have many liaisons," the Elf-knight answered, unperturbed. "I have one lover."

"And are you here now by your own choice, or by the Prince of Hell's? Or perhaps I should say, how is it that one once given in the teind is free to walk the earth again?"

"This is not the earth."

"Nevertheless." They exchanged a smile, understanding one another, and walked on. The ground was springy, worm-honeycombed under the rustling leaves.

"Ah. Now that is a complicated question." Murchaud's broad gesture took in the beechwood, the glade beyond, the valley down to the furrowed earth beside the bridge to mortal realms. "Did you know that stands of quaking aspen are all one plant? They connect underground like horsetail ferns, out of sight, unseen. The trunks may be damaged, but the parent organism survives and regrows, for thousands—perhaps millions—of years."

"These are beeches," Keith said. "Quaking aspens are a New World tree."

"Irrelevant to my point," Murchaud answered with a smile.

"You're constructing an analogy."

"Indeed," he said, pleased. "Thus it is with the Morningstar. You cannot hope to comprehend what lies beneath the surface of his plotting and counterplotting."

"But you're going to tell me anyway?"

"Hah! I can impart no such enlightenment. There is a geas."

"There always is. Is this your roundabout way of telling me that you are here in the service of Lucifer, Murchaud?"

"No. It is my way of suggesting to you that I am here of my own free will, and went to Prometheus as an agent of Hell."

Keith swallowed. "How does one return from the tithe?"

Murchaud turned his face up to the sunlight. "One is permitted to leave. The Morningstar is not such a bad master."

"So what does he want?"

"What we all want. The love of a just and generous Deity. Not to be cast out of Heaven, and the sight of God."

It should have surprised Keith to hear an Elf-knight speak such words so easily. But really, little was surprising anymore.

Arthur crossed the vale toward me and I stood up to meet him, untangling my hand from Ian's. He smiled at me as I went, and Hope smiled too. I forced one in return and went to talk to Arthur. "I'm coming with you," I said as I pulled the baldric off my shoulder and offered him the blade.

"I can't allow it," he said.

I smiled. "You can't prevent it. Do you know how to find her cave?"

"The Merlin will show me. I spoke with her."

"And I've spoken with her since. Arthur. We won't intervene. But Carel and I will come and bear witness to this thing you do."

He shook his head, crow's-feet in the corners of faded blue eyes. His beard seemed more gray through the red in the few days since he had awakened, and he looked tired. "I will not risk your life, Your Majesty."

I couldn't remember the last time I'd lain down to rest. My wedding night? The green power of Annwn filled me and lightened my step. I rubbed my aching arm. "My life is mine to risk."

He raised the hand that didn't cradle sheathed Excalibur, and stopped. He studied my face, Arthur, King of Britain, and let a slow breath trickle out of his nostrils. "It will be as you wish it. Get your things."

The three of us paused by the entrance of the cavern and I smiled up at the blooming and twining vines. As gnarled and thorny as the black iron bridge, they still put me in mind of something else entirely. "Third time's the charm," I whispered.

Carel pushed the vines aside for Arthur and me. "Aren't Kings for slaying dragons?" she asked.

He laid a hand on the hilt of Caledfwlch in its ill-fitting sheath. "There are many sorts of dragons," he answered, and went forward into the darkness as if without fear.

Carel and I shared a look, and she shrugged and followed him. I came up beside her, briefly laying a hand on her arm. She said nothing, and I answered the same way.

We followed the sinuous underground highway down and down, through the mist and the darkness, aided as before by a conjured light. I let it fail when we rounded the corner into flame, and I could feel Carel trembling beside me. Her last trip here had put the fear of Mist in her, as well. "Be of good courage," Arthur said without turning. I wondered how he knew.

Because he's a King, of course. I pressed the heels of my hands against my eyes, and we walked up to the end of the tunnel and stood three abreast, looking down into the cavern of the Mother of Dragons. She lay silent, her chin on her knuckles, and I felt the heat rising off her. Arthur blinked and ducked his head, resting his chin on his chest. I saw him square his shoulders. *He means to die,* I realized. *That's what he meant about sacrifices. That's why he didn't take the scabbard.*

Arthur Pendragon opened his eyes and drew his storied blade into his strong right hand. "Mist," he called into the echoing spaces. "I've come to help you."

She lifted her head—now a serpent's, now a lizard's, now a horse's head festooned with tendrils and streamers, red flesh glaring under shifting black scales like Ian's heart shining between my fingers, like magma gleaming beneath the spreading edges of the world, somewhere too far under the sea for the water to have a hope of boiling. "Help . . . *me?*"

Mockery and disbelief. Amusement and a smile. "Arthur Pendragon. Best beloved of all my servants. And the Merlin. And you, Queen with no Name. Greetings and welcome. Few come to see me a second time, or . . . a third."

"Show me your chain and I will strike it off," Arthur said. "I've come back to you for a reason, Mother of Dragons—mistress of worms and serpents, from the smallest crawlers that renew the loam to the world-girdling monster devouring his own tail."

"Mother of more than Dragons, Dana," I said.

I swear that Dragon looked me in the eye and winked. "My chain?" She leaned back on her haunches, and turned away.

I sat down on the floor.

The black iron ring sunk into the flesh on both sides of her spine must have been as thick as Arthur's powerful thigh, and each link of the chain that braced it was the size of the span of a big man's arms. "It would cripple me to tear it loose," Mist said. "I'd recover, of course. Your kind would not survive my struggles. Think better of your intention, King."

Arthur swallowed and held up his black-bladed sword. "Excalibur," he said. "Caliburn. A sword made of iron fallen from a star."

"I know it," Mist said, licking her lips. "You couldn't get close enough to use it, mortal King."

Arthur pressed his free hand to his side, just below the rib cage. He closed his eyes. I flinched, and thought of boar spears and bear spears. They have a crosspiece lashed on them, to keep the beasts from charging up the length of the spear and slaughtering their murderers . . .

. . . as Arthur had done, when Mordred, mounted, had driven his lance through the armor and into the side of the unhorsed King. "I can endure it," Arthur said softly. "Show me the way down."

Carel reached out as if to lay her right hand on Arthur's shoulder, and I caught hers in mine. She looked at me, startled, and I nodded, and couldn't say a word. *This is why he's remembered.*

"Arthur Pendragon," the Dragon said. "Bear of Britain. Aptly you earn your name." She gestured with one streamered wing, tracing a line in the cavern wall. Living rock flowed like water, reshaped itself into steep and narrow stairs. "You two"—her eyes gleamed like fractured crystal—"stay where you are."

Carel nodded. I held tight to her elbow, and she squeezed my hand. Almost languidly, Arthur turned and smiled at each of us before he started down the stairs.

It seemed to take him an eternity to travel that distance and then wade across a sea of gold and jewels, chalices and coins and crowns undamaged by the weight and flame-heat of the Dragon. *More magic, of course.* He strode along the wall, as far from Mist as possible, and she lay down again and rested her head on the gold, her wings spread wide. She seemed to grow darker, blacker, as I watched, shrinking slightly, as if she cooled and solidified.

"Sweet hellfire," I whispered as Carel squeezed my hand.

"I can't watch," she said.

"You have to write the songs about it, Merlin. You will watch." I made my voice cool and crystalline, and she seemed to draw strength from it. "And I will watch with you," I continued, and tasted blood as Arthur came forward and set his boot upon the extended leather of

Mist's obsidian wing. "Don't move an inch," he said to the Dragon, "or you'll throw me." We heard him clearly amid the echoes of his voice, which seemed very small and far away.

I saw him flinch, but he didn't pull his foot back, and a moment later I smelled scorching leather. "Jesus," Carel whispered, and I bit back bile. I didn't bother to remind her.

Moving quickly, careful of his balance, Arthur threaded the length of Mist's wing to her spine, and made his way down the length of her back, walking between the jagged bony spikes that decorated her hide. I could see the smoke rising now, and imagined that any moment flames would lick the soles of his feet. He limped, but kept walking, and once he stumbled and slipped and caught one of her spines to right himself. I saw the blood from the wound on his hand and heard him grunt loudly, although I could only imagine the blood running into his beard as he bit his lip, only imagine the lines of concentration creasing his brow.

"Arthur." Something stung my eyes, something cold and hot. I smelled searing flesh now, and Carel whined like a dog in pain. It might have taken a minute. I would have sworn it took him an hour.

Arthur reached the anchor point of the chain. It was almost invisible against the roughened char of Mist's dark hide, and the rest of it vanished under the litter of gold and jewels by her feet. He paused, for a moment, and raised Caledfwlch in both hands. Fire kissed his ankles and trousers. His feet burned in their boots, and he somehow stood, steadying himself on the vast iron ring welded into her spine. He kicked the chain to one side, and I could see why; even with a sword like that, the massive ring was too thick to part with one blow, and he'd have to put all his back behind it to burst the chain. If the blow went through and severed Mist's spine . . .

"For Britain!" he roared, burning, and brought his blade down.

Mist howled and reared up, her blood springing forth and smoking over Caledfwlch, over Arthur's face and hands as the King fell, screaming now that his task was done, sliding down the Dragon's blazing side and—engulfed in flames—tumbling bonelessly the vast, hard distance to lie among the treasure scattered on the floor. The chain slid down beside him and pooled there, bright with the Dragon's blood.

Mist threw her massive head back and bellowed pain, bellowed grief and triumph and fury.

Carel turned to me and buried her face against my neck, but I felt no wetness of tears. I put an arm around the Merlin and watched as Mist remembered and set her pain aside. She turned and breathed over Arthur, a cloud of cooling vapor. The flames flickered and died, but the fallen King did not stir.

Mist raised her head, impassive as dragons are. "Hail, Arthur Pendragon," she said. "Hail, the Bear of Britain."

"I can't write this song," Carel said, helpless.

"You will," Mist answered, and bowed her head. "Ask me a boon, Queen with no Name, in return for this service."

"Destroy the Magi," I answered promptly.

Mist chuckled. "I won't. But ask another."

"Will you fight for Faerie, then? Or Hell?"

"No a second time. Do you have another?"

The Merlin looked up again. "Third time, right?" she said to me, and I nodded. "Fly," Carel said to her Dragon. "Go into the sky, Mist, as you used to do, and fly from one place to another, in daylight and by moonlight, and do not rest until you have circled the globe and every nation has seen you."

"Done," Mist said, and spread her wings. "You'll want to leave the cavern before I go."

I swallowed hard. *And that's why she's the Merlin and you're not,* I reminded myself. *Because the Dragon listens to her.*

"Keep the sword," I said, and tugged Carel's hand, bringing her away.

Chapter Twenty-Five

There were willing hands to help Matthew back to the workroom. There was clean water and there were fresh clothes; Jane came into the men's room with him, barricaded the door, and made a point of seeing to it that he washed and changed. And there was an ache like slivers under Matthew's skin, an itch like the itch of an old half-forgotten scar.

He did as Jane bid, bathed and dressed himself, followed her into the antechamber and sat down in one of the steel-gray modern chairs, drank the whiskey-laced tea she shoved into his hands. He pushed the sleeve of his borrowed pullover up and rubbed at the tattoos winding his wrist: just so much ink now, black and stark against the blanched paleness of his skin, as empty as print to an illiterate.

"I would rather it had been me," he said, a sentiment so trite that he laughed. And laughed harder when Jane answered the only way she could.

"I'm glad it wasn't. You're going to hate me for a while."

"Probably."

"I'd make book on it." Jane crouched in front of him, knees tidily together, one hand splayed on the floor for balance. Prometheans drifted about the cool white room behind her, aimlessly meandering or moving into knots for quiet conversation. There had been a ritual here too, while the remote team had been in Times Square. All that power they'd squirreled away had needed to be released, focused, channeled. There had been work enough for all. Matthew drained the last of the tea and set the cup on the floor. To hell with it. Tonight, somebody else could clean up after him.

There was a fleck of blood dried on his glasses, a perfect round spot. He pulled them off and scratched at it with his fingernail, spat on the glass and polished it on the borrowed pullover before he remembered it wasn't his. He slid the spectacles back up his nose and took a deep breath. "I want to go inside."

"Matthew—"

He lurched to his feet so abruptly that Jane jumped back, barely keeping her balance. "You brought Kelly's—you brought Kelly back. I want to see him."

She stared at him, worrying her lower lip with her thumb, and after a moment she nodded. "Promise me you'll stay calm—"

"I'd be a fool to promise that when I can't deliver it," Matthew said in measured tones, running both hands through his hair so that grimy unwashed strands caught in his rings. He yanked them loose, harder than he should have, feeling each trapped hair stretch and break. "You'll just have to trust me, Jane." *Like I trusted you.*

She offered him her hand without visible hesitation, and then paused abruptly and reached into her jacket pocket. "Phone." She pulled it out, the vibration blurring her fingers, and squinted at it to push the green button. "Jane Andraste."

A line appeared between her eyebrows almost instantly. Without lowering the phone, she caught Matthew's eye and jerked her chin and her thumb toward a control panel on the wall. He understood and moved toward it, his sudden silence and efficiency drawing the eyes and attention of colleagues who had been allowing him privacy in his grief. He thumbed a switch; a panel slid aside, revealing a flatscreen television as long as Matthew was tall.

"Put on CNN," Jane said.

Matthew obeyed and stepped back, at first not quite able to comprehend what he was seeing. Image after image, obviously shot in different nations at different times, showed vivid footage of enormous black wings and eyes like magma slipping across a series of dawning skies.

Enormous beasts, no two quite alike, the time stamps showing a steady progression of movement from east to west.

"Christ," Matthew said. "What's that?" He turned to look at Jane.

The cell phone was still in her hand, but her hand hung at her side. Her jaw tensed as she swallowed. "The gauntlet thrown back, Matthew. We're in it now."

Keith looked up from his maps and his charts, spread on a wooden trestle in the early-morning sun, and rubbed the crease between his eyes with his thumb knuckle. "Why New York?"

"A little bird told me," Elaine answered, pausing before his tent. She pulled off her gloves and slapped them against her thigh. "A pigeon, in matter of fact. Pigeons, it turns out, know all sorts of things. A Central Park pigeon."

Keith pushed the map away, flat-handed, and sat back as his wife came to stand beside him. She looked up, across the bridge. He said, "Weyland's not doing any better than we were. You don't think they'll let him just tear it down."

Smokeless heat rippled from the forge Weyland Smith had set up by the bridge. He whittled away at it with fire and steel while Hope and Whiskey helped as they were able, ice and chill winds at their disposal. Everyone else stayed well away. "I thought about climbing it, Jack up a beanstalk," Elaine said.

Tents and pavilions were springing up around the vale and up the hillside—a regular encampment. The table Keith worked at stood by the door of his command tent, which was hung with red and saffron banners.

"It's Hallowmas, in this realm and that," Keith said, trying to keep the distance in his heart from coloring his tone. "The calendars are matched, and at midnight the clocks will be as well. They'll come tonight."

"And we'll be taking the fight to them. New York City. Times Square."

"It seems strange that they didn't press their advantage after raising this," he said, gesturing to the bridge.

"Three things—"

"It always is."

"Touché. First, I imagine it wearied them, and they want to be strong for the fight. And second, it leaches our strength. The longer it stays there, the more it drains us. Although they reckoned without the Mebd's sacrifice, and Arthur's."

"And third," Keith said, sliding an arm around Elaine's waist, "Mist may be keeping them busy."

"And third, what's days in Faerie currently is but a few hours in New York. I'm sure they'll be along presently." She leaned her hip against his shoulder. "But yes, Mist is. I've been in and out of the mortal world with Carel while you've been drilling your armies. I'm a little concerned they may resort to nuclear weapons in an attempt to halt her progress."

"Would that hurt her?"

"Not in the long run." Elaine sat down on the bench beside him and leaned her face against his shoulder. "She seems to be starting in the Far East and working her way west."

"That makes sense," Keith said, and kissed his wife's neck. He longed to comfort her and knew it was futile, and had just enough sense to stay silent. *Arthur and Gwenhwyfar had a long time together, before the end . . .* which was a fresh grief all its own. *I wish I had known him better, Arthur of Britain.* Keith sighed and closed his eyes. "It doesn't answer my question, Elaine. Why New York?"

"Where else? Where else in all the world?"

"Kuala Lumpur? Hong Kong? Palo Alto? London?"

"Palo Alto makes a lot of sense, actually. But New York City is where the kings of commerce reign. The others are regional capitals at best. Besides, I trust what pigeons tell me." She shook her head, slumping against him as if exhaustion weighed her bones. "Something else. The mortal media is in an uproar."

"Yes?"

"In addition to the dragons—and they think Mist is many dragons, not one, because they haven't realized she never looks the same way twice—and the preachers prophesying the end times, it seems that there've been sightings of mythical beasts. Centaurs and griffins. A wyvern or two. The willow tree in the center of Carel's campus up-rooted itself the other night and walked off; the official explanation is vandals with a crane."

"I see." He grinned. It crinkled the corners of his eyes and made her smile in return. The sadness in her eyes told him the truth. For a chilly moment, he felt the coldness that passed for love in her, then he closed his eyes and bent and kissed the back of her hand. Then he looked down and busied himself weighting his papers with smooth-washed rocks.

"We won't win," she said.

"No," Keith said, standing and drawing her up with him. "But if I can echo the steps of my forebears, Elaine, then neither will they. A turning point. That's all I have to give."

"A rock they cannot break."

"Exactly. And it took more than one Dragon Prince to shatter Rome, you know." A rolling shrug. He squeezed her hand. "When are you leaving, and who are you taking?"

"Sometime around moonrise. I'm hoping the battle will be joined here first, and we can flank them. I'll take Whiskey and Carel. Hope. Jack-in-Irons. And perhaps my father."

"A nice cross section. I'll be frightened for you." He stroked her hair, ignoring the calculated way she leaned into the caress. It was the best she could give, and he would take it as she offered: in faith. He tilted her head to kiss her nose. "Elaine. Come inside with me." He gestured to the tent.

"Now?"

He read protests in her eyes. *We have things to do. Plans to lay. Troops to drill.* It didn't matter. "Who knows when we'll get the chance again?"

Or if. He didn't need to say it.

She glanced down the hill, her attention drawn by the ringing of Weyland's hammer on iron. Whiskey stood beside him, holding a wooden-handled wedge as if it weighed nothing. The water-horse looked uphill as if feeling eyes upon him. He met Keith's gaze, and per-haps Elaine's. He nodded, once, and turned back to his task.

Keith squeezed Elaine tighter as she stiffened. "All the comforting things a normal husband would say right about now are lies, Elaine."

We'll get through this somehow. We'll always have each other. I'm here for you. It will be all right.

"I know," she said, and led him into the shadows of the tent, the door flap cutting the sunlight when she let it fall between the two of them and the day.

The sun was going down crimson over the beechwood that evening when I called Whiskey away from the fireside and slung my leg over his spine. I leaned down close to his neck and took comfort in the warm, oceanic smell of him. He no longer seemed wild and strange, but like an old and faithful friend. He whickered and stamped. I stroked his smooth-curried mane before I guided him out of the firelight and toward those dark and ruined woods. We passed through the encampment along the way. Jack-in-Irons crouched hulking on the shattered bole of a tree four feet thick, dragging a whetstone as big as my head along the moon-arc of his blade. The crescent was not reflected in the sky overhead, and I wondered if I would live to see the old moon in the new moon's arms on the morrow. The Unseelie camped apart from the rest of the Faerie host, with Keith's pack arrayed between them. A stocky blond wolf I recognized as one of Keith's closer attendants raised a short blade in salute to me as I passed, and I nodded in return. "Hail, Shadowhand!" he called, and I heard a few more voices echo. *"You are among the heroes now."* The gesture distracted me, but not enough to miss Ian in the shadows. I shifted my weight on Whiskey's back to bring him to a stop. Ian came forward and laid a hand on Whiskey's shoulder.

It was a strange thing, like being half blinded, and I wasn't yet used to not being able to sense things all around me, an eye in every shadow. I'd traded the powers of the Seeker for the powers of the Queen; some gifts go with the office. Another would have to watch the shadows for me now.

"Mother." He smiled, and the hand he reached up to lay over mine was warm to the touch. "I've been meeting the pack."

"What do you think of them?"

He sighed and shook his head, silhouetted in the twilight. "I have so much to learn." His hand squeezed mine. "And—you were right about Hope. And thank you for stopping me."

It stung that his words didn't mean more to me than they did. Whiskey snorted and his tail flickered, however, as if he felt my pain for me. He probably did, at that. *Oh, I have done you a disservice, Uisgebaugh.*

"You're welcome," I said, and bent down to kiss my son's hair and tuck an elflock behind his subtly pointed ear. "Fight well tonight, if it comes to that."

"You too, mother." He stepped back, releasing Whiskey and me to the failing light. "Mother. If you were going to name a child, what name would it be?"

Oh, Ian.

I looked away, into the darkness and the blasted wood. "Ask Morgan," I said. "And never tell me." I turned back so he would see me smile through the shadows, and Whiskey bore me into the trees before I so much as shifted my weight.

"I'm sorry, Elaine," my stallion said when we were out of earshot of the camp. "I'm sorry. I will try to endure this better, for you."

"Hellfire." It came out with no force behind it. I wanted to tell him that it was my fault, that he was never meant to be burdened with the worries and loves of a mortal soul. I said something else entirely. "We'll spill that blood tonight, Uisgebaugh. They'll sing of this destruction for a thousand years, and some will call us heroes for it."

"And some will curse our names."

"I haven't one to curse," I answered, and lay against his neck as he moved like a pale wandering ghost among the trees.

"I'll bear the curses for you," he said, and spoke no more until we came to a clearing among the broken wood. I sat back and he halted, restive, his white hide glittering in the gloom. I slid down over his shoulder and stood for a moment, my face pressed against the warm muscle of his neck. A moment later, and his arms were around me.

"Love is a threefold curse for you," he said. I smiled through the pain of it, wondering if I would forget, over the centuries, how much less it hurt now than it would have before, or if I would always bear the memory of mortal frailty.

" 'If I had known, if I had known, Tam Lin,' " I said into his chest. His skin was warm against my lips. "Sing it for me, Uisgebaugh?"

And he did so. He held me, and he sang. *"And Tam Lin on a milk-white steed, with a gold star in his crown . . ."* and the purity of it pierced my heart with a mortal pain, and I understood at last why the Mebd would never hear the song sung. To care so much, to feel that pain: it might have shifted a heart, even, of stone. "The Ballad of King Orfeo" reveals that secret, that the Fae will pay any price to one who can move their hearts.

Morgan came out of the trees a few moments after he finished, and after I was done with weeping. I had seen her in the shadows. She had been waiting for some time.

She wore sage trousers cut close to her skin, and a sweater of claret wool. Evèr and Connla paced her, watching me with eyes wiser than they had any right to. But then, dogs have always known us better than we know ourselves, and loved us in spite of the truth.

Unlike wolves, in whose eyes we see the judgment of something too like ourselves, I suppose. I pulled away from Whiskey and went to meet her, stepping over tangled roots in the dark. "Grandmother. What brings you into the woods at night?"

"You do, Elaine." She took my hands and led me back to Whiskey, who shifted restlessly from foot to foot. The dogs stayed where they were, smiling their wise and secret doggy smiles. "You promised me something, not too long ago."

Oh. Dear. "The answer to a question."

"Yes." I heard the pleasure in her voice.

"Will you answer one for me as well?"

"Perhaps." She leaned back against the rough trunk of a tree, half-invisible in the twilight except where it caught in glimmers on the titian of her hair. I found myself looking at her profile: straight, proud nose and an arch expression. Her lips curved. "You first."

I sucked my lip and leaned back into the strength of Whiskey's calm embrace. I meant to ask a better question, a careful question, but the one that finally passed my lips was a child's exhausted and bewildered "Why?"

"Why not?" Her eyes flashed with humor. "All right. You deserve a

better answer than that." She looked away, and then up at the periwinkle sky. "I made some mistakes, Elaine."

She was quiet for a long while, and I almost went to her, but she held
up her hand to forestall me and when she looked back down, tears
gleamed on her cheeks. "The cost. I've stayed stronger than the others,
but I've also been changed. From darkling goddess, seductress and
battle-raven, mother and murderess, seer in the bowl of blood, to the
wicked Queen and the malicious sorceress, the ender of empires. Or,
sometimes, even though it was men who wrote the stories down, they
remembered a little of what their mothers had woven into the tales: that
it is dangerous to wrong a woman simply because she seems weak. And
that women wronged are not like men. Women who are pushed to a certain point will do what they must."

"Yes," I said, understanding.

"All these things live in me. But we are more than the total of their
fears and longings, Elaine. We are what we are, like Mist. Under the
layers and the legends, there is a core of . . . reality. Or else how could
we surprise them, and ourselves, and each other?"

I nodded to encourage her to continue, but I think by then she was
speaking more for herself than for me.

She paused for a breath, and looked down at her boots, sunk in the
leaf litter. "A woman wants what a woman wants," she finished. "And
she'll do what she must to ensure it. And if that's the blood of my sisters,
the cruel and the bright, spilled on the snow, so mote it be. And if it
costs me my brothers, well. It has cost me more than that, in its time."

"What do you want, Morgan?"

"I answered one question," she said with a smile. "And now it is time
to claim my price."

I am not ashamed to say I was afraid of what she might ask me. I
would have taken a step away from her, but Whiskey's arm was like a
steel bar supporting me, and I managed the appearance, at least, of
courage. "Ask me."

She looked back and met my eyes. "What do you want, and what are
you willing to pay to get it?"

"That is two questions, Morgan."

"I'll consider the second one a favor to be repaid, then," she offered, and tossed her hair back over her shoulder.

My mouth worked. *What do I really want? Beyond anything.* I blinked. "Ian safe," I said, what seemed hours later. Whiskey's arm tightened on my shoulders, and he drew me closer. I felt no fury in him, no betrayal. Only love and support. *What have I done to him?* "And anything."

Morgan paused and knotted her hands in front of her hips. "And I think in that, Elaine, you'll find the answer to your question of me, as well. And the reason I needed to arrange to have my elder sister . . . done away with. A woman does not forgive someone who costs her a child, no matter what the child's part in the matter. Also, like the Mother of Dragons, I'd rather see neither half of my heritage eradicate the other."

"I was your weapon."

"You are my beloved grandchild, Elaine. And I am proud of you, and I grieve for you, and I will be here for you whenever you call on me, until the day you die."

She turned to go, her wolfhounds silent, graceful shapes alongside her, one red and one silver in the darkness. I heard a tolling, not too far away—the sound of Weyland's hammer—and then the unmistakable sound of a roaring ocean when no ocean was near enough to hear. Battle was joined. The Magi had arrived.

"What about Mordred?" I think the words crossed my lips before I so much as thought them.

Morgan le Fey paused in the shadows. Slowly, slowly, she turned to look over her shoulder, the fall of her hair kissing the high bone of her cheek. "That was my fault as much as Arthur's," she said. "And I have paid for it, Elaine. And paid again, I think, not a short week since." She bowed her head, then, and folded her hands before her, and walked away.

I couldn't have called after her. My throat was full of thorns, and no words could have gotten past.

Matthew had left Jane and the rest in the antechamber surrounded by fabulous art, blinking like so many penguins in front of a seemingly endless stream of poorly focused images of immense mythical beasts confounding mortal skies. Sydney, Tokyo—even in Matthew's current state, he could see the humor in that—Morocco, Addis Ababa, Baghdad, Capetown, Moscow . . . the list went on.

He'd gone into the workroom instead and seated himself on the iron stair. Kelly's body lay at the foot, face covered and arms swaddled in hastily wrapped blankets, laid out on a row of metal folding chairs that must have come from a storage locker somewhere. Kelly looked almost straight and tall, wrapped up like that, as if his twisted bones and ruined feet had been healed in death. Matthew left the broad doors cracked open; the voices of the others carried to him very well, enhanced by high ceilings and the inlaid hardwood floors.

He tried not to look at those floors. The inlaid dragons were too much of a taunt, and he could half imagine that their steel claws and eyes flickered with a bloodred tint.

"Kell, I haven't been a very good brother, I'm afraid." Matthew scooted down two steps, until he was sitting on the second one from the bottom and could lean forward and smooth the blankets across Kelly's face. His tattoos still itched. He didn't really mean to—although he didn't mean not to, either—but he found himself drawing a corner of the swaddling back, to give himself one last look at Kelly's face.

He paused when his fingers brushed smooth, cool flesh. Then he settled himself and twitched the cloth aside.

It wasn't what he had expected to see. Kelly looked young, a mere few years older than Matthew. His eyes were closed over a placid, dreaming face, his gently parted lips full and plump, with only the start of crow's-feet strengthening the corners of his eyes. Matthew leaned forward, one hand outreached and his other elbow resting on his knee, holding his breath, unbelieving.

Healed. Healed and dead.

The twisting unease that had been his constant companion since he brought Kelly home from the hospital solidified, settled like iron in the pit of his belly. The unicorn healed Kelly. And killed him. And Jane had summoned the unicorn . . .

. . . which meant she could have healed him at any time in the last fifteen years. Except it hadn't been *her,* had it? It had been the unicorn. A creature of magic and . . .

. . . a Fae thing. A beautiful, terrible thing with eyes like a forest night and a horn of Damascene steel, and Matthew could not find it in his unicorn-pierced heart to think the animal evil. His blood. Kelly's blood. Promethean magic, and a unicorn's horn.

Why would Jane let Kelly suffer like that when she could have healed him at any time?

The answer was as obvious as the iron rings on his hands. *Because she's been planning this since he was taken. Because an elf-touched Mage was just the bridge they needed to break into Faerie. Because he was my brother, and the magic in our ink bound us together.*

And because my fury at the Fae over what they did to Kelly made me blind.

The television still muttered in the other room, broken by the occasional voices of Magi. Soon the sun would rise on Halloween, and the Prometheans would try to find what rest they could. The invasion would begin at midnight.

Matthew balled his hands into fists, veins standing out on his forearms and the rings biting into his fingers. *And where will you be at midnight, Matthew Magus?*

Cool twilight grass tickled Keith's neck and back as he threw himself down in the shade of the tent fly, mopping sweat from his chest with a shirt too soaked to be much use as a towel. He panted, thinking of cold water. *If you were a real King, you'd have someone playing fetch and carry for you.* He grunted and got an elbow underneath himself, meaning to go plunge himself face-first in the convenient spring Elaine's mount had kicked in the turf upslope. He opened his eyes, and almost jumped out of his skin. "You're too damned quiet," he said to Vanya.

Vanya dropped a leather bucket down on the grass beside him. He grinned, a tight wolf-grin. "Already so old you're losing your sense of smell, Sire? Or does the stink of your own sweat just cover it?"

"You came from downwind," Keith accused. He dipped his hands into the bucket and cupped water to his mouth two or three times, then upended the rest over his head. Vanya jumped back, laughing, and pointed over Keith's shoulder. "There goes your wife. She's pretty."

"You can tell from this distance?" Elaine, mounted on her piebald stud, was retreating under the shade of the beeches.

"But can she dance?"

Keith laughed and turned to his brother wolf. From this angle, Vanya's shaggy yellow hair obscured his eyes, giving him the look of a myopic sheepdog—hardly the image of a noble wolf. "Not very well," he admitted. "But she can ride."

"That's more important in the long run," Vanya admitted. He crouched, digging his fingers into the rucked, raw ground, turning it over and rubbing it between his fingers. "Fyodor says the pack is ready. And he may not see what you're doing, Keith MacNeill, but I do."

Keith coughed, and stood. His trousers clung to his skin. He stepped inside the tent and started to strip them off, still talking through the wall to Vanya. "I wish I could run," he said. "I wish I could strip off and put all four feet down on the earth and run until I left the hounds behind."

"Pity it is a new moon," Vanya said, dryly.

"Pity indeed." Keith left his soaked trousers on the floor and slid into a pair made of tough hide. Dry socks followed, and then he stamped into boots. Elaine's sword hung from the centerpost, jammed into Caledfwlch's ill-fitting sheath with a handspan of blade showing. Keith belted it on over his trousers and cast about for a vest and the shirt of mail Puck had made him promise to wear. "Were you watching the scrimmage?"

"Scrimmage?" Vanya mouthed the unfamiliar English word thoughtfully. "The practice combat?"

"Yes." Keith tossed the blond wolf his mail shirt, grinning like a human as the metal slipped like water between Vanya's broad, capable hands. "How did it look?"

Vanya shrugged and crouched to pick the hauberk up. The sun had set and silver rings shimmered coolly in the gloaming. "If the Daoine Sidhe and the Unseelie don't kill each other, you might have an army. And don't think you've distracted me, Sire."

"Vanya?"

The light made his blue eyes shadowy and strange. "Fyodor Stephanovich, Elder Brother. I know why you saved his life."

"Don't you think he would have beaten me?"

Vanya nibbled his lip. "I think he was fated not to, Sire. I think it had nothing to do with skill, or who might be fitter to lead. And I think—"

"Speak freely." Keith turned his back, buttoning his shirt against the chill in the air.

"I think you saved his life so he can take your place when you are dead, Dragon Prince."

Keith scuffed a bootheel on the turf, turning around, pulling his swordbelt out to tuck the shirttails into his waistband. "Am I so transparent, Vanya?"

The blond wolf smiled, standing, the hauberk stretched out between his hands so he could assist Keith on with it. "It will be years, of course, before that becomes a worry. You may be old and gray by then."

"Unless we die tonight." Keith shrugged. "I should probably wear the swordbelt over the mail shirt. Don't you think?"

"I've never worn a mail shirt. I don't know." And then Vanya's head came up, sniffing the breeze, at just the moment that it carried the sound of hoofbeats to Keith's ears. He turned, seeing in the twilight better than a human would have, although in shapes and movements and shades of gray, and caught sight of Carel standing in the stirrups of her trotting bay. *Somebody should teach her to post,* Keith thought. *Or at least ride a trot. She looks like a marionette.* Unfair: she was riding halfway well, for a woman who hadn't been on a horse a few Faerie hours and less than a mortal day before.

"Merlin," he called when she was within earshot, and went to meet her. "A message of some haste, I take it?"

She nodded, beads clattering, the scent of a forge hanging around her as she shoved escaped braids out of her eyes with the hand that did not hold her reins. "We need to make ready," she said. "I can feel them. They're coming."

A little before midnight, in fact, Matthew was still sitting on the iron stair, chin resting on his interlocked fingers, pondering his future. Jane found him there when she led the rest of the group into the workroom. She laid a hand on his shoulder, a motherly gesture that made his skin crawl. "Are you ready, Matthew?"

"As ready as I'll ever be," he said, and stood, carefully not looking at Kelly's blanket-wrapped body as helpful Magi came to move it to the side. "So we're beset by dragons, are we?"

"Apparently," Jane answered, helping him to his feet.

Matthew rolled his shoulders back. His spine crackled. "How many casualties?" At least if there were a strain in his voice, it could be blamed on the evening he'd endured. In fact, he decided, a note of re-strained fury wasn't out of line.

"None, so far." Jane shrugged. She dusted her hands down her skirt. Matthew wondered if her palms were sweating. His were, itching under the rings. "Doesn't that seem unusual?"

"It does." He shrugged and walked with her to the door. More Prometheans than he had ever seen in one place were wandering into the workroom now, familiar faces and ones he had never seen filling it to capacity and beyond. Some of them wore military uniforms. Most carried firearms. "Where did all these Magi come from?"

"All over the world." She eyed him carefully. "Matthew, you don't have to go tonight. You've done enough, you and Kelly. Stay here with me." Her hand on his arm was like a mooring rope, a promise of harbor.

Except I'm the Flying Dutchman, *now.* "No," he said. "It'd be silly to turn back now." He patted her on the arm and walked away to join the ranks of Magi assembled around the base of the massive spiral stair.

"Matthew, stay—" she called after him, but she didn't follow. And he went.

There was no chime. No one raised a voice or cried "Go!" Instead, a ripple swept the crowd, a sort of *knowing* that prickled hair on necks and arms, and people simply started walking. Deasil: with the clock, with the sun.

The room was rectangular. Eddies of Magi collected in the corners, rejoined the spiral when there was a gap. There was no marching, no lockstep footwork. Just a casual amble, spiraling like the stair and fad-ing inward, ever inward, as Prometheans—three abreast, in a steady stream—readied their weapons and began to climb the stair. They were clad for war, protected by Kevlar helmets and body armor modified with iron sigils and strung about with protective wards. Prometheans from around the world were represented. Matthew saw talismans made of granite, and ivory, and jade, and brilliant jungle-bird feathers among the qabbalistic and thaumaturgic ones. Prometheans were never shy about appropriating symbols.

They carried semiautomatic weapons, the ones who could handle them, and some had hung steel swords between shoulders or from hips, or wore daggers strapped to thighs. It was startling that Jane hadn't managed to find a way to bring a tank or two, now that he thought about it.

Matthew's foot was on the first tread before he knew it. He climbed, on the left-hand margin of his group of three, one step behind the woman in front of him. He felt eyes on him. He didn't turn to see if they were Jane's.

He didn't have a weapon in his hands, and it occurred to him how pitifully little he'd bothered to know about this spell, this task. *We'll build a bridge and go and get the children back, and cut Faerie out of contact with the mortal world so they can't trouble us anymore.*

It sounds so simple when you put it that way.

Jane never intended me to go, did she?

The man on his right side stumbled on a step edge. Matthew caught his elbow. He seemed to have been climbing for a long time, but when he glanced down, he could still see the workroom floor, thick with twining dragons, their steel eyes glittering lava red. He glanced up, and saw mist like lowering clouds. He walked up into it, clenching his hands at his sides.

He thought they'd come out into a firefight, that the Fae would be waiting to pick them off as they stepped off the stair. Except it didn't seem like a stair, at this end, but rather a gargantuan wrought iron helix with razored edges that he didn't dare touch, dimly lit with starlight. The Fae were well back, as if they had been expecting something to happen and did not want to risk proximity to that much iron. The earth was soft as if mole-chewed under Matthew's boots. He stepped aside, expecting another rank of Magi to follow him out of the mist and shadows, and then stopped, as he fully comprehended the size of the group surrounding him, and the nature of the army they faced.

Torchlight, witchlight, St. Elmo's fire lit the enemy in neon reflections of red and green and blue. Natural luminescence—if you could call it natural—provided eerier colors: lime, corpse-flower, a dappled blue like the skin of a poison arrow frog. He took a breath and smelled harrowed earth and something rotten, and the ozone thrill of an approaching storm. The night was so silent he thought he could hear the enemy's horse-harness jingle: no shouts, no chants, no challenges. *For we are beyond all that, you and I.*

How do you fight a war without any weapons?

That's very easy, my boy. You go and die like a soldier.

Around him, the Magi massed like a beast gathering itself to spring, silent still except for a slow, unified breathing. The Fae waited, the advantage of the slope behind them. Brave thoughts or not, Matthew found himself slipping back through the ranks, back between pressing bodies of strangers and people he had known, all of them straining forward like dogs on a leash. He laid a hand on the hard iron root of the bridge, rubbed his fingers into rust made sticky with old, dried blood. *Kelly's blood,* he thought. *The blood we all paid into this thing. And here it is.*

Just doing its job. He breathed in. He breathed out. *"Oh, how full of briers is this working-day world,"* he quoted to himself, and pressed his back against the bridge as Prometheus shouted with one voice, moved with one strength, and burst forward onto the field of battle. The crash when the ranks came together sounded like ships of the line colliding, tearing metal and clashing metal and the rapid-fire discharge of semiautomatic weapons like rivets popping out of a stressed seam. A storm slammed down on both armies like the angry hand of God, and all Matthew could see for some little time was the flickering lightning, as he crowded into the rain shadow of the bridge. He couldn't track the battle; it ebbed and flowed, and shapes as strange and wicked as demons moved in the half-light, in the flickering darkness and occasional, actinic brilliance of lightning or a hurled bolt of wrath from one of the Prometheans.

Those tricks didn't work on earth anymore, although Matthew had studied them as well as the next Mage. But apparently they still sufficed in Faerie.

Matthew closed both hands on his trouser legs and sank to the ground. He would have buried his face in his hands, was moving toward it in fact, but someone touched his shoulder and he lifted his head to see who it might be.

A wizened old man stepped out of the shadows along the ridged stem of the bridge, naked except for a leather apron, white hair growing in tufts from his ears and his beard braided in forked strands and looped over the apron belt. He held an iron hammer in one hand, and Matthew blinked. Blinked and looked quickly down at his own hands, to be sure the rings were where they belonged. They were, and here he was up to his neck in Faerie, a war raging not a hundred meters off, and his fingers didn't hurt at all.

"How is it you can touch iron?" Matthew shouted, above the swell of combat.

The old Faerie man looked from Matthew to his hammer, and laid that same knotty hand on the twisted trunk of the bridge. "I'm the Weyland Smith," he said. " 'Tis what I do. Now tell me, laddy. How would I go about tearing down this little construct of thine?"

Chapter Twenty-Six

Whiskey and I rode out of the woods and into the confusion of battle. Torchlight and witchlight lit the scene for our part, turning the Fae armies into a horde of misshapen shadows, while at the base of the iron bridge I made out something like a thousand human shapes clad in camouflage, jean jackets, leather, Kevlar, and ceramic armor. Flashes of light stitched from among them — weapons fire, although I couldn't see if any of it made contact among the Fae. I couldn't, in fact, see much of anything at all but shadows moving in the darkness.

Whiskey stopped, solid as a statue, and I knelt up on his back, balancing myself against his crest. Jack-in-Irons I recognized, a headless, rattling shape backlit by fire and wreathed in smoke, swinging an axe as long as a man. He waded among the Magi, who scattered, and I saw his huge form shudder as bullets broke the corona of moon-colored light surrounding him. They must have been steel-jacketed slugs, because the giant sagged to his knees, still striking out wildly. Magi went down around him like mown wheat, and I saw other shapes, Elf-knights on horseback and what must have been the pack, afoot, charging in to fill the gap he had created.

I couldn't see Keith. But I picked out Carel, high on the hillside, the foxfire surrounding her hands matching the torn light that half shielded Jack-in-Irons and flickered from place to place, marking the muzzles of guns and drawing the fire of Fae archers. I marked a figure hurrying up the hill to stand beside her—*Morgan*—and wondered that they did not find themselves targets of the mortal Magis.

Wondered a second too soon, as a fevered, electric arc lanced the width of the battlefield. I shouted and felt Whiskey tense, ready to charge in among them . . . but the levinbolt twisted aside, scorched earth harmlessly, filled the air with the tang of ozone and burning soil. *Hope,* I wondered, *or Morgan?*

No matter. Hope was here. I smelled the storm rising, and the breeze that brushed my face was cold and heavy with rain.

"Whiskey, bring me around to Morgan." I slid back, forking my legs around his barrel, and grabbed a handful of mane. I hadn't ridden bareback so much since my childhood at the ranch . . . which reminded me of what my father had said, about visiting my mother. Soul-sold or not, if I couldn't feel love, I could feel duty all the more sharply. Duty, and guilt.

Whiskey extended into a hard run, skirting the battle. Snatches of song came to me, and mortal cries of pain. Gunfire, the hiss of arrows, the clash of blades. Darkness slid across the stars. "Gharne," I said into the rising wind, wondering if his name could still bring him to me, wondering if I dared to leave the Cat Anna unattended, bound or not.

Hell. It will all be over soon, one way or another. And I've bargained Hell out from under her.

Jack went down, earthshaking in his fall, a huge dark shape outlined in dying light. The Magi swarmed over and around him. I looked away. I'd meant him for my part of the battle, and things would be harder without. I couldn't take Morgan; she was needed here. Hope and Carel were too, dammit. We all were. I saw the Fae hosts falling, the Magi a tight knot pushing forward now, the gap in their ranks scabbed over and healed without a trace. Whiskey stretched low and ran faster as the first drops of rain stung my face and thunder rolled, barely audible over the clamor of battle. Lightning danced, more golden than the levinbolts that wove among it, and the stench of ozone and burning meat grew unbearable.

Keith.

Ian. I wondered if my son was out there, fighting with his arm in a sling, or if Keith had ordered him into the rearguard. And if Ian had gone where bid. The flashes and foxfire and the flames, hissing in the sudden downpour, made an intermittent brightness that revealed the battlefield as plainly as a strobe freeze-framing a dance floor, and all I could smell was electricity and blood.

Whiskey snorted and dug into the hillside; Morgan looked up as we came. She stood beside Carel's horse, fingers clenched tight on the reins; the bay mare danced and snorted. Carel herself had both hands knotted on the pommel, and her face looked ashen in the television light. Morgan leaned on the reins as Whiskey skidded to a halt beside them, clods and mud flying from his hooves. "Where's Hope?" I shouted over the noise, and Carel shook her head and pointed at her ears, not glancing away from the battle. Another corona of moonlight, watery through the increasing rain, flared around a target, and that target fell. I couldn't see what Morgan was doing, but her lips were moving. She lifted her arm and pointed.

Hope stood in darkness a little beyond, gowned in black or indigo and unhorsed so I hadn't seen her. The lightning didn't much reveal her, which made me smile tightly around the taste of rain. I heard more gunfire and winced, but Morgan shook her head. "I'm glamouring," she said. "Most of what they shoot is unreal. The only problem is, the Magi bear iron, which shatters the glamours as fast as I build them, and they've already laid warfetter on half our troops."

Blinded, deafened, or simply made too weak to stand: a magic so old it's recorded in the Táin Bó Cúailnge. "Hell," I swore. "Morgan, I need Carel and Hope."

"Take them," she said, unhesitating. *It will cost us lives.*

Yes, and it might save us all. Gamble, or play the safe cards and have no chance at all. I nodded, and grabbed the reins of Carel's mare. Morgan held them up. "Gharne, where are you?"

"Here," he said, yellow eyes hanging in the night. "And none too soon. Your Cat Anna is a dull sort. Is this the war?"

"Part of it," I said. "Can you find Murchaud in all that?"

"No problem."

"Do it. And if you see Keith, tell him I'm leaving. Go carefully, and meet me in New York if you can."

"I understand," he said, and the amber of his eyes winked out as the stars had, before.

Carel blinked and seemed to shake her body back on as I turned her mare and led it toward Hope. "Elaine?"

"We're taking the battle to them," I said, and tossed her the reins. She caught them awkwardly, but her seat had improved with practice. "Come on."

She followed. I came up on Hope from an angle that let her see me, not fancying a lightning strike if I surprised her. She stood with her hands by her sides, holding the heavy fabric of her skirts away from her legs, the rain streaking her dark hair down her cheeks. Lightning hammered here and there, wherever her eyes rested, striking the bridge, coruscating in brutal opposition to the Magi's levinbolts. I gulped in awe at the power she wielded, and wondered who her father was. She didn't take her eyes off the battle when she spoke, shouting over the now ceaseless crackle of her storm. "What?"

"We're going to the city to break some things," I called back, unable to hear my own voice.

She must have, though, because she shook her head. "Ian's out there."

"So is Keith," I snapped.

Then she did look at me, and scintillating light reflected in her enormous eyes. "Ian isn't doomed."

Damn her. And damn her twice for being right. I heard hoofbeats, and Carel didn't shout so I didn't bother to turn. "Come on. Maybe we can save them both, at least until tomorrow."

Her eyes rested hard on mine for a moment, and then she jerked her gaze away. Murchaud drew rein beside us, his steed a black, batwinged thing that bore the same kinship to a horse as Gharne did to a falcon. "That's all there is, right?" Her words were bitter, and so soft I wasn't sure she meant me to hear them, but they fell into a lull in the storm. "Push the end back another day."

"Yes," I said. "And hope our children do the same."

She sucked her lips and nodded, and held out her hand to me. I hauled her up behind me, Whiskey steady as a bronze statue, and glanced from Carel to Murchaud. "New York City," I said. "And ride!"

We chirruped our steeds into a gallop, breakneck across the slippery turf, away from the iron bridge as fast as a running horse could carry us. Carel called moonlight out of nowhere to guide our steeds; it turned each leaf of grass into a construction-paper representation. The rain fell behind us, although lightning still tore and flashed, and in a few moments we entered the second valley, beyond the shallow hill. It was Carel who opened the passage under the thorn trees, and Carel who led us into it.

Her mare shied and snorted, but the presence of Whiskey and of Murchaud's un-horse were comfort and pressure enough to move her forward into the tunnel under the earth. "I promised you no caves," I said as the Merlin sealed the hill behind us, hoping to provoke a laugh.

"I promised you nothing," she answered, and the way opened before us into light-rippled shadows and the torn edges of reality. Carel put her mare into a trot, and we followed for some hours. Until big trees arched over, and Whiskey's hooves clopped on packed earth and roots. "Inwood Hill," Hope said over my shoulder. "Brilliant."

"We still have a long way to ride." Carel leaned forward in her saddle. "Heya! Follow me!"

The bay mare leapt forward and Whiskey and the un-horse surged after, two abreast as the earthen trail gave way to pavement, headlong down the hill, under the tunneling, half-leafed trees. I judged it late evening, dry and crisp, cold for October. Traffic noise drifted up to us, the bean sidhe shriek of an ambulance announcing a death.

Carel led us through a small park at the bottom of the hill, past a baseball diamond and a small, gawping group of mortals. Whiskey flicked his tail at them, silver-shod hooves ringing like glass bells on the pavement. "Thank you for the shoes," he said over his shoulder.

I didn't answer, but I smiled.

Carel turned us east. The racing steeds hurdled vehicles and knocked aside pedestrians, careless and savage in their grace, and people stopped, pointed, and shouted. Whiskey drew even with Carel's steed, despite the mare's lighter burden, and laughed in delight at his prowess. The Merlin clung to her saddle gamely and let the mare have her head. I risked a backward glance when I heard Hope gasp, and my laughter turned into something else.

Murchaud's batwinged stallion had taken to the air, and glided behind us on unholy slow beats of leather wings wreathed in flame.

Just a few blocks, and Carel turned southward. Whiskey paced her. The sirens were behind us now, and ahead. Whiskey grunted and staggered when one forehoof, trailing slightly on the side where his shoulder had been wounded, clipped the edge of a Cadillac going over, and the Seeker might have winced at his pain, but I laid a steadying hand on his neck and urged him forward. He didn't need it. He was game, and he ran as if his heart alone were enough to carry him, each stride jarring my bandaged knee and spiking pain all the way to my teeth.

This street was wider, and ran diagonally, a great slice cut across the orderly grid of Manhattan. Broadway. A Faerie Rade down Broadway. Carel did indeed have a certain inimitable style. "Times Square, right?" she yelled over her shoulder. I nodded and shouted something wordless back. The beating heart, as it were, of the capital of the Promethean World.

Carel had given up on the reins entirely and clutched her mare's black mane, laughing like a maniac and singing between the gasps. I caught a word or two over the wail of sirens, the thunder of hooves, the leathery stroke of the un-horse's wings: something about broken hearts and lights on Broadway.

The Merlin's sense of humor would be the death of me yet.

Southward, and the traffic grew, and the honking grew, and all around us glistened white lightbulbs by the millions. Whiskey staggered, lather flying, and caught himself. Hope clutched my waist and I clutched his mane. Flashing lights splashed us with red and blue and amber, and I couldn't hear Carel singing over the shouts and the screams. Something wet struck my lips. I wiped blood and froth onto my sleeve, and still Whiskey ran. There is no courage like the courage of horses.

The lights in front of us flashed like Christmas, and the horses ran faster than horses had any right to. I wondered if the police meant to give us speeding tickets.

More than a hundred and fifty blocks, over iron roads. Carel's horse seemed to withstand it better; there must have been mortal blood in that mare. I could feel the pressure of the city on me like an iron pin in every joint, like a thousand eyes turned toward me. Shouts to stop and then bullets whistled past us. There was a black van parked across the road, and men in blue before it. "Don't kill the cops," I yelled into the water-horse's ear, and then wondered why it mattered. We were here to break things.

Whiskey gathered himself, and I set myself and felt Hope lean into it too.

Neon, then, and the thud of hooves shattering pavement, the crawl of lights across the billboards, and the glass wall of a television studio across the way. Carel reined her horse around, and Whiskey sat back on his haunches in a gymkhana spin that almost cost me Hope. I turned to see the un-horse sail through a firestorm of bullets that spattered off his hide and, judging by the shouts, fell back among the shooters in a molten rain.

He glided over our heads as well, and settled behind us. Mortals fell, scurried and ran, a hellrider too much even for a New Yorker's composure.

Hope released her hold on my belt and raised her hand, and—rainless, thick with lightning—her storm slammed shut over the sky. Electrical discharge crackled from building to building, a latticework across the heavens. Whiskey reared up, storybook charger, and threw back his head with a stallion's high, ringing challenge. His hooves clattered on pavement when he came down, and the scabbed shoulder split, threading crimson over his lathered hide.

I looked up at the lightning; the wind from the un-horse's wings stirred my hair. My heart thumped in my chest. Carel Dragonborn, the Merlin, sat up on her bay mare beside me. SWAT officers from the van, regular police, trained twenty or fifty firearms on us.

"I could kill them all," Hope said. "That would make an impression."

"It would," I answered, and swallowed hard. Carel turned to me, a haunted look. I shook my head and said, "I have to try."

"It won't work," Hope said. She slid down Whiskey's side and grabbed my boot. "They're mortal. You know what they'll do."

"Yes," I said, and moved Whiskey forward, toward the men with the guns, a little too fast to hear whatever it was that Carel was chanting under her breath.

"Elaine," Hope called after me, in the tones of someone who doesn't expect to get another chance to say something. "Elaine. It's a girl."

I didn't turn back to smile at her, because I wouldn't have kept going if I did.

Keith should have been in the thick of the fight, leading from the front the way a wolf should lead. Instead he sat his bay horse on the hillside, surrounded in darkness, Morgan on his left side and wounded Ian on his right. They were spread out so as not to make one target and screened behind a row of Daoine Elf-knights, but the sorceress stayed within earshot of him. It was Fyodor down there with the pack, and that was wrong. It itched in his blood, on his skin. His blood bay picked the tension up and shifted, snorting, tossing his head to try and shake the reins loose from Keith's trembling hands.

Keith soothed the animal, stroking his mane flat with the palm of his right hand, coarse strands catching on his calluses. "Easy, boy." *Think of the battle in front of you, and not of your wife, lad—*

Not quite his father's voice, which might have been why it didn't steady him. He glanced left, caught Morgan's profile in reflected light. "We're failing," she said, as if she felt his eyes upon her. "Dragon Prince, it's not enough—"

"And I'm stuck here watching it and shouting orders," he said bitterly. "This is it. This is everything we have."

"Near enough," Morgan said, turning her head to watch as her raven soared over the battlefield, grown to three times his natural size. The Magi were pushing outward, out from the root of the iron bridge, pushing the Faeries back. Bodies littered the field, which was lit with the ropes and lights of sorcery and the gunfire of the Prometheans.

Petunia whinnied and backed a step as bullets splattered off the wall of air that Morgan had set before them, and Keith steadied him again and stroked Excalibur's sheath where it banged against his leg.

It was down to a crawling battle now, the Fae advancing where they could against the overwhelming gunfire of the enemy. "I should be down there," Keith said again. Fyodor *was* leading the pack. Keith could see them like a dark wedge among the gaily colored Fae, giving as good as they got. They moved as if they made up one animal clothed in different hides. They had no recourse to wolf shape, here on the dark of the moon, but like the Magi they carried firearms and unlike the Magi they had no fear of base metal bullets.

And still the Magi advanced. Wolves wouldn't die of iron, but they would if struck by magic, and the flat valley around the bridge gave no cover. It should have hurt the Magi too, but arrows and slings were no match for automatic weapons. Faerie blood soaked the harrowed earth; Keith could smell it over the reek of cordite.

"Christ," Keith said, frowning an apology when Ian flinched. "Ian, stay with Morgan. I'm going."

"Sire —" Ian said.

Keith shook his head. "Even the bard is down there. It's where I should be too."

"I wish the Merlin were here," Ian said.

"Yes," Keith answered, drawing his wife's sword from Arthur's sheath. "I wish she were too." And then he trapped the sheath between his knee and the stirrup leather, so it touched his red horse too. He clucked to Petunia, gave him all the rein he wanted, and touched him with his heels.

The horse leapt forward as if struck from behind. Keith raised his fey blade and shouted—no. *Howled.* "To me! To me! To me!" And they came. They ran, Fae and wolves alike, falling into his guard and fanning around him like a crescent moon. He looked down and saw Eremei Fyodorovich maintaining a long easy lope at his stirrup, holding what looked like a Kalashnikov.

A halo flickered around Keith as he rode, shouting: Morgan le Fey's ward and guard. Magi's spells shredded off it like waves off the bow of a ship. He waved his sword wildly over his head and shouted again, driving down upon them, driving forward to split them apart and send them running in dismay. Bullets struck him; they stung like pebbles as they passed through his body; the wounds healed bloodlessly. They struck his brave red horse as well, and the stallion pressed forward, unfazed by the impacts, Arthur's scabbard healing the wounds as fast as they could be dealt.

Keith spotted Cairbre in the press, standing over the body of his horse, laying about himself with a mace and a buckler and roaring songs like a wild beast. No one could strike him; no one could get close without being struck down in a red veil of blood, and his music stopped the bullets in midair. They hung there like swarms of bees until they were bashed aside by the arc of his mace or the swing of his cloak. It was breathtaking.

"To me!" Keith shouted, riding down the cluster of Magi to Cairbre's left. "To me!"

The bard glanced up as Keith rode down on him. He transferred his hair-clotted mace to his shield hand as Magi scattered, then pulled something from the saddle on his fallen horse. Petunia skidded in the bloody mud and slowed to a prancing walk, shaking foam from his bit. Wolves and Fae closed around them, surged past them. Blades clashed on bayonets; they stood in a momentary lull in the eye of the battle, a paltry shelter of flesh and bone. "Up," Keith said, offering Cairbre his hand.

"It's not every day an Elf rides pillion behind the King," Cairbre said, and instead of giving Keith his hand he gave him a hide-and-wood-cased harp. Keith looked at it curiously, and Cairbre stepped up behind him as easily as if he had walked up a mounting block. The bard settled his cloak and reached around Keith to take the harp, to open the case and hang it on Petunia's saddle. The wood of the instrument gleamed red, despite the flickering green of Morgan's witchcraft: a red so dark no light could alter it.

"The Red Harp," Keith said. "Can it help us?"

"It can't shatter guns the way it can blades," Cairbre said, his rich baritone hoarse with shouting. He shifted against Keith's back, hooking his mace onto his belt. "And the time for mending hearts is past. But what it can do it will do, aye, my King." He took a breath, braced the harp between his thigh and the saddle, and ran his fingers down the strings.

Something took root in Keith's breast: a seed of hope, a thread of heartening strength. He drew a breath and glanced around. The Magi had broken under the madcap charge but had not fled the field. Rather they'd regrouped in front of the tree line, more bunched than before, ready to receive the Fae. A shattering green bolt of power burst overhead, splattering against the shield of Cairbre's music like acid thrown against glass. Keith turned his head to watch the rivulets run down the inside of the sky.

He glanced left and right, at the ragged assemblage of Fae and wolves, and shook his head. "Sorry excuse for an army," he said, but the magic in what Cairbre played made it come out fondly, and he could see the strength returning to disheartened and exhausted shoulders.

Keith raised his sword again. Witchery reflected the length of it, so it looked like a stroke of lightning in his hand. "Forward!" he cried, pressing his knees to Petunia's sides. The bay curvetted, tossing his mane, and danced forward. Keith's army moved around him.

And suddenly, savagely, the world went blind and dark.

There was a battle raging not ten feet off, and no one even looked in their direction. Matthew crouched beside the Weyland Smith and ran his fingers up and down the metal of the bridge. "You want this taken down?"

"Yes." The bandy-legged smith hefted his hammer, crouched so low his knees rose up beside his ears.

"You know I helped to put it here."

"Aye," the smith said. "And it's my task to cut it off at the root, and I cannot give over until my task is completed. Such is my geas." He blinked at Matthew shrewdly through the darkness. His eyelashes were long and black, weird against the shaggy white beard and brows that framed his face. "And judging by the look on you, son, if I may say so, you seem unhappy at the manner in which your own geas plays itself out."

"I haven't any geasa," Matthew said. "I'm a mortal man, free to make my own fate."

"The old people believed that even mortal men had geasa, Matthew Magus."

"How do you know my name?" Sharper than he'd intended, and he jerked back when the old man reached out and gripped his wrist, but his fingers were like welded chain.

"It's written in your eyes," Weyland said, his own eyes glittering like water in deep caverns. "Now tell me how to tear this old bridge down."

"Blood," Matthew said, and stopped trying to pull his hands away. Instead, he turned them over, showing smooth palms callused from the weight room and not much else. "My blood tempered it. You use my blood to tear it down."

Weyland let go. "I knew I could count on you, son."

Trembling, Matthew fumbled his pocketknife out. He opened the blade, checked to make sure the thumb lock was set, and held it out to Weyland, handle first.

"You do for yourself, lad," the old man said kindly, his eyebrows waggling over glinting eyes. A levinbolt splattered against thin air off to Matthew's left; he risked a glance and saw the Fae surrounded, a red-bearded warrior on a great red horse urging them forward, a black-haired Fae cradling a harp riding pillion. The image struck Matthew with its absurdity and power. He laughed and shook his head. "It's all madness, isn't it? Why should I let you tear this down, when my brother gave his life to build it?"

"Because your brother gave his life to build it," Weyland answered. "Here, dab your blood on this hammer. We'll bring the house down. It's too late to save your friends if we do this thing, Matthew Magus."

"I know," Matthew said. A ragged cheer broke out from the Promethean ranks. The big redheaded man had slumped forward in his saddle, the sword fallen from his hands as he clutched his eyes. Other Fae fell to their knees, tripped and sprawled full length on the ground. The ragged dome of light that glowed around them had torn, Matthew saw, its greenness sickly now rather than rich and deep. The storm that had raged earlier had broken entirely, and when he craned his head straight back he saw the bridge standing twisted against a field of stars. Razored blue edges glittered, and he blinked and sighed ruefully. "More fool I," he said, and folded the knife tidily and put it in his pocket. "This blood won't do it. I ought to know that—"

"Matthew Magus?"

"—I touched a unicorn." Matthew reached up, standing on tiptoe. He could almost brush one of the unblunted edges with his fingertips. " 'Do as thou wilt shall be the whole of the Law,' " he muttered. "And when was the last time I listened to *that* advice?"

He crouched, knowing that the smith moved away around the circumference of the bridge, not caring. He closed his eyes and drew a deep breath.

Off to his left, only the rippling, failing light and the savage tones of the musician's harp kept the Prometheans at bay. The Fae had fallen, or were stumbling about, blinded and deafened. Warfetter, and whoever had cast it, had gotten every last one of them except the bard, and whatever fey sorcerers hid in darkness, managing the barrier that kept the Prometheans from their fallen comrades. Matthew tried to imagine the power behind that manifestation, and failed.

He sprang directly upward, his shoulder striking the iron of the bridge a breathtaking blow, his hands stretched upward like a drowning man's, his right hand striking the embedded blade and slicing cleanly down to bone, severing muscles and tendons. Hot blood fell on Matthew's face before he landed, spattering his borrowed shirt, dripping on the harrowed earth.

It hurt. He gasped with the pain, falling forward, cradling his right hand in his left. He pushed it forward when it would have curled itself against his chest, offering it to Weyland, his blood and his pain. "There," he said. "That's the blood to do it."

Weyland did not answer. He held out his hammer, and Matthew smeared it with the dripping blood. He stripped his pullover over his head and ripped a sleeve off and wound it around his hand, knotting it with his teeth. It might not stop the bleeding, but it would soak up the blood.

"You'd better stand back, son," Weyland said, considering the bridge with a craftsman's eye. "I expect this thing will come down hard."

Times Square is a triangle: a strange hex-sign marking Manhattan like a rune carven into the blade of a knife. I put the Times Tower at my back and moved forward to claim the center of that space, stiff and up-right though iron dragged me down. Water oozed from Whiskey's every footstep. "Tonight it is good Halloween / The Faerie Court will ride." The Merlin raised her voice as I passed her, her mahogany bay pranc-ing in a nervous spiral as the mare tried to watch the strange lights and buildings and the armed, swarming men in blue all at once. I thought of monster movies and I thought of rubber suits. *No one will ever believe this. Never believe a word of it.*

Murchaud's voice joined Carel's, heartbreaking and pure, the song of an angel of Hell, and Hope's voice rose up a moment behind it. Cairbre the bard chose her for a reason. And then I smiled, bittersweet, and knew who Hope's father was, and how Cairbre had come to be where a Promethean might capture him. *"Jenet, she's kilted her green kirtle well above the knee / And ta'en herself to Miles Cross as fast as she can go."*

"Shit," I murmured under my breath. "It always ends at the cross-roads."

"That's because they're magic," Whiskey said. He leaned from hoof to hoof, light on the forehand, his ears pinned flat. Frightened, which surprised me.

Reflecting the rippling neon as if he were cast in chrome, my shin-ing pale steed moved forward, and the bay and the black flanked him on either side. Carel turned her head to grin at me. Lights and images flashed on every side, hung on the weary stone of buildings old by New World standards, and on the shining steel and glass curtain walls of skyscrapers. JVC. ABC. WB. Neon and flickering light, a thousand col-ors, an aurora that blotted out the stars—a glamour of light and color and modernity, I suddenly realized, over the ancient truth of the city. The city, a beast all its own: a beast of stone with iron teeth and a heart of hot meat, pulsing living blood through its arteries and avenues. Times Square and neon, bustle and media, blinking lights crying "buy, consume, desire." Peter Jennings with his hair blown out of order standing outside the ABC television studio, beside a camera crew, gawking like the rest of them and then suddenly straightening his tie, slicking a hand through graying locks, and turning back inside to do his job.

Broadway and Seventh Avenue. The nerve center of the beast. The beast the mortals think they've chained, and tamed.

The Dragon whose pearl is the heart of the world.

"Fuck me," Hope said softly, as they finished their song. "I never meant to return here."

The last strain of Carel's voice died away into a silence, a silence unholy for New York City. No sirens, no shouting, no loud conversation. The sound of weapons cocking fell into that hush. Whiskey snorted blood.

"Hope," I said to the woman beside my stirrup. "Carel. Shut it down."

"Your Majesty," they answered in unison, and as the un-horse unveiled his flame-shot wings behind me, electricity hissed and Carel raised her hands as if in surrender. Sparks geysered from billboards and LED screens as Hope brought her lightning down like a lance—once, twice, and again.

And the lights went out on Broadway.

I expected screams in the darkness that followed, or gunfire, but the cameras were our ally. *Those* lights stayed on, flooding the scene with a sharp-shadowed unreality that reminded me of the grass under our hooves in Faerie. Those lights, and the lights in windows and inside buildings. Garbled words through a bullhorn, and then clearly, "Keep your hands where we can see them." Police were trying to move bystanders along and hustling the media inside, but it was too much, too fast, and they didn't have control.

And I needed to act before they did.

I smiled and held up both hands, riding toward the SWAT van. Moonlight surrounded me and lightning crackled overhead, the air stinking of ozone. A deeper hush greeted me as my companions let me ride from between them, broken only by the measured tones of

Whiskey's hooves upon the asphalt. I gnawed my lip, chewing back a frantic laugh. *Klatu verata nikto.*

"People of New York City! I am Elaine Andraste, Queen of the Daoine Sidhe, and I come as an emissary from the kingdoms of Faerie and of Hell. We wish to treat with your leaders. We come in peace, and in proof I remind you that while your men fired their weapons first, we returned no harm."

I winced at my tone. I'd forgotten how to talk like a mortal.

Someone cleared his throat. Floodlights seared the night and I thought a scuffle might break out between the camera crews—three of them now—and the cops. "Fairies," someone said. "We're supposed to believe you're *fairies?*"

Not exactly approved negotiation technique. I lowered my hands, but kept them spread wide. "Fae folk and a Duke of Hell, sir." I couldn't see past the lights. I wondered how the battle was going in Annwn, and how long I had before the Magi sent someone to deal with me. I wondered if it would be Matthew.

I didn't want to kill Matthew. I half liked him, and I could certainly see his side of the argument.

"I see." He couldn't keep the dryness from his voice. "You want to talk to the mayor. I imagine he's a little busy dealing with the blackout, Elaine. Do you mind if I call you Elaine?"

Ah, that's more like the textbooks. He's getting his feet under him. Time to knock them out again. "Hope."

She must have been frightened. Lightning hammered sky to earth and sky again, a bolt so blue it seared images across my vision. My hair lifted in the wind and sparked, end to end. Two of the floodlights shattered, spewing glass and fire. They weren't the camera crews' lights. Clever girl.

"No," I said civilly. "I don't mind at all." I let my hands fall to my side. *This is going too well. They'll send a professional negotiator next.*

I was wrong. "Look," said the man behind the lights, "this is some kind of publicity stunt, right? Halloween and people dressed up like devils and fairies."

"I wish it were," I said. I could feel him grappling with the evidence of his own eyes, versus the problem of what he *believed* to be true. Your average modern rationalist doesn't *understand* the scientific world. He simply places faith in it, much the same way he places faith in what his doctor tells him, or his priest. All that belief is a powerful thing. At least Hope's lightning was keeping any helicopters at bay. *How do I make you believe in me? And quickly? Before the Magi get here.*

The answer was the same one I'd come to before, and tried to find a way around. *You break things.*

And then I heard another voice over the bullhorn, one I barely remembered: a woman's voice, rich with age. "Elaine. And Murchaud. I'm not surprised to meet you two here."

I looked back over my shoulder. "My *mother?*"

Murchaud caught my eye through his visor and tilted his head to one side. "I did try to tell you. All your talent comes from somewhere, Elaine. From Jane Andraste."

My mother's voice continued, mechanical and distorted. "There's still a place for you with us. The fight in Annwn is going well. Come over to the winning side."

I ignored it. My father rode up close beside me. "I thought it came from Morgan . . . from *you.*" I wrestled cold emptiness and a sucking disbelief: that terrible realization that the world goes on and changes around you, and you don't always get the memo.

He shrugged under his armor, crimson cloak rippling from his shoulders in wind-scattered folds. "It never crossed my mind that you didn't know what she was. That she hadn't told you."

Maybe not, but I'll bet that ring Kadiska owes me that Morgan knew. My mother is one of the Magi. My mother is how Matthew knew my name. "I suppose it's your fault she signed on with them, father?" I turned back to the lights and the guns.

"She was a Mage when I met her."

Somewhere, not far away, I heard shattering glass and the wail of sirens. Gunfire stitched the night. *Rioting? Looting?*

I couldn't think about that now. I dropped my chin and closed my eyes. "Mother," I said. "Come and talk to me."

She still held the bullhorn dangling from her hand when she walked out of the maze of police cars. Whiskey danced in place, and I gentled him, knowing he was only doing what I, myself, would like to do. She should have been in her seventies, but she looked trim in a violet suit, discreet diamonds glittering in her ears. Her shoes were sensible for walking.

She laid the bullhorn by her feet. Hope let her lightning fall quiet; only the floods lit the scene. She was my mother, and she smiled at me, and held out her hand. "Come home."

"I wanted to," I answered. "But I can't."

"They took you from me," she continued, coming closer. I looked down into her eyes, and they were neither green nor gray, but a brown as dark and clean as river water. "It killed your father. And you never came home."

"I couldn't stand to. And the war is older than that. Mom."

"Take your soul back. Bring your friends. You know you're doomed to betray your Dragon Prince anyway. Sooner or later."

"And you are right, and Faerie is wrong?"

My mother laid her hand over my hand, reaching up to where I held Whiskey's mane to do it. My wedding ring pinched my finger as she pressed down. "Can you deny it? Take back your soul, and tell me what you have done is not *wrong*."

Whiskey stood still as a board. He loved me, and he would go with me if I chose. Carel looked across at me, stricken. Bound to me, and by more than tangles in my hair. Hope clutched my boot on Whiskey's near side, and on his off side . . .

I looked down into the face of the woman who came to treat with me. She was my mother, and she smiled at me, and she held my hand. I looked over my shoulder at Murchaud.

"Hell would take an alliance offered, and you know it," he said. "You are the Queen of the Daoine Sidhe."

I spoke for Fae, then, and for Hell. And for all the Unseelie, for I bound them through their Queen. We had survived centuries of paying the seven-year's tithe and more. We had subjugated ourselves before to survive. There would be so much less blood if I simply nodded, and did what my mother asked. And betrayed my husband, as I was born to do.

My mother tugged my hand. *"She's pulled him down into her arms / And let the bridle fall."*

Janet won.

I nodded. I imagined my mother's arms around me. Imagined the home and the family I'd not seen in thirty years. My father's grave, which I had never seen. My father. The man who raised me, who put me through school. Not the man who got me on a mortal woman, like many an Elf-knight before him. *You are wrong, and we are right.*

The mortals like to believe that.

I looked at Carel, and down at Hope. I tugged my hand out of my mother's and squeezed her fingers before I let them fall. "All right, Hope," I said, and felt her flinch. And I smiled and kicked Whiskey forward. *"Bring it all down on their heads!"*

My mother fell backward on the stones, and suddenly a light surrounded her that owed nothing to lightning: the gleam of neon, a thousand colors and a hundred writing shapes. I heard the un-horse shriek, and Carel's wild cry as she raised her hands and tore down stones and signage as if with clawed fingers, raining them into the crowd. A camera smashed. I could not see if the operator died with it. I kicked Whiskey again and rode him up the hood of a police car and into the midst, I expected, of a storm of bullets that would tatter the blue moonlight surrounding me, shouting, "I dedicate this battle to the Mother of Dragons!" knowing Hermann the Cheruscan must have shouted something similar, two thousand years before.

There was no gunfire. Whiskey landed hard amid running men, shouldered a police horse aside and kicked out at something I did not see. Then there were flashes and bangs, a sound like a string of fireworks on the Fourth of July. Whiskey startled and half reared, expecting the impact of bullets on our flesh as surely as I did. I knotted a fist in his mane, but the bullets were aimed outward rather than in. Metal crunched and fiberglass shattered, and now I heard screaming. The remaining camera crews scrambled to take in the new situation; as they swung their lights around, I threw my fist in the air and cheered.

The SWAT van skidded aside, its ribs staved in. A squad car followed it, tumbling, officers diving aside. I saw clearly now as Hope raised her hands and lit the scene with livid purple balls of lightning. A low wind moaned through the buildings and then picked up, bitter cold and stinging with sprays of ice. Over the wail of the wind, the scream of tearing buildings, the hurt-hawk shriek of Murchaud's un-horse, I heard something deep and terrible rising up as if from the belly of the earth, the subway tunnels and the rock underneath. Singing.

Deep and terrible, singing. Singing to shake the bones of the world.

Lurching down Seventh Avenue, scattering taxicabs and prowl cars, shrugging aside bullets like so many butterflies, marched an army. An army of willow trees. Their roots slithered over the pavement; it groaned and sprouted trails of steam and geysers of water in their wake. Whiskey snorted and danced backward, leaving bloody puddles on the concrete of the sidewalk. He charged through the gap and bore me in among the willows, up alongside their leader. The tree's long, leafless fronds reached down to smooth my hair, as they had before. "Old Man Willow," I said, and he laughed under his song and said, "Elaine."

"Hoom," he commented further. Whiskey nickered approval.

"Who read you that one?"

"Many and many," he replied. "It is nice to be remembered even a little."

"Water, Uisgebaugh," I said low in his ear, pointing to a shattered hydrant, and he tossed his mane and bent the spray in among the rallying officers, bowling them over. The wood walked down Seventh Avenue, and not a bullet passed through their branches to threaten Whiskey or me. We faced the others who had first come with me now, and I saw Murchaud grin grimly across the Square, his helm off and his face red-lit by the flames that danced around his hellsteed's neck. My mother lay motionless on the stones at the fell thing's feet, and as I watched the un-horse's mighty wings opened wide. The force of the rising wind lifted it as easily as if it were a scrap of black paper burning at the edge. Hope shouted, but I thought she shouted at the storm, and Carel gestured amid shattering lightning. Glass burst in tiers and fell like daggers. Over the crash rose screaming.

The lights went out in the television studio; gunfire embroidered the night. I couldn't see Hope, though I shouted her name. White as an ibis, a unicorn picked its way over the rubble and bowed to me, glimmering in the darkness, droplets of crimson tracing the steely spiral of its horn. It shied, stung by a bullet, and whirled into the shadows.

I turned my face away.

"What do we do, Queen Elaine?" Old Man Willow asked me. Travelers used to fear his kind.

I reached out and leaned one hand on the rough bark of a low bough. "Tear it all down," I said. "No stone upon a stone." My breath tasted like bile. *We are right, and you are wrong.* "There are no innocents in this world," I continued, more to my mother than to my companions. "They'll remember us now."

I moved Whiskey forward, marching into Times Square among singing trees, some dozens or hundred of them, to break the glass and hew the stones. *Kristallnacht.* The thought should have made me shudder, but instead I shrugged and raised my hand to point. "That building there. Begi—"

—which is when the sky turned red, and Hope's storm blew out like a candle, and Carel tumbled from her horse to lie upon the pavement, motionless. The bay mare bolted, and even Whiskey shied like a green-broke stud. The trees cowered around me.

I smelled burning stone and heated metal, and fought the urge to bury my face in Whiskey's mane. *Someone will have to tell the story.* A voice like the iron roots of mountains, raised in a wordless roar, shook more stones loose from the damaged facades. Still air groaned under the weight of her wings.

Whiskey fell to his knees among the stones. I saw none of the others. Nothing but Mist, her wings arced high and symmetrical over her head, settling onto the roof of the Warner Brothers store and frowning down on us. Fire and vapor licked from her nostrils, outlining the shape of her face.

"Children," the Dragon said mildly. "Really." Her head swiveled side to side, seeking like a serpent's. She tasted the air. "Queen with no Name. Come out of those trees."

I did as the dragon instructed, and walked out into the center of

Times Square, smoothing Whiskey's mane before leaving him to struggle to his feet alone. I splashed through water and picked my way over
rubble and came out of the shadows beside Carel, who was oozing
blood from a dozen cuts. Carefully, my eyes still raised to Mist, I
crouched down and took the Merlin's pulse. Thready and slow, but she
lived. I could not see Hope. I could not see my father.

"Mist," I said, standing up. My mother also lay among the stones, and
I couldn't decide if I was relieved or disappointed that her heart still
beat. "Is this what you wanted?"

The Dragon smiled. Lava dripped smoking from between her teeth,
puddles and spatters of fire. The night should have been moonless, but
a full moon had risen behind her, and it lit all the city in silver. I heard
footsteps, and hoofbeats, and looked from my left side to my right. I expected Hope or Murchaud, but they were nowhere in sight. Whiskey
limped up beside me. Glass crunched underfoot. Mortals too came forward: newsmen, and the camera crews, and police in torn uniforms,
blanched faces set with human courage.

I heard a sighing as the willows lurched forward and we all stood in
a group, looking up at the Dragon who perched on the crenellated roof-
edge and crumbled not a stone under the massive weight of her talons.
"You called. Our Merlin commanded my presence. Now choose," Mist
said, very plainly. "Choose your future, Queen with no Name."

"What do you mean?"

The Dragon's enormous head dipped, her neck so long that her muzzle brushed the ruined square. In the strange blue glow of that unnatural moon, it all seemed very real. Camera lights flickered back on,
painted her starker in shadows. She blinked at the newsmen lazily,
flickered her tongue across my mother's still form and then Carel's.

"Choose one," she said. "Which magic would you have in the world?
The Merlin or the Mage?"

I swallowed. "What happens to the other?"

The Dragon's breath upon my face smelled of hot metal and cool
earth. She smiled. "What do you imagine? I am a Dragon, after all."

If we could put you away, I thought. *Really and for all, put you away. Put the
Dragon out of us, and become . . .*

What would we be, without the Dragon?

Mist spread her moonlit, red-hot wings over the city and seemed, for a moment, to embrace it.

We'd have to make another Beast to take her place, I realized. *Hell, we already have. I'm standing in its belly.*

"I have to choose a sacrifice?"

"You are to choose a future."

"Remember when the time comes. Remember." "Someone once told me," I said, the dryness of the words filling my mouth, "that in the end, you go to judgment naked, clad only in what you were born with and what you have earned, lessened only by what you have sold or given away. That those things which are taken by force, for good or for ill, go unconsidered. Is that so, Mother of Dragons?"

"It is so," she said.

I nodded. I looked down, at the Merlin and at my mother. I knew what the choice entailed; it was more than the sacrifice of a woman that Mist asked of me, and until that moment I could have told her without hesitating what my choice would have been. First one way and then the other. I would have known.

I looked around the ruined Square, the wreckage of neon. Mortal lives, or Fae? I wondered if Keith yet lived, or Ian. There was blood on the stones around me. Innocent blood, and not nearly as much as I had meant to shed, this night of all nights.

"Who am I to choose?"

"You are the only one who can," Whiskey said. He laid a hand on my arm. "You stand between worlds, Elaine." I looked up at him and knew he stood ready to pay the price for what he was made to be.

Somewhere nearby, a baby wailed like a siren. I closed my eyes. I wished Murchaud were there, but still he did not come forward, and then I remembered something about tithes, and what it meant if they went willing. *Balance grows out of struggle.*

"Take me," I said before I could change my mind, and stepped forward, putting myself between Carel and my mother and the Dragon. "I'll stand payment for both sides, Mist, and all they've done."

I expected Whiskey to protest, but he made no sound.

The Dragon's smile grew wider. "Done," she said, and opened a mouth lined in teeth long as swords, dripping liquid gold-red flames. I steeled myself for the pain, and then the emptiness, and barely made a sound as the Mother of Dragons angled her head straight down and closed her maw over me.

Chapter Twenty-Seven

First darkness, and then the music. Keith struggled against it, bore down, teeth in his lip and a wolf's white passion to be free. He'd gnaw his paw off before he stayed in a trap. Could he do less now?

And there was the music, the music to follow. The music and the light.

The big bay shifted underneath him. He felt the reins knotted in his palm. *I am not mad. I am not blind. I am ensorceled. And I still have a wolf's nose on me.*

He forced himself to calm and touched his heels to Petunia's flanks. He dropped the knotted reins against the horse's neck. *Trust the horse.*

Cairbre was still behind him. He felt the harp prod the small of his back when he leaned back in the saddle. The bard's hands were moving, a rhythmic, facile stroking of his instrument. Vibrations touched Keith through the saddle, and he leaned into them, grateful for anything.

Anything.

Anything.

The deep tolling like a hammered bell that rattled his teeth and trembled his heart, for example. The swell of his mount's breath between his legs. The delicate notes of—

He heard music.

Keith lifted his head and cast for the scent. Cairbre. Cairbre was playing. Playing to wake the dead.

"No," Keith tried, and felt his voice box vibrate. He leaned on the pressure that held him immobile. "No!"

Something broke, with a palpable *snap* like glass pressed with a cutting blade. He blinked hard, rubbed his eyes.

All around him, Fae and wolves did the same. Keith turned in the saddle and saw flickering light. A tolling as of some great bell, vaster than imagination, shook him in the saddle; Cairbre's music rose over it, consumed and subverted it.

Around them, other Fae sat up. Wolves found their feet. Keith saw Vanya, who must not have given himself up to the warfetter, pulling Eremei up. Keith swallowed, his throat too dry, and worked up saliva to swallow again.

The Prometheans were still on the other side of the light, pushing forward, unable to push through. Keith heard hammers on iron, turned his head and saw the Weyland Smith swinging his mallet overhead like a cartoon railwayman. He brought it down again — again — again — tolling the bridge like a bell. No delicacy now: just *force*.

He couldn't possibly affect the massive spiral of the bridge. And just as Keith thought that, something rumbled and something tore, the sound of fatigued metal giving way echoing from hillside to beechwood. It shook Keith from the last of his stupor. He'd dropped his sword. He raised his empty hand instead. "To me," he shouted, reining the horse once more at the clustered Magi. "To me! To me! The day is ours!" and then he took a breath and said the thing he had to say, to claim his place under the Dragon's wing. "I dedicate this battle to the Dragon, Mist!" he shouted. "Leave none alive!"

Cairbre clutched at his belt, and he kicked the bay forward to the harmony of rending metal as the bridge began to sway overhead like a wind-whipped pine.

It hurts for much longer than I expected. *Arthur,* and I try to coil into a ball against the pain. *If he can do it, so can I.*

Make it stop, make it stop, make it stop.

I imagine acid etching my skin, peeling it back in sheets and laying bare nerve endings open. My hair burns away. Lips, cheeks, eyebrows. I had thought it would be quick. *I thought it would be over quickly.*

I hear an answer—the rumble of Mist's voice through ears I feel searing, blackening, charred stubs and then bare bones. *It never is. Over quickly, Queen with no Name. The pain will go on. I can end it for you if you ask.*

Does the sacrifice count, if you do?

No.

I shall endure. My eyes melt down my cheeks like tears; I think of salt water, think of Whiskey. *I wish I'd gotten a chance to say farewell to Keith. Does this count as a betrayal?*

Everything you do, Mist replies, the weight of her attention staggering even through the pain, *is a betrayal. There are no innocents.*

There is a unicorn.

That seems to silence the Mother of Dragons for a moment. *There is,* she agrees at last. *There is a unicorn. And she has blood on her horn.*

The flesh burns on my bones, searing like a roast in the oven, leaking gravy through blistered cracks. Blind, and my bones burning, my heart cooking in my breast. *This is what Hell is like,* I understand. *Burning, and never ending. In the belly of the Beast.*

Wolves are innocent, I argue. *They are what they are, and if it is bloody, so be it. And what about dogs, servile beside their masters' fires?*

Servile? Known many dogs, Mist? They trust. It's different.

As men do, when they give their conscience into the keeping of their leaders? And shall I end your pain?

Bones crumble into ash, and I feel every instant. Taste my own burning, rank smoke and incinerated meat. I would scream if I had throat and tongue left to do it. *No. And yes, men trust their leaders. Too well, sometimes.*

And now Mist smiling, the Dragon surrounding me, burning my body away. *Does that make it right, Queen with no Name?*

What they have done? What we have done? No. No heartbeat, my brain boiled away inside my skull, blackened bone crumbling into a gritty ash, mingling with the Dragon's acid saliva. Burning, failing, melting, gone. *Nothing makes it right. But you are the Dragon. What do you care for right and wrong?*

And the pain continues. How can it continue? Worse than the stag's antlers. Worse than childbirth. Pain both sharp and deep. Pain that can only be borne, because there is no way to end it.

I care for enduring, the Dragon replies. *Wisdom of old, and foresight for the future, and treasures guarded by monsters in the bottom of your mind. What will you endure to reach them?*

Haven't I endured enough? I give you your sacrifice.

Are you ready to give in, then? Let me end the pain?

Never. I will hold fast.

I am the Dragon, Mist answers. *I am your Mother, and I am as cruel and kind and arbitrary as all the world. Do you see yet, Queen with no Name?*

I feel her. Feel her body as my own, as if I shrugged into her shadow. Feel the vast sheltering spread of her wings, the ragged teeth of her jaws. The flame dripping, crisping, and the shattered kindness in her eyes. I see her drawing back from the sword, dragonblood running like magma down her face.

You destroy what you touch, I say, remembering Arthur.

It might appear so.

I am inside the Beast when she spreads her wings. Small figures cluster and break below me: Fae and mortal forms, and the little damage they have done me itches, itches like the throne's deep gouge in the palm of the hand I no longer have. Among the trees, walkers and riders, little beings move on my skin, even as I look down on them. So fragile.

I blink. Mist's eyes blink with me. Blood moves through my veins, except it isn't blood, not quite, and I hear the pulse of my own enormous heart, a spinning mass of iron and nickel and the hot brief elements that burn and change whatever they touch. Burn, as I am burning still, bodiless in the body of the Dragon.

The injury itches, low on my back beside the iron ring still welded to my spine. I want to scratch it, rub it like I rubbed the healing wound in my hand. Mist draws back, observing what I will do. I reach. My vast clawed hand hesitates. I rise, and the shattered facade of a building crumbles as the earth shifts and complains beneath it. I know what would happen if I laid my taloned hand against this little, irritating wound.

The Dragon's body flows around me. I feel as if I animated a statue:

the limbs are heavy, the movements ponderous unless they are lightning fast. I grin, and her lips peel back from her fangs.

Mist. Trickster.

Dragon, she answers quietly. *How do you like your choice now, Queen with no Name?*

It is dangerous to lie to dragons. It is even more dangerous to try to bargain with them. *There is no choice,* I answer. *You are all that is dark and bright in us, Fae and mortal, wolf and dog. White hart and black, Queen and King, Merlin and Mage. We are the same.*

I know the answer now, around my unending, unendurable pain. *The Beast has a thousand Names. Maat is only one of them, and I could not have bound you with it. They're us. We're you. All the Beasts there are, and there is only one Dragon.*

Then what is my Name?

New York City.

Yes, she says. *That is one of my names. When you know them all, only then can you can make me do your bidding. Do you fear me now, Queen with no Name?*

I am not afraid.

Then you are a fool.

Perhaps I am, I say, and if I were more than ash in the belly of a dragon I would laugh, and laugh, and laugh. *Like goddamned budgies in a cage. That's why the Dragon Princes. That's why the sacrifice, and the betrayal. You must admire the irony in going to war and realizing that we are fighting a mirror.*

She turns in the air, shows me destroyed Times Square and the crumbled billboards. *And I'm not sorry I hurt you.*

"Go home, daughter," the Dragon said, and spat me out among the stones of a crossroads in ruins—spat me out whole and shapely in every limb and garbed in clean white linen.

Weyland swung his hammer again, and the whole sky shivered. Matthew scrambled back into darkness, pressing his right hand to his chest. Gooseflesh pimpled his shirtless back. His own blood drying on his skin prickled; his right hand was a dull, severed ache as long as he kept pressure on it. He held his own fingers shut around the cloth. They didn't want to bend.

He didn't know where to go. There was a wood a little way off. The reaching branches were silhouetted against the stars, and it didn't seem as if the fighting had ranged among the trees. He heard shouting, metal squealing as it tore. A pale yellow glow surrounded Weyland, sparking like the aura of flame over a bellows-fed forge. The Faerie smith cocked his head back, calculating the sway of the bridge. When it was at the nearest point of its oscillation, he swung his hammer again. The span rang like a gong. The sound of straining metal intensified to a vast, twisted, ripping shriek.

Matthew put his head down and ran for the tree line. Shouts from Fae and Prometheans told him that the battle had turned to a panicked rout. The flickering lights were dying, and he recognized some of the voices crying out in the darkness. He didn't turn. He didn't look.

The shock wave of the falling bridge knocked him off his feet before he reached the wood. He fell intelligently, taking it on his shoulder and rolling, and could have come up to his feet if he'd been able to use his hand. Instead he ended in a crouch, one knee bent and the ball of the other foot planted, dirt clotting his hair and sticking to the blood drying down his torso, dappling his body so that he vanished in the shadows.

The bridge had fallen. The Prometheans were dying.

Matthew stood, and limped into the wood.

He knew he should have kept walking, but he was so tired, and the wood so dark that he feared falling over a root as he plowed through autumn's fallen leaves. He sat down in a drift of leaves with his back to a silver birch, the bark just rough enough to rasp against his skin. Shivers ran the length of his body. He hugged his legs tight, pressing his face to his forearms, and burrowed into the leaf drift as well as he could. The leaves made as good a symbol of notice-me-not as anything, and he needed their warmth, but he didn't expect to sleep.

When the sun rose, he'd have to figure out how to get back to the mortal world. Assuming he could. Assuming he wasn't going to end up another mortal Mage trapped in Faerie. And he'd have to come up with a plausible excuse for what happened to his hand, and get himself to an emergency room.

And then he'd have to figure out what to do with the rest of his life. Because like Hell was he going crawling back to Jane Andraste.

He was cold. The shivers started between his shoulders, a clenching sensation as his muscles contracted. He gritted his teeth to keep his jaw from rattling, and forced himself not to keep glancing at his watch. He could still hear calls and conversation from the battlefield, Fae voices that seemed almost human and others that were deep and strange or high and crystalline, as if they were the voices of woodland glades and foundation stones and cracked glass bells. And something else, soon — a susurrus like a wind through a wheat field, and a creaking like the mast of a sailing ship.

And singing, a singing that trembled the earth under Matthew's ear and got into his bones and shook him out of chilled and fitful slumber into wakefulness. The leaves kept some warmth close to his skin, but not enough, and he raked more over himself with his left hand. The right one hurt worse now, but the bleeding seemed to have stopped. He imagined the improvised bandage must have scabbed to the wound; he didn't look forward to getting it loose.

The sky at last began to lighten, the warmthless gray light of false dawn creeping up the sky beyond the bare fingers of the beeches. The earth seemed to shiver and stretch. Matthew rolled out of the leaves in the bone-deep chill and rubbed his eyes with his left hand. Not too far away, a big dog barked joyously, answered by another. He huddled closer to the tree, working a little lace of magics to keep them off his scent. The insignificant effort left him trembling with exhaustion.

He needed water desperately, as much to wash the blood and filth off his skin as to drink. He didn't know where to find it.

And you can't drink water in Faerie in any case, Matthew Magus. Not if ever you wish to go home.

A crashing through the leaves drew his head up. The very air was graying now, that quality of light where the atmosphere seemed to lose its transparency and hold up veils between observer and observed. Something glimmered nearby, white enough to glow through the dawn — flashing the first rays of sun off a blue like steel.

Matthew forced himself to his feet, knowing who came. He rubbed his eyes again, determined to meet the unicorn with whatever dignity he could salvage.

But it wasn't a unicorn.

It was a woman. Tall, her red hair braided into a single straight tail down her back, wearing blue jeans, boots, and a bloused shirt of linen bleached white as a goose feather and sewn with tiny clear crystals over the yoke, a fillet across her brow with baroque curves worked in knife-blue steel instead of gold or platinum. Her eyes were the color of win-tergreen leaves, and a red dog and a gray dog trotted at her heels.

"Matthew Magus," she said, with a smile that brought out all the pleasant lines in her face. "You're hurt. Won't you come home with me? I'll see you tidied up and doctored well, I vow."

He swallowed and straightened up, eyes on her fillet, clenching his left hand into a fist to feel his useless iron rings. "What happens to me if I don't?"

She gestured upslope and over her shoulder. "I take you where the thorn trees are, and I show you the way back home."

"And if I do?" His voice was steady, suddenly, his hand hurting less. As if her presence gave off strength that he could use. She came closer, seeming undeterred by the blood and filth that crusted his skin.

"How long are you going to wait for your unicorn?" she asked, and when he blinked in surprise she leaned forward and kissed him on the mouth.

Her mouth was soft and hot; her tongue sent a shiver of necessity down his spine. He found himself leaning into the kiss, his bandaged hand gentle on her hair as hers were not gentle in his. She smelled of rosemary and bitter herbs he didn't know the names of, and she tasted of honey and ale. She was soft and certain in his arms, and it tingled in his belly and along his spine when she pressed her body close. It was fire, and when he came out the other side, he was remade.

And not in the way she had intended. "I know your name," he said, when she leaned back.

"You know so many things," she said, and laid her long hand flat against his filthy chest. The mud and blood that smeared him hadn't touched her. She still shimmered white as a princess in a fairy tale. He couldn't feel her hair against the fingers of his injured hand, but the longing in his breast was powerful enough to ache. "And so do I. We should share them with each other, Matthew-with-no-place-to-go. Come with me."

"Morgan le Fey," he said, and shook his head because it was too hard to say the next thing he should say. She smiled: smiled more when he pried the iron rings off each finger of his damaged hand, pulled the ones on his left hand off with his teeth. He reached up and fumbled his earrings out left-handed, tearing his earlobe, but what was a little more blood at this point? He knelt down and dug in the soil with his left hand, his good hand, meaning to pry up leaves and woodlot flowers and horsetail ferns and bury that iron in the earth, where it could not trouble him again. His hand closed tight over the iron, though, and he frowned down at it, suddenly unable to remember why he had planned what he had meant to do.

He stood. He shoved his hand with the rings in the pocket of his trousers and dropped the rings there. They rattled on each other like change. Morgan watched, amused, her steel fillet gleaming on her brow.

Matthew shook his head again, harder, and answered, "Morgan le Fey. I am honored—"

A wry smile from the Faerie, rather than the wrath he had been half-afraid of. "But."

"—but send me home."

Chapter Twenty-Eight

Whiskey must have carried me back to Annwn, for I don't remember anything between the stones hard against my face and the softness of Keith's cloak under and over me, the smell of green grass and the shade of a willow tree. Someone sat beside me, and even as I turned and raised my head I knew from the smell that it was Keith. He put a hand on my shoulder to press me back but I sat up against it, looking out at the cool, bright morning. And swallowed.

I barely recognized the vale and the devastated beechwood beneath a grove of willows that had taken root in the furrowed ground. I reached out, feeling the iron settled in the earth. The bridge wasn't visible, so I knew Weyland must have succeeded in gnawing it off at the root, but that root still sank a taint deep into the soil. "A problem for another day," I said, and realized I had said it aloud when Keith slid his arm around my shoulders and squeezed. "What news?"

"Stalemate," he said. "They may be back."

"If they are," I answered, "it is my fault. I could have destroyed them, in New York."

He nodded and helped me stand. "It wouldn't have saved me in the long run."

I shook my head and leaned against his shoulder. "And I lost my binding on the Cat Anna. My hair . . ." I ran my hands through it. It was thick and soft and untangled, and felt freshly washed. "She can't be made to go to the teind now. She's been freed of a binding."

"Worry about it later, Elaine," he said. He turned me to face him and then let his head roll down his neck, studying the smooth grass under his boots. Pale skirts blew around my calves. Mist had garbed me in a dress unlike anything I'd worn in Faerie before: white linen, soft and fine, the neck high and simple and the bodice cut to flare into a gored skirt. A very modern sort of dress, with buttons up the front from hem to collar. I fussed with the hang for a moment, so I wouldn't have to look Keith in the eye. "Who?" I said at last.

He rubbed his face before he answered. "Your father, Elaine. I'm sorry. More than half of the Daoine, and perhaps two-thirds of the Unseelie court. They fought hardest, and rode at the front. And seventeen of the pack."

I knew he wasn't finished. It didn't hurt enough yet, under the layer of ice and fire that numbed my heart. I reached out and took his arm. "Who else, Keith?" *Not Ian. Please.*

"Hope," he said, after a long time. "And Robin."

"Robin *fought*?" *Hope. Dead.* Bullets? Or the falling buildings? And did it matter, in the end? *No. No. No.*

"Everybody fought by the end of it," he said, and then he buried his face in his hands and stood before me, swaying like a willow in the wind, his breath whistling through his fingers.

Hope, and her daughter with her.

I never should have . . .

"I shouldn't have let her go," Keith said, and let his hands fall to his side. He looked down over the willow wood, dry-eyed and haggard, and I reached out to touch him and drew my hand back before I could offer the cold mockery of comfort that was my own. *No.*

"Keith," I said, the words chillier than I would have meant them. "We did what we did. And we'll carry it."

He turned to study me, the yellow branches of the willow brushing his hair fondly. "I imagine we will," he told me. "What will you do now?"

"Are the bodies buried?"

"They've been washed and laid out, as best we could. Ours and theirs. Damn the distinction. The willows said they'd handle the burials. You want to say good-bye?"

"Yes." I twisted my wedding ring on my finger. It was wearing a place already. I scuffed a bare foot through the grass of Faerie, the greenest in any world. "Carel? And my . . . mother?"

"Mist brought them to me." He opened his hands as if pouring water. "I let your mother go. The Kelpie told me your bargain, and Jane seemed willing to abide it. All things considered. I understand the toll was worse than she imagined."

"It was worse than any of us imagined," I said.

Keith shook his head. "We killed them all, Elaine. Every last one who came to Annwn. Men and women. Some of them were very young." He turned away, looking down over the tossing sea of willow crowns below the rise of the hill. "I wanted to teach them a lesson."

"You're a Dragon Prince," I answered. "It is what you were born to do."

"And what I'll die doing too," he answered. "That doesn't excuse it."

"No," I said. "It doesn't excuse anything."

"Elaine," he said. "I still love you."

I couldn't lie to him. I turned away, trying to hide my smile and my sorrow both.

The rows of white-wrapped bodies stretched endless under the bower of the willows. Side by side, with just enough space to walk between them. Dozens. Hundreds, with red stains blotting the white linen of their shrouds and their dead eyes closed against the filtered light of the sun. The shadows of budding leaves moved across their faces. I imagined the earth would just open up and receive them when the willows were ready.

"Thank you," I said to the trees, and they whispered things in return. Soft things, forgiving things. There were rows of bodies, and rows beyond those. I walked along them all. Gharne came out of the trees, his wings unlike the heavy wings of the Dragon, and he settled on my shoulder. Unseelie, Daoine, men. Tidy and white as snowdrifts, blossoming with red flowers. I knew their faces and I knew their names.

I found Matthew laid out among them and knelt down by his side. His hands were wrapped tight to his breast, folded one inside the other.

Through the linen, iron from the rings still on his fingers stung my hand. His hair had come loose from the ponytail. I smoothed it back from the ruin of his face. Something with a clawed foot had opened his flesh from temple to chin, and I saw the white nuggets of his teeth through four slashes in his shredded cheek. The blood had been washed away; his skin was pale and waxen. "I could have known you," I said, and tucked the loose strands of his hair inside the shroud.

And then I drew my hand back, startled, and nibbled on the inside of my cheek. "You're not Matthew Szczegielniak, are you, sir?" No. I pushed the linen wrappings back, and all the details were correct: the straight blond hair, the startling dark eyes, the intricate details of the ink under his skin. But this man wore no earrings, and there was nothing to show he ever had.

It was a simulacrum. A changeling, like the ones Kadiska and I had left in many a baby's bed. The body of another, witched to look like the body of the Promethean.

Clever, Matthew Magus, to turn my own tricks back on me. And I bid you go in peace, Mage. But know I will be looking for you, if you should happen to come for me.

He even smelled like Matthew, somewhat. A relative?

I wondered what his name had been.

Finding Robin hurt more. By some hard coincidence, they had laid him beside my father, but when I knelt down between them no tears blessed me. His strange little ear was shredded. His glinting eye was dark. Murchaud looked all but unmarked, but there were stains on the cloth wound over his breast. I closed my eyes so they matched my father's, and sang to the wind. " 'Mother, mother, make my bed. Make for me a winding sheet. Wrap me up in a cloth of gold, and see if I can sleep.' "

"You won't," my mother said. She crouched on the other side of Murchaud's cold body and stroked one hand across his eyes. "Not much, and not often."

"Jane."

"Sweetheart." Her eyes seemed very deep. I couldn't tell if it troubled her that I called her by name. "I'm sorry."

"Why?"

Her lips pursed, fine lines spiderwebbing alongside them. She seemed much younger than I would have expected. "Why fight Faerie?" she asked.

"Because it needs to be fought," I answered. "No. I understand that. But why all this?"

She tilted her head, gazing up at the sky. "There's no other way to fight a war," she answered, and touched my face with a hand still cool from my father's cheek. "Diplomacy amounts to nothing; it all comes down to blood and iron in the end."

"Don't misquote Bismarck at me." I stood and stepped away. Her suit was stained and torn, patched with blood and dust. "Will we be able to talk?"

She shrugged and sat back on her heels, shading her eyes with a black-bruised hand. "Well, we seem to have something like an armed truce going. Heaven and Hell aren't much for détente."

"Heaven and Hell can go hang," I answered. "What about you and me, Mom? Are we burying enough here? Or are we just like all the bloody fools before us?"

"I don't know," she answered. "As long as Annwn stays under the protectorate of the Morningstar, as long as you steal our—children, steal mortal men and women too . . . No, I think. We're not different at all."

"Did it trouble you that the Devil plays both sides of the game, mother?"

She paused, and pursed her lips. "Yes," she said. "It troubled me."

"I see," I said. "Good-bye, mother." And turned my back on her, trying not to trip on the root-bulging ground as I strode unsteadily away.

I knew where Hope lay before I came up on her, by the slender figure in black velvet who sat on the ground beside her. Ian looked up when I walked round the trunk of a willow, and looked quickly down again. "Mother," he said. "You don't belong here."

"Ian . . ."

He stood, a fluid movement, one hand on the hilt of his sword, the other still bound up in a splint and a sling. "This is your fault," he said. Dead and cold, and he pressed one hand to his chest as if his heart would burst through the walls of his body and fly away. His mouth worked bitterly.

I thought of Arthur and Morgan, and the break that came between them and took fifteen hundred years to heal. Hope looked very pale in her white linen wrapper. It was easier to look at her still face than Ian's eyes. I looked up at him anyway.

"Yes," I said. "My fault. My fault, Ian. And I am sorry."

"Maybe someday," he answered, "that will be enough. For now, though, leave us be."

Gharne shifted, twisting his tail around my neck for balance when I turned away. And then I looked back, frowning. "Ian. One last thing."

I chose to take his silence for permission.

"Arthur and Morgan, Mordred and Lancelot. You said it once, and I say it to you now in return. They didn't know, Ian. They didn't know what would happen. Whereas we . . . well."

I wanted an answer. I wanted him to look up and squint and say *Maybe that will help me forgive you someday.*

I waited a long time for him to find his voice, his one hand twisting like a white banner in the wind. "I've lost my child," he said, and turned to face me, finally, with human grief in his eyes.

"Ian. Don't take mine away as well."

But he shook his head and looked to the horizon, and gestured me away.

I went, walking and not sure where I was walking to. The willows had come to rest in the scarred earth, making wide avenues and wandering lanes. I walked uphill, and left the dead behind me.

Willows are the trees of death. "Will you stay in this wood?" I asked them, not expecting an answer.

"Tomorrow and the day after," someone answered, over the sound of a trickling spring. "Many of them." I recognized the place; Whiskey had struck the earth here, and now the cold water ran between the roots of a thirsty tree.

"Old Man Willow," I said, and leaned against his trunk. "Are *you* staying?"

"Do you wish it?"

"Yes," I said. "I miss you." And then I hesitated. "You're needed where you were, though, aren't you?"

"I offer comfort," he said, brushing my shoulder.

I smiled. "I'm not supposed to need that."

I heard the hoofbeats before I saw him, and I stepped away from Old Man Willow's embrace. Whiskey shifted as he came to me, a blur of motion, ivory, jet and seafoam-white among the shadows of the trees, his cuts all scabbed and crusted closed. The whole of the wood lay around us, silent as hallowed ground. "Whiskey," I said, and he drew me into his arms and held me tight when I would have thrust him away. It was warm and comfortable there in his embrace, and a little while went by before I lifted my forehead from his shoulder. "I've changed again," I told him.

He nuzzled my neck as if looking for sugar cubes. Gharne hissed halfheartedly and hopped out of the way. "I was—frightened for you, Elaine."

Wrong, and wrong again. "I can't take it back, Uisgebaugh."

"I know," he answered, stepping back and tossing his forelock out of his eyes. His hair had grown. "I know. The Merlin is looking for you."

I opened my mouth to comment. His blue eyes fixed on me, stopping the words before I shaped them. Old Man Willow stroked a weeping bough down my hair. "It's not done yet," I said. "I meant to pay the tithe. Pay it off forever, pay it with my own blood and the blood of the other Queens. We'll have to carry on as we have been, raiding Fae half bloods from among the humans and shrinking slowly into nonexistence. Or. There's another answer."

"You did a lot on Hell's behalf," he answered. I tried to pull away a second time, and he held my forearms, gently but firmly. "Look at me, Elaine."

"That is not my name."

"No," he said. "You are not Elaine. You're not Seeker anymore, either. You change in my arms and change again, and all I can do is hold you."

I looked at him. Looked carefully, and saw him worn around the edges, thin and sallow-seeming. "How long since you fed, Uisgebaugh?"

"Recently enough," he lied. He took my cheeks between his hands and kissed my mouth, hard and sweetly. I gasped, and he held me fast and warmed me in his arms, finally leaning back enough to search my eyes. I closed them, smiling with a sort of passion that left me cold and distant inside. Mountain peaks, ice in the sun. Smiling unconcern, and a ruthless certainty. Somewhere under it, magma shifted and passion burned, but I could not touch it—only feel it far away, like stroking the fur of a wolf with gloved hands. Like feeling the earth under hooves shod in silver, I imagined, rather than warm, living feet.

At last, I thought, *you know what it means to be Fae.*

I kissed Whiskey back, and drew him down by the spring on the blood-fertile earth. Gharne flew up into the tree's branches and left us in what passed for privacy. Old Man Willow, I imagined, had seen it all before.

The white dress wouldn't take a stain, and rode up around my thighs like a blanket of daisies while Whiskey bore me uphill. I headed him out of the ghost-riddled wood, but before we came back into the sunshine something dark strolled deliberately across our path and turned to stare at me. *Gharne*, I thought at first, but it wasn't.

The black dog paused in a framing beam of sunlight, and at first I thought it was a Great Dane or boarhound that had wandered into the wood. It gleamed in the sunlight like oil on peat-stained water, and I almost slid down Whiskey's shoulder and went to it, hand extended. But my stallion's ears pinned and he danced back a step, snorting, and the giant dog's eyes flamed golden and orange.

I knew what I was looking at then. "Black Shuck," I murmured, and if Whiskey had been wearing a bridle my hands would have tightened on the reins. "Which of us do you suppose he's here for?"

The stallion snorted. "At least it's not a bean sidhe." His voice was low and worried. I flinched at the tone. He backed away slowly, his hooves soft on the fallow earth, and turned away. "Is he following?"

I looked over my shoulder. The black hound watched us go, tongue lolling. "No," I said.

Whiskey stepped carefully, slowly away. "Marked for Hell, then," he said, when the hound vanished behind us with a final glimpse of glaring eyes.

"What else is new? Must it be us?"

"Us," he said. "Or someone near us." He snorted, finally tossing his head up and braying wildly, shaking his mane. A sharpness grated in his laughter.

I finally interrupted through the frost that had settled over my heart. "Don't tell Keith about this, Whiskey."

"Keeping secrets already?" Serious now, with a trace of the old edgy mockery in it. "I wouldn't dream of betraying you, my lady. To your husband, or anyone else."

The doorman opened the spiral-worked doors, and Carel and I entered the throne room.

The white-horn throne still stood uncovered, slightly to one side of the dais, the velvet drapes drawn back. Somebody had removed the pall I'd torn off of the Queen's deadly chair; I imagined it neatly folded away in a cabinet somewhere, labeled, in a white linen sack.

"Elaine."

"Carel," I said, and looked at her. "I'll survive it. And the Daoine Sidhe must have a Queen. Until I sit in that chair, I'm nothing more than a pretender. And I've tasks to undertake that only the ruler can. Besides . . ." I pushed my hair from my eyes. "It can't hurt more than being swallowed by a dragon."

She sucked her full lips in. The silken flesh of her throat dimpled and smoothed as she swallowed hard. I looked away, up the dais at the throne that crouched there, waiting for me. I thought I saw it breathing, the breaths I couldn't feel swelling my own breast, and moved toward it.

"Elaine."

Not Carel's voice. My husband's, taut with fear.

"What do you think you're doing?"

"I'd hoped to keep you away until it was done," I said, and spun on the ball of my foot to look into his eyes.

"Then you shouldn't have sent a page for the crown," Keith answered, and strolled out of the doorway and across the green-and-azure tiles. "Elaine. Don't do this."

"Are you ordering me, Your Majesty?" I half hoped he would. I turned away and eyed that throne, poised like some predatory beast, its base just at eye level.

"Yes. I forbid it."

I began to argue, but—"Indeed." Carel stepped in between us. "Forbid it. Go ahead. She'll do what she must," the Merlin said, prophecy dripping from her voice. "Stand in her way. See what it nets you."

He walked across the stone tiles, bootheels clicking, and laid a hand on the cold flesh of my arm. "I know better," he answered, and went down on one knee. "Elaine. No. Please."

My hand was in his hair before I knew it. Carel looked away; I pulled Keith's mouth up to mine and kissed him hard, tasting the softness of his lips. Wine. Sorrow. "Will you stop me, my King?" His eyes on mine were greener than I had recalled. I smiled into them, and I didn't think he saw it.

"Go," he said, this man, my husband. I heard agony in his voice. "Go. I won't stay to watch it."

I kissed him again, lips and forehead. His hair was coarse between my fingers. *I loved him once.*

It seemed a very long time ago.

"I wish I could love you like I used to," I said. "You will not stay?"

The door swung open silently and Wolfsbane the page sneaked in, bearing the crown tucked under his arm like a bolster. I hated to see Keith flinch, and reveled in it. "Enough blood," he said. "Enough for one fucking day, Elaine."

"Is it ever enough?" The dress clung to my thighs when I turned, sticking to sweat. I shook it loose. Wolfsbane thrust the crown, not into my hands or Keith's, but Carel's. She would not look at me. At either of us. "You don't have to stay," I said then, as the page slunk toward the massive doors.

Keith touched the underside of his fingers to his lips. I felt the pressure of his eyes on me, then dropping away. "I wasn't there for you last night," he said, quietly as water droplets falling into a pail.

"Nor I you." One step up, and two. I felt as if the throne pressed me away from it. I leaned into the pressure, while Carel went to stand before it, feeling nothing. "Go on, Keith. It's not fair to ask you to stay."

"It's not fair to leave," he answered, and that was the end of it.

I reached the top of the dais and turned to face him, my back to the chair like a pile of ivory daggers. I shook as if a hard cold had settled over the room. Perhaps one had. I could not feel it. Carel handed me the crown.

"Fair has nothing to do with it," I said, and sat down on the blood-stained chair.

Mist's white dress was red in every stitch when I managed to stand from its embrace once more.

I'd like to say that throne seemed as nothing after my rebirth in the jaws of the Dragon. There are limits to pain, and truthfully it wasn't as bad as burning, but it was bad enough. When Carel helped me to stand, I felt my injuries sealing themselves behind the passage of the tines. The crown was heavy on my brow when Keith came forward to receive me; strength filled me, subtle and vibrant, and I felt all of Annwn stretched over me living and rich as my skin. My husband took my hand and turned it over to see the new scars marking my flesh. He raised it to his mouth and kissed a healed wound at my wrist.

"How does it feel?"

"Alive," I said, the heartbeat of Annwn twinned to my own. "And now for Hell," I said. "See a messenger sent, Carel, please. Tell them their emissary has perished, and that we wish another."

"Of course," she answered. I could not read whatever was in her face. She turned away, and I let her go.

"You were going to send the Queens to Hell," Keith said, when the doors swung closed behind her. I turned and trailed a thumb up one of the antler tines. It didn't part my skin this time, and I smiled.

"To pay off the tithe. Yes. I thought to force the Cat Anna. It can't happen now, though. No one who has been bound and freed can be made to go. And we're a day late anyway. The tithe is due on Halloween."

"You were going to go to Hell."

"*Am* going. I can endure it. Break with the Unseelie, Keith. Let them pay the damned tithe and stay beholden to Hell. I'll pay the price. You win us free, Dragon Prince." *Even when they break me and send me to betray you.* That was how it would be. How it had to be.

"Elaine, it's not worth—"

"It's worth what it will buy. What it will buy: a Queen gone willing . . . I'll make Hell see that it is enough."

"I know," he said. He brushed a hand across my cheek, smoothed a strand of hair back under my crown. "You're unfair to Carel, you know. And the Kelpie as well."

"Who ever said life was fair?" I heard my mother's tone in my own and laughed like choking. We stood in silence for a little while, and I thought I heard my blood running through the drains under the dais, sticky and dark, down into the hungry belly of the earth. We all feed our blood to one heart or another. We all feed the Dragon in the end.

He pulled me close. I leaned my forehead against his neck. His breath came evenly, counterpoint to the rhythm of his heart.

"Elaine. I wish . . ."

I leaned back on my heels and examined the line of his jaw through the growing beard. "Would you set your son in my chair, then, Wolf Lord? Discard the child to keep the lady?"

"Take your name back from the Kelpie. He would return you your soul in an instant, to be free of the grief it brings him. I'll give you the scabbard. It would be hard but it—"

I pinched the bridge of my nose to keep the sting out of my eyes. *I will never weep again.*

" —would keep me alive on the chair? Keith. If I do, then I am Elaine again, and can be bound. And if I can be bound, I cannot be Queen. The Mebd named her heir quite clearly, in the hearing of all the hall—" My hair brushed the neckline of the tattered dress. His hand knotted in it, rested on my shoulder, drew me back.

"Lady," he said, "you are confused. If you go to the teind, you cannot rule, and Ian takes the throne anyway. He's a wolf, though; I imagine he will survive it, heart intact."

"Then who goes to Hell, if not me?"

He sighed. "All I want is your love, Elaine."

"And it's the thing you may not have." I smiled, like that could make it right. "Keith. You have my loyalty." *Until Hell's through with me.*

"Ian may hate you more for leaving him."

"Children hate their parents," I replied, thinking of Mist rather than my mother. Or even Morgan, for that matter. "You've spilled your blood, Keith, and I've spilled mine. Let me bear the burdens for what I've done, rather than passing them on to our children. And Ian—" I sighed. "Ian was ready to turn loose the Wild Hunt. I'm not comfortable with the idea of him as King Under the Hill. You'll have to take the throne, Dragon Prince. Can you do it?"

He sighed, and shook his head. "I would not sacrifice you in his place. Or him in yours. I am not Fae, Elaine. I cannot rule here. And you know what Ian wants."

Something my mother told me when I was little rose to my lips along with an ironic smile. "Children should not always have what they want, Keith. He has a heart now. He can grow." I stepped close enough to taste his breath and put my palms against his face. " 'I can get other sons,' said Arthur, when he ordered the babes of a kingdom set adrift on the cold man-murdering sea. But Gwenhwyfar was barren, and Arthur lost what he lost. His innocence, if you believe in such a thing. And lost as well the love his sister might still have borne him. And we know what that mistake cost him, Arthur of Britain, King."

"You compare me to Arthur."

"I will not be the last." I reached up to take the crown off and hang it on the spikes of my throne. It tangled in my hair, and Keith silently helped me free the strands.

"There is always a price. Did it have to be you?"

"Be grateful," I replied. "It is as nothing, compared to the prices your forebears paid."

"I haven't paid them all yet."

"May the day be long in coming, Dragon Prince. May the blood spilled in your name content the Dragon. And see that your mistakes are less than Arthur's, lest you find yourself lain on his old bier, awaiting your own chance at redemption." My voice pealed cold and clear as flowing water, a rill unfrozen in winter. I felt my face calm over my bones as I turned my eyes to stare out the window.

Keith straightened his shoulders, and I realized he had been bending toward me. "As you wish, my lady. Keep your crown, and your cruelty. Love me not. I will go."

"You are my husband, Dragon Prince," I answered. "We rule together, or you rule not at all."

He rubbed at his forehead as if trying to erase the narrow lines that dappled it. "No," he said. "I mean that one Ard Ri should pay a debt as surely as a pair of Queens. If I am overlord of Daoine and Unseelie alike, surely my flesh can stand surety to their debt."

I didn't understand him. I didn't want to understand him.

"I'll go to the tithe." he said, and turned his back on me. "It will be enough. I'll release you from the marriage. Faerie needs Queens. Not a Dragon Prince, not anymore. And you cannot love me."

"No," I said. I closed my eyes. "No. It is my place to go."

Pay the teind. Forever and ever. Amen.

"The Mebd swore me fealty," he whispered. "You will do as you are bid."

"If I had known, if I had known, Tam Lin." I clutched his arm. "No."

He only smiled, and the silence stretched like molten glass until I could hold it no longer. It cooled, brittled, and shattered while I cast for words, for an answer. "Murchaud came back from it."

"So did Fionnghuala," he said, as if I should know the name.

"I'll wait for you."

"Do you suppose the Mebd made Murchaud that promise?"

Blood and dragonfire burned through my veins, unholy bright as liquid iron. I looked past him, up at the throne. "Yes," I said. "She said the same." *And my mother didn't come to pull Murchaud down from his steed at the crossroads, did she?*

If I took my soul back, I could win Keith away from the teind. As Janet won Tam, through love. And Ian would get what he wanted: that chair. The temptation burned me for an instant. Longer than an instant. But—*Ian safe. And anything.*

"She promised she would wait."

"She didn't keep it, did she?"

He knew the answer as well as I did, written in every line of blood on her throne. "Of course she did," I said, and kissed him, and walked away.

"Where are you going?"

"I'll meet you in a little," I said. "I'm going to care for my horse, and then I need to arrange for an emissary from Hell."

Taking care of his horse seemed like a better idea than anything he was likely to come up with on his own, and certainly superior to brooding about the desolate castle. He rather imagined that Elaine and Whiskey would not be in the stables, in any case, but Petunia was, and more deserving of apples than any horse alive. Keith patted the scabbard on his hip, grateful to it for saving the big bay from his— Keith's—rashness.

He detoured through the kitchens and liberated a pocketful of apples, ignoring the sow-headed cook's threat to smack him with a three-foot wooden spoon. He smiled and ducked away like a spoiled boy, and thought she grinned through spotted teeth. The curious lightness in his chest as he strolled outside might have been relief at a decision made and met, he thought. Or it might have been simple, irrational hope.

It didn't matter; he'd take it. He entered a stable redolent with the rich smells of hay and horse manure, and collected combs and brushes and a chamois from a dwarfish Faerie with long, knobby arms and hedgehog prickles along his spine. "Thank you, ah—"

"Vasily," the Faerie said, picking up another brush and walking down the row of stalls. Bits of straw and hay stuck between his spines. "All stable hands named Vasily in Faerie, yes? Is good you care for own horse. Is good King does."

Keith pursed his lips, at first amused to find Russian horse-Faeries at work *here*, and then saddened to realize how depleted the Fae things had become. *Many countries*, he thought. *One nation.* He shook his head and ducked into the stall.

Petunia had been groomed, of course—enough to get the sweat and blood out of his hide—but it hadn't been a careful job. There were too many dirty horses in need of attention, and the spined stable-lads and grooms were still giving each animal a lick and a promise to make it comfortable before coming back to finish as time permitted.

Petunia whuffed softly as Keith slipped into his stall and latched the half door behind himself. "Do you smell the apples, handsome?" Keith pulled one out of his pocket and broke it against the bars, feeding Petunia the more crushed half and taking a bite out of the other half himself. The horse crunched, dripping juice, and reached determinedly for the rest of the apple, his upper lip curling like a beckoning finger. "All right," Keith said, and gave it to him, moving around to the near side and slipping his hand into the loop on the stiff-bristled brush.

He worked steadily for fifteen minutes, occasionally bribing Petunia with apples. The dense yeasty smell of the big animal calmed him. He leaned into Petunia's shoulder and drew deep breaths, scrubbing the hair and dirt from his brush with the currycomb.

The scent of wolves alerted him to company; he glanced up to see Vanya and Fyodor approaching the stall, Ian between them. All three moved softly enough that he wouldn't have heard them if he hadn't been listening.

He'd known he couldn't escape for long. "Hello," he said, plying his brush with enough vigor to send a cloud of dead hair and dust glittering into the sunbeam that fell through the high stall window. A sparrow flew past, chirping, or perhaps it was one of the birdlike Fae.

"Sire," Fyodor said, tilting his head just enough to show his throat and the mocking glitter in his eyes. "Sire," Vanya echoed, without any little displays. Ian just met Keith's eyes and nodded.

Keith did not set down his brush. Petunia's coat whorled across his chest, and Keith crouched to give the sweat dried there particular attention. "Gentlemen. I hope you don't mind talking over the stall door."

"Not at all," Fyodor said.

"How did you know where to find me?"

The black wolf chuckled. "A stable full of vasily, and you wonder who told the Ukrainian wolf where you were?"

"You can't trust anyone," Vanya offered helpfully. Out of the corner of his eye, Keith saw Fyodor shoot him an amused sideways glance.

"I've come to talk to you about your pack, Sire."

Keith shook his head and blew a sweaty lock of hair out of his eyes. "It's your pack now, tovarisch."

Fyodor leaned forward on the stall door, his forehead wrinkling with interest. "What do you mean?" His tone was amused, silky-sweet, but Keith caught the worry under it.

Keith ducked out from under Petunia's neck and let his hands fall to his sides, still holding the brush and currycomb. "Let's not play games, Fyodor Stephanovich. You've come to see me, three abreast, because you know what I told Elaine."

"You're going to Hell," Ian said. "You're volunteering for the teind. I want to know why."

The bay lipped Keith's shoulder as he glanced down, picking a jet-black strand of mane as coarse as wire out of his brush and blowing it up into the shaft of light. "Because I can put an end to it forever," he said. "And I'll be back."

He met Ian's gaze directly, turned his attention to Fyodor, and ended with Vanya, who nodded slowly. "The King is the land," Ivan Ilyich said. "The land is the King."

"Precisely. I go to Hell and I buy Faerie free."

"And you dodge the price of being a Dragon Prince." Ian, wry and bittersweet and sounding so adult that Keith looked twice to be sure it was actually Ian speaking. There were shadows like thumbprints under his eyes, and Keith looked down again. *Are you sure you're not just running away again, Keith MacNeill?* Morag's mocking voice, but in his head this time.

"However it's paid, it's paid," Keith said. He licked his lips and forced himself to meet Fyodor Stephanovich's eyes. "Take care of Morag," he said. "The crumbling heap is yours now, Ian. If Faerie gets a bit much, it might be nice to have someplace to go." The boy nodded; he caught it with his peripheral vision, even if he didn't look away from the Ukrainian wolf. "And you, Fyodor Stephanovich."

"Sire."

"The pack is yours," Keith said firmly. "Keep it out of genocides if you can."

"That's not how it's done—" Fyodor protested, stepping away from the stall door.

Vanya caught his elbow and led him back as Keith settled his brush into his hand again. "It is now."

"Father—" Ian said, and Keith heard, finally, what was in his voice.

He scrubbed Petunia's nose with his palm, set the brush on the ledge beside the water bucket, and unlatched the door. Fyodor stepped out of his way as he came into the aisle. Ian backed away, glancing down at his shoes, flinching when Keith reached out and put his hand on Ian's arm. "I'd stay if I could," he said. The boy shook, flinching again, pulling himself away.

Keith closed his fingers tight on Ian's doublet—thinking that a wolf would grasp a cub so, by the scruff, careful never to break the skin— and dragged him into an embrace.

Stiff, so stiff, like twigs wrapped in wire. Keith thought he would struggle, would bite. Instead he stood, trembling, stiff as a statue. "I'm sorry," Keith said, stroking Ian's hair.

Fyodor came up behind him, a wolf among wolves, and pressed his body against the boy's narrow back. Vanya moved back, shifting from foot to foot, an anxious whine hovering low in his throat. Ian shivered harder, Keith and Fyodor holding him tight, arms around each other's shoulders, eyes meeting as Ian buried his head in his father's shoulder and folded into the embrace.

"I'm sorry," Keith repeated, quite helplessly, wishing Fyodor would look down. The black wolf didn't shift an inch. Of course. "I'm sorry I have to go."

Sunset, he said. Sunset on All Saint's Day: a day later than tradition demanded, but that seemed appropriate. I took Keith away to my rooms for hours and we spent them alone. I slowed the course of the sun in the sky as much as I dared. I guessed he noticed, but he didn't say a word.

When the light began to grow golden and slant across the garden, I bathed him and dressed him in the finest clothes I could find, and myself in black for mourning. I crowned him with a golden circlet as befit a King, and had the blood-bay stallion brought to the stable-yard. Keith tried to hand me Caledfwlch's sheath, with my misfit sword still stuffed into it, and I pushed it back at him. "You may need that later."

"You're right," he said. "I may." He looked at me, and I looked at him, and there didn't seem to be anything further to say, so I held the stallion's reins while he mounted. The horse tossed his head and sidled. Hoofbeats clattered on the cobbles.

Whiskey dipped his head over my shoulder. "You'll want to ride," he said. I gestured to my gown, and he came a half step forward. I saw him fitted with a sidesaddle and jeweled blanket, his mane and hide groomed and oiled until they shone.

"No bridle?" I joked, but my heart wasn't in it, and the sidelong glance of his china eye told me he knew. He dipped a knee so I could mount more easily, and Keith reined his mount out of the way.

Carel had already sent the messenger, so Keith had an escort for his departure. The promptness pleased me; I must have impressed some-one. Side by side, my husband and I rode through the palace gate. Keith put his hand out to take mine, and thus we left the courtyard and went into the twilight. I hadn't told anyone what Keith intended. I had thought we'd go alone: the red steed and the white, out among the emissaries of Hell.

Riders lined the road up to the gate on either side, and at their head sat Carel and Morgan. I saw Cairbre and Kadiska. I wasn't surprised not to see the Cat Anna present, but I had hoped for Ian, once I saw the crowd.

Too much too soon.

Whiskey curvetted like a parade horse. The red destrier paced beside him, calm and unworried, despite the tremble in the hand with which Keith stroked his mane. My husband looked at me, and I at him, and I drew my cold, dry hand from his. We came to the end of the honor guard; it hurt to look at the shifting shapes in fire and smoke that waited at the bottom of the hill. One among them stood taller than the rest, his steed like a wall of red-hot iron under him. Flames wreathed his horned iron crown, and I shuddered. *Queen,* I thought, and forced myself not to look away from his gaze, and his smile, and his nod as he did me the dignity of a very small bow.

"This is it," Keith whispered. I nodded, not ready to trust my voice. He cast one long glance back over his shoulder as the blood bay finally seemed to realize himself on display and picked up his feet. I knotted my hand in Whiskey's mane and set my face in the mask that was becoming my habit and ward.

Keith seemed to take a long time covering the distance.

"Go after him," Whiskey murmured. His ears were up, tail high and caught on an evening breeze. Overhead, I saw the old moon rising in the new moon's arms, a sliver like a horse's hoofprint on the sky. "Go after him. Love him again, and take this pain from me."

"Whiskey," I answered, leaning forward. I felt him shift under me, gathering himself, tasting the wind. *The Arabs say Allah made horses of the south wind, but the Celts say they came out of the sea. And both have the truth of it. That's the wonder of the thing.* I laid my other hand on his mane. Carel's eyes were on me, and Morgan's over her calculating frown.

In the end, it was the Queen of Cornwall's solemn gaze that broke me.

I jerked the coarse, shining strands between my fingers. "Let him go. Take me back inside, Uisgebaugh."

Two lines of riders peeled in behind us as we rode all the length of the long, lone lane up to the gates: followed at a distance, but still alone. Storm clouds were covering the slender clipping of a moon when the doors swung closed behind us. Carel rode up beside me. I stared straight ahead and didn't notice her until she reached out and laid a strong hand on my arm.

"It's permanent," she said.

I blinked at her in confusion. "Keith leaving?"

"The binding of Annwn into the mortal realm. There's unicorns on the six o'clock news."

"You went home?"

She looked up at the changing sky. "Briefly. Time is still moving much faster here. Next time you ask, Elaine, you'll get the president. And he'll be pissed at you."

I shrugged. *I'll worry about that tomorrow.*

"What about the emissary?"

I glanced back over my shoulder, ignoring the searing grief and the iron resolve in the look Cairbre directed at me. *This is only part of the price.*

I'm sorry about your daughter, master bard. I hoped he read it in my eyes, for I could never say it. "Find the Duke of Hell a room," I said to Carel. "And let him know I'll receive him on the morrow. I am too weary for politics tonight."

It was Whiskey who took me to my bedroom. My bedroom. The Mebd's bedroom, now, and not my own chambers. I couldn't have borne the sight of my own unmade bed.

The Mebd's was tightly pulled and dressed in velvets, silks, feather beds, pillows larger than I was and draperies heavy as the touch of the rain-wet wind through the windows. Whiskey opened the black jet buttons glittering the length of my spine—buttons that Keith had done up so little a time ago. Something stung my eyes, so I closed them. Queens do not weep.

He opened my gown with gentle hands and brushed the loose fall of my hair aside. His hands touched here and there across my shoulders, down my back. Soft, pained whickers told me he was touching the pale new scars that covered my skin like crescent moons in a twilight sky. "You wear no braids," he said.

"Nor ever will," I answered. He slid my gown to the floor and lifted me out of it, sat me before the mirror and brushed out my hair. "Uisgebaugh, how can you bear it?"

I saw him kneel behind me. Saw him lower his head and kiss and rekiss my scars. "I can't," he answered. "But I do it anyway. What's this?" He reached out then and picked up something that lay on the black marble of the vanity: a crimson ribbon, and knotted onto it with a goosenecked loop, a simple circle of polished resin that caught and held the candlelight like a sliver of the sun. An amber ring.

"Payment on a bet," I said, and took it out of his hand. It felt like nothing, airy and weightless as the light it represented. I parted the two sides of the ribbon and pulled it over my head.

I looked in the mirror and watched my eyes shift from green to lavender and then to gray, changing as the sea, changing as an olive leaf turning in a wind. Uisgebaugh lifted the black locks of my hair out of the confines of the crimson strand. Kadiska's payment fell between my breasts, and hung there like a reminder of summer, and sunlight, and things that were growing once and now are frozen.

"Do you love me, little treachery?"

"Aye," he said. "All unwilling. And I am not sure I would trade it back to you now if you asked me."

"Give it a few hundred more years," I answered, and as the storm broke outside the window I blew the candles out.

The darkness could not disguise the sound of tapping on my chamber door, the scratch of Gharne's claws unmistakable as he slithered through wood and stone and blinked his lamplit eyes. "Elaine?"

"My friend?"

He laughed; the Fae do not have friends. "Your son is in the hallway, my Queen. He says he wishes to speak with you."

If my true love were an earthly knight
As he's an elfin gray
I would not give my own true love
For any lord here today

The white horse that my true love rides
Is lighter than the wind
With silver he is shod before
With burning gold behind

— *"Tam Lin,"* Traditional

ABOUT THE AUTHOR

Originally from Vermont and Connecticut, **Elizabeth Bear** spent six years in the Mojave Desert and currently lives in southern New England. She attended the University of Connecticut, where she studied anthropology and literature. She was awarded the 2005 Campbell Award for Best New Writer.